UNFINISHED BUSINESS

"You have a debt to pay, my lady," he whispered against her lips. "It may not be your debt, but you will pay it all the same."

"I don't understand," she said, trying to make some sense out of what he was saying.

"You make my blood burn. I can hardly wait to feel all the delights your body has to offer." His voice was no more than a soft whisper, but the sound of it seemed to echo against Season's subconscious.

"No," she pleaded, turning her head from side to side, trying to escape the lips that were arousing sensations she didn't want to feel.

The Raven grabbed her chin in one hand and covered her lips with hot kisses. Against her will Season surrendered as he forced her lips apart and became master of her flesh.

At that moment, The Raven knew he had won. Season became soft and pliant in his arms and her hands moved around his neck to tangle in his hair.

Season had no feeling of what was right or what was wrong. It was as if their bodies had been destined for one another. In all of her girlhood fantasies, she had never dreamed a man could make her feel so alive. The Raven was not her enemy—he was the one for whom her body had been created!

W9-BXG-024

VELVET CHAINS

CONSTANCE O'BANYON

ZEBRA BOOKS
KENSINGTON PUBLISHING CORP.

ZEBRA BOOKS

are published by

Kensington Publishing Corp.
475 Park Avenue South
New York, NY 10016

First printing: August 1985

Printed in the United States of America

To my son, Jason, the youngest member of my family. You fill my heart with love and my life with song. You give me time to stop and smell the roses.

Velvet Chains

Velvet chains bind securely though they cannot be seen;
Velvet bondage holds me prisoner even in my dreams.
Upon the sea the wind does blow to carry me away . . .
I strive to find my life and soul at end of dying day.
I have no life besides this man who hides his face
    from me;
I am obsessed with him—I love that which I cannot see.
I seek to find my freedom, I pray for my release.
Velvet chains—my bondage—will I never be at peace?

Constance O'Banyon

Chapter One

New York—January, 1779

Although it was still early in the evening, the cobblestone streets were dark and deserted. It was a cold, damp night, and a dense fog moved over the town, bringing with it the salty aroma of the sea and spreading a cloak of eeriness in its wake. Out of the darkness came a lone horse-drawn carriage. The sounds of the horses' hooves were muted and were soon swallowed up by the dense fog.

A dark, shrouded figure detached itself from the shadows and crossed the street toward the only pinnacle of light that pierced the ominous blackness. A sudden gust of wind picked up the man's dark cloak and swirled it out behind him, giving him the appearance of a sinister bird of prey. Sounds of lusty laughter came from The Duck and Hound Tavern, so the dark figure avoided the front entrance and instead made his way down the side street toward the back door. He kept well within the shadows so he wouldn't be detected by any passers-by. The man's boots made no sound as they struck the wet cobblestone street. His movement was as silent as the shadows that surrounded him.

Stopping before the back door of the tavern, he rapped three times, paused, and rapped three more times. He then stepped away from the door and waited in the shadows, impatient for someone to answer his knock so he could be admitted.

Hearing the rap on the door, Amos Duncan wiped his hands on the soiled apron tied about his ample waist. Anxiously he glanced over his shoulder, toward the taproom where many British soldiers seemed to be enjoying themselves. Hurrying through the kitchen and past the back stairway, he hoped fervently that the redcoats wouldn't ask for him in his absence. When the patriots had needed a place to hold their weekly meetings, he had gladly volunteered his attic. Lately, however, Amos had begun to wonder if he had made a mistake. If the men were caught in his establishment, there would be hell to pay.

Lord, not another one, he thought. He prided himself on being as good and loyal a patriot as the next fellow, but these weekly meetings above his tavern were beginning to play havoc with his nerves. There were a dozen or more redcoats in his taproom at that very moment. In the past it had amused him to attend to the enemies' needs. He had served them ale and laughed at their jokes, pretending to be loyal to the crown, when in truth secret meetings were taking place above the redcoats' heads.

A loud burst of laughter reached Amos and he

smiled to himself, thinking that in their ignorance the redcoats were enjoying themselves.

By agreeing to allow the patriots to use his upstairs storage attic, Amos felt he was striking a blow for liberty and freedom in the only way he could. Of course, he was honest enough to admit that at first he had become a patriot out of necessity rather than from a sense of honor or outrage. The British taxes and tariffs were especially harsh on anyone who was in business for himself. Amos had only recently acquired his true patriotism, because the British were bleeding the Colonies dry for what they termed God and king. The colonists were treated with contempt by the Crown, and the injustice of it all made Amos' blood boil.

Removing a lantern from the hook where it hung in the dim hallway, Amos turned up the wick and walked to the back door cautiously. The meeting upstairs had been going on for well over an hour, and he was leery of latecomers—even if they knew the signal. He quickly shot the bolt and opened the door, ready to face whoever waited, be he friend or foe.

At first Amos thought his eyes must be deceiving him! He gasped at the tall figure draped in black and wearing a leather mask to conceal his face. The man stood a good head taller than Amos, and with the black leather helm hiding his identity, his appearance was ominous. His full-length cape fell almost to the ground, concealing its wearer's shape among its generous folds.

The tavernkeeper felt the hair on the back of his neck stand on end, and the hand that held the lantern trembled. He quickly fumbled beneath his apron and withdrew his pistol, pointing it at the man.

"If it be ale and a good time you seek, you'd best try the front door, stranger," Amos said, thinking his voice sounded far braver than he felt at the moment.

"I seek neither ale nor pleasure, my friend," came the raspy reply. "The eagle has flown."

Even though the man in black had just given the tavernkeeper the correct password, and had known he must rap three times on the door to gain entrance, Amos was suspicious of him.

"You have the password, friend, but you come among us hiding your true identity. Who are you? How do I know you ain't a spy?"

"It isn't important that you know my identity, Amos Duncan, for I know you and I'm aware of your loyalty," came the deep reply.

Suddenly Amos' mouth fell open in awe. "Well, hell and damnation, I know who you are! You are The Raven!"

The cloaked figure roughly pushed Amos aside and entered the room, quickly closing the door behind him and shooting the bolt home.

"Amos Duncan, take me where the meeting is being held." The mask muffled the order.

Although the man had neither confirmed nor denied that he was The Raven, Amos knew he could be no other. Before him, in the flesh, stood the legendary hero that young lads worshipped and old men discussed in hushed tones. The Raven's many daring exploits had been told and retold. He was held in high regard by all true patriots, and was hated and feared by the British. Mystery surrounded The Raven. No one seemed to know his true identity. Yet somehow he always managed to acquire valuable information from the enemy, and he passed it on to help the cause of the patriots. Amos could hardly believe he was facing the famous Raven and actually talking to him!

"Forgive my caution, Raven. A man can't be too careful in this day and time," he said, as an apology. "What could be so important that it would bring The Raven himself out into the open?" he couldn't help asking.

"I didn't come here to pass pleasantries with you, nor am I inclined to answer your questions. Take me up those back stairs to where the meeting is being held," The Raven said in an authoritative voice. Amos could tell by The Raven's tone that he was a man who was accustomed to giving orders and to having them obeyed without question.

The tavernkeeper replaced the gun in his belt and nodded his head. "Follow me, but have a care. The place is crawling with them redcoats tonight." Amos led the way up the back stairs, followed closely by the figure in black.

The shadows in the hallway flickered into light as the tavernkeeper raised the lantern over his head to light the way. After they reached the second-floor landing, Amos led the way up another stairway, to what was obviously an attic room. He stopped before the doorway and was about to rap when his hand was caught and held fast by The Raven.

"It will be best if you return to your guests. We wouldn't want them to miss you and come searching for you, now would we?"

Amos was reluctant to leave. His curiosity was piqued and he wanted to find out what could have brought The Raven to his tavern. However, as he stared at the black mask, he became unnerved, knowing The Raven was watching him closely. So he nodded his head in agreement and quickly retraced his steps down the hall, thinking that The Raven's mission must be mighty important to bring him out into the open.

The dark figure watched until Amos disappeared down the stairs. The hallway was now in total darkness since the landlord had taken the lantern with him. Slowly turning the knob, The Raven opened the door and slipped silently inside. Once he was in the room, he clung to the shadows, not wanting to reveal his presence just yet.

The room was smoke-filled and dimly lit, with no less than a dozen men gathered about a table, talking in hushed tones. The Raven took note of each man as he stood in the shadows. Silas Dunsberry, a prominent merchant, was trying, with little success, to bring some semblance of order to the meeting.

"Silence, please, gentlemen," Silas said. "If you all try to talk at once, we shall never accomplish anything. Each of you will have your turn to speak. Wallace Tuddle has something of great importance to relate to you. I suggest we give him the floor at this time."

The Raven studied each man's face carefully, knowing many of them were prominent citizens—merchants, printers, farmers. The British would willingly pay a goodly sum to see any one of them uncovered as a spy.

Wallace Tuddle stood up and cleared his throat while the others waited for him to speak. "I have news which will sadden you all. I have been told that George Dale has been captured by the British and accused of being a spy!"

Tuddle's announcement brought an immediate outcry of protest and anger. A man named Harvey Bailey jumped to his feet. "Are you sure? Can there be no mistake?"

"It is the truth . . . I have it on good authority. Dale is in the hands of the enemy," Tuddle answered with assurance.

"Will he talk, do you think?" another man queried.

"If he were of a mind to, he could name everyone in this room," another added.

"We don't know what he would do under torture. He might betray us all!" a third man cried out.

"I know Dale very well," Silas Dunsberry said. "I don't believe he will name any of us. He is a man of strong principles, a man of honor. Dale is as dedicated to freedom as any one of us in this room."

"I'm sure what you are saying is true, but under torture even the bravest man will crack," Tuddle said, studying his companions' faces closely.

The room became silent as each man contemplated what discovery would mean to him and his family. They were all so deep in thought no one heard the soft, booted steps of the cloaked figure who came forth from the shadows and made his way to the center of the room. No one knew The Raven was among them until his raspy voice swept across the room with the intensity of a whiplash.

"I can assure all of you that George Dale did not reveal any of your names."

An audible gasp escaped from someone as all eyes turned to the dark, hooded figure. The intruder was dressed all in black, and his leather helm and long flowing cape disguised his identity. The two slits in the helm that allowed the man to see gave him an ominous appearance.

Seconds passed and no one spoke. Tuddle's eyes darted nervously about the room, then settled on the newcomer.

"Who are you? What do you want?" one of the men asked, voicing the question that was on all their minds.

"My name is of no importance," the dark figure said. He seemed to loom out of the darkness in the poorly lit room, almost as if he were a part of the shadows.

"Are you friend or enemy?" someone asked.

As the cloaked figure walked slowly and deliberately toward the table, silence enfolded the room once more.

"If you stand for truth and justice, if you are a true patriot who wishes to see this land purged of tyranny and injustice, then I am your friend," was the raspy reply.

Wallace Tuddle stood up, clearing his throat. "Gentlemen, gentlemen, allow me to have your attention. I know this man. As he told you, he is a friend to us all. This is none other than The Raven himself. I circulated the word that I wanted him to come here tonight. Evidently he received my message."

The silence that followed Tuddle's announcement was tense. Each man stared at the legendary figure they had all heard of, wondering why he had come.

16

Silas Dunsberry stood up, being the first to find his voice. "Why have you come among us tonight, Raven?"

The Raven walked slowly around the table. Finding an empty chair, he raised his black-booted foot to rest it on the seat.

"I have two reasons for being here tonight. First of all I regret to inform you that George Dale is dead! He was hung this noon by the British. Rest assured he didn't reveal any of your identities."

There was an immediate outcry of disbelief and anger. Silas held up his hand to restore order; nonetheless he had to shout to be heard above the din.

"Gentlemen, keep your voices down! I have some questions to ask of The Raven." Finally the gathering quieted and Silas was able to speak. "Raven, are you quite sure Dale is dead?"

"I witnessed his hanging personally. There was nothing I could do to help him," the raspy voice replied.

"You are sure he didn't talk?"

"You have my word, Silas Dunsberry. Dale went to his death without betraying the cause."

Silas nodded slowly. "My friends, today we lost a brave and valiant ally. I know you all feel the tragedy as deeply as I do. I suggest we adjourn and go to our respective homes, since I'm sure none of us feel like continuing with the meeting," Silas said sadly.

"Wait!" the raspy voice commanded. "I said I had two reasons for coming here tonight. I have not yet revealed my second reason. What time is it?"

Silas pulled out his pocket watch, flipping open the

catch. "I make it to be almost eight-thirty," he said, pocketing the watch.

The hooded man nodded. "I have come here tonight to expose a traitor among you! A man you call your trusted friend has betrayed you to the enemy!"

"How can this be?" someone asked.

"Surely not one of us!" cried another.

Again silence descended, and it hung heavy in the room as each man looked at his companions, wondering just who the traitor might be.

"Do you know this for a fact?" Silas spoke up.

"Yes, I have it on good authority. One of you in this very room is a Judas. One of you has sold out his fellows for money."

"Tell us who the man is!" Wallace Tuddle demanded. "Reveal him to us so that we might put an end to his miserable life!"

"Yes, tell us," everyone agreed.

"Raven, do you know who this man is?" Silas asked grimly.

"I know," came the deep reply.

"Expose him to us!" the man called Dawson cried out, waving a pistol in the air, only to have it wrenched from his hand by The Raven.

"Would you fire off your piece here and have the red-coats come swarming into the room?" The Raven said, shoving a befuddled Dawson down into a chair.

Each eye was trained on The Raven as he walked leisurely around the table, studying every man's face with eyes that seemed to burn through the slits of his helm. The occupants of the room could feel the tension mounting. Each one waited for The Raven to speak again.

At last The Raven stopped in front of Wallace Tuddle, who seemed to cringe visibly before the close scrutiny of the man behind the hood.

"Here is your traitor, gentlemen. Wallace Tuddle!"

Tuddle's mouth gaped open as he shook his head, seeming to have lost his voice for the moment.

"How can that be? I have known him for twenty years," Silas said, coming to Tuddle's defense. "All of us here know him well—he is one of us. He would never betray us." Others nodded their agreement.

Tuddle stood up slowly, never taking his eyes off The Raven. At last he found his voice. "How can you accuse me? Was I not the one who sent word for you to come here tonight? My God, would I have asked you here if I were the traitor you accuse me of being?"

Deep menacing laughter came from behind the hood. It wasn't a pleasant sound and it held no humor. "Do you think me a fool, Tuddle? I happen to know you think when that clock strikes nine this room will be rushed by redcoats and every man here will be arrested as a spy . . . all but one. You, Tuddle! No doubt the rest of us would have suffered the same fate as George Dale, each dangling from a hangman's noose.

Wallace Tuddle looked upon the faces of his contemporaries, reading doubt and distrust in their eyes. "You all know me. Hell, most of you have dined at my home or I in yours. On the other hand, what do you know of this man that calls himself The Raven? My God, how can any of you take the word of a man who hides his face against mine?" Tuddle cleared his throat nervously. "Listen to me. I charge that he is the spy, not I!"

Before anyone could answer, The Raven grabbed Tuddle in a fierce headlock and swung him around to face the other men. A dagger appeared from somewhere among the folds of The Raven's black cloak, and he held it at Tuddle's throat.

"I have to give you credit, Tuddle. If your plan had worked tonight, you would be hailed as a hero by the British. How much did they pay you to set up your friends? Thirty pieces of silver?" The Raven hissed. "Did you wish to sweeten the pot by handing me over to them as well?"

"Raven, are you quite sure of your allegations?" Silas asked. "Could there be no mistake?"

Again they heard the ominous laughter. "It is well that you question me, Silas Dunsberry. We live in dangerous times where friend turns against friend. It is not wise to take a man at face value, as Tuddle has proven. Let Tuddle speak of his own guilt." So saying, The Raven applied pressure to the dagger he held at the throat of the unfortunate Tuddle, drawing blood. "What say you, Tuddle? Do you die with a lie on your tongue, or do you speak the truth and cleanse your treacherous soul?"

By now the helpless Tuddle knew that he faced certain death. He began to whimper and whine. "What is the difference? You will kill me anyway!" he cried, staring up at the dark, hooded figure of The Raven.

"Of course you will die," The Raven stated matter-of-factly. "But . . . if you speak the truth, you will have a chance to defend yourself. Otherwise I shall end your miserable life here and now."

The other men in the room watched in disbelief. Each of them aware of The Raven's reputation with the rapier. Tuddle would have no chance in a match against him. Obviously the luckless Tuddle knew it too, for when The Raven released his hold on the man, Tuddle fell to the floor in a heap, grasping the black cape.

"I'm a dead man," he whimpered. "A dead man, with no one to stand in harm's way for me."

"Who knows, perhaps you can best me," The Raven said lazily. "Speak the truth and I will give you even odds," he whispered softly.

Tuddle scrambled to his feet. He could see by the faces that surrounded him, that everyone was now beginning to believe him to be guilty. Not a one of them would come to his aid. Suddenly he experienced overwhelming hatred toward the men he felt had deserted him in his hour of need. The need for revenge seemed to burn intensely within his body.

"I will see you all dead!" he raged. "Yes, I told the king's men to come here tonight. I also arranged for The Raven to be present. None of you will escape, for the hour of nine is upon you. You are all doomed!"

Someone at the back of the room muttered a loud oath and aimed his pistol at Tuddle's heart. The weapon was quickly knocked away by Silas Dunsberry.

"Let him be. He will receive his just reward from the worthy hands of The Raven," Silas said with feeling.

George Tuddle studied each face. He saw hatred mixed with disbelief on the faces of the men he had called his friends. He now knew his only salvation lay in stalling for time. He pulled his watch from his pocket and saw it was five minutes before nine. At any moment the redcoats would come swarming into the room. The Raven seemed to sense Tuddle's thoughts.

"Time is against you, Tuddle. Admit why you committed such a treacherous deed before I run you through," The Raven hissed, unsheathing his rapier and placing the sharp point at Tuddle's throat. "Face the men you have betrayed," he said softly. "Let them hear from your own lips how the deed was done so there will be no doubt in anyone's mind that you are guilty."

For the first time, Tuddle felt shame as he looked into the eyes of the men he had known most of his life. There wasn't a man among them that he hadn't supped with. He knew all their family members by name. He began to feel dismay at what he had done. Unable to look into the accusing eyes of his fellow patriots any longer, he turned his gaze to the man in the black leather helm. Suddenly he felt unbridled anger toward The Raven who had dashed all his hopes. He hadn't intended to be unmasked as a traitor. The plan had been that he would be arrested with the others and later released. In the beginning it had seemed so simple and impersonal. When he had planned for tonight, he hadn't known he would experience these feelings of shame and guilt. He had thought only of the money the British would pay him and of what it would mean to his family.

"It's true that I sent word to the British to come here tonight, with a message that I would turn over to them a nest of traitors. I also told my contact that I would try

22

o have you here when they arrived, Raven." Tuddle ried to look past the hood to the man underneath. In a panic, he wondered how The Raven could have gotten vind of his plan. He had been very careful not to tell anyone what he was about. Did The Raven have some unholy power that permitted him to see into a man's oul? Tuddle wondered frantically.

"It will do none of you any good to try to flee. I gave ny contact each of your names. There is nowhere you can hide. I'm willing to bet that at this very moment he tavern is swarming with redcoats, that they have he place surrounded." A satisfied smile came over Tuddle's face. "You would all do well to place yourselves in my hands. Perhaps I can convince the British o be lenient with you. Think of your families."

"You swine," Dawson shouted, moving across the room and grabbing the traitor by his coat front to shake him violently.

The Raven stepped forward, dislodged Dawson's grip, and shoved Tuddle down onto a chair.

"What shall we do?" Silas asked, looking to The Raven for guidance.

"Kill the traitor," Dawson cried out. "If what Wallace Tuddle said is true we have nothing to lose. Let he British find him swinging from the rafters when hey burst in on us! Let his miserable life be a substitute for the life of George Dale—though a poor substitute it s."

"That will not be necessary, my friends," The Raven said. "May I suggest that each of you leave now in the least conspicuous manner. Go straight to your homes and have no fear. I can assure you the enemy does not know your identities, save Tuddle's and before too long he will be past harming anyone.

"How do we know we will not be set upon when we leave this room?" Dawson asked, voicing the concern of the others.

"You will just have to trust that I know what I'm talking about," The Raven assured them. "Have no fear for your safety, and leave me to deal with Tuddle."

The room became silent as each man weighed The Raven's words. There was something about him that did inspire trust, and after all hadn't he revealed Tuddle's treachery to them?

At that moment The Raven seemed larger than life. Although he was surrounded by mystery, he somehow seemed worthy of their confidence.

Silas Dunsberry was the first to react. He walked over to Tuddle and stared long and hard into his eyes. "I denounce you as a traitor. You received friendship from everyone in this room, only to flaunt that friendship before the enemy. If there is a lower form of life than you, I am not acquainted with it!"

Tuddle had the good grace to lower his eyes, unable to face his accusers.

"Silas Dunsberry, if you will do me the favor of leaving your rapier, since Tuddle doesn't seem to have one of his own, I would be in your debt," The Raven said in his disturbing voice. "I will ask that each of you leave now. As I said before, I shall deal with Tuddle in my own way."

Without reluctance, Silas handed over his rapier, knowing that Tuddle carried no weapon to defend himself. He felt some regret that the traitor's family would be forced to face alone the hostility occasioned by Tuddle's disloyalty because he doubted that Tuddle's wife, Sarah, or his daughter, Mary, knew anything about tonight's dealings. Silas raised his head and looked at The Raven.

"I am loath to think how his family will suffer because of Tuddle's dishonor, Raven."

"I will handle all the details. Rest assured no innocent person will be made to suffer unduly."

Once again a hush fell over the room as the men began to take their leave. Each man believed The Raven's assurance that no harm would come to them or their families.

Tuddle felt great fear as the room began to clear. His lips were so dry he had to moisten them with his tongue. He would have risen from the chair he was sitting on, but The Raven kept a restraining hand on his shoulder.

When the last man had departed, The Raven walked over to the door and shot the bolt. He then turned to face Tuddle who seemed to shrink visibly. The Raven took his rapier and the one Silas Dunsberry had given him, and threw them to the middle of the floor, where they landed point-down in the wooden floor and swayed drunkenly in the dimly lit room.

"I give you leave to choose the weapon with which I will end your life, Tuddle," the hooded man said softly and without feeling. The sound of his raspy voice was enough to send poor Tuddle down on his knees.

"I beg you, sir, have mercy. I have a wife and daughter who will suffer grievously if I should forfeit my life. Allow me to live, for I have seen the error of my ways,"

25

he pleaded.

The Raven seemed to swoop across the room, his black cape fanning out behind him, giving him the appearance of the bird from which he drew his name. Grabbing Tuddle by the coat front, he raised him into the air and dangled him there as if he weighed nothing.

"I liked you better when you didn't act the sniveling coward. I will show you the same mercy you would have shown your friends tonight, had not your plan miscarried. You are craven as well as traitorous. Arm yourself before I run you through," The Raven hissed.

Tuddle realized he would receive no mercy from this cold-hearted man. The only way he could survive would be to destroy him. The Raven lowered Tuddle to his feet and gave him a shove that sent him in the direction of the swords. The hooded man seemed in no hurry, and he waited patiently, allowing Tuddle to choose his weapon.

"But for you, I would be a wealthy man, Raven. My family and I would soon be on our way to London!" Tuddle cried, as he grabbed up a sword and lunged at the unarmed Raven. The Raven had anticipated Tuddle's move, however, and he quickly side-stepped the thrust. Laughing insultingly, The Raven grabbed the remaining rapier, and locked swords with his opponent.

"Had your plan worked tonight, Tuddle, you wouldn't have found the British as generous as you thought." The Raven taunted. "For all their faults, they like a traitor no better than I do."

When Tuddle struck, The Raven always anticipated him and easily parried his thrust. It soon became apparent to the now-desperate man that The Raven was only playing with him, humiliating him. The Raven was tireless. He deftly side-stepped or parried every move Tuddle made. Such a man was no match for The Raven, a master of swordsmanship who had the cunning of a fox.

When at last The Raven tired of toying with the traitor, he ripped the rapier from Tuddle's hand with the tip of his sword and sent it flying into the air to clatter on the floor some distance away. He then placed the tip of his blade at Tuddle's throat.

"If you have any last requests, Tuddle, I would suggest that you voice them now." The Raven's sword swooped down slicing the brass buttons from Tuddle's coat with such art that the fabric of the coat was unharmed.

Tuddle licked his lips. "Who are you? What demon from hell lent you its power? What devil allows you to see into a man's soul? From what do you draw your strength?"

The Raven stood with his blade poised at Tuddle's throat. "I grant you your last request. It is only right that a man should look upon the face of the one who is the instrument of his death." The blade at Tuddle's throat was lowered, and with one swift motion, the leather helm was removed. Tuddle gasped at the tall figure that now stood unmasked before him.

"My God, it cannot be!" he gasped. "You are the last one I would ever have suspected!"

The Raven bowed politely. "You are among the privileged few who have seen me unmask. Not many have knowledge of my true identity."

Tuddle made a sudden dash for the door, but The Raven was too quick for him. He caught the traitor by the shoulder and spun him around.

"When I came to you today, you allowed me to tell you all about the meeting here tonight. You smiled as I named names. I thought you were pleased to learn about the nest of traitors to the Crown and all along you were laughing at me!" Tuddle cried.

"You never dreamed today when you sang your song to me that you were signing your own death warrant, did you, Tuddle?"

"What is the difference between you and me?" Tuddle asked, dropping to his knees. "You aren't what you pretend to be any more than I am." The frightened man's voice rose hysterically.

The Raven's blade slashed the front of Tuddle's coat, revealing the bare skin underneath.

"I haven't the time or the patience to point out the differences between you and me, Tuddle. What you did was done in the name of greed and personal gain. What I do is done so that the people of these United States may one day lie in freedom without answering to a foreign power. I do it so an American like your daughter can grow up in a place where she can speak her mind."

"It's easy for you to speak of freedom; you are already a wealthy man. I wonder how patriotic you would be if you had to grub for a living," Tuddle said accusingly.

"Enough! I tire of this conversation. Have you any other request?"

"I am a dead man then?"

"Yes, the deed is all but done," The Raven said, showing no sign of weakness or pity.

Tuddle arose to face his death with a surprising lack of the fear and cowardice he had displayed earlier. For some reason it had become important that The Raven should not think him a coward. "I would prefer my wife and daughter not be told about tonight's happenings."

The Raven inclined his head. "They shall be told that you were killed by the enemy which will be the truth. It will be said that you met death as a brave man. It has never been my practice to punish the innocent."

Wallace Tuddle's death cry was muffled as the rapier sliced through his heart. The Raven felt no remorse for the deed, no pity for the man who would have sacrificed his friends' lives in order to acquire a degree of wealth.

The Raven removed his cape and wrapped the dead man in it, knowing it would not go well for the tavern-keeper if Tuddle's body were found anywhere near The Duck and Hound. It might raise too many unanswered questions.

Replacing the leather helm on his head, he hoisted Tuddle's body onto his shoulder. The Raven then left quietly by the back stairway and was soon lost in the dark shadows.

A thick fog swirled about The Raven as he made his way down the back street. The hooded man knew he had done the right thing in ending Tuddle's life. He had been forced to act quickly before too many innocent people had been made to suffer. Still, tonight's business left a bitter taste in his mouth. This was the kind of war that had no appeal for him. He much preferred to be aboard his ship, seeking out the enemy in a fair fight. But he couldn't allow himself to feel sympathy for a man who would betray his country and sell out his friends.

Chapter Two

Silas Dunsberry refused the mulled wine his house-keeper offered him, choosing instead a liberal amount of brandy before sending her off to bed. His nerves were on edge after the incident at The Duck and Hound tonight. Even now he couldn't believe that Wallace Tuddle had turned traitor and betrayed his friends.

Silas took a large drink of the brandy and felt it burn a path down his throat. He cursed himself for leaving the tavern before he'd made certain of Tuddle's death. Should Tuddle somehow overcome The Raven, there would be grave consequences.

"No, it's not possible," he said aloud. "Tuddle is no match for The Raven."

The clock in the hallway struck the eleventh hour, and still Silas waited. In the dim firelight, his face showed traces of his growing concern. As the door opened a sudden gust of wind fanned the flames in the fireplace, causing them to leap higher and warning Silas that he was not alone. Someone had just entered his study by way of the garden door.

Turning his head slowly, the old man saw a dark, hooded figure move out of the shadows to stand before him.

"Is the deed done then?" Silas asked.

The dark, hooded man nodded.

Silas let out a relieved sigh. "Lord, what's the world coming to, when a friend turns on you? Before tonight, I would have numbered Tuddle among my most trusted friends."

The Raven sat down opposite Silas and stared into the fire.

"His last request was that his wife and daughter be spared any hurt. I told him they would be told only that he died at the hands of the enemy, which in truth he did."

"Yes, there is no reason to cause them hurt. It will be hard enough for them to learn of his death. I feel certain they weren't privy to his deed tonight."

"So he indicated, Uncle Silas. If that's brandy you're drinking I wouldn't say no to a glass."

"You'll have to pour for yourself; my gout is paining me tonight," Silas said, waving his hand in the direction of the side table where the brandy decanter stood.

The older man watched The Raven stand up and walk across the room to pour himself a brandy. Only he knew what it had cost The Raven to go to The Duck and Hound tonight. His eyes followed The Raven as he returned to the chair and sat down, crossing his black-booted legs.

"My God, have you any notion of the thoughts that

went through my mind tonight when you showed up? Are you crazed to expose yourself so?"

The Raven took a drink and turned to Silas. "I had little choice. Not one of you would have believed that Tuddle was a traitor unless I accused him openly. I had to force him to admit the deed so there would be no doubt in anyone's mind as to his guilt."

"I am at a complete loss. How is it possible that you found out about his plan? Are you convinced that he told no one else our names?"

"I can answer both your questions at once. Imagine my surprise today when Tuddle called at my lodgings, asking to speak to me in private. Once we were alone, he told me about the weekly meetings above The Duck and Hound Tavern. He called you and the others by name, and I even wrote your names down to be more convincing."

Silas could hear the amusement in The Raven's voice. "We were damned fortunate that he chose you to spill his guts to. Had he chosen another, tonight might well have turned out quite differently."

"The deed is done. It's best to put it behind us," The Raven said, removing his gloves and then his leather helm, and tossing them on the floor beside him.

"I have been getting an uneasy feeling lately that you are taking too many chances," Silas stated, staring into the unmasked man's eyes. "You seem to thrive on danger without weighing the consequences. Should you be discovered, it would be a great loss to the cause. Tonight is a clear example of that. Suppose Tuddle had come out on top tonight? You would now either be

dead, or in the hands of the British. My dead sister
would turn over in her grave if she could see how her
son continually mocks death."

The Raven studied his uncle's face. It was a kind
face, but one which was careworn and etched with
sorrow. Silas had lost his wife and only daughter
because of the British, and he had never recovered from
the blow. The Raven thought back to the time when his
aunt and cousin had been visiting a friend in the village
of Fairfield, Connecticut, when it had been burned by
the British. The British had used the excuse that the
town harbored spies; they had left very little untouched
that day. Silas' wife and daughter had lost their lives in
the fire along with several other women and children.
That was one reason why The Raven's uncle now
worked against the British in any way he could.

"I cannot credit that you worry about me, Uncle. I
can take care of myself," The Raven stated matter-of-
factly.

Silas rose, his face red with anger. "Sometimes I feel
some people give too much to the cause, while others
not near enough. Good lord, every day you place your
life in danger! You are too foolhardy, always laughing
in the face of death. One day you will make a wrong
move, or trust the wrong person, and that will seal your
end." Silas looked down at his nephew, who was a
handsome rogue, as many a fair maiden could attest.
He was the son Silas had never had, and he loved him
more like a father, than an uncle.

"I don't consciously test fate, Uncle, although I will
admit, I have chosen a dangerous profession in being a

privateer." He smiled devilishly. "It does have its moments, however."

"You would have me believe you are risking your life for the fun of it, but I know better—you can't fool me. There isn't a better patriot in this whole country than you."

Again his nephew smiled. "There would be some who would dispute that."

"I have to admit this double life you live has lost me many nights' sleep. I fear each day to hear you have been exposed, and you know the penalty for being a spy. Already the price on your head is high. Give up this madness. Allow The Raven to disappear," his uncle argued, not for the first time.

"I cannot do as you ask, Uncle. You, more than anyone, know of the valuable British plans to which I am privy. I must continue to pass on the information I acquire to the Continental Congress. I feel it is my duty to walk the fine line between treason and honor."

Too many times Silas had tried to persuade his nephew to give up this dangerous game, now, as always, he met with stubborn resistance. Deep inside he was proud of his nephew, but he feared for his life. Silas knew from past failures, however, that it was useless to pursue the matter further, so he changed the subject.

"Where is the *Andromeda* anchored?"

"She's off the Jersey coast. I have found a way to add two more knots to her speed, thanks to a British ship I took as prize."

Silas sat down, and his eyes sparkled with interest.

The older man had only sailed on the *Andromeda* once, and on that occasion he had enjoyed himself enormously.

"How was that accomplished?"

The Raven smiled, knowing he had caught his uncle's undivided attention. "It was simple really when you stop to think about it. I had a layer of copper sheeting placed on the hull. It not only increases the *Andromeda*'s speed, but discourages marine growth on the hull as well."

Silas remembered the summer he had sailed to France with his nephew. It was an experience he had never forgotten; even now it stirred his sense of adventure. In a way he envied his nephew for having the courage and ability to strike at the enemy. He had a crew that had been hand-picked; to a man they were loyal to The Raven.

The *Andromeda* was as legendary as the dark master who sailed her. She was a privately owned vessel that had once belonged to an English merchant. Before the war, Silas' nephew had purchased her, never dreaming she would be used in battle. She was a sharp and rakish ship with long clean lines. She had been built for speed, with a sharp bow and an undercut stern, and she had then been modified by his nephew who had made her one of the fastest vessels afloat. What Silas didn't like was the bounty the British had placed on her captain's head—a reward of five thousand pounds to anyone who would provide information leading to the capture of The Raven.

"I would have thought copper sheeting would slow

her down by adding to her weight," Silas said reflectively.

"No, not at all. In fact, the opposite is true," his nephew answered.

Both men lapsed into silence as they stared into the crackling fire, each lost in his own thoughts. At last Silas spoke. "I have a letter for you. It was hand delivered a week ago. Although it has no return address, I suspect it's from Captain John Paul Jones."

Silas stood up, moved to his desk, and removed the letter from the top drawer where he had placed it. He handed it to his nephew and sat down in front of the fire once more.

The Raven broke the seal and began to read.

"Yes, it's from John Paul," he said, scanning the letter and then tossing it into the fire. He knew it would be dangerous to leave such a letter lying around. Both men watched the hungry flames lick at the parchment. "Jones is in France waiting to be outfitted with a ship."

Silas snorted. "He will do better getting a ship from France than from our own country. He has powerful enemies in Congress who are too blind to see Captain Jones is the best damned sea captain they have."

The Raven nodded. "He wrote of hardships, mutiny, and petty jealousy."

"What else does he say?"

"He hints that if I come across someone who is of great importance to the British Crown . . . someone who could be captured and later held for ransom, it would be in our country's best interest."

Silas leaned forward. "Good lord, in what respect

would that be of any help to the United States?"

"It seems that when our ships are captured by the enemy, the crew are imprisoned as traitors, under the most deplorable conditions. Some are even pressed into the British Navy and forced to work aboard their ships."

"Yes, I have heard that also," Silas admitted. "But I don't see what can be gained by capturing some high English official."

"John Paul wrote that the navy is abominably short-handed. He has been obliged to take on Spanish, French, and even Russians to man his ships. It's not being short-handed that he minds so much, but rather the cruel and inhuman treatment our sailors are receiving at the hands of the British."

"Is he asking you to do this deed then?"

"I believe he is . . . although he states that if he's ever asked if it was his idea, he will deny any knowledge of it."

Silas raised his eyebrow. "Will he now, by damn. It would seem he is willing to place your head on the block and hand the enemy an ax to lob it off with!"

The Raven laughed deeply. "It's not as bad as you may suppose, Uncle. John Paul himself tried to take the Earl of Selkirk as hostage. But on arriving at St. Mary's Isle, he found the earl to be away from home and had to abandon his plan. He says it was the most embarrassing situation he has yet had to endure."

Silas looked at his nephew suspiciously. "Are you planning to do as the good captain suggested?" Silas asked, fearing his nephew might be considering Jones's foolish notion.

"I don't think so, Uncle Silas. I believe John Paul's plan has merit; however, I have no stomach for kidnapping. I wouldn't be surprised if John Paul tried again to take some highborn Englishman and then demand the release of our sailors for the man's return. I would imagine all he needs is another likely candidate!"

Silas' face eased into a smile. Can you imagine John Paul sailing all the way to St. Mary's Isle to take the earl prisoner, only to find the man away from home? Dammit, if that's what our navy has come to, I'm glad you aren't a part of it. I'd sooner see you scuttle the *Andromeda* and retire her from the sea than use her in such a harebrained scheme."

The Raven merely looked at his uncle through lowered lashes. "When America is free and we no longer have to worry about that tyrant who sits upon his throne in England, perhaps then I can retire from the sea," he stated lazily. "Until that time, we all do things that are distasteful to us."

"You are a fool if you think this war hinges on anything you do. The war will be won or lost without your help or interference."

The Raven nodded his head and laughed, amused by his uncle's blunt observation. "I suppose you are right, but I do what I can, however small the contribution."

Silas looked into dancing eyes and couldn't help smiling himself. "You are a devil and you seem to thrive on causing me worry. I will no longer belittle the effort you are making on this country's behalf. Just be careful, that's all I ask of you."

The Raven drained the brandy glass, then he stood. "I must take my leave now. I don't know when I will see you again. Watch your own health, Uncle."

Before Silas had time to reply, The Raven had gone through the door as silently as he had entered earlier. The old man walked to the doorway and stared out into the darkened night. He wondered what new and daring adventure his nephew would attempt next, and secretly he wished he could go with him.

Chapter Three

England—February, 1779

Lady Season Chatsworth stared at her image in the mirror. She knew she was pretty, but she had never found much satisfaction in that fact. So far, her beauty had proven to be only a curse. Of late, her hand had been sought by many titled gentlemen, yet Season still couldn't believe her father had betrothed her to the odious Earl of Ransford.

At the tender age of nineteen, Season felt as though her life was over. She shuddered in disgust, remembering the touch of the earl's sweaty palms sliding down her arms and over her breasts. Lord Arthur Ransford was always correct and respectful when her father was present, but whenever her father left the room, Ransford would touch her in the most disgusting and intimate ways. Season remembered the feel of his wet mouth on hers and closed her eyes, trying to block the dreadful experience from her mind. She remembered

41

the time she had escaped from him by running into the garden, only to have him follow her. He had been delighted to have her alone, and he had pulled her into his arms and kissed her. In trying to free herself, Season had bitten the earl on the lip. She had felt no guilt for having done so. Indeed, she had felt great satisfaction from drawing blood that day. Afterward, Lord Ransford had angrily declared that she wouldn't act so high and mighty once she became his wife.

Season frowned at her image in the mirror. Her skin was creamy white and she had been blessed with high cheekbones. When she smiled, dimples appeared on either side of her cheeks. Her hair was a vibrant golden color, and when the sun struck the shiny mass, her curls came alive with red highlights. Her father had once laughingly told her that there was distant Viking blood running through her veins, thus explaining the color of her hair. Season was tall for a girl and, she thought, much too thin, but her body was appealingly curved, though very firm from the many hours she spent on horseback.

Although Season found her eyes were too large for her face, she was pleased with their deep green color. Unlike many women with light-colored hair, Season's lashes weren't pale in color, but long and dark. They were complemented by her delicately arched brows. Her mouth was full and generous, but at the moment it trembled as she pondered her future.

Lord Arthur Ransford was a widower who, it was rumored, had long been searching for a young wife to bear him the children his barren wife had been unable to give him. Season shuddered, remembering the earl's assurances that he could father children. He had mentioned several bastards scattered about his estates as proof of his virility.

On many occasions Season had begged her father not to give her hand in marriage to the odious earl who, in truth, was more than ten years older than her father. On those occasions her father had raged at her, accusing her of being an ungrateful chit and declaring she should feel honored because the earl had asked for her hand. No amount of pleading on Season's part could sway her father. He was determined that his daughter would be Countess of Ransford.

As the date for the wedding drew near, Season became almost desperate to save herself from the lecherous old man. The young girl thought that if her mother were still alive she might have taken her side in the matter, but Season's mother had been dead for twelve years. The girl had been left motherless at an early age.

Season's father was very rarely at Chatsworth Castle. He placed great importance on his seat in The House of Lords and spent the majority of his time in London. He took very little interest in his daughter or his country estates. Season had learned long ago that she was little more than an afterthought where her father was concerned.

The coach accident that had taken her mother's life twelve years ago had also killed Season's only brother, and since that time her father had changed from a gentle, caring man to a cold one who hardly ever smiled. He didn't seem to concern himself overmuch with the welfare of his only child. Season hadn't been to

London since she was ten years old. For that matter, she'd rarely gone farther than the village at the foot of Chatsworth Castle. It appeared that her father had all but forgotten her existence.

Season was often lonely because she had no companions of her own age. Most of the time she could be found riding her favorite black gelding, Cinibar. She spent many hours racing across the vast Chatsworth estate, her golden hair flying in the wind, Cinibar her only companion.

Yet for all her father's disinterest in her, he hadn't neglected her education. When she had been younger he had employed a strict governess who had taught Season all the finer graces that befitted a lady of her high station, and as she had grown older, her father had engaged a tutor, a dance instructor, and a music teacher. Season now realized that her father had been grooming her for an advantageous marriage.

Unlike most young girls her age, Season loved to read, and she spent hours pouring over the tomes in her father's vast library. Her favorite reading was poetry and romance. The Lady Season Chatsworth was a hopeless romantic. She often dreamed of a handsome young man who would carry her away with him. Yet Season knew her dreams would never be. No young gentleman had come to sweep her into his arms and declare his undying love for her, and Lord Ransford fell far short of the dashing young hero she had created in her mind. She was young and alive and couldn't stand the thought of being shut away from the world in Lord Ransford's dark castle.

While she was growing up, Season hadn't been entirely unhappy. She had been surrounded by servants who looked after her every comfort. Indeed, she would be perfectly content to live out her days at Chatsworth Castle . . . if only she could meet the man who would sweep her off her feet and fulfill her girlhood dreams.

Two weeks ago, Season's father had sent a dressmaker from London to make her wedding trousseau, and if it weren't for the fact that she was being forced into a marriage she didn't want, she would have been elated by all the new gowns. In the past, a seamstress from the village had made all her clothing. Now her father had sent a Frenchwoman from one of the finest establishments in London to see that she was properly gowned. Season was being outfitted with evening gowns, morning gowns, riding habits, nightgowns, and robes. She had shoes to match each outfit, along with bonnets, gloves, capes, and shawls—everything a new bride would need to take to her new home . . . everything, except a man she chose to marry, and perhaps a kind word from her father.

Season looked again at her reflection in the mirror. She was dressed in a simple, light blue gown with white puffed sleeves. The bodice was tightly laced across her breasts and the waist was fitted to call attention to her eighteen-inch circumference. For all her new finery, Season sometimes preferred to dress simply, especially when she was grooming her horse, Cinibar. What did it matter how she dressed, she thought, biting her lower lip. There was no one to notice how she was gowned.

45

"'Tis said, oh shame to be sacrificed for fame!" she said aloud, quoting one of her favorite poems. There was no doubt in Season's mind that she was being sacrificed by her father to the Earl of Ransford. The reason for it she could only guess. Perhaps her father wanted to be rid of the responsibility for her upkeep. In the past she had pleaded with him to take her to London so she could be presented at court, but he had refused her so often that finally she had given up asking altogether.

It was a lonely, solitary life at Chatsworth. The young girl was never invited to attend any of the village functions, since it would be unseemly for the Lady Season Chatsworth to socialize with the locals. She sighed heavily, and reflected that she didn't seem to belong anywhere. She had grown up without benefit of family or friends.

Pushing an unruly lock of golden hair away from her face, Season bit her lip. She had only a short time of freedom left. In three weeks she would become the wife of Lord Ransford. If only there were some way she could save herself from this marriage, she thought unhappily.

Shaking her head, Season picked up her straw bonnet, tied it under her chin, and walked out the door of her bedroom. If nothing else, she would enjoy her last three weeks of freedom to the fullest.

As she made her way to the stables, Season decided she would groom and curry Cinibar. Perhaps after luncheon, she would ride to Chatsworth Village. The people of the village always seemed genuinely happy to see her. They were always warm and friendly to their lord's daughter.

Season patted Cinibar's black coat, which gleamed from the brushing she had just given him, and gazed out the stable door, allowing her eyes to move over Chatsworth Castle. The aged white brick structure was the only home she had ever known. She felt an ache deep inside, knowing she would soon be leaving it behind. The huge castle was made up of two different architectural styles: the oldest part had been constructed during William the Conquer's time, and boasted nine Norman towers; the latter wing, added in time of Henry VIII, represented the Tudor era. At one time there had been a moat surrounding the castle, but it had been filled in with earth during Season's great-grandfather's life; he had complained of the stench that came from the foul, stagnant water. However, a huge lake was located behind the castle, and in warmer weather a large number of white swans drifted lazily over the water.

Looking up at the sky, Season noticed it was a bleak, overcast day. It looked as if snow might fall before the afternoon ended.

"My lady," Tom, the stableboy, said, coming up beside her, "there be a coach drawing up in front of the main house. I think it's the Lord Ransford."

At first Season thought Tom must be mistaken. Not even Lord Ransford would dare visit her while her father was away in London and she was unchaperoned.

Peeping around the stable door, she saw it was, indeed, he. She felt fear, knowing there was no one to protect her from the earl. Lately he had become very bold in his advances toward her. How would he behave with her father away?

"He is not alone," she said, observing the two other gentlemen who stepped from the coach.

Season frowned, remembering the last time Lord Ransford had visited Chatsworth. On that occasion he had told her he couldn't wait to show off his young, innocent bride-to-be to his friends.

Her eyes flashed with anger. How dare he come to her home when he knew very well that she would be alone and unchaperoned! Yet this act was so typical of him, she wondered why she was so shocked by his behavior. Did he think he could parade her before his friends as a fine catch? Season knew her father well enough to realize even he wouldn't be overpleased by Ransford's untimely visit. She hoped he would be furious at the man's audacity.

Suddenly a devilish plan began to form in Season's mind. Knowing what a prideful man Ransford was, she knew he would want her to make the best impression on his friends. Unmindful of the far-reaching consequences of thwarting the earl, she decided this would be the perfect occasion to rid herself of the hateful man.

"Tom, tell Simms to inform Lord Ransford and his friends that I am in the stable. Tell him not to inform Ransford that I know he is here. When you have delivered the message return to me, posthaste." Season smiled to herself, awed by her own daring.

She watched Tom rush away to do her bidding,

feeling a prickle of guilt. She intended to use the poor unsuspecting stableboy in her plan to be rid of Ransford. Tom's father was the innkeeper in the village, and for the last six months Tom had been helping out at the Chatsworth stables. Season wasn't sure of his age. Though he was tall and muscular, she judged him to be no more than sixteen.

When Tom returned and told her he had delivered her message to Simms, the butler, Season almost changed her mind. Tom's blue eyes were sparkling so innocently she couldn't seem to bring herself to use him so shamelessly, and she was in the process of leaving the stables, when Lord Ransford's voice reached her ears.

"Wait until you see my lady love. She is scarcely out of the schoolroom. She has lived in the country all her life and hasn't acquired the wicked ways so many London maidens have," Ransford bragged to his contemporaries.

"I have heard it said that she is a real beauty and will bring with her a large dowry. You are indeed a fortunate man if the stories one hears about the Lady Season are true," one of the men speculated.

"You are damned lucky, Ransford. Would that I were the one to take such a young innocent to the marriage bed." The lewd remark came from the third man.

Season felt her face burn with indignation and embarrassment at hearing herself discussed in such a crude way. In that moment, the young girl knew she would have to go through with her plan. She could never marry a man who allowed his friends to make sport of her innocence. Glancing at Tom, she read the pity in his bright eyes, and setting her jaw stubbornly, Season mentally prepared herself to act a part.

"Oh, she's innocent all right, I would never give my proud name to some flighty, promiscuous miss," Ransfored declared.

As the stable door was pushed open, Season sprung into action. She propelled herself against a startled Tom, knocking him off balance, and sending them both tumbling into a pile of fresh hay.

"Forgive me, Tom," she whispered. "I am desperate— please help me!"

Poor Tom was just getting over the shock of the lady of the manor landing atop him when her sweet lips covered his. Raising her head, Season's green eyes held a beseeching glint in their misty depths.

"Please, Tom, kiss me," she pleaded.

Tom didn't stop to consider. He knew there would be hell to pay over this day's incident, but he couldn't resist her plea. His arms slid about her slender waist, and he rolled her beneath him, seeking her lips. He knew if it were not for the audience that would soon descend upon them, he would have felt that he had died and gone to heaven at the taste of the beautiful Lady Season's honeyed lips. He would have been willing to wager that nowhere in all England was there so fair a maiden. She was as far above him as the sun was from the earth.

However, since everyone on Chatsworth knew of the lady's trouble—being betrothed to the ancient earl— Tom realized immediately that she was playing a game and trying to free herself of the Earl of Ransford. At that moment, however, the stableboy would have died for her had she asked it of him.

"Here, what's this?" Lord Ransford's enraged voice boomed out.

Season braced herself for whatever was to come. She pretended to be shocked as she pushed Tom away and sat up, pulling a piece of hay from her tumbled curls.

"My lord, I . . . had no notion you were coming. I did not expect to see you." She was surprised at how guilty her voice sounded. She hadn't known she could be such a convincing actress.

Lord Ransford's face was red with anger and indignation. "You sly baggage," he choked. "I will never give my name to a harlot such as you!" He couldn't look his companions in the eye, knowing they were as shocked as he was. He had wanted Season as his bride. He would still have wed her, had it not been for the fact that she had shamed him before his good friends.

"How long has this been going on behind my back?" he demanded to know.

"Oh, my lord," Season said, standing up and nervously pressing a wrinkle out of her gown. "Please do not think I behave this way at all times. Besides Tom here, I have been with no more than six other men," she said, playing her part to the hilt. "I thought you might well appreciate having a wife with some experience." Delighted by her own daring, she could hardly contain the joy she felt at the stricken look on the old lord's face.

"You, miss, are the most unscrupulous tart of them all. You haven't heard the last of this. Your actions today will not only reach your father's ears but also the ears of the king!" He turned his anger on the boy, Tom.

51

"You, young man, will pay a high price for tossing this lady in the hay! I wish you a good day as well as good-bye. He turned abruptly and stalked out of the stable, followed closely by his two stunned friends.

Season stood motionless for a moment. It had been too easy. She knew there would be reprisals from her father and realized she hadn't heard the end of today's deed; still, she smiled. No matter how angry her father would be when he heard about what had occurred, she felt her heart lighten. She was free of Lord Ransford!

The Lady Season turned slowly to face her accomplice and smiled slightly. "Tom, I hope you do not believe I am promiscuous as did Lord Ransford. I doubt that you understand why I acted so brazenly."

"But I do, my lady. We all on Chatsworth know that you ain't been happy." He grinned rakishly. "If you don't mind me saying so, and meaning no disrespect, my lady . . . it was a real pleasure to help you out."

Season couldn't help but laugh at his bold reply. "Be that as it may, Tom, I have brought trouble down upon your head. My father will not be well pleased when he finds out what happened here today. It would be well for you to be gone from here when he returns home."

Tom ran his hand through his sandy-colored hair. "Well, my lady, I have this powerful itch to see Dublin. My father has long had his mind set on me visiting my aunt who lives there."

Season nodded, wishing she had somewhere to hide from her father's wrath. As she walked out of the stable, she watched Lord Ransford's departing coach roll down the driveway. She knew he was on his way to London to see her father.

Tom came up beside her, and they both watched the coach until it was out of sight.

"I suppose after today my reputation will be ruined," Season observed softly. "It seems a high price to pay for one's freedom."

"No one will hear about today from me, my lady," Tom stated loyally.

Season smiled inwardly as her spirits began to soar. It didn't matter what trouble resulted from today's actions. Whatever happened, whatever price she would have to pay, being rid of Lord Ransford was worth it. She gazed at the winding tree-lined roadway, where only the dust created by Lord Ransford's departing coach remained as a grim reminder of his visit.

A cold wind was blowing, and a light snow had begun to fall. Season lifted her face to the sky, feeling free and light-hearted at last. She wouldn't worry about the kind of punishment her father might choose to inflict on her. Nothing he could do to her would be as bad as being forced to marry Lord Ransford!

Chapter Four

As it happened, Season had to wait in fear and uncertainty for a fortnight before her father finally came to Chatsworth. During that time, the castle was unusually quiet; even the servants seemed to be on edge and spoke only in whispers. No one mentioned the incident that had taken place in the stable except Season's personal servant, Molly. The maid had tended Season since birth, and she said things to Season that no one else would dare express. Molly had not hesitated to make known her views regarding Season's conduct with Tom, and she was sure the roof would cave in on them all when the master returned home.

Season was out riding Cinibar when her father arrived. Upon her return, she saw her father's coach and six being unhitched by the new stableboy. She swallowed the lump in her throat and made her way to the house.

Fear gnawed at her insides when Simms gave her a sympathetic smile.

"Your father is waiting for you in the study, my lady. He asked to see you at once."

As Season approached her father's study she had to force one foot in front of the other, and her hands were trembling when she reached the heavy, nail-studded oak door. Squaring her shoulders, she rapped lightly.

"The door's open," her father's voice boomed out.

Season took a deep breath and entered the room. Her father was seated at his desk, and his eyes pierced her with an angry glare. Her heart seemed to plummet as he drummed his fingertips on the surface of the desk.

Lord Mason Chatsworth was a handsome man. His face was finely chiseled, and his body was still firm and hard. His hair was devoid of powder, but otherwise his appearance was immaculate, as always. His pale blue satin cutaway coat had pearl buttons down the front, and his matching knee breeches had white trim down the side seam. He stood up slowly and motioned Season into a chair, while his angry green eyes never once left her face.

Season still clutched her silver-handled riding whip in her hand as she sat on the edge of a red velvet chair, watching her father's every move.

"Hello, Papa," she said in a small voice. "I'm glad you are home."

He walked the length of the room and back before he stopped in front of Season. "Are you, miss? Are you indeed glad to see me?" he asked in a strangled voice.

Season lowered her head. "Yes, Papa. I am always glad to see you."

"You know why I'm here?" he demanded, reaching out, gripping her chin, and raising her face so she was forced to meet his eyes.

"Yes, Papa."

"Lord, I must be cursed to have such a daughter. I am thankful that your mother isn't alive to witness the shame you have brought upon this family. However, I suppose I have no one to blame but myself; I trusted you to act in a manner which would befit your station in life. I should have been more strict instead of being so indulgent with you."

Season blinked in astonishment. By no stretch of the imagination had her father ever indulged her. True, she had been given everything that money could buy, but she had never had the pleasure of her father's company save for a few short weeks in the summer. Never had she had his love or indulgence.

"Do you have the slightest notion what you have done, miss?" he asked pointedly.

She raised her chin proudly. "Yes, Papa, I know exactly."

"I don't think you do. Allow me to enlighten you. Because of your disgraceful performance, Lord Ransford has withdrawn his marriage agreement, and who can blame him?"

"I was sure he would," Season said in a voice hardly above a whisper. Her father seemed to loom over her, bigger than life, and she didn't know what punishment he had in mind for her.

"That's not all. Ransford has spread the most ungentlemanly tales about you, miss!"

"I'm sorry that you are angry with me, Papa, but I'm not sorry that Lord Ransford has canceled his marriage contract with me. I decided I just couldn't marry that awful man."

Her father's eyebrows shot up. "It wasn't your decision to make, Season. You are too young to know what's good for you."

"Papa, I tried to talk to you about Lord Ransford, but you wouldn't listen to me. When you weren't looking, he would put his hands on me and make the most lewd statements. I . . . hated him."

Lord Chatsworth's eyes darkened. "I suppose there was no reason to hope he would act charitably toward you. Perhaps he had already gotten wind of your reputation and saw no reason to treat you with respect. What is done cannot be undone, but you will rue the day you shamed me, miss."

"Papa! I never allowed a man to . . . I didn't . . . you don't understand." She was horrified that her father should believe she had behaved in an unmaidenly fashion. "I'm sor—"

"Stop saying you are sorry. You don't yet know what the word sorry means—but you will, Season. By God you will!"

"What are you going to do to me?" she asked, raising frightened eyes to him.

"You might well ask. I will tell you in good time, but first I want you to know what a scandal you have caused in London. Your conduct has even reached the ears of the king!'"

Season couldn't remember ever having seen her father so angry. Her fondest wish had always been to please him and make him proud of her. She would have done anything to gain his approval—anything but marry Lord Ransford. She had always known she had been a disappointment to him, because she, his daughter, was alive, while his son and heir was dead.

Now as he towered above her, Season could see his nostrils flare. "Ransford has blackened your name, miss, and in doing so, he has blackened my name as well. I called him out, but he refused to fight, saying you weren't worth his life or mine. What do you think of that, Season?"

"Oh, Papa, I didn't think about you calling him out. I would never have forgiven myself if anything had happened to you," she cried, tears streaming down her face. Her father had always been a proud man, and she hated the fact that she had shamed him before the whole world. For the first time she wished she had willingly married Lord Ransford.

"You can spare me your tears, Season. They will neither soften my heart, nor the stand I have been forced to take on your behalf. Do you have any notion what's being said about you in London?"

"Yes, I assume it's being said that Lord Ransford and his friends found me in the hay . . . with the stableboy."

"Yes, that and more. I couldn't believe that my own daughter would behave in such a disgraceful manner." He seemed to shrink visibly. "You look so like an angel, Season."

"Papa, I never . . . I would never—"

"Dammit, girl, stop stuttering. If you have something to say, say it! However, I don't see how you will find anything to say in your own defense, though God only knows I wish you could."

Suddenly Season became angry. Her father believed her guilty. How could he have so little faith in his own daughter? Tears of frustration blinded her as she stood up, looking her father squarely in the eyes.

"How can *you*, my own father, believe what Lord Ransford told you about me? My greatest guilt lies in staging a tête-à-tête for Lord Ransford's benefit. I would hope that as my father, you would have more faith in me."

Mason Chatsworth's eyes gleamed dangerously, but Season saw something besides anger in their green depths. Could it be that she saw pride in her father's eyes? "You had better explain yourself, Season. What are you telling me?"

"I am telling you that before that awful day I had never been so forward with a man. I used poor Tom, the stableboy, to my own advantage. I was angry because Lord Ransford had come to my home while you were away. I wanted to make the earl think I wasn't worthy of being his wife. Nothing happened between me and Tom but a harmless kiss. It was all staged for Lord Ransford's benefit, Papa."

Season saw her father's lips dip into an almost smile, and she did see a glint of pride in his eyes. "By damn, did you now? I always thought you were sweet and mild like your mother, but by heaven, I'm finding out you have some of me in you."

Season was astonished. She had always been in awe of her father. Thinking he wanted her to be a proper lady, she had tried to please him with her soft manners. On the rare occasions when he had been at home, she had always tried to act timid to make him like her. She wondered how different their relationship might have been if she had just been herself.

"You aren't mad at me, Papa?" she asked in a voice

filled with wonder.

"Oh, yes. I am furious with you, but I can see that there may yet be hope for you. It seems you will not allow anyone to push you around, including me—will you? You fought me on this, and dammit, you got your way!"

"I didn't mean to fight you, Papa," she said meekly.

"Oh, yes, you did, Season—but I'm afraid your victory will be short-lived," he told her almost reluctantly.

"What do you mean?" she asked, fearing her father had somehow convinced Lord Ransford to forgive her conduct and continue with the scheduled wedding.

"I mean, miss, that King George was not at all pleased when this unpleasant incident reached his ears. He sent me home to settle your future." Season's father studied her lovely face for a long moment before he spoke again. "How would you like to see the American Colonies, Season?"

Season was astonished. "I haven't given it much thought. There is a war going on in the Colonies, and I have no wish to be scalped by wild Indians."

"Heaven help the Indian who would come up against you," he said laughingly; then his face turned serious. "You will pack your belongings immediately. I have made arrangements for you to take ship for the Colonies in three weeks time. When you reach your destination, you will be married to your cousin, Edmund Kensworthy."

Season's mouth flew open, but her throat seemed to close off before she could make a reply. How could she go to the Colonies and marry a man she hadn't even met? She was being sorely punished for her behavior. Her father was sending her to the end of the world to marry a stranger. Would it not have been better to marry Lord Ransford? At least had she married him, she could have remained in her beloved England.

"There's a war raging in those British holdings. The colonists don't like us," she said in a futile attempt to change her father's mind.

"So there is. If you are fortunate, you will arrive in the Colonies without incident. Pray your damaged reputation doesn't precede your arrival."

Season gripped her riding crop tightly in her hands. She was doomed! Surely this punishment far out-weighed her crime. She feared she would be swallowed up in the wilds of the Americas, never to be heard from again!

As Season's father had promised, no less than three weeks later she boarded the frigate *Good Hope,* bound for the American Colonies. Her numerous trunks were stowed below, and she was offered the best accommodations on the ship. Her father had accompanied her to the ship to make sure of her comfort and to introduce her to Mrs. Tibbs, who would be her chaperone for the duration of the voyage. The short, chubby, Mrs. Tibbs was joining her husband, who was a colonel in the dragoons. It had been arranged that Season would be staying with the Tibbs in New York, until such time as she could be presented to her cousin, Edmund Kens-worthy, as his bride.

When Mason Chatsworth took leave of his daughter, he bade her a brisk farewell and then left the ship without ceremony.

Season stood at the railing of the *Good Hope,* feeling alone and deserted. As she watched the shores of England fade in the distant fog, tears of hopelessness blinded her. She had no one to blame for her predicament but herself, she thought miserably. Molly, Season's faithful servant, stood at her side, crying into a handkerchief and declaring her poor lady had been banished from England forever.

As the days passed into weeks, Season was surprised to find she was enjoying the voyage. She was certain that if her destination were not America she would indeed feel happy. She was young, and her heart was full of adventure. Season tried, without success, to block out the thought of the stranger who awaited her arrival.

She found the captain and his crew to be very respectful of her. She had lived so long in the country that she hadn't realized her father was such an important man. She had always known that her father was a personal friend of King George III, but she hadn't known what importance others placed on that friendship. The realization only made her feel worse since her actions had cast a shadow on her father's good name.

Season tried to remember everything she had heard about her cousin Edmund. All she really knew was that he was the youngest son of her father's uncle, Hugh, the viscount of Pennyworth. She had no notion how old he was or what he looked like. Her father had told her he was a captain in the guard and had a brilliant future ahead of him.

Season had overheard the first mate of the *Good Hope* talking to a fellow officer. In their conversation, it became clear to her that everyone was wondering why the daughter of the Duke of Chatsworth would marry the youngest son of an improvised viscount.

Season pondered her situation. Perhaps it would be best just to take one day at a time. If the ship didn't sink, and if they weren't set upon by the enemy, all her questions about her cousin would be answered upon her arrival.

Mrs. Tibbs wasn't weathering the voyage very well. She spent most of the time in her cabin, burdened by seasickness. Season had sympathy for the poor woman, but was glad she herself hadn't succumbed to that malady. Each time Season would visit the unfortunate Mrs. Tibbs with an offer of help, the woman became nervous and agitated, blaming herself for not being a proper chaperon for the young girl. Mrs. Tibbs was overcome by the honor that the Duke of Chatsworth had bestowed upon her by allowing her to chaperone his only daughter. Indeed, the woman made Season feel uncomfortable with her continuous gushing and bowing.

Season was grateful that neither Mrs. Tibbs, nor the ship's crew traveled in her father's circle of friends, because it was apparent that no one aboard the *Good Hope* had heard about her situation.

One thing was certain, Season had become humbled by her disgrace and had decided she would behave like a proper daughter and marry her cousin, no matter how disagreeable he might turn out to be. That was the least she could do for her father after ruining his good name by her foolish actions. She worried about whether the rumors regarding her and Lord Ransford would reach her cousin Edmund's ears. She hoped not.

Chapter Five

Sir Edmund Kensworthy, captain of His Majesty's Guards, entered the rose-colored ballroom, searching the faces of the crowd. He spotted Lucas Carrington, a distant cousin on his mother's side. As he made his way across the room, many of the ladies stared at him, admiring the cut of his red army coat with the gold epaulettes on his shoulders. He did make a dashing figure in his bright coat and the snowy white knee breeches which suited his muscular form. In the current fashion, his hair was powdered and pulled back in a queue. His eyes were a light blue that sometimes appeared almost gray. Edmund was accustomed to receiving admiring glances from the fair sex. He smiled now at a lovely lady he passed, but he didn't stop to chat with her.

Lucas Carrington was talking to General Henry Clinton, but he watched Edmund's approach out of the corner of his eye. Lucas, unlike his flamboyant cousin, was dressed inconspicuously. He wore a white lawn shirt with ruffles at the wrist. His black velvet trousers fit to the knees and white silk hose covered his legs. His black velvet jacket was unadorned except for silver buttons. Unlike the other gentlemen in the room, Lucas wore his hair unpowdered, and his gold-colored eyes were alert and intelligent. His handsome face was unreadable as he listened intently to General Clinton speak.

"Lucas, my boy, I could use someone with your talent in my service. You know the countryside, perhaps you would be beneficial to us in our intelligence service."

"I'm flattered by your offer, General, but alas, I am only a simple planter. It is my belief that he who feeds the army, also serves," Lucas said lazily.

"Quite right, my boy, quite right. It takes an enormous amount of food to feed the troops, and you have contributed greatly in that respect."

Sir Henry Clinton was the commander of the British troops in America. To date he had managed to hold New York and wage a successful blockade of America's northern coast. He liked Lucas Carrington, who had descended from a proud old English family on his mother's side. Sir Henry didn't hold Lucas' father against him, even though he had been born on the American continent.

"I wonder, Lucas, if there is anything you *do* feel strongly about?" Sir Henry asked, eying the young gentleman closely.

"Excuse me, Sir Henry," Edmund said, interrupting the conversation, "I am told that my cousin, Lucas, feels strongly about the opposite sex."

General Clinton laughed deeply. "I have heard you fare well in that department yourself, Edmund."

"Modesty prevents me from answering, sir," Edmund said, a twinkle in his eye.

"Perchance your carefree days are over, Edmund. I have heard your betrothed will be presented to you later in the evening," the general said with mirth.

"Yes, it would seem so, my lord. I wonder, have you seen her? Can you tell me what she looks like?"

"Of course I have seen her. How could I allow Lord Chatsworth's only daughter to land in New York without paying my respects to her."

"Is she fair of face, sir," Edmund asked.

"Well," the general said evasively, "good looks aren't everything. After speaking to her I found her very well informed. We spoke of the books we have read, and I found her to be most intelligent."

"Good lord, a bluestocking. I can already tell by your description that she is not fair to look upon. Pray, she doesn't have a wart on her nose!"

"What is this, Edmund?" Lucas Carrington broke in. "Am I to understand that you are to take a bride?"

Lord Clinton chuckled to himself and walked off, shaking his head. He enjoyed a good jest as well as the next fellow. He thought it wouldn't hurt young Edmund to squirm a bit.

Edmund gave his cousin, Lucas, a woebegone look. "Let's find a place where we can talk privately," he said, leading the way out of the noisy, crowded room.

Lucas gave Edmund a quizzical glance as they entered the morning room and found it to be empty; then he turned to his cousin. "Now, tell me, Edmund, what's this about you getting married?"

Edmund seated himself on the sofa and leaned his head back against the soft cushions, staring at the ceiling. "You have heard me speak of my uncle, the Duke of Chatsworth?"

"Yes, of course I have. I met him once while we were at Eton together."

"Well, it seems I am to marry his daughter," Edmund stated flatly.

Lucas laughed and lowered his tall frame onto a gray brocade chair. "I must say you don't sound too happy about the event. Am I to gather you aren't looking forward to a life of wedded bliss?"

"My feelings don't count in the matter. It seems the duke paid a visit to my father, and between the two of them, it was decided I would marry my cousin, the Lady Season Chatsworth," Edmund said sourly.

"Good lord, an arranged marriage. I am well pleased I am only related to you on our mother's side. I don't believe I would want to be under the thumb of the illustrious Duke of Chatsworth."

"You can mock him if you like, Lucas, but my uncle is a very powerful man in England. It is said he is second only to the king. Had I been consulted in the matter, I might well have said no to the arrangement, but I doubt that my uncle's wishes have ever been thwarted."

"Am I to take it that you have never seen your bride-to-be?" Lucas asked in a disbelieving voice.

"I am sure I must have seen her at some family gathering, but she didn't seem to leave a lasting impression on my memory. From the way General Clinton spoke of her, I assume she is no great prize," Edmund said ruefully.

"Still, Edmund, she is the daughter of a duke. That's reaching high, is it not?"

"You haven't heard the worst, Lucas. A letter arrived from my sister, only this morning. She wrote me of the gossip going around London concerning my betrothed. It seems the Lady Season was pledged to marry a Lord Ransford, until he caught her in a very compromising situation with a stableboy. The talk is she isn't too selective about whom she beds. She is no innocent maiden."

"That could explain many things. Do you think you are being used to cover the rumors about the lady's past . . . indiscretions?"

"Damned right! I'm being made the scapegoat. By marrying her, I give her respectability."

"You could always say no," Lucas suggested lazily.

Edmund shook his head. "No. That is a luxury I can't afford. I was told by my father that the lady brings with her a large dowry, and I'll be assured of a promotion in the army. My father suggested it wouldn't be wise to offend my uncle by not accepting my cousin's hand in marriage."

Lucas studied his fingertips. "Oh well, take heart, Edmund. You can always keep your little wife in the country and visit her as infrequently as possible. I have never put too much importance on marriage vows."

Edmund looked at his cousin sourly. "That's easy for you to say. You aren't being forced to take a wife against your will."

"Let's just say that I, like you, enjoy the free life. I

refuse to be tied down to just one woman. Cheer up, being married doesn't mean you have to be the model husband."

"Dammit, Lucas, in my mind's eye, I can already see her! Most probably she has a horse face and twitters or giggles excessively. I can only imagine that she is a wretched creature if her father sent her from England in disgrace."

"Well, as for myself, I would never allow anyone to force me to marry—especially if the lady's reputation were tarnished. You had better consider long and hard before you give your final consent, my friend," Lucas warned.

"Would you take the lady in question as your wife if you were offered a country estate of two thousand acres and a yearly income of fifty thousand pounds?" Edmund wanted to know.

"No, my friend, not even then. If I ever do get married, it will be to someone of my own choice."

"Let's talk about something else," Edmund said, changing the subject. "Why didn't you accept General Clinton's offer this evening? I'm having very little doubt he would see that you got a worthy commission."

"It doesn't suit me to be a soldier. As I told the general, I am but a humble planter from Virginia."

Edmund frowned. "If you are a humble planter, then I'm a Whig sympathizer, Lucas. There has never been anything humble about you."

"Don't associate me with your ambitions, Edmund. You are the one who won all the honors at swordplay when we were at Eton—you are a natural-born soldier."

Edmund stood up. "Let's join the ball. There are some pretty misses with whom I would like to dance, and I have little doubt that my intended bride will arrive shortly. It wouldn't be wise to keep her waiting."

The coach stopped in front of the large stone mansion where the ball was already in progress. Sounds of music and laughter drifted through the air as Colonel Tibbs led Lady Season Chatsworth up the steps. When they reached the top, Season took a deep breath. She felt very young, and frightened. It had been her wish to be introduced to her cousin at the formal ball, since she had been nervous about meeting him in private. She now wondered if that had been such a good idea. Tonight she was in a foreign country, surrounded by strangers. One of those strangers would soon be her husband.

Season had dressed carefully, hoping to make a good impression. Her ice-blue velvet gown was adorned with yards and yards of silver trim, and silver lace flowers were sewn along the hem. In the center of each flower was a tiny seed pearl. Season's matching floor-length cape was lined with rich mink, but she felt no warmth from it at the moment. She didn't know if her hands trembled from the cold or from fright. Molly had arranged Season's hair atop her head, except for one long curl which hung over her shoulder, and although Season had given in with ill grace when her maid had insisted on powdering her hair, she knew she had seldom looked better. Indeed, she had rarely been dressed as fashionably and she had never been to a ball such as the one she was attending tonight.

Season wished Mrs. Tibbs hadn't taken ill. She would have preferred her company tonight. A hundred butterfly wings fluttered inside her stomach as they approached the double doors, and Season felt the chill wind sting her cheeks as the doors were quickly opened and the colonel ushered her inside. A butler in full military dress and powdered wig took Season's cape and requested their names before leading them into the grand ballroom.

Edmund was deep in conversation with Lucas when the butler cleared his throat to make his announcement. The servant's voice rose above the music since he was introducing such an important guest. "The Lady Chatsworth, and Colonel Tibbs," he boomed.

Season could feel all eyes turn in her direction and she nervously clutched her silver lace fan tightly in her hand. She smiled weakly at General Clinton as he moved forward to take her hand.

"You are the loveliest young woman I have seen since leaving England, Lady Season," he said, beaming at her.

Season was unaccustomed to receiving compliments and made no reply other than a soft "Thank you." She was acutely aware that somewhere in that sea of faces was the man she was to marry. She laid her hand lightly on General Clinton's proffered arm and raised her head proudly, hoping she would present a picture of elegant sophistication. She did not want to reveal the frightened young girl she felt herself to be at the moment.

General Clinton smiled down at her in a fatherly manner. "Come, my dear. I have it on good authority that Edmund Kensworthy is anxious to make your acquaintance."

The music had ceased, and the crowd seemed to move aside to allow them free passage. Season couldn't help but overhear some of the remarks people made as she passed. "Imagine, a duke's daughter," someone declared. "What an exquisite gown," someone else was heard to say. "She is beautiful," another whispered. Season felt anything but beautiful at that moment. She was terribly frightened.

She caught a glimpse of two men standing at the end of the long line of people. Her eyes went first to the taller one. His imposing presence seemed to cast everyone else into shadow though he was modestly dressed in black velvet. He was tall and broad shouldered. Season couldn't help but notice that his handsome face was deeply tanned and his hair was unpowdered.

As she drew near she could see that the man's eyes were the startling color of liquid gold. He didn't smile, but instead looked at her boldly, almost insolently, causing her to lower her gaze.

Season's heart was beating rapidly as General Clinton stopped before the two men. She waited for what seemed an eternity for the general to make the introduction, meanwhile she dared to steal another glimpse at the imposing stranger through half-veiled lashes. This was the man of her girlhood fantasies. Handsome was too tame a word to describe him. He was alive and virile. His brilliant golden eyes were half amused, half mocking. Oh, please, please, she prayed silently, let this man be my cousin, Edmund Kensworthy!

As Lucas watched the Lady Chatsworth walk gracefully toward him he thought the blue of her gown gave her skin the appearance of silken alabaster. As she drew nearer, he noted her lovely, delicate features and her unusual green eyes. Surely nature had erred in painting her eyes; never had he seen such a brilliant green. Although the lady's hair was powdered, Lucas instinctively knew in its natural state it would be golden in color. Lucas was a man of the world and had seen many beautiful women, but he had not seen one who rivaled this lovely vision. He remembered the story of her tarnished reputation. Why does she appear so shy and frightened? he wondered. She must be a very adept actress, he thought, because she certainly seems to be an innocent. She appears as pure and untouched as an angel. He reminded himself that she was a trollop, and reflected that he had thought she would be older. His eyes rested on her slightly parted lips that seemed to invite a man's kiss; then his gaze dropped to the modestly high neckline of her gown and he noticed how snugly it fit her full, firm breasts. When he looked back at her face, he could have sworn the blush that stained her cheeks was genuine.

General Clinton interrupted the silence. "Lady Chatsworth, may I present to you your cousin, Edmund Kensworthy." The general smiled at Edmund's confusion.

Season had paid no heed to the man to whom Lord Clinton had just introduced to her. Now he bowed politely. In a bold display, he took her hand and raised it to his lips. She felt a fool as he brushed her fingertips with his mouth.

"I am indeed honored to meet you, my lady,"

74

Edmund said, smiling brightly. He could hardly contain his joy or believe his good fortune. His future bride was the most beautiful woman he had ever seen!

Season faced her future husband with a sinking heart. Why was she feeling such overwhelming disappointment? Edmund Kensworthy was a well-set man with a sincere light in his blue eyes. She would have considered him handsome had he not been standing next to the dark silent stranger.

Season looked once more into those golden eyes as if beseeching their possessor not to allow all her girlhood fantasies to die so suddenly. She tried to find her voice, but even breathing seemed difficult. In her distress, she tried to hide her confusion by turning back to her cousin Edmund.

"I . . . am pleased to make your acquaintance, sir," she said, hardly above a whisper.

"I look forward to the time when we shall come to know one another, my lady," Edmund said, his good humor at finding his bride so pleasant to the eye obvious.

"My father sends his regards," she said, for want of something better to say. Her whole being was attuned to the tall stranger who was still silently appraising her.

"I am pleased indeed that my uncle should think of me," Edmund replied, suddenly noticing where his bride-to-be's attention was focused. As always, Lucas seemed to draw the eyes of any female away from him. Edmund was perturbed that it should be so with his intended bride. Good manners dictated that he should present Lady Chatsworth to Lucas, however, so he had no choice.

"My lady, may I present my cousin, Lucas Carrington. Lucas, Lady Season Chatsworth."

Season's eyes widened in surprise. "If the two of you are cousins, does that mean I am also related to you, Mr. Carrington?"

"Lucas inclined his head. "I fear it isn't the case, my lady. You see Edmund is related to me on his mother's side, while he is aligned with you through his father. I am loath to tell you that I am no more than Edmund's country cousin from America."

Lucas Carrington's voice was deep, and the sound of it sent shivers down Season's spine. She could read insolence in his eyes and she realized that Mr. Carrington was trying to be insulting to her. His rudeness fanned her anger to life, and she gave him her haughtiest glance.

"What a pity," she said. Watching his golden eyes light up with amusement, she began to blush with maidenly shyness, and to cover her confusion she turned back to face Edmund Kensworthy.

"You do not look anything like your American cousin, and he speaks with a strange accent," she told Edmund. Season felt herself flush again, and she was afraid that she was babbling like a silly schoolgirl. She heard deep laughter behind her and realized Lucas Carrington was amused by her foolish statement.

"I am what you would term a colonial, my lady—thus the accent. If you will excuse me, I see a friend. It was a pleasure to meet you, my lady. Do enjoy your stay in my country." He bowed curtly and walked leisurely away. Season watched as he approached a lovely lady, took her hand, and led her away from the crowd.

76

"I hope you will forgive my little jest earlier, Edmund," General Clinton said and laughed jovially.

Edmund's laughter joined his. "You did have me squirming on tenterhooks for a while, sir," he admitted.

Season paid little attention to the conversation Edmund held with the general; she was intent on watching Lucas Carrington take his partner out the side door to what she supposed would be the garden. Perhaps he is married and that woman is his wife, she thought, wondering why that speculation made her heart feel so heavy. She was having a strange reaction to a man she had met only a few moments ago.

"I wonder if you would do me the honor of being my partner for the next dance?" General Clinton asked, breaking into Season's thoughts. "As your future husband's commanding officer, I feel it is my right."

Season nodded her agreement and offered him her hand. She found that she and the general danced the minuet well together. It was the first time she had danced with anyone other than her dance instructor, and she was pleased to find that she had been taught well. At least she hadn't embarrassed herself by being clumsy.

Later Season danced with Edmund and found him a delightful partner—smoother and more agile than the general had been. She was beginning to relax and enjoy herself.

"What do you think of the Colonies?" Edmund asked when they came together at one of the turns.

"I have seen very little of it so far. Mrs. Tibbs, the lady who is my chaperon, has been ill and unable to show me around."

They drew apart; Season curtsied to her new partner and then moved back to Edmund.

"We shall have to remedy this situation," Edmund told her, smiling. "I have a week's liberty and would be glad to show you around if you would allow it."

"Thank you, I would like that," she said, beginning to warm to the man who would soon be her husband. He was indeed handsome and had a most charming manner. Season began to think he would make a very admirable marriage partner. She realized he wasn't the man her young heart had dreamed of, but he was far better than the odious Lord Ransford.

When the music stopped, Edmund took her about the room, introducing her to his friends. Few of them had ever met the daughter of a duke, so they appeared stiff and formal when, in truth, they didn't know how to address Season.

She felt most uncomfortable and was glad when Edmund led her to the morning room where the two of them could talk in private. He settled her on the sofa and then took a chair across from her.

"I am aware of how difficult it has been for you to come to this country and to be thrown in with so many strangers, my lady."

Season was immediately warmed by his kindness. "Please call me Season," she urged.

He chuckled. "I think that would be most wise under the circumstances—will you call me Edmund?"

"Yes, of course, Edmund."

His eyes drifted across her face, and he couldn't help but draw in his breath at how lovely she was. "As I told you earlier, I have a week's liberty. Would you consider it bad form if I were to ask you to marry me this soon?"

Season opened her fan nervously and closed it with a snap. "I . . . hardly know you. Could we not wait until we are better acquainted?"

Edmund smiled. "Of course. Perhaps it would be wise. I will want to find a suitable house for you. I know everything here is new to you, including myself. We will wait until you feel more at home." His eyes fastened on hers. "I hope you will not delay too long."

Season saw something in his eyes that she couldn't define. It was a deep searching look, and suddenly she knew he had heard the rumors that had been circulated about London by Lord Ransford.

"Edmund . . . I am aware that there is talk about me, but let me assure you—"

"Do not speak of it, my lady," he said hurriedly. "We shall close the chapter of your past and make a new beginning. Before I met you tonight, I wasn't too happy about the prospect of making you my wife." He took her hand. "Now that we have met, I will feel honored to be your husband."

Season couldn't help but be confused by this man. If he believed the wicked lies about her, why would he want to marry her? "You are very kind. I would like to tell you about myself, however. I believe I owe you that much."

Edmund raised her hand to his lips. "I will not ask for your confession."

Before Season could react, Edmund moved to sit beside her. His hand slid down her shoulder to boldly rest against her breast. For a moment she looked at him in shock, too stunned to react. As his fingers began to trace a pattern across her breast, her anger soared.

"How dare you, sir!" she cried, pushing his hand away and quickly rising to her feet. "You take liberties that are not allowed!"

Edmund jerked himself to a standing position. "Don't try to play the innocent with me, cousin. I can assure you, your reputation has preceded you."

Season shook her head. "I don't understand. You were so kind a moment ago."

"Oh, I shall be kind to you, Season, but I will never trust you. Don't you think I was aware that you couldn't keep your eyes off Lucas Carrington tonight? Don't you think he was aware of it also?"

"I . . . didn't . . . I thought he was you."

"Listen well, Season. Lucas is my cousin and a friend, but that friendship doesn't mean we will be sharing your favors. When you take my name, I will expect you to honor me. I will not be the laughingstock of the regiment—do I make myself clear?"

Season glared at the man's audacity. She had been willing to tell Edmund the truth about herself, but now her lips were sealed. She couldn't bear to think of being married to a man who didn't trust her. She had only met Edmund tonight, yet already she could feel his possessiveness and jealousy. If he was this bad now, what would he be like when they were married?

"If you do not wish to marry me, I release you from any obligation," she said, hoping he would, indeed, release her.

Before Season knew what was happening, he pulled her against him and forced her to look into his eyes. "Oh, no, Season, I will never release you. You will be my wife, and if you should ever play me false . . ." His hand tightened on her chin, and Season blinked at the pain.

She tried to move away as he lowered his head, knowing he was going to kiss her. She struggled as his lips covered hers. Season remembered the time Lord Ransford had tried to kiss her and she had bitten his lip. She didn't hesitate to do the same to Edmund. He swore loudly as he shoved her away.

Her breasts heaving, Season clenched her fists tightly together. "You are a monster! I wouldn't marry you if you were the last man on earth," she whispered through trembling lips.

"Yes, you will. You have no choice. It will be my good name which will bring you respectability. Do you think now that I've seen you I will let you go?"

Angry words tumbled to her lips, but before Season could utter them, a young corporal appeared at the door. "Begging your pardon, sir, but Sir Henry would like to see you in the study."

Season watched as Edmund dabbed at his lip with a lace handkerchief. He waited until the corporal left the room before he spoke. "We will settle this later, Season," he said before stalking out of the room, his back straight and his face livid.

Season felt her legs go weak. What manner of man was Edmund Kensworthy? Placing her trembling hands over her eyes, she held back her tears. So much for girlhood dreams of undying love. Something about Edmund frightened her more than Lord Ransford ever had. What could she do—where could she turn for help?

Sitting down on the sofa, she buried her face in the soft cushion. She was in a war-torn land among strangers. Suddenly Season yearned for the comfort of Chatsworth. She was so miserable that she didn't hear a man enter the room. In truth she thought herself to be alone until she heard a deep voice.

"Is there something amiss, Lady Chatsworth," Lucas Carrington inquired.

Season's head snapped up and she stared into the face of the disturbing stranger. "I . . . no, nothing."

Lucas sat down beside her, still gazing into her teary green eyes. He thought nothing could be so lovely and so unsettling as misty green eyes. This woman's unhappiness tugged at his heart. She seemed so young and innocent that he had to remind himself for the second time that night that Lady Chatsworth was not what she seemed.

"I think differently, my lady. Something has caused your tears—or should I say someone?"

"It is nothing for you to be concerned over," she told him, wishing he would go away. "I am but homesick."

"Ah, perhaps there is a young gentleman in England that you pine for," Lucas suggested.

"You have no right to ask that of me," she said, thinking he too had heard the vicious rumors about her. "You are far too bold, sir. I wish you would just go away and leave me to myself."

"I think perhaps you need a friend, just now," he said, showing no indication that he would honor her wish for him to leave.

"I just need some time alone," she said, swallowing hard. In truth she didn't really want to be alone. She desperately needed to talk to someone and Lucas Carrington seemed willing to listen.

"So you miss your home," he stated, dipping his head so he could catch her eye. When she looked at him and nodded, he smiled crookedly. "I know everything is different to you here. You are not accustomed to our ways."

"It's not just that. I don't like being in the city. I was raised in the country where I was allowed to feel free. I feel that I will suffocate with so many people about."

Lucas' smile deepened. "Yes, I suppose one can have more freedom in the country away from prying eyes."

Season looked at Lucas. Did his statement have a double meaning? she wondered. Was he aware of her tarnished reputation? "Do you perhaps live in the country, Mr. Carrington?"

"Yes, as a matter of fact I do. I have a plantation in Virginia."

"I have read about Virginia. It is lovely, is it not?"

"I think so, my lady. I would compare it to your English countryside."

"You have been to England?"

"Yes, on several occasions. My mother was from England, and I attended Eton with Edmund."

Suddenly Season realized that it was improper for her to be alone with Lucas Carrington. She remembered Edmund's warning and knew she was committing a serious breach of etiquette. She did not want to start tongues wagging about her here in the Colonies.

"I must go," she said, rising to her feet.

"Must you leave?" Lucas asked, standing up and towering above her.

"Yes, I'm sure it isn't proper for us to be seen together. It wouldn't be wise to start tongues to wagging. Gossip can be very cruel." Season lowered her head so she wouldn't have to look into those disturbing, golden eyes. When she looked up, she saw amusement behind his lowered lashes.

"Have you found that to be so, my lady?"

"Yes, of course . . . I mean I have seldom been alone with a man. . . . I didn't have too many gentlemen callers since I lived in the country."

Season was startled when Lucas Carrington took her hand, and she could feel her face flush. The strong charge of electricity that flowed between them upset Season.

"Maidenly blushes become you, my lady," he said in a deep voice.

"Insolence doesn't become you, sir," she chided, jerking her hand from his grip.

Deep laughter filled the room. "Tell me, underneath all that powder on your head, is your hair perchance red as your temper would indicate, or is it a brilliant golden color?"

"You go too far, sir! If you are representative of the men from the Colonies, then I can well do without your acquaintance. I can tell you didn't benefit by your education at Eton." Season's temper was rising by degrees.

Still he seemed amused by her. "It's true, I have not the pretty manners of your English-bred gentlemen, but take heart; you will find I am not the rule, but the exception. My fellow countrymen would be able to hold their own with a beautiful lady, such as yourself." A smile played on his sensuous lips, and his golden eyes

84

sparkled with mirth.

Season gathered up her gown and brushed past Lucas Carrington. "I will bid you good-bye, sir."

His laughter followed her out the room.

When she reached the ballroom, Season searched the crowd for Colonel Tibbs. The whole evening had gone from bad to worse as far as she was concerned. She was to marry a man who was insulting and who couldn't keep his hands off her, and she wondered what she had ever seen in Lucas Carrington. She was aware that he had been talking down to her with hidden remarks and innuendos. He was an egotist and a scoundrel, and it had been apparent that he did not think much of her.

At last she spied Colonel Tibbs and headed in his direction. When she reached his side, he was deep in conversation with another officer, so she waited, not wanting to interrupt them.

"Did I hear you say The Raven was sighted last night?" Colonel Tibbs asked.

"Yes. He was spotted near the docks by two of my men," the other officer confirmed.

"Good Lord, he grows bolder with time. I assume he made his escape as he always does?"

"Yes, I'm afraid so. My men gave chase, but The Raven seemed to disappear into thin air."

"Of whom do you speak?" Season asked, interested.

"No one you need concern yourself with, my lady," Colonel Tibbs assured her.

"You spoke of a Raven, but I gather you weren't speaking of a bird," Season said, refusing to be put off.

"That's true," Edmund stated, coming up beside

85

Season and giving her a slight smile. "The Raven is a great irritant to us. He sneaks about in the shadows, and it is said he sails on a phantom ship called the *Andromeda*."

By now Sir Henry Clinton had joined the group as had several of the ladies. "The Raven is more than an irritant to the crown, Edmund," Sir Henry declared in his boisterous voice. "He seems to be in two places at once. Somehow he always knows how to strike at us where he can do the most harm."

"Is he a pirate?" Season asked, her eyes wide.

"He is a pirate, a traitor, and many other names I could never say in front of a lady," the general replied.

"What does he do?" Season pressed.

"In the past six months, The Raven has been responsible for taking five of our merchant ships which were loaded with uniforms and badly needed supplies. He is a most unscrupulous villain," Sir Henry declared.

"Do you know who he is?" Season's curiosity was aroused.

"No," replied Colonel Tibbs. "Whoever knows his identity, isn't telling it. He wears a black hood which hides his true face.

"That's correct," agreed Sir Henry, "but I have high hopes that we will soon capture the traitor. Only this afternoon my men arrested a man called Silas Dunsberry. It is thought that this man knows the true identity of The Raven."

Lucas Carrington joined the group and his eyes locked with his cousin Edmund's.

"Who knows, perhaps I am this villain you speak of," Edmund said, a grim expression on his face.

"Most unlikely, Edmund," Sir Henry retorted. "You wouldn't then have so much time to spend in the company of ladies. . . ." Sir Henry's voice trailed off as he realized his remarks were most unseemly. He cleared his throat as Season sent Edmund a scalding glance.

Suddenly Season had had enough of this ball. All she wanted to do was leave. "I wonder if you would mind taking me home, Colonel Tibbs? I seem to be frightfully weary," she stated to her escort.

Sir Henry summoned a lackey and sent him to fetch Lady Season's wrap. "I wish you farewell, my lady," the general said gallantly. "I take ship tomorrow," he added, taking her proffered hand and raising it to his lips. "I will hope to see you at a later date—perhaps, at your wedding."

Season raised her eyes to see Lucas Carrington staring at her with something akin to hatred burning in his golden gaze. His glance sent shivers down her spine, and she looked quickly away. She wasn't even aware that Edmund stood beside her until he reached for her hand.

"I will call on you tomorrow morning, if that is agreeable to you," Edmund said, taking Season's cape and placing it about her shoulders. Season knew it was no accident that his hand brushed against her breast.

"I'm sorry, but I plan to sleep quite late tomorrow," she replied, scalding him with her green gaze.

Edmund's eyes narrowed and he took her by the arm, steering her toward the door and out of earshot of the others. "Very well, Season, I will see you after luncheon."

87

"No, that will not do. I promised Mrs. Tibbs I would spend the afternoon with her—she hasn't been feeling well." Season raised her chin and challenged Edmund with her eyes.

By now they had been joined by Colonel Tibbs, and Edmund turned to him. "Do you think it would be possible for your wife to forego the pleasure of Season's company tomorrow, so she and I could become better acquainted?"

"Oh, to be sure. I will speak to Edna about it when I arrive home."

Season knew she was trapped. Realizing that she could no longer object without causing a scene, she relented. "I will expect you after luncheon, then Edmund."

Her words were sweetly spoken, but Edmund could read the defiance in her glance.

He smiled slightly, but his blue eyes were as cold as ice. "I look forward to tomorrow." With a curt bow he turned and walked away.

On the coach ride home, Season had many things to ponder. Tonight she had met a man who was handsome enough to make a young girl's heart soar on the wings of love. Yes, Lucas Carrington could fulfill her maidenly dreams, except that he was arrogant and opinionated, and he caused Season's temper to rise. Furthermore, she had discovered that her intended husband, Edmund Kensworthy, didn't hold her in the highest regard.

The two men were nothing alike, and yet each had

touched her life in a different way. Season was discovering that it wasn't much fun to be the daughter of a duke. Perhaps, had she come from humble parentage, she would have been allowed to fall in love and marry the man of her choice.

Season's first week in America was drawing to a close. So far it had been disappointing in every respect. If only Edmund had not turned out to be her intended bridegroom . . . if Lucas Carrington had been her betrothed . . . What a promise of pleasure and fulfillment his golden eyes had offered her tonight, but why had they turned so cold by the end of the evening?

Season turned to Colonel Tibbs. "Tell me, Colonel, is Lucas Carrington married?"

"No, my lady. It is said that no woman can tie him down, though if rumor is to be believed, many have tried."

Season felt relief wash over her, although she wondered why she should care whether or not Mr. Carrington was married. Most probably she would never see him again.

Stop it, she chided herself. Lucas Carrington isn't for you. Stop being a dreamer and face facts. Edmund Kensworthy is your chosen bridegroom, and this time you will obey your father's wishes. Still, she felt wretched knowing that before the month was out she would be Edmund's wife.

Chapter Six

Season sat before the vanity while Molly draped a white cloth about her shoulders. Her eyelids were heavy as she watched her maid unpin her hair and brush the powder from her golden tresses. Season coughed and held her nose as the thin white powder filtered through the air, threatening to choke her.

"I liked it much better when we lived at Chatsworth and I didn't have to bother with powdering my hair, Molly," Season exclaimed, her eyes stinging from the flying particles.

"Now, my lady, you mustn't mind the powder. It's the fashion, and you no longer live in the country," her maid reminded her.

"I still think it a frivolous waste of time," Season stated, covering her eyes with her hands.

"Do you know what my mother told me was the beginning of ladies powdering their hair?" Molly asked, in a jovial mood.

Season covered a yawn. "No," she said, wincing in

pain as Molly brushed a tangle from her hair.

"She told me the style must have gotten its start when some lady of quality didn't like the color of her hair and wanted all other ladies to look as dowdy as she did."

Season smiled at Molly in the mirror. "Your mother was a wise woman. It could be that there is some truth to that statement."

Molly held the hairbrush suspended while she studied her lady's face. "What was your cousin, Edmund Kensworthy, like? Was he handsome?"

Season's eyes locked with Molly's, and the maid could read unhappiness and disillusionment in her glance. "I cannot say that I like him overmuch. He reminds me of a younger version of Lord Ransford." Season hadn't meant to be so blunt, but she had always felt close to Molly. In the past she had confided many things to her maid. "Perhaps I am being unfair to Edmund. He would be considered handsome . . . I suppose."

"You may not like Mr. Edmund, but something or someone has put the blush to your cheeks," Molly observed with her usual uncanny perceptiveness. Molly removed the white cloth from Season's shoulders, taking care not to spill any of the powder on the floor, all the while eying her young mistress.

"It was the cold night air that put the color in my cheeks, Molly, nothing more."

"Hmm, I wonder?" the maid said, grinning.

Season stood up, allowing her maid to unfasten her laces so she could breathe more freely. Next, layer after layer of delicately embroidered petticoats were removed, then the two whalebone rings. Season pulled a white lace nightdress over her head and slipped between the bed covers.

Clamping her hands about her legs, she bit her lower lip reflectively. "Molly, do you believe that there is such a thing as instant love?"

The maid, who had been putting Season's clothing away, paused to look at her lady. "I suspect there might be something akin to instant lust, but I don't know about the love part. To my way of thinking a woman can be as happy with one man as another—long as he don't beat her and is good to her."

"Have you ever seen a man with golden eyes?" Season asked dreamily.

Molly walked over to the bed and peered at Season intently. "I once saw a bird with golden eyes, but never a man. Why do you ask?"

"No reason. I was just curious, that's all." Season lay back against a fluffy pillow. "Gold is a strange color for eyes, is it not?" she reflected.

"Who are you talking about, my lady?" Molly asked suspiciously. I hope it's your cousin who has brought that dreamy expression to your face, but something tells me it ain't."

"No it isn't Edmund. Molly, I met the most extraordinary man tonight. His hair was as black as midnight—he had broad shoulders and was extremely tall. His golden eyes seemed to look deep inside me to some secret place that I never knew existed."

Molly sat down on the edge of the bed and took Season's hand. "Oh, my lady, this cannot be. This man is not for you. Who is he?"

"A planter from Virginia."

"A Colonist!" Molly said, her voice filled with horror as if Season had just announced that the man had the plague. "You could never marry a common man, your father would never allow it."

Season sighed heavily. "This man would never ask me to be his wife, Molly. For some unknown reason he seemed to view me with contempt. I don't know why. At first he was friendly enough, but later on he looked at me with such . . . loathing."

"It's just as well," Molly said, standing up. "It appears to me you had best put this man out of your mind and think more about the man you are to wed. No good can come over mooning after something that can never be."

"It was strange," Season continued, not heeding her maid's warning, "when we first met, it was as if we weren't strangers at all. When he looked at me I felt all funny inside, and it frightened me. His name is Lucas . . . Lucas Carrington, a planter from Virginia."

Molly shook her head. "Uh-huh, I know the feelings you're talking about. If you want my advice, you'll put this Lucifer out of your mind."

"His name is not Lucifer, Molly, it's Lucas—Lucas Carrington."

"Same thing if you ask me. I'm warning you, there ain't no good gonna come out of your thinking about him."

Season looked perplexed. "You are always preaching gloom and doom to me, Molly. I hoped when I told you about Mr. Carrington you would understand my feelings."

"I understand better than you do. It wasn't love that

attracted you to that man; it was lust pure and simple—or unpure and not so simple," Molly stated firmly. "I know his kind, and they bed a different woman every night. You are just too young and inexperienced to deal with a man of this cut."

"You haven't met him. How could you sit in judgment of his character?"

"Oh, I know him all right. I have lived twenty years longer than you have, my lady. As me mother would say, I have been around the bush a few times. Heed my words and forget about this man."

"Snuff out the candle, Molly. I don't want to talk to you any longer," Season ordered sourly.

Molly did as she was told, mumbling all the while about some people not wanting to hear good advice.

Season closed her eyes when she heard Molly leave the room. She knew deep inside that much of what Molly had said made sense. Still . . . Lucas Carrington had struck a cord inside her heart that had never been played before.

Season had no way of knowing that at that very moment her future was being taken out of her hands. She was unaware of the dark, cloaked figure that stood beneath her bedroom window and waited for the house to darken.

The Raven had anchored the *Andromeda* in a secret cove off the New Jersey coast for over two weeks, not daring to bring her into New York harbor because it was bottled up by the British. His ship was very vulnerable to the guns of the British fleet. Only a mission of great importance would have caused him to risk his vessel and the lives of his crew.

Raising his face to the window on the second floor, The Raven watched as the light was extinguished and the room became dark. Quickly, he pulled his dark hood over his head to conceal his identity. After a few moments passed, he placed his foot on the trellis that led to Lady Season Chatworth's bedroom, testing it for sturdiness.

How easy it had been to find out which of the bedrooms Lady Season occupied. He had spent thirty minutes with the upstairs maid, and she had gladly given him all the information he required. He smiled to himself. The maid, Doreen, had been a delight in more ways than one. He had had the added pleasure of bedding the saucy little wench.

The trellis seemed well able to support The Raven's weight so he climbed silently toward his goal. In no time at all he had reached the outside ledge of Lady Chatsworth's window. The window was unlocked so he cautiously slid it upward.

Hearing a noise, The Raven glanced below him and spotted the sentry who was guarding the house. He wasn't worried, however. He had anticipated a guard when such an important guest was staying at the Tibbs's house. He smiled as he watched Doreen make her way toward the unsuspecting man on guard duty. Her hips swayed enticingly and she carried a jug of drugged ale. He laughed silently, thinking the maid would have no trouble distracting the sentry long enough for him to accomplish his mission.

Suddenly Season opened her eyes, fully alert. She could feel a cold draft coming from the open window. She sat up, knowing the window had been closed before she'd drifted off to sleep. She remembered that the Tibbs's maid, Doreen, had come in to make sure it was locked. Season knew it was highly unlikely that Molly had come in and raised the window since it was extremely cold outside.

Slipping out of bed, she made her way toward the window, intending to close off the draft. She never made it that far. Suddenly she was engulfed in the folds of a dark cloak, and a hand was clamped over her mouth!

Season twisted and turned, trying to free herself, and finally managed to push the cloak away from her face. She strained her eyes in the darkness trying to see her assailant, but all she could make out was a dark blur. Never in Season's life had she known such fear. Her stomach churned, and her heart pumped at a furious rate. With renewed strength derived from her fear, she kicked and twisted; but the person who held her was of a superior strength.

The gloved hand clamped over her mouth cut off her air supply, and only muffled sounds came from her throat. Suddenly she was clasped tightly against the man's body, and a deep raspy voice spoke next to her ear, sending chills up and down her spine.

"It will do you no good to struggle. If you do as you are told you will not be harmed. Do you understand?"

Season nodded her head. She would agree to anything, if only the man would remove his hand from her mouth so she could breathe.

"I'm going to remove my hand now, but should you make a sound, it will be the last thing you do before you die," said the deep voice. You needn't worry, she thought wildly. She was positive her fear would not allow her to make even the slightest noise.

True to his word, the man removed his hand, and Season took a deep gulp of air into her lungs. Her slight body was trembling so badly that when he released his hold on her she fell to her knees.

Tense moments passed as Season knelt, her head bowed, trying to regain some of her lost courage. Finally she forced herself to look up at the intruder through a curtain of golden hair. She could see nothing but a dark menacing form which seemed more shadow than man.

Season wished she dared to ask the man what he wanted with her, but she was having difficulty finding her voice. At last she managed a painful whisper. "Did you come to rob me?" she managed to ask.

"Silence!" came the raspy reply.

Season complied immediately. She watched the black shadow move across the room, apparently gathering up objects and throwing them onto the bed. The man *had* come to rob her, she thought with relief. Well he could just take what he wanted, she certainly wasn't about to stop him. Let him take what he would as long as he didn't harm her.

Standing upon shaky legs, Season leaned against the bedpost for support.

"Not one word, my lady," warned the voice. It was a voice that represented sudden death to her.

Season watched as the man wrapped his bounty in the bed covering and tied it into a bundle. "Are you leaving now?" she dared to ask.

"Yes, my lady," came the reply.

Before Season knew what was happening the man pulled her toward him and tied something about her mouth. She tried to struggle, but soon found the effort to be futile. Deep, menacing laughter rumbled from inside the man's chest as he pulled a cloth over her head, shutting out what little she had been able to see in the darkened room.

When Season felt herself being lifted onto the man's shoulder, she renewed her struggles. He wasn't just going to rob her—he was going to kidnap her! She struggled with every ounce of strength she possessed, but when he whacked her hard across the bottom, she became motionless. Suddenly she couldn't breathe; it seemed as if her air supply had been cut off. She became limp, lost consciousness, and was unaware that she was being carried down the trellis and across the courtyard.

The Raven stepped over the unconscious sentry who was sprawled on the walkway. Doreen stepped out of the shadows and The Raven bent his head to give her a quick kiss.

"Well done, my dear. Go back into the house and tell no one what has occurred. In the morning, pretend ignorance," he said hurriedly.

"Will I see you again?" she asked.

"It wouldn't be beyond the realm of possibility that our paths might cross again," he called over his shoulder.

Doreen watched The Raven disappear amid the night shadows before she turned and quickly made her way into the house. She had met many men in her life, but never one who had given her so much pleasure. She would die rather than betray The Raven. After all I am as good a patriot as anyone, she reckoned.

Seeking the shadows at the side of the long driveway, The Raven spotted the waiting coach. He placed the Lady Chatsworth on the seat and dropped her belongings on the floor. Motioning for the driver to move on, he seated himself in the coach, smiling at a job well done. Reaching out, he pulled his cape from the Lady Chatsworth's head and removed the gag from her mouth. Shaking her gently, he finally succeeded in bringing her around.

Season opened her eyes and tried to remember where she was. Something had happened, but for the moment she couldn't remember what it was. She became aware that she was in a speeding coach. She heard the sound of the horses' hooves on the cobblestone street, and the swaying motion of the conveyance almost unseated her.

"I apologize for my ungentlemanly behavior, my lady, but, you see, I knew of no other way to convince you to accept my hospitality." The deep raspy voice brought back Season's memory.

"Who are you, and what do you want with me?" she blurted out. Her thoughts seemed to be tumbling over one another. If this man hadn't meant to rob her, what was he after? She strained her eyes in the darkness, trying to see the man's face, but she could see only black on black.

"Forgive me for not introducing myself earlier, my lady. I am known both far and wide as The Raven. I doubt that you have heard of me, since you have so recently landed on our shores," he drawled.

Season drew in her breath as a new fear replaced the old one. God in heaven, she had been captured by the same man General Clinton and Colonel Tibbs had been discussing this very evening! A shudder racked her body, and Season cringed in the corner of her seat, getting as far away from the man's menacing presence as she possibly could.

"If it's information you want from me, I know nothing about our defenses. Even if I were privy to that information, I would never tell you."

"Nay, my lady, I do not ask you to betray your fellow countrymen. Instead, you will be the instrument that I will use to save one of mine."

"I don't understand. How could I possibly be of help to you?"

Again Season heard the sinister laughter that played on her already overwrought nerve ends.

"You have nothing to fear from me, my lady. Just do as you are told and no harm will befall you."

"If it's riches you are after, my father will pay handsomely for my release," she offered.

"Remain silent!" The husky command came from somewhere among the dark shadows.

"No, not until you tell me where you are taking me," she demanded.

"I'm warning you, my lady. Do not push me past my limit," he snapped.

Season swallowed convulsively and then cringed when The Raven propped his black-booted foot up on the seat beside her. But as he leaned back in a relaxed position, Season's anger overruled her fear. How dare this man come into her bedroom and take her away by force. He was nothing more than a barbaric pirate while she was the daughter of the Duke of Chatsworth. Propelling herself across the seat, she threw her weight against him and began to pound her fists against his chest.

His amused laughter made her angrier still. He caught her flying hands and held them firmly against his chest. Lifting her up as if she weighed nothing, he pulled her across his lap. She was pinned so tightly against his chest that she could scarcely move.

"What a spirited little wildcat you are," he whispered against her ear. "Do not force me to clip your claws, my lady; I can assure you, you may not like my method."

Feelings not unlike those of fear tightened Season's stomach muscles. "You are a brute!" she said, trying to free her hands.

"How do you like your men, my lady? Weak and fawning, or strong and masterful?" he asked insultingly. "If you prefer weak and fawning, you will have to look for your pleasure elsewhere."

"How dare you speak to me thus, sir. I am not one of the tavern wenches to which you are most probably accustomed. My father will kill you for this!"

Again Season heard the laughter that was beginning to tell on her nerves. "We are in agreement that you are nothing like a tavern wench. However, as to your father, he is a long way from here, my lady. I have it on good authority that he sent you to America for a speedy marriage to curb your . . . appetites."

Suddenly all the life seemed to go out of Season. She wondered how it was possible that this man knew so much about her. General Clinton had said The Raven seemed to know everything that was going on, and she was beginning to believe that.

"But for men, I wouldn't be in the position I now find myself," she said, with more spirit than she felt. "I hate all men!" she declared, burying her face against the dark folds of his cape. She was too tired and weary to care if he ravished her on the spot.

"From what is said about you, my lady, the opposite is true."

"Why should I care what you think?" she said, closing her eyes. The rocking motion of the coach and the warm, hard body she was held against soon lulled Season into an exhausted sleep.

The Raven stared into the darkness. He did not like the part he was playing that night. It went against his instincts to mistreat a woman—even if she were a worthless bit of baggage, as well as the enemy. The price for just one of her gowns would probably feed Washington's army for a whole month, he thought bitterly. He closed his eyes, trying not to think about the soft body that rested against him. That was difficult to do for he readily admitted to himself that he admired the lady's spirit and he reluctantly admitted that he admired her beautiful face and body.

Again he reminded himself that the woman he held in his arms was the enemy. He didn't have the time or the inclination to cater to her whims.

His only purpose in taking her captive was to use her to bargain for his Uncle Silas' life. Just this evening he had learned that the British had taken his uncle prisoner. If they harmed him, this lady might well pay with her life! The two countries were at war, and he

103

couldn't allow himself to be soft just because this enemy was a woman. All he could allow himself to think about at the moment was his uncle who was locked away in some dank cell and was probably being tortured by the British to make him talk. The Raven knew his uncle would never succumb. Silas Dunsberry would die before he would betray either his nephew or the cause.

As the coach passed a tavern, The Raven looked down and watched the lights from the establishment flicker across Lady Season Chatsworth's face. He could observe her to the fullest since she was asleep. Yes, she is beautiful, he thought. But he had long ago learned that beauty could be very superficial, as he suspected it was in her case. He pulled his cloak tighter about her, wondering why the lady's loose morals should bother him. Too many times he had enjoyed a loose-moraled woman.

Why, he wondered, is there such an air of innocence about this particular woman? Probably that is part of her charm, he reasoned bitterly. The Raven had no intention of falling under this lady's spell. He did not wish to be one of the many who had bedded her. This was the first time The Raven had ever abducted a female, and doing so didn't sit well with him. If it weren't for his uncle's predicament, he would have sent her right back to Colonel Tibbs.

Season awoke, slowly becoming aware that the swaying of the coach had stopped. Before she had time to reflect on where The Raven was taking her, she was pulled from the coach. The man took her hand and led her in the direction of the pounding waves that washed against the shore. She could just make out a small boat some distance ahead. She was cold and miserable, the wind off the ocean stung her cheeks, and the beach sand hurt her bare feet.

Season stumbled. Immediately she was lifted into strong arms and carried to the waiting boat.

"Please, I don't want to go with you," she pleaded, realizing her destination was to be the sea.

"Remain silent," came the low hiss near her ear.

The Raven placed her in the boat and climbed in beside her.

As the small craft caught the waves, it rocked about drunkenly until the six men aboard plied their oars and propelled the boat forward.

"You chose a fine night for your business, Captain, there be only a half-moon tonight. The British will never know we sailed in right under their noses," one of the crew members declared.

"Hold your tongue," the dark captain ordered in a whisper. "You know sound carries on the water."

Soon all that could be heard were oars slicing through the water and waves lapping at the small craft. It seemed to Season that they had been in the boat for hours; her body was numb and cold. In the far corner of the boat she pulled The Raven's cloak more tightly about her and shivered, staring into the darkness. The moon was covered by clouds. She was frightened, but she knew there was nothing she could do about her plight for the moment.

Season was her father's daughter and did not easily admit that she was beaten. Having a strong will and a sense of survival, she was determined that no matter what happened she would never grovel at the feet of the man who called himself The Raven. Was she not superior to him by birth and breeding? Wouldn't it be wise to show him how an English lady of quality acted? She was determined to bury her fears and to meet whatever demands this man made on her with strength and dignity. Season had taught herself to swim on the lovely summer days she'd spent in the English countryside, and she was a good swimmer. Perhaps, she thought, I will be able to break away and swim for shore. Thinking of escape will keep me from loosing my sanity, she told herself.

Suddenly a huge ship loomed before them through the dense fog. Season could just make out the figurehead, it was shaped like a raven with wings spread, ready to take flight. She closed her eyes, trying not to think about all the stories she had heard about how pirates treated their captives.

When the small boat bumped against the hull of the ship, The Raven hoisted Season onto his shoulder and climbed the rope ladder. Once he reached the deck, he placed her on her feet and assumed command of the ship.

"Hoist the riggings, Briggs. We sail on the morning tide," he called out.

"Aye, aye, Captain," came the reply, as the crew began scurrying about, making ready to sail.

"These are tricky waters, Captain, I fear we might run aground in this fog," the man Briggs called out.

"Have no fear, I know these waters like your own mother knows your face. I will take the helm until we are out to sea," came the raspy reply. "Take the lady below, to my cabin."

"Aye, aye, sir."

The man called Briggs turned to Season. "Come with me, little lady. I'll see that you are made comfortable."

Season gave in gracefully, knowing she had no other choice. Briggs led her down the companionway and into a dark cabin.

"I'm sorry you can't have no light until we are safely out of these waters, my lady. Here give me your hand and I'll lead you safely to the bed."

Season stubbornly refused to give the man her hand, so he took her by the arm and led her forward. Reaching out in front of her, she felt the bed and sat down. She heard, rather than saw, the man leave, and she recognized the sound of a key grating in a lock. Season knew she was now the prisoner of the ominous Raven.

Unable to see the cabin, she feared it was filthy—the bed might even have lice, she thought, jumping to her feet. Sniffing the air, she couldn't smell any offensive odor, only the bracing aroma of the sea.

Sighing heavily, she sat down on the bed. She was so weary that she soon lay back and curled up, pulling the covers over her, no longer caring about the condition of the cabin. Sleepily she closed her eyes.

She could hear the wind catching a bit of canvas and the waves lapping against the ship. Too tired to care about anything, Season drifted off to sleep.

The Raven had removed his black hood and he now stood at the helm of the ship. His first mate, Briggs, stood beside him, watching him maneuver the huge ship through the water with little fear of jagged rocks and sand bars—the hazards that preyed on unsuspecting sailors in these waters.

"You have the gift, Captain. You handle the ship as easily as if you was on a Sunday stroll."

The Raven did not reply.

"Did you have any trouble this evening, Captain?"

"It was too simple. No man challenged me. No one will know Lady Season Chatsworth is missing until the house awakens tomorrow."

"Did she give you any trouble?" Briggs wanted to know.

The Raven stared into the thick fog. "She seemed willing to accept the inevitable after a fashion."

"What's our destination, sir?"

"We set course for the open sea and safe waters. There we await the signal that my uncle has been released. If all goes well I will set the lady ashore by tomorrow evening. I left a note pinned to her pillow. I am certain the British will not hesitate to exchange my Uncle Silas for Lady Season."

"Let us hope so, Captain. I have a great fondness for your uncle."

The Raven gripped the helm tightly. He had taken desperate steps tonight, but he had been backed into a corner and had had no choice. He had very little doubt that General Clinton would be shown his note tomorrow. Tomorrow night the *Andromeda* would again sail close to the New Jersey shore to receive the message of his uncle's release. The Raven knew that General Clinton was planning to take ship himself in a few hours, but he had no doubt that the man's fear for Lady Season Chatsworth's safety would keep him on land long enough to see that Silas Dunsberry was released.

Chapter Seven

Molly came running down the hallway, screaming at the top of her lungs. "My lady, my lady, they've took my sweet, innocent lady!"

Mrs. Stiles, the housekeeper, who was just coming out of the Tibbs's bedroom grabbed Molly's arm and tried to make some sense out of her raving. "What are you talking about? Is something wrong with Lady Season?"

"What's all this commotion?" Mrs. Tibbs asked, poking her head around her bedroom door. "Do you want to awaken Lady Season with your carrying on?"

"My lady has been taken away. Someone came into her bedroom last night and spirited her out of the house," Molly cried hysterically.

By now Colonel Tibbs had heard the loud carrying on, and he came out into the hallway, tying the sash of his purple robe about his waist. Here now, what's all this about? Your shrieking would wake the dead," he said in a commanding voice.

Molly dropped to her knees before him. "Oh, sir, my lady has been taken!"

"What's this? What are you saying, woman!" the colonel asked, hauling the hysterical Molly to her feet and shaking her soundly.

"When I went into my lady's room like I always do—she's an early riser and if she isn't already awake, I awaken her—"

"Yes, yes, get on with it," the colonel commanded in an irritated voice.

Molly dabbed at her eyes with her apron. "When I went to her room this morning, there were signs of a struggle, and she's missing!" Molly declared, grabbing the colonel's hand and practically dragging him toward Season's bedroom.

The colonel caught his wife's eye. They both knew that if anything had happened to Lady Season while she was under their protection there would be all hell to pay.

Colonel Tibbs looked about the cluttered room with the practiced eye of a soldier. He noticed there was clothing strewn on the floor, but Lady Season Chatsworth's jewelcase was on the vanity, seemingly untouched. He glanced at the curtains blowing in the wind and deduced that the intruder must have climbed through the window.

"By the saints," he roared. "Someone will pay for this piece of work." He scanned the room, looking for some clue as to the lady's disappearance. Mrs. Tibbs's voice had joined Molly's, and the two women put forth a fearful howl.

Colonel Tibbs's eyes fell on the rumpled bed, and he

noted that the coverlet was missing. Then he saw the note propped against the pillow. He grabbed up the parchment and saw that it was addressed to General Clinton. Hurriedly ripping it open, he began to read aloud.

General Clinton,

I regret to inform you that the Lady Season Chatsworth is a guest of mine until such time as you can procure the release of one Silas Dunsberry. The lady will be shown every courtesy and I will expect the same treatment of Mr. Dunsberry. I will be in touch with you, but meanwhile, may I suggest you seek Silas Dunsberry's release with the utmost haste. I know he is being held somewhere in New York. Remember he must be unharmed or you will never see Lady Season Chatsworth again. You are being watched—I will know if you play me false.

The Raven

"Damned impudence," Colonel Tibbs raged as he pushed past his wife and ran downstairs to dispatch a quick note to General Clinton.

A short time later General Clinton paced the floor, raising his fist in anger. "This time that upstart has gone too far. Before he was a damned nuisance, but now he has overstepped the bounds of decency! He will swing from the gallows for this piece of work!"

111

"I fear for my cousin at the hands of such a mad man," Edmund declared angrily. "How was it possible for him to spirit her away right under our noses?"

Colonel Tibbs turned a shamed face toward Edmund Kensworthy. "You have every reason to be put out with me. It was my duty to keep your bride safe until the wedding. I was lax in my duty and will take full responsibility. I can only guess what Lady Season's father's reaction will be when he hears about this atrocity."

General Clinton waved Tibbs's statement aside. "There is no time for recriminations. The utmost priority at the moment is to make sure we meet this man's demands. After Lady Season is safely returned we will deal with this pirate! Believe me, when this is over, heads will roll."

"Let's hope that The Raven's head is the first to go," Edmund spoke up.

"Perhaps he will do as the note says and release Lady Season when Silas whatever-his-name-is is set free," the general's aide spoke up.

"Dunsberry," Colonel Tibbs offered. " Silas Dunsberry."

"You do intend to give The Raven this man in exchange for my cousin, don't you, General?" Edmund asked.

"Hell, yes. I have no choice. I have already sent a man with orders to release the prisoner. We cannot afford to make any slips. The Raven has ears everywhere. It goes against everything I believe to give in to this blackguard, but my hands are tied. At this time, all that matters is that we get Lady Season back safely."

"I am in agreement with you, sir," Edmund said.

112

"I'm half out of my mind with worry over Season."

"I know you are, my boy—we all are. I am upping the reward on The Raven's head. I will make it so high that his own mother would turn on him to collect. Soon there will be nowhere he can hide!"

Season awoke to the sound of a key grating in the lock. Sitting up, she noticed it was morning and sunlight was streaming into the cabin through the high, oval-shaped porthole. She had lived through her ordeal and by some miracle she was still alive.

When the door swung open she grabbed the bedcovers and pulled them up to her throat, expecting to see the mysterious captain of the ship enter. She blinked her eyes with relief as a short, sturdily built man with salt and pepper hair entered and smiled brightly at her.

"My name's Briggs, my lady. We met briefly last night when I showed you to this cabin, but there weren't no time to pass pleasantries then. I brought you something to eat."

Season gave the little man a scalding glance. "I have no intention of eating your food. I wish to see your captain at once," she demanded, while giving him what she hoped would be her most authoritative look.

"I'm sorry, ma'am, but I can't honor your wish. The captain's a busy man. I'll just put the tray down here on the desk. You might feel hungry later."

"I will not change my mind. You are a pirate, and I will never partake of your food." Season's anger soared when she saw that her words only brought a sad smile

113

to the little man's face.

"Now I can see how we might look like a motley lot to you, but I can promise you we aren't classed as pirates, my lady. With my captain in command, you will be as safe as you would be if you was back in your own bed in England." His soft blue eyes moved over Season's lovely face, and he laughed. "I wonder if my captain will be safe from you, though?"

"You may leave now," Season declared, turning away from Briggs. She had seen nothing to fear from this man who spoke so respectfully to her and seemed to have the kindest blue eyes.

Briggs nodded his head and swept her a graceful bow before departing the cabin. Season heard the key grinding in the lock once more and knew she had been locked in again.

Easing herself off the bed, she walked over to the desk and glanced down at the breakfast tray. The ham smelled delicious, and her mouth watered when she saw slices of melon and two generous pieces of bread spread with creamy yellow butter. She closed her eyes against the tempting aroma of brewed tea.

"I won't weaken," Season said aloud. "I will not eat that man's food!" She decided she would rather starve to death than put one morsel of food in her mouth, and closing her mind to her hunger, she paced the length of the floor and back.

She couldn't help but notice that the cabin wasn't filthy as she had feared last night. In fact, it was spotlessly clean. The oak deck gleamed brightly, reflecting the sunlight off its smooth surface, and the dark wall paneling smelled of lemon oil. The bedcoverings were snowy white. Season doubted that there was a speck of dust in the whole cabin.

She walked back to the heavy, hand-carved desk and flipped open the lid of a small mother-of-pearl box she found sitting there. Inside the box she found several cheroots. Turning around, her eyes swept the cabin. There were shelves running along the length of one wall, and she saw that they were crammed with maps.

She gripped the edge of the desk so tightly her knuckles whitened. There was no doubt in Season's mind; she was in the captain's cabin! She felt panic! Only moments ago she had told Briggs she wanted to see the captain; now she was afraid he *would* come to see her!

Glancing down at her thin lace nightgown, Season looked about for something with which to cover herself. She spotted the bundle on the floor, and knew she would find some of her clothing inside.

Going down on her knees, she loosened the knot and found to her relief that the man had brought several of her gowns. The Raven had not robbed her as she had supposed; he had merely picked out what he thought she would need. From the looks of the bounty, he had left nothing out. There were shoes, hairbrushes, underclothing, and even a bar of soap.

Sitting back on her heels, Season wondered why The Raven had brought so many of her belongings. Evidently he intended her to be on this ship for a long time. She was now more frightened than if he had merely stolen her jewels. Where was he taking her? Would she ever be free again?

Season feared The Raven would enter the cabin at

any moment, so she quickly slipped into one of the three gowns she had to choose from. She found that the captain had overlooked one important item; he had not included a hoop in the bundle. Her green velvet gown dragged on the deck, and she would have to be careful not to trip on it.

Picking up her ivory-handled hairbrush, Season began to brush the tangles from her hair. Just because she was a prisoner didn't mean she couldn't look her best. She would not cower in the corner like some lost soul. When The Raven did come, he would see that she wasn't intimidated by him.

Hours passed while Season paced the cabin floor restlessly. She remembered the time her father had taken her to visit the king; she had been no more than ten. It had been the only time her father had taken her to London and she had been filled with excitement. One afternoon, one of Queen Charlotte's serving ladies had taken her to visit the wild animals that were kept in cages near the palace. That day Season had watched a magnificent lioness pace the length of her cage. She remembered feeling sad that such a magnificent animal should be kept in a cage. She now knew how that lioness had felt. Season was restless and could feel her calm slipping with each passing moment. She was accustomed to roaming free at Chatsworth. She realized that the one way to break her spirit would be to cage her for a long period of time.

Her footsteps lagged, and she sat down on the soft bed, burying her face in her hands. She would not give in to the weakness of tears; no matter what The Raven did to her, he wouldn't break her spirit. She was determined that she wouldn't show weakness while in his presence.

Season heard the grating of the key in the lock, and she almost jumped out of her skin! Watching the door swing open, she clasped her hands tightly together and waited for whoever was about to enter. She was relieved to see it was only Briggs. He was carrying a tray of food, so Season surmised it must be nearing the noon hour.

Briggs clicked his tongue when he saw the uneaten breakfast. "You really must try to eat, my lady. A wee little lass like yourself could just waste away to nothing in no time at all if you don't eat. The captain wouldn't like you to become ill from lack of food."

"How I choose to treat my own body is of no concern to you or your captain," Season said, tossing her golden mane in defiance. "If you want that food eaten, then eat it yourself."

Briggs merely smiled kindly and shook his head. "You won't be hurting no one but yourself if you don't eat, my lady. You haven't seen the captain when he doesn't get his way. I've seen grown men cringe when he's out of sorts."

"What do you expect of me, Mr. Briggs? Should I say 'Yes, Captain', 'No, Captain', 'Whatever you want, Captain.' I didn't ask to be put on this ship. I have no control over my life, except to say whether I will or will not eat!" she stormed defiantly.

Briggs made no reply. He placed the lunch tray on the desk and left with the breakfast tray. Season watched him leave and listened to the key turning in the lock.

The delicious aroma of the food assaulted Season's senses. She tried to think of something that would take her mind off her hunger. For some reason unknown to her, she was being held prisoner by The Raven. Her father was a wealthy man, and she realized the colonists must have heard about her arrival in New York. She supposed that by taking her captive they were striking a blow at the English aristocracy.

Season smiled bitterly. If The Raven were to demand a ransom for her safe return, she knew her father would pay. How long would it take for word to reach her father in England, and how much time would pass before he could deliver the money to The Raven? Today was the first day of her captivity, and she was almost out of her mind already from being locked in this cabin.

Perhaps she deserved to have this happen to her, Season thought, weighing her guilt for the first time. In the past hadn't she only been interested in her own wants? Not once had she considered her father's feelings. Twice her father had arranged marriages for her, and twice she had balked. Had her father been right when he had called her an ungrateful child? Wouldn't marriage to her cousin, Edmund, be preferable to the situation she now found herself facing?

Season walked over to the desk and stared down at the food. Her eyes were drawn to the roast chicken, which had been served in a fruit sauce. As she eyed the thinly sliced baked potatoes, she could feel her stomach react in protest.

Crossing the cabin, she stood beneath the porthole. It was too high for her to look directly through it, so she watched the sunlight shining through its crystal panes and shrugged her shoulders, wishing she had something to do to make the hours pass more quickly.

Glancing at the shelves where the maps were kept, she crossed the room and removed one of them. Dropping to her knees, she spread the map and studied it for a moment, but knowing next to nothing about geography, Season soon tired of looking at the charts which made no sense to her.

Irritated, Season rolled up the map and shoved it back on the shelf. That was when she spotted the book. Someone had placed the book at the back of the shelf as if wanting to hide it away. When she turned it over in her hands, Season was shocked to find it was her favorite volume of French poetry! She climbed onto the bed and began to read. Before long she was caught up in the haunting poems of love and honor. She couldn't help but reflect on how strange it was for an American pirate to have a book of poetry, even stranger that he would be able to read French. This discovery only served to deepen the mystery that surrounded The Raven!

Season soon became drowsy, and the book slipped from her hand and dropped onto the bed. She laid her head back and fell into a deep sleep.

Chapter Eight

The Raven unlocked his cabin door while balancing a tray of food in one hand. When he entered the cabin he saw Lady Season asleep on his bed. Setting the tray aside he stood over her sleeping form and studied every detail of her lovely face.

He had somehow known that her hair would be blond, but he hadn't expected the mass of golden curls that tumbled across the pillow. As the dying rays of the sun filtered through the window, her hair seemed to come alive with flaming red highlights. She looked so young and childlike that The Raven felt his heart contract.

Had he been wrong to believe the stories he had heard about her escapades in England? He stared at the long silky lashes resting against her pale cheeks. Then his eyes were drawn to her breasts which rose and fell with each breath she took. Her bosom was full and rounded and the bodice of her gown was stretched tightly across the soft mounds. Her mouth was soft and full, tempting him to see if it would taste as sweet as it promised.

The Raven felt desire stir in him, and he knew he wanted this temptress as he had never wanted any woman before. Was she a devil that could drive a man mad with her sweetly curved body, or was she an enchantress who could lure men to their deaths for want of the touch of her lips?

He watched, spellbound, as her lashes fluttered and she looked at him with her emerald-colored eyes.

Season quickly scrambled to her knees and moved to the far side of the bed, trying to get as far away from the hooded man as she could. When The Raven saw that she was frightened of him, he felt a pang of sorrow.

"Why are you here?" she asked in a choked voice as her eyes moved over the man dressed in black. Last night he had blended into the shadows, but now she could see him only too clearly. He appeared more frightening than she could have imagined, and she couldn't control the shudder that shook her body. The black hood he wore had slits where his eyes and mouth should have been. His black shirt was tucked inside black tight-fitting breeches. Shiny black boots reached to his knees, and his overall appearance was frightening and sinister.

"I have come to personally see that you eat a proper meal," came the deep, raspy reply.

Season pressed her back against the cabin wall. "I . . . told your man Briggs that I had no intention of eating your food," she said in a small voice. Season was surprised that she could speak at all with The Raven hovering over her like some awesome bird of prey.

The Raven picked up the tray and sat down on the bed beside Season. Her heart was pounding loudly and she couldn't seem to move. Her deepest instinct warned her not to defy this man.

"I think you *will* eat, my lady, if I have to spoon-feed you every bite."

"You wouldn't dare," she exclaimed with indignation.

"Would I not? Come, eat like a good girl, and if you clean your plate, I will take you for a stroll on deck so you can get some fresh air," he cajoled, as if speaking to a wayward child.

Season considered his proposal. She was tired of the inside of this cabin. It would be wonderful to walk on deck and breathe in the fresh sea air. "Are you saying if I don't eat you will not allow me to walk on deck?" she asked, not knowing how childlike she appeared at that moment.

He nodded his head affirmatively. "I believe we understand one another, my lady."

"Give me the tray," she said with ill grace. "I just want you to know I am eating because you forced me to and not because I want to."

The Raven placed the tray within her reach and smiled behind his mask. Season watched him stand up, and her eyes followed him across the room. He picked up a chair, turned it around, and then straddled it. Season doubted she would be able to swallow a bite of food while he was watching her so closely.

"Must you stay here while I eat?" she asked with a toss of her head. She had no notion how lovely she looked as her golden hair swirled about her.

"Yes, I must. You see, I don't trust you. Besides I would not want to hand a malnourished bride over to her intended bridegroom."

Season's heart lightened when she sensed the man's good humor. "You are going to release me?"

"You don't think I want to keep you indefinitely—do you?"

Season took a bite of what appeared to be chicken, but actually tasted nothing like it at all—in fact, it was like nothing she had ever tasted before.

"What is this?" she asked, spearing a piece of meat with her fork.

"Do you like it?"

"I don't know. You tell me what it is, and then I'll tell you if I like it or not. I have heard it said that you colonists have been known to eat very strange things."

"It is called turkey—a fowl that is native to the United States," he answered in an amused voice.

"You mean the Colonies, don't you?"

"No, my lady, I mean the thirteen United States of America."

Season decided to let that pass. The last thing she wanted to do was antagonize the man since he had hinted that he would be releasing her. "Is this a meat-eating bird? I can assure you if it is, I will not eat another bite."

"No. The turkey is not a predatory bird. In the wilds it feeds on grains and berries. Many farmers raise the turkey very much the same as one would the chicken. I am told that the turkey is the least intelligent of God's creatures. It is said they will often drown in a rainstorm, simply by looking toward the sky."

"You are making that up, are you not?"

"No, I can assure you it's the truth, my lady. Your neighbors, the French, have added the turkey to their diet. It is said that the king and queen serve it often at Versailles." The Raven noticed that Lady Chatsworth had begun to relax and had lost much of her apprehension.

"Ugh, the French," she said, making a face.

"Let me see if I have this right: you don't like us Americans, and you are not overly fond of the French—who do you like?" he asked, watching her take a bite of the turkey.

"I did not say I do not like the Americans, although I have met only one of you."

"Not so, my lady. You have met myself and Briggs," he reminded her.

"But there you are wrong, sir. I was never formally introduced to you, and Briggs is most probably a pirate and a cutthroat, the same as you," she dared to say.

Season took another bite of fowl and found it to be indeed delectable. She wondered if she really liked the meat or whether the lure of a walk on deck—and her hunger—made the turkey taste so good.

"If the American you spoke of meeting is not myself or Briggs, who is it? Perhaps the person will be an acquaintance of mine."

"I doubt that you and I travel in the same circles. It is not likely that you would have met any of my cousin Edmund's friends."

The Raven watched her bite into a slice of apple and smiled. "I am intrigued, my lady. Tell me of whom you speak."

"You wouldn't know him. He is a gentleman by the name of Lucas Carrington. I don't think he would associate himself with you," she stated, taking a bite of sweet golden corn which was seasoned with melted butter.

"I know Lucas Carrington as well as anyone, my lady. He is a planter from Virginia. I have found him to be a most disagreeable fellow."

"Tell me what you know about Mr. Carrington," Season urged, raising her eyes to his.

Deep laughter shook The Raven's tall frame. "Lucas Carrington is a man without a purpose. He neither stands for one side, nor the other, but leans more toward the middle. Most probably he is a coward. I have heard it said that he sells his crops to the British. In my way of thinking that goes under the heading of aiding and abetting the enemy."

"I don't believe him to be a coward. You are just jealous of him because he is a gentleman and you are not," she stated flatly.

"So, the lady defends the American. I wonder why you are so quick to come to his defense. I would venture to guess that Edmund Kensworthy doesn't know about your attachment to Mr. Carrington."

Season's face became flushed. She devoured the last bite of turkey and then lowered her head so the curtain of golden hair would hide her embarrassment. "I am not interested in Mr. Carrington as a man. I am merely curious because he is the first colonist I have met."

"I could tell you about your cousin, Edmund, if you wish," The Raven offered.

"I don't wish to hear what you have to say about him.

126

You would only present a distorted picture."

"You might be surprised by my assessment of your intended bridegroom. I know him to be an honorable man; unlike Lucas Carrington, he has his loyalties. If you don't know him very well, let me warn you that you cannot always judge him at face value. Give him a chance, my lady, for I'm sure he will make you a good husband. Do not always judge a man by your first impression. Edmund is impulsive sometimes, but he is always sorry when he acts unwisely."

Season glanced at the slashes in the black hood and knew The Raven was watching her closely. Why was he defending Edmund to her? He spoke as if he knew what had transpired between her and Edmund in the morning room on the night of the ball.

"I do not think what takes place between my cousin and myself is any of your affair," she said with as much dignity as she could manage. "All I want from you is to know when you will let me go."

The black-clad shoulders shrugged indifferently. "I will let you go, my lady, when—and only when—I have what I want."

"What do you want—money?" she asked in a contemptuous voice.

The Raven was silent for several moments. Finally he stood up. "I see you have cleaned up your plate like a good little girl. I will take you for a stroll on deck as I promised. I would suggest you bring a cloak since it is bitterly cold topside."

Season scrambled off the bed, showing a flurry of white petticoats in the process.

The Raven saw the eager look on her face, and was

once more reminded of her youth. She didn't look at all like the *femme fatale* she had been accused of being, but rather like a frightened young girl who was unsure of her future. He somehow wanted to assure her that he would do her no harm, but he remained silent.

Picking up her cloak, with the intention of placing it about her shoulders, he noticed her reluctance to come too near him so he tossed the cloak to her. Crossing to the door, he waited for her to join him.

Season quickly pulled the blue velvet, fur-lined cape about her shoulders and hurriedly walked toward The Raven, fearing he might change his mind and not take her for a walk on deck. She followed him through the companionway and then up onto the deck.

Season took a deep breath of invigorating salt air. The wind was cold, but it felt good against her face. It is wonderful to be alive, she thought, turning around in a circle.

She watched with interest as the crew scurried about tying off ropes and working on the riggings. Some of the men smiled at her and doffed their hats. Season remembered how much she had enjoyed the voyage to the Colonies, and she decided that if she had been born her father's son, instead of his daughter, she would have sailed the world.

Season had completely forgotten that The Raven stood just behind her until she felt his hand on her shoulder. She flinched as he took her arm and would have pulled away, had his grip not been so firm. She made no objections as he led her to the ship's railing.

Glancing at the horizon, Season noticed that the sun had gone down, leaving a bright red glow in the sky which made it appear that the sea was being swallowed up by the sun.

Season's hood had fallen from her head, and the rosy glow in the sky seemed to cast its light on her golden hair, making it appear as though it were on fire.

The Raven resisted the sudden urge to push a stray wisp of golden hair from Season's face. Where is the seductress? he wondered. Where is the woman who is supposed to have shared her charms so readily with a stableboy? Could an enchantress be locked inside the innocent face of this angel? The Raven was confused. Could this girl have two personalities—could she change her face as easily as she changed the color of her gown?

"How old are you?" The Raven asked bluntly, staring at the lovely childlike face.

Season turned her face away from the sunset and gazed at the hooded man beside her. "A gentleman should never ask a lady her age, sir," she said indignantly.

"I thought we had already established the fact that I am no gentleman."

"That's the one thing we are in agreement on," Season spat out.

Amused laughter came from behind the black mask. The Raven had never been so charmed by a woman before. She amused him and she made him laugh. She was witty and brave; she would fight him at every turn. He began to feel a deep admiration for this girl who hardly came up to his shoulder.

"No matter. I have always been a good judge of a woman's age. I would say you will never see twenty-five again."

Season bristled instantly. "How dare you insult me, sir. I have but celebrated my nineteenth birthday this last November."

The Raven's deep laughter seemed to dance on the night air. "It is as I thought," he said in his disturbing, raspy voice, "Although I would have placed your age more at the sixteen-year mark. You look hardly more than a child, my lady."

Season turned angry green eyes on The Raven's face. "You are a trickster, sir. I am not amused by your cunning sense of humor!" she declared heatedly.

"Be that as it may, my lady, I am very amused by you. I can almost find it in my heart to envy Edmund Kensworthy."

"I do not wish to talk to you any longer. I would rather go below than suffer your presence another moment," she stated angrily, brushing past him and heading for the companionway.

Season feared that she might have said too much when he grabbed her arm and turned her around to face him. He seemed to loom above her like an ominous shadowy figure.

"You may go below later. First you will take a turn about the deck," he declared in a voice of authority.

"I do not wish to be exposed to you and your band of cutthroats. My guess is that each and every one of you are unsavory characters."

"Do you really think so?" came the amused reply. "Briggs you have met; he is my first mate. Did you find he treated you with less than kindness?"

"No, he was . . . kind," she admitted. "Perhaps he is

the only one aboard who knows how to treat a lady."

The Raven's hand tightened on her arm and he steered her about the deck. Near the quarter-deck he stopped beside a young boy who was winding a long length of rope. "My lady, may I present James to you. I will not give you his last name for obvious reasons. He is the ship's cabin boy and is sometimes called Jim. I wonder, does he fit your description of an unsavory character?"

Season looked into the face of the young boy. His hair was a mass of brown curls and his blue eyes were shining brightly as he bobbed her an awkward bow. "I'm pleased to make your ladyship's acquaintance," he said, hurriedly removing his cap and tucking it under his arm.

Season didn't acknowledge the introduction, but turned her back to study the other crew members. It was true none of the men seemed to fit her concept of a pirate. They either avoided looking at her or smiled politely when she caught their eyes. They appeared to be neat and clean. In truth, this ship was far cleaner than the *Good Hope* on which she had sailed to the Colonies.

As Season assessed the crew members, she saw no eye patches, pegged legs, or hooked hands. Turning her glance back to the dark captain, she wondered what he would look like if he were stripped of his disguise.

"Do you fly the skull and crossbones?" she asked.

"I have on occasion flown the Jolly Roger, my lady, as I have sometimes flown the Union Jack. You should know that a pirate owes his allegiance to no country and no flag. I will now allow you to go below, my lady.

Jim here will accompany you," he declared in a voice of authority, putting an abrupt end to their conversation.

The young cabin boy appeared at her side and waited for her to go below. With one last glance at The Raven, Season swept past him and walked away. She was confused. The captain had as much as admitted to being a pirate, and yet there was a small doubt nagging at her. Somehow he didn't fit the part.

When they reached the cabin, the door was open, and Season swept inside. James followed her and smiled brightly. His brown curly hair hung down his neck, and she thought he could do with a haircut, otherwise he was neat in appearance. She would judge his age to be somewhere between ten and twelve years of age.

"Why did your captain send me below?" she asked.

"I can only guess it was because the weather is so cold," he replied earnestly.

"James . . . will you stay and talk to me for a moment? I am very lonely."

The young boy closed the door and stood stiffly before Season, not knowing how to handle her request. She sat down on the bed and motioned for him to be seated in the chair.

"Why are you at sea and not home with your family, James? Surely you are too young to be exposed to a bunch of cutthroats and pirates."

James sat on the edge of the chair and turned his blue eyes to Season. "We who sail aboard the *Andromeda* are not pirates, ma'am. The crew are all good honest men who fight for freedom," he told her with conviction.

"Do you call holding a lady hostage for money fighting for freedom, James?"

The young boy stood up quickly. "The captain won't be getting no money for your release, ma'am."

Suddenly Season's eyes filled with tears. The ordeal of the last two days had finally taken its toll on her. "What then does your captain intend to do with me? I have been frightened half out of my wits. It isn't pleasant to be held captive, James."

The young cabin boy shuffled his feet uncomfortably as he watched tears roll down the beautiful lady's cheeks. He had never seen anyone as lovely and graceful as she. He wished there was something he could do to assure her that his captain would never harm a hair on her pretty head.

"Begging your pardon, ma'am, but the captain will see that no harm will befall you. He's a good man and there ain't one sailor aboard this ship who would do you ill—even if you are the enemy."

Season wiped her tears on the back of her hand and managed a weak smile. "How did you come to be aboard the ship, James? You seem so young."

"I been sailing on the *Andromeda* for nigh on three years, ma'am. The captain seen me on a fishing dock once and he sat down beside me to inquire if I'd caught anything. We got to talking, and I told him about my ma recently dying and that my pa ran off before I was born. When he learned I had no family and I was sleeping in the back of the tavern, he asked me if I'd like a seagoing life. He took me in and now each night I go to bed with a full belly and I feel like I belong to someone. The crew is all my family."

"Oh, James, you are so young to have suffered so greatly. I wish it were within my power to help you, but I can't even help myself." Season could easily relate to the young boy. While she hadn't known the poverty he had been exposed to, she had never had a sense of belonging to anyone.

"Don't you go being sad for me, ma'am. I have a good life, I have. I wouldn't want to trade places with nobody in the whole world."

"Then be sad for me, James, because at the moment I have no life to look forward to. I don't know what your captain will do with me."

James took a hesitant step toward Season. She is a finely dressed lady, he thought. He was willing to bet that her gowns alone had cost more than he would earn in a lifetime; yet he still felt her sadness like a knife in his young heart.

"I'd best be going topside, ma'am," he said, thinking he had better leave before he started crying himself. "I 'spect the captain will be wanting me."

Season watched the young boy leave the cabin, wishing he could stay with her a while longer. When she heard the key turn in the lock, she lay back on the bed and lost herself to the misery of tears.

James made his way to the quarter-deck, where he found the captain gazing out to sea. The young boy thought the captain wasn't aware of his presence until he turned to him and spoke.

"What kept you, Jim?"

"The lady wanted to talk, Captain. She was kinda

lonesome and I felt sorry for her."

"What did you talk about, Jim? I warned you about revealing anything to her."

"She weren't prying, sir. She was just wondering why I was aboard ship." James looked at the unmasked face of his captain. He all but worshiped this man, however, seeing the beautiful lady so miserable made him question his captain's reasons for kidnapping a woman.

"Captain, sir, couldn't you let the lady go free. She is very sad and frightened. I couldn't stand it when she was crying."

The Raven turned his gaze on the young cabin boy. "Beware of a woman's tears, Jim. Always be on the lookout for the tender traps laid down by a lady. Older and wiser men than yourself have been caught in a beautiful lady's alluring web—especially this lady's."

"Have you ever been caught in a beautiful lady's web, Captain?"

The Raven laughed, showing his flashing white teeth in the lantern light. "Not yet, Jim, but I have come mighty close a few times."

Suddenly The Raven grabbed up the lantern and blew out the flame. The *Andromeda* was nearing the New Jersey coast so he fastened his eyes on the shore. Suddenly a flashing beacon of light pierced the darkness.

Briggs joined them on the quarter-deck. "It's the signal, Captain. What does it say?" the first mate asked.

The Raven took a deep breath and let it out slowly. "It says that my Uncle Silas had been transferred to Boston, but Lord Clinton has given orders that he is to

135

be brought back to New York immediately. He has agreed to the exchange!"

"That's good news, Captain!" Briggs said, beaming. "We've won, haven't we?"

"Never underestimate the British, Briggs. They may yet have some trick in mind. I think we will call on the help of our friend to see what he has learned about my uncle."

"Captain, how is it that you can always find out what the British are doing?" Jim wanted to know.

The captain smiled and clapped the boy on the shoulder. "I have a spy among their numbers, Jim. He is someone they would never suspect. He keeps me informed of the enemy's every move. That's all you need to know."

Edmund Kensworthy climbed the stairs of the fashionable Horse and Groom Inn where his cousin, Lucas, lived when he was in New York. He rapped on the door of the suite and waited for an answer.

"The door's unlocked; come on in," Lucas called out.

Edmund found his cousin sitting in a chair with a glass of brandy in his hand.

"Help yourself to a drink," Lucas said, swirling the dark liquid around in his glass.

Edmund poured himself a stiff drink and sunk down in a chair. "He'll never give her back, Lucas. I don't trust The Raven."

"Have there been any more messages, Edmund?"

"No. Nothing since the note that was found in Season's bedroom." Edmund's blue eyes narrowed. "If he harms her, I'll hunt him down. I won't rest until he has been brought to justice. This is not some nobody he has abducted. The Raven reaches high when he kidnaps the Duke of Chatsworth's daughter."

"If he harms her, I'll help you hunt him cousin," Lucas said with feeling. "I was packing to go back to Virginia when I heard about Lady Season being abducted. I immediately canceled my plans and stand ready to help you in any way I can. Please don't hesitate to call on me if there is anything I can do for you."

"I appreciate the offer, but at the moment all any of us can do is wait. We are all at the whim of that damned Raven!" Edmund declared sourly.

"You were always the one who secretly admired The Raven, Edmund. I told you all along that he was out for himself, but you insisted he was doing it for a cause. I suggest his cause was, and is, to line his own pockets," Lucas said, taking a drink of his brandy and then setting the glass down on a side table.

"Yes, even though he is the enemy, I always admired his courage and daring. I damned sure didn't think he would stoop to using a woman to get what he wanted."

"I have learned not to trust anyone, least of all a man who claims to be one thing but proves to be the exact opposite." Lucas stared at Edmund lazily. "Take you, cousin. You appear to be the devoted king's man, but I wonder how far that loyalty goes!"

"My loyalty goes a hell of a lot farther than your loyalty, Lucas. You can't even decide which side of the war you want to be on."

"Wrong, cousin. I lean toward the British, since they will win in the end. I draw the line at backing a losing cause. The rebels will never win."

"Have you heard what The Raven has demanded for Lady Season's release?" Edmund asked, studying Lucas' face closely.

"No, I assumed he asked for money."

"He asked for the release of Silas Dunsberry!"

Lucas sat up straight and his hands tightened into fists. "What are you saying?"

"You heard the other night at the ball that the crown had arrested our Uncle Silas."

"Yes, but I decided it wouldn't be wise to admit kinship at that time. When I inquired about his arrest from the captain of the guard, I was told they would be releasing him in a few days, Edmund. Why would The Raven want to interfere in this?"

Edmund stared into his cousin's face. "Perhaps one of us is The Raven."

Lucas smiled lazily. "That's an interesting thought. Suppose I were to admit to being The Raven? Would you turn me over to your superiors?"

Edmund stared into his cousin's strange golden eyes. "Without hesitation, but first I'd teach you a lesson you wouldn't forget," he said, reaching up and touching the hilt of his sword. "On the other hand, suppose I told you I was The Raven, Lucas? Would you turn me over to my fellow countrymen? I understand the one who delivers The Raven will receive a substantial reward for his troubles."

Lucas smiled as he picked up his glass of brandy, downing the remainder in one swallow. "On the contrary, Edmund. I would salute you for your ingenious cunning."

Edmund half smiled, but his eyes bore into Lucas. "I know you aren't The Raven, because I have had you watched these last two days. You haven't left these rooms. A widow by the name of Lady Lorona Southerland has been here with you."

Lucas smiled. "You are far too clever for me, Edmund. I had no notion you took such an interest in my love life. I would prefer, however, that you leave the lady's name out of our conversation."

"Dammit, Lucas, you are a cool one. Someday you are going to have to come to terms with this war and decide which side you are really on."

"I am called an American by accident of birth, Edmund. My father came from a fine old English family as did my mother. Where does that leave me?"

Lucas stood up and walked over to the sideboard. "Come, Edmund, have another drink."

Edmund reached out for the brandy Lucas handed him and drank deeply. "You know Lady Season seemed to prefer you to me the other night, Lucas."

"I think not. Do you find that your heart is engaged now that you have met your intended bride?"

"I can't tell you how I felt when I first saw her. I had no notion she was going to affect me so strongly. Good lord, Season is beautiful enough to have any man she wants, yet she is meant to be my bride. Still, for some reason her past life bothered me, and I made some very foolish blunders the night of the ball. If I do get her back, I'll make it up to her."

"Edmund, I doubt that The Raven will touch the lady. Let's hope that when our uncle is released he will send her back to you unharmed."

"That's what I keep telling myself, Lucas," Edmund said, draining his glass.

"Let's get out of here. What you need is another woman to take your mind off Lady Season. I know just the one to help you forget for a few hours."

"I can't, Lucas. I have to return to headquarters and find out if there has been any more news."

"If you should change your mind later on, you can still take me up on my offer," Lucas said, walking his cousin to the door.

Edmund paused. "Season really was taken with you, Lucas; I could tell. It has always been so with the women I have known; they have always liked me untl they met you. Take care that you don't encourage this one in her folly, cousin."

Suddenly Lucas' golden eyes narrowed with anger. "I'm going to think that your concern for the woman's safety has caused you to speak rashly, Edmund. I have never taken that which belongs to you."

"Yes, but this time it's different. I saw the way you looked at Season. Don't let her come between us, cousin. You know I'm the better swordsman."

Suddenly Lucas' good humor returned. "Then take comfort in that fact, cousin."

Edmund left, shutting the door quietly behind him. Lucas walked over to the window and peered down at the street below. He smiled to himself when he saw the two British soldiers standing guard out front. He knew there would be two more stationed at the back of the inn.

Lucas laughed aloud and picked up his drink, knowing his cousin didn't trust him.

Chapter Nine

During the night the sea became rough, and the *Andromeda* swayed and pitched as heavy waves splashed against her sides.

Lady Season Chatsworth tossed and turned restlessly in her sleep. Then she awoke suddenly and sat upright in bed when a huge wave smashed into the hull of the ship. The *Andromeda* seemed to bob up and down in the restless waters like a tiny cork.

Season grabbed hold of the wooden bedpost and screamed out in terror as the ship rolled, but her grip slipped, and she rolled out of bed onto the hard floor.

She was so terrified that she was only half aware of the hands that reached out to her from the darkness and helped her to her feet.

"It's me, ma'am, James. The captain sent me below to tell you there ain't no danger. He thought you might be scared, since you are a female."

Season clung to James's hand as if it were her life line. "The storm is bad, isn't it, James. I fear we will sink!" she cried out in a strangled voice.

"No, ma'am, this ain't bad. I've seen much worse. This here storm will blow over by morning," he declared, just as another wave slammed against the *Andromeda*. The impact sent them both tumbling to the floor, then slammed them against the wall.

It was as dark as pitch, and the ship groaned and creaked as Season groped for James's hand.

"Are you hurt, ma'am?" the boy asked, trying to help her stand.

"No, I'm not hurt,"—her answer came from trembling lips—"but I have very rarely been so frightened."

"It would be best for you to sit on the middle of the bed and hang on," James instructed.

"Stay with me, James!" she cried, tightening her grip on his hand, and as the lad helped her across the cabin, Season hoped they would reach the bed before another wave sent them sprawling onto the deck.

When Season felt the bed beneath her, she grabbed hold of the bedpost and held on for dear life.

"The captain said I was to stay with you, ma'am," James said, reaching out and touching her arm.

"Climb onto the bed with me, James," she said, taking his hand and pulling him toward her. Her body trembled and she couldn't seem to keep her teeth from chattering.

James wished he could assure her that there was nothing to fear. Then, as Season pulled him tightly against her, the boy thought how soft she was and how sweet the fragrance that clung to her skin was.

"You needn't have any fear, ma'am. The captain's at the helm. There ain't no better captain on all the seven seas, than The Raven."

Season drew very little comfort from James's faith of his captain's ability. When another wave broke over the ship, she clasped the boy tightly against her. She feared they would both be at the bottom of the ocean before this horrible night came to an end.

The Raven watched the sea become calm as the first rays of sunlight touched the horizon. "See to the broken riggings, Briggs," he said, handing the ship over to his first mate. "I'm going below to see how our passenger rode out the storm."

When The Raven reached his cabin, he opened the door and his eyes swept the room. The cabin was in disarray; maps had spilled from the shelves, and everything that hadn't been battened down, was scattered about. His eyes moved to the bed, where Lady Chatsworth lay fast asleep with James curled up beside her.

He shook the young boy by the shoulder, and when he awoke, The Raven nodded for him to leave. Jim sleepily rolled to his feet and padded out of the cabin.

The Raven sat down on the edge of the bed, feasting his eyes on Season's beautiful body which was clad only in a thin lace nightgown. The neck of the gown was open, revealing the gentle swell of her creamy white breasts. As if against his will, his eyes slid over her softly rounded hips and followed the line of her long shapely legs to rest on her delicately arched, dainty feet. He felt an ache deep inside him, and he knew she was the most beautiful woman he had ever seen. Her lovely hair fanned out about her head like a golden halo. In sleep there was a slight frown on her inviting lips.

The Raven's hand trembled as he reached for the coverlet and pulled it over her body. Reluctantly, he walked away from her. Leaving the cabin and locking the door behind him, he tried to erase Lady Season from his mind. There was work to do—he had to assess the damage the storm had done to the *Andromeda*.

General Henry Clinton became red in the face as he stared at the note which had just been handed him by his aide. The young aide watched his commander with growing concern, as did Edmund Kensworthy.

"What does the note say, sir?" Edmund asked.

Sir Henry Clinton looked up as if he had forgotten there were others in the room besides himself. He sat down heavily and shook his head.

"Damnation, there will be hell to pay for this incompetence," he roared. "I'm sorry, Edmund, but you must realize that none of this was my doing. God only knows what Lady Season's fate will be now!"

"What do you mean, sir?" Edmund asked in an uneven voice. "Has something gone amiss?"

Suddenly the general looked very tired. Silas Dunsberry was executed but two hours before my man arrived with the orders for his release!" Lord Clinton's announcement fell heavily on the room. Several of the officers present began murmuring among themselves.

Edmund stood, stone-faced. He couldn't show the grief he felt for his uncle because no one in this room knew that Silas Dunsberry had been his uncle.

"What will The Raven do when he learns about the death of Silas Dunsberry, Sir Henry?" one of the officers wanted to know.

"I hate to think. For the moment it is best if word of his death doesn't leave the room. I need time to decide what to do next. This must be a closely guarded secret; is that clearly understood?"

Edmund snapped to attention and clicked his heals together. "I request permission to take my leave of you, sir," he stated, solemn-faced.

"Permission granted, Edmund. Go home. I'll send word to you if something should come up."

Edmund didn't go to his lodgings, but instead found himself before the door of Lucas' suite. Not bothering to knock, he threw the door open and entered the sitting room. Looking about the room, he saw no sign of Lucas so he called his name loudly.

Lucas came out of the bedroom and immediately noticed the stricken look on Edmund's face. "Something has happened to Uncle Silas, hasn't it?" Lucas asked in a sharp voice.

"Yes, I was only just informed that he was executed! Dammit someone will pay for this, Lucas. I had to stand before Sir Henry acting as if I were hearing of a stranger's death. We have both known for a long time that Uncle Silas was a Whig. We have both begged him to have a care or he would be caught. Even though it was my duty to turn him over to the Crown, I looked the other way. My God, he was my uncle! How could I betray him?"

Edmund was ranting and raving so fiercely that he didn't notice Lucas' golden eyes were stone cold. He didn't see his cousin's hands tighten into fists.

"By whose authority was our uncle executed?" Lucas asked in a quiet voice.

"Who can say?" Edmund replied, dropping into a chair and staring into the fireplace. "It was none of General Clinton's doing. He was as shocked as I to learn about the deed. The general thinks we should keep Uncle Silas' death a secret until he can decide what to do. He wants to keep the knowledge of his death from The Raven if at all possible."

Lucas shook his head. "That may not be possible. As you know The Raven has eyes and ears everywhere. I fear for your lady," Lucas said through clenched teeth. "The Raven is a black-hearted bastard or he would never have taken Lady Season in the first place."

Edmund studied his cousin's face. "I see no grief in you for Uncle Silas' death. Are you so damned cold-hearted that you can't feel sorrow over the death of someone who is of your own flesh and blood?"

Lucas smiled. "Perhaps I wasn't as close to Uncle Silas as you were. If I were you, I would forget about the dead and concentrate on the living. As I said before, I fear for your lady!"

Under full sail the *Andromeda* caught the evening tide and made for an unknown destination. The dark master of the ship stood at the helm, staring into the wind. His heart was filled with grief and hatred. A voice deep inside him cried out for revenge. The man who was responsible for his uncle's death would pay, and pay dearly. Lucas already suspected he knew who had ordered Silas' death, and he swore that the deed would cost that man his life!

"I'm sorry, about your uncle," Briggs said, as he watched The Raven turn the *Andromeda* windward. There was a loud snap of canvas as the evening breeze caught at the white sails, puffing them out like a huge fluffy cloud.

"Did you see that my message was delivered to General Clinton, Briggs?"

"Yes sir, Captain, but I don't see why you don't let the young lady go free. She had no part in your Uncle Silas' death."

"If I want your advice, I'll ask for it. You are first mate on this ship, not my conscience, Briggs," came the sharp reprimand.

"What are you aiming to do with Lady Season, sir?" Briggs pressed, not in the least intimidated by The Raven's harsh words.

"I have not yet decided the lady's fate. When I do, you will be among the first to know," The Raven said angrily.

"Begging your pardon, Captain, but she is such a sweet little thing, and I wouldn't like to see her come to harm. I have known you for many years, and I've never seen you take out your anger on a lady. I know how you are grieving for your uncle, but she is innocent in all this."

"Do you take me for a fool? As you said, I have never yet harmed a lady, but don't be too sure this one is innocent." The Raven's voice was harsh and dry.

"I never did think you a fool, sir, but I have never seen you like this before either."

"Do not be deceived by the lady's innocent looks, Briggs. I happen to know behind that angelic face is a black-hearted wench. There is no accurate record of the men's lives she has ruined with her . . . soft manners."

Briggs knew his captain well enough to realize there was no point in continuing the conversation, so he changed the subject. "Where do we head, sir?" he asked.

"I'll let you know later. Take the helm and hold a steady course. I'm going below to talk to our passenger."

Briggs took the wheel and watched as his captain slipped the soft leather hood over his head.

"Keep the wind at our back, Briggs. Steer in a northerly direction. We will not stray too far from the New Jersey shore," The Raven said before leaving the quarter-deck.

Briggs hoped his captain's temper would cool before he faced the lady. He had never before seen The Raven in such a rage. Briggs knew that a fire was smoldering inside his captain, and he feared that the little lady might be the outlet for that anger.

Season and James were sitting in the middle of the bed, playing a game of cards, when the captain entered the cabin. Although Season couldn't see The Raven's face, she could sense in him a strong feeling of anger.

"How many times have I told you that this door must

be kept locked at all times, Jim?" The Raven demanded to know in a low voice that was laced with anger.

James scrambled off the bed. "I forgot, Captain. It won't happen again," the boy replied, shamefaced.

"Leave us," came the raspy command.

James gave Season a look of pity before he turned and hurriedly left the cabin, shutting the door behind him.

Tense moments passed as Season stared at the black mask. She could feel The Raven's eyes burning into her, and she couldn't guess why he was acting so strangely. Up to now, he had left her alone and she had slowly begun to feel less frightened of the man. Now, she had a strong sense of danger and wondered what was amiss.

Season's hands were unsteady as she began to gather up the cards. Indeed, she trembled so badly that the cards slipped from her fingers and scattered across the floor.

Searching for something to say to the silent, menacing man, she voiced the first thing that popped into her head. "I would like a bath," she stated in a trembling voice, knowing she was desperately trying to distract him. "It has always been my habit to bathe daily."

"What are your other habits?" the raspy voice whispered.

"I . . . do not know . . . what you mean," she replied. Season had the strong feeling that she was in mortal danger, but she didn't know the reason why.

She watched, almost fascinated, as The Raven bent down, picked up the scattered cards, and laid them on his desk. The silence between them was so thick that

Season licked her dry lips nervously. She watched, her heart pounding, as he bent to blow out the candle, leaving the cabin in total darkness!

"I could scream," she said, moving off the bed, only to come up against the barrier of a human wall.

"Scream then, my lady. Who will hear you?" he whispered close to her ear.

Season felt his hand on her shoulder, and she began to struggle. When he picked her up in his arms, she became paralyzed with fear! She was shocked when he placed her on the bed. She tried to scream but couldn't find her voice, and she shuddered when he covered her body with his, pressing her into the soft mattress.

She realized that The Raven had removed his leather mask when she felt his lips against her neck. "Please don't do this," she pleaded. "I have done nothing to deserve this treatment from you."

He wound her hair around his hand and jerked her head forward. She could feel his warm breath against her lips.

"Have you not?" he whispered.

Suddenly Season felt the full weight of his body. She was sure she would be crushed. "Please I implore you—let me up." Her fear was deeper now, for she knew what he had in mind.

"I have heard it said, my lady, that you are no lady. What difference then if I take what you have so often given to other poor fools? I could make you want me, shall I prove it?"

"No! I have . . . never done . . . no one has ever . . ." Her words were choked off as his hand ran softly across her cheek, then down to rest against her neck.

All at once her fear was replaced by a deeper and more frightening sensation. She felt his teeth nibbling at her earlobe, causing tiny shivers of delight to skirt across her skin, and she seemed to go weak all over as he brushed his hot mouth against hers.

Season tried to remember that she was a lady, that this man was nothing more than a black-hearted pirate. She was about to voice her objections, when his hand brushed against her breast and caressed it with a slow circular motion. The only sound that escaped her lips was a low moan.

Her lips trembled as his tongue circled her mouth. Season was aware that his hands were unfastening the laces at the bodice of her gown, but she didn't seem to have the will to stop him.

In no time at all he removed her clothing, with a masterfulness that led her to believe he had performed the deed many times before.

"No, no," she moaned, just before his scorching mouth settled on hers. At first Season was shocked and tried to pull away, but soon she became aware of a deep ache in the pit of her stomach. She had never been kissed in such a way before and she didn't know how to react. His hands were roaming over her hips and she felt a slow burning sensation wherever they touched her skin.

"Open your mouth," he whispered against her lips. His voice was deep and husky and sent her senses reeling.

"No," she pleaded, turning her head from side to side, trying to escape the lips that were causing her to feel things she didn't want to feel.

He grabbed her chin in one hand and covered her lips with hot kisses. Season could feel herself surrendering against her will as he forced her lips apart and plunged his tongue inside the warm sweetness of her mouth.

At that moment The Raven knew he had won. She became soft and pliant in his arms, and her hands moved around his neck to tangle in his hair.

Season was overcome by the new feelings that ran through her untested body. She felt the whole world had no substance; nothing mattered to her but the dark Raven who, in his impatience, was stripping the shirt from his own body while his lips caressed and teased Season's tender mouth.

Season was experiencing many new and different sensations, but the one that seemed to render her mindless was the feel of the rough hair on his hard chest brushing against her swollen breasts.

She was locked in a warm cocoon of darkness, where only the feelings aroused by the man who was becoming master of her body mattered. There was no world outside this room. She clamped her mouth together tightly as his hot lips traveled down her arched throat to move slowly over her breasts. When he encircled a silky peak with his tongue, she felt her body respond even more. She couldn't control the tremor that shook her.

Season now had no feeling of what was right or wrong. It was as if their bodies had been destined for one another. In all her girlhood fantasies, she had never dreamed a man could make her feel so alive. The Raven was not her enemy—he was the one for whom her body had been created.

No, this isn't wrong, she thought, as a warmth spread through her body. What harm was there in allowing him a few kisses? He could feel her naked body, but he couldn't see her. Season knew she wasn't thinking rationally, but that didn't matter—nothing mattered but the feel of those sensuous hands moving across her stomach as softly as butterfly wings.

Season felt momentary confusion as he moved off the bed. She could see nothing in the total darkness; she could hear only The Raven's heavy breathing. Suddenly she felt him beside her again, and he pulled her against his hot body. She heard a low groan escape his lips, when hot naked flesh fused with hot naked flesh.

"No, this is wrong," she whispered, feeling as if her breathing had closed off.

"You have a debt to pay, my lady," he whispered against her lips. "It may not be your debt, but you will pay it all the same."

"I don't understand," she said, trying to make some sense out of what he was saying.

"I'll say one thing for you, my lady. You are the best I've had up to this point. Someone taught you very well. You make my blood burn. I can hardly wait to feel all the delights your body can offer." His voice was no more than a soft whisper, but the sound of it echoed in Season's mind.

She didn't know what he was talking about, but she didn't care. She moved her body against his and felt a deep satisfaction when he groaned and clasped her tightly against his lean hard body. She could feel his swollen shaft against her inner thigh and touched it with her hand. She heard The Raven gasp and could feel him tremble.

"I will have you, even if I die for it," he groaned in her ear. "I could sooner die than stop now. You are in my blood, and have been since the first moment I saw you."

His mouth sought and found hers. Season felt her head swim at the intensity of feeling that passed between them. She knew instinctively that The Raven was as moved by her as she was by him.

She had no notion as to what the mating of a man and woman would be like, but she knew she was about to find out. Would the meeting of their flesh be as consuming as the kisses and caresses The Raven had bestowed on her? she wondered. Suddenly she was impatient to find out. She felt his hands on her knees as he easily spread her legs apart. When he paused above her Season wondered what new sensation awaited her.

His hand moved over her inner thigh and Season bit her lip to keep from crying out. Surely his hands have magic in them, she thought as his fingers brushed against her.

Suddenly she could feel him tense. "It has to be now, my lady, he whispered. "You are driving me out of my mind. I need to feel myself deep inside your body."

Season cried out as he thrust his swollen manhood into her. Pain ripped through her and she gasped for breath. She hadn't known there would be pain!

She felt him stiffen, and he grabbed a handful of hair and jerked her head up to him. "Damn you to hell! What trick is this? You have never been with a man before! You were a virgin."

"Let me go, you are hurting me," she cried, trying to

pry his hands away from her hair. "You are a brute!" she sobbed, pounding against his chest.

The Raven was totally confused. He suddenly wanted to draw her to him and comfort her. Her first time with a man should have been handled gently and patiently. He realized how wrong he had been about her, and how he must have hurt her. What monster had spread the lies that she was a soiled dove? As his lips moved over her face, he could taste the saltiness of her tears, and he felt the fire within his body intensify. He knew he wanted her more than ever. For some reason he found great satisfaction in knowing he was the first man to be with her.

"If I had known . . ." he whispered against her trembling lips. "But the damage is done; I see no reason to stop now. I would be doing you no favor if I stopped at this point. It might do you more harm than good."

"No, I don't want—"

"Listen to me, my lady," he said, touching her face softly. He still rested inside her and it was hard for him to concentrate. "If I do not complete the act, you might shy away from men in the future. Trust me when I tell you there is pleasure beyond the pain."

Before Season could voice her objections, he dipped his head and found her honeyed lips. Slowly and gently he began moving inside her. Season didn't know when the pain ceased and the pleasure began, but suddenly she arched her hips and met his forward thrust, feeling as if she were floating in a deep, warm void where only pleasure and wild sensations dwelled.

"Sweet little virgin," he breathed against her ear.

The sound of his raspy voice reminded Season that

this man was not only her enemy but a pirate as well. She struggled against him trying to push him away!

"It will do no good to fight, my lady. It would be far more enjoyable if you would go with your feelings," he urged softly.

"Never! I will see you dead before I succumb to your beastly appetites. I will fight you with my dying breath!"

Soft laughter rumbled deep inside his chest. "The time for maidenly protests has passed. I think you will not fight me," he said in an amused voice.

Season hated him for being so sure of his domination of her. She closed her eyes, knowing he was too strong for her to fight him. She would just lie passive; surely he wouldn't want her that way.

He started moving inside her again, but this time it was different. Whereas before he had been gentle with her, he now thrust forward forcefully, penetrating deep into the depths of her womanhood. "I think you will give me all I ask and more," he breathed against her satiny breast.

"Please, Raven," she said in a throaty voice.

"Please what, my sweet, sweet lady?"

"I don't want this," she groaned.

"Pity you are so young and inexperienced, my lady, but I know just how to make you want me."

"No, never," she said, not realizing her passion-laced voice lent the lie to her claim.

"Never is such a pessimistic word, my lady," he said, thrusting forward with such intensity that her arms slid around his back and she dug her fingernails into his skin.

Instantly, Season swallowed her pride, knowing she no longer wanted to fight this man. Pleasurable feelings flowed like the stormy sea through her veins. Her untrained body was reacting urgently to his masterful manipulation. When his mouth sought hers, her parted lips welcomed his kiss. How easily he had won her over, she thought, unable to stop her hungry body from trembling.

The Raven's kiss deepened as her soft yielding body seemed to set him afire. He had long ago lost count of the number of women he had bedded. Lately the women he had known had been nothing more than objects on which to release his pent-up emotions, but this time it was different. His whole being seemed to tremble as a lock of her sweet, scented hair brushed against his lips.

Closing his eyes, he tried to close his heart to the new feelings that seemed to entrap his whole being. There was danger in the silken arms wound about his neck. He had sought to revenge his uncle's death by taking Lady Season, but perhaps it was she who had extracted the revenge. She was casting a spell on him, and he feared it was a spell that would never be broken. The Raven was angry with himself for wanting her, angry with her for making him experience these unwanted feelings. But it was too late to run now. He had a sensation not unlike that of drowning, and he knew she had extracted his heart from his body!

As his lips tasted the salty tears on her face, he realized he was being too rough with her, so he gentled his movements. Where was the victory in striking out at her as at an enemy? Just then his body reached the highest plane of satisfaction. He shuddered. No, he thought. I have not conquered the enemy—she now holds me captive! In truth, the Lady Season Chatsworth had answered a hunger deep inside him that he never had known existed.

"My lady, my lady," he murmured over and over. It sounded to Season's ears as if he were calling her *his* lady.

In that moment she experienced a new and deeper feeling. Her body seemed to erupt, and she felt her whole being tremble. Never had she felt so at peace with the world, never had she felt so fulfilled and alive!

For a long moment neither of them moved, the only sounds their heavy breathing and the lapping of the waves against the side of the *Andromeda*.

Season reached up to shyly touch The Raven's face, and he kissed her hand, but suddenly he tensed and shoved her roughly from him. Aware that he had moved off the bed, she wondered why he had changed toward her. Season strained her eyes in the darkened room, but she could see nothing. The hopelessness of her situation seemed to hit her like a physical blow.

She was in disgrace! She had wantonly allowed The Raven to take what she would never have given to another man. Season couldn't even claim rape! What little effort it had taken to break down her defiance. Now the things that were being whispered about her in private drawing rooms was true. She was a soiled woman!

"I am ruined forever," Season cried out, burying her face in her hands.

"Don't take it so hard, my lady. You have merely

lived up to your reputation," came the cruel reply.

"You took advantage of me!" she accused, as some of her spirit returned.

"That might have been true in the beginning, my lady, but after a bit you were willing enough."

"You are a beast, and I will hate you until I die!" she cried. Hot tears scalded her face, and Season pounded her fists into the soft mattress. "If only I were a man, I would see you dead!"

"If you were a man, there would be no cause," came the amused reply.

Season heard The Raven cross the room and open the door. She knew he had departed when she heard the key grate in the lock. For the longest time she lay, dry-eyed, staring into nothingness. Her body felt so different now, as if it no longer belonged only to her.

She laid her head on the soft pillow and a ragged sob escaped her lips. After tonight she would never be the same. She had been changed from a young girl who had dreamed of a man who would sweetly love her to a woman who felt betrayed by a dark figure with no name and no face.

"He will never touch me again," Season cried out to the dark room. Then she wept until she fell into a deep, exhausted sleep.

A steady wind was blowing as The Raven stood at the helm of the *Andromeda,* staring out to sea. He turned his unmasked face upward, locating the North Star. Drawing in a ragged breath he closed his eyes. Never before had he forced his attentions on a woman.

He'd always followed an unwritten law and never bedded a virgin. He could argue that Lady Season had been willing when he finally took her, but that didn't excuse the deed. He reminded himself that she was English and the English had killed his Uncle Silas, but that didn't soothe his guilty feelings either.

He remembered how sweetly she had surrendered to him. How would he ever be able to get her out of his mind? She had reached deep inside him as no other woman had; Lady Season Chatsworth had touched his heart!

Never had he felt so alive. He felt as if he were a part of the stars that twinkled in the ebony skies. Even now, he could remember the feel of Season's satiny skin and the scent of her silky hair.

The Raven knew if he didn't exercise restraint over his emotions he would take her again. Lady Season Chatsworth had awakened a hunger in his body that no other woman would be able to feed. His hands gripped the ship's rail. If he wanted to do the right thing, he would set a new course and take her back to New York.

"Plot a course south by southwest, Briggs. We sail for the Barbary States!" The Raven ordered.

The first mate felt sorry, knowing that The Raven had decided not to give the lady her freedom, but he didn't hesitate to obey his captain's command.

Chapter Ten

Season pulled the chair over to the porthole and climbed onto it so she could see outside. It was a bright warm day, and she could hear the wind snap the canvas sails. She had no notion where the *Andromeda* was sailing, but one thing was certain, they had left behind the bleak cold weather in favor of warm sunny days. She wondered if they might be sailing for some exotic South Sea island or perhaps they were sailing to some distant pirate stronghold.

Season hadn't seen The Raven since that awful night two weeks ago when he had so artfully relieved her of her maidenhood. She had feared that he would seek her out again and the deed would be repeated, but when he hadn't come to her, she had begun to relax.

She tried her best to put that night out of her thoughts. In the daytime she was partially successful, but sometimes at night she would dream of a deep raspy voice whispering in her ear and she could almost feel his caressing hands touching her body. Season couldn't understand what was happening to her. One part of her wanted The Raven to seek her out again, but another was shamed at what had happened to her. And her body was alive with a new and sometimes frightening awareness.

James came daily to the cabin. He and Season spent their time together playing cards, or sometimes she read to him from The Raven's one book. Each evening Briggs took her topside for a stroll on deck. At those times she always feared she would encounter the dark captain, but thus far he had not appeared. Season found herself searching the deck for The Raven and was confused by her growing need to see him.

Time lay heavily on her hands, and some days she would pace the floor restlessly. She remembered the peaceful, lazy days she had spent at Chatsworth, riding Cinibar across the green meadows, feeling free and light-hearted. Those days were gone forever. She felt she would never see Chatsworth, or England, again.

Season did not understand why The Raven had taken her prisoner. She didn't know if he had presented a ransom demand to her father. She wondered what plan he had in mind for her. Had he taken her for his own pleasure, or did he plan to harm her in some way? It was hard for her to believe that the hands which had caressed her so gently that night could one day deliver her a death blow.

Now Season rose from the chair and began to pace the floor. Somehow she couldn't seem to curb her restlessness. She had read and reread The Raven's book of poetry many times. She had even spent hours poring over his maps.

It is well past the noon hour, and yet the tray which contains the remains of my lunch still sits on the desk, she was thinking absentmindedly when she heard a rap on the cabin door. Season hesitated to answer, fearing it would be The Raven.

"Who is it?" she asked.

"It's me, James, ma'am."

"Come in," she called gratefully. She welcomed his visit because time seemed to lie more heavily on her hands than it usually did.

Season heard the key grinding in the lock, and the door swung open to reveal James's smiling face. "I brought you some lemons," he said, wrinkling his nose, knowing how she always detested the bitter fruit.

"I don't want them. You can either eat them yourself or throw them into the sea," she said with ill grace.

"You know it's the captain's orders. He don't want you coming down with the scurvy. He told me to see that you had at least one lemon a day."

Season did not want to go against The Raven's orders because to do so might bring him to the cabin again. She took the fruit and bit into it, shivering at its bitter taste. She knew the captain had ordered every member of his crew to eat a lemon each day, but she didn't particularly like the idea.

"I see you didn't eat much of your lunch, ma'am. The captain won't like it none if he finds out," James said, concern in his voice.

"I would think the captain would have better things to do with his time than worry about whether I eat or not." She squeezed the lemon so hard the juice ran through her fingers. "Do you report everything I do to

The Raven, James? I thought you were my friend."

"I am your friend, ma'am, but the captain always asks me about your health and if you're eating properly. I have to obey his orders."

"What or how much I eat is no concern of your captain's. I am not a child that needs to be looked after," she said, licking the lemon juice from her lips.

James stared at Season, dumfounded. He had grown to admire her in the past few weeks. He had never before criticized The Raven's judgment, but he couldn't understand why he was holding Lady Season against her will. Silas Dunsberry was dead, and there was no longer anything to be gained by keeping the lady a prisoner.

"Sit and talk to me for a while, James. I am so lonesome. Talk to me about anything; I want to hear what you have been doing."

James nodded his head and sat down cross-legged on the cabin floor. He was always glad for a chance to talk to Season.

"I been busy helping patch the sails. The captain says we're in for a big blow sometime tonight."

Season looked toward the window. "It won't be as bad as the other storm, will it, James?" she asked, remembering the storm that had terrified her beyond belief.

"I fear this storm's gonna be a bad one, ma'am. The captain said I was to remove everything from this cabin that wasn't battened down."

Season's eyes darted about the cabin fearfully. "You are making me very frightened, James."

"There ain't nothing to fear. I will stay with you like I

did the last time if you want me to."

Season stood up and walked over to the porthole. She climbed onto the chair so she could see out. "The sky looks clear, James. I do not see any sign of a storm."

"If you was able to look leeward, ma'am, you would see the dark storm clouds that are gathering, and the sea is already getting choppy."

"Will we be in danger, James?"

"No, ma'am," James said confidently. "When the captain's at the helm, there ain't nothing to worry about."

Season's green eyes seemed to cloud over at the mention of the captain. The crew of the *Andromeda* seemed to think he could do anything. They rushed around to obey his slightest command, but fearing him as she did, she would well imagine why none of them wanted to cross the dark captain. She stepped off the chair and sat down, resting her chin on her folded hands.

"Tell me about your captain, James. What is he really like?"

James shifted uncomfortably. "There ain't much I can tell you about The Raven, ma'am. He's a good patriot and has taken many English ships as prize." James's face flushed and he reluctantly looked into Season's eyes. "Begging your pardon, ma'am, I sometimes forget that you are English."

Season laughed. "Don't bother apologizing, James. You may forget that I am English, but I can assure you I never do. I would expect you to be loyal to your captain, although how you can think so highly of a man like him is well beyond my comprehension."

"He's a good man. There's not one of the crew who would consider serving under any other captain. Every one of us would fight to the death alongside him."

Season could see the admiration shining in the young boy's eyes. "Perhaps your notion of a good man differs from mine, James. How do you excuse his taking me captive?"

"When the captain kidnapped you, ma'am, he was desperate. A man called Silas Dunsberry had been arrested in New York. It was the captain's intention to exchange you for Mr. Dunsberry."

"Why was the exchange never made, James?" Season wanted to know.

"The exchange couldn't be made, ma'am; Silas Dunsberry was hung by the British."

Season felt a prickle of uneasiness. "When did your captain find out about the execution of Mr. Dunsberry, James?"

"It was two weeks ago today, ma'am. I remember it well, 'cause the captain was in an awful rage."

Season closed her eyes, remembering the night he had come to the cabin and ruined her life. She realized he had taken his revenge out on her that night.

"What will happen to me now?" she wondered aloud.

"I don't know what the captain's plans are. He was powerfully close to Mr. Dunsberry. You don't need to worry though. He would never harm a lady."

Season wondered what James would think if he knew his captain had already harmed her beyond repair, but she decided it would be best not to talk about her own situation. "Tell me why your captain hides his face behind a disguise. Have you ever seen him without his mask?"

"Aye, the captain does not wear his mask when he's on board the *Andromeda*."

"What does he look like, James?"

"I can't tell you that, ma'am. We of the crew are honorbound not to reveal his identity to anyone. There isn't a man aboard who would betray the captain," James said, avoiding her eyes. He knew he had already said too much.

Relief washed over James when he heard a rap on the door. He was glad to see Briggs had come to help him remove the loose furnishings and carry them below to be stored until after the storm.

It was just after sundown when the *Andromeda* began to roll and pitch drunkenly. The howl of the gale force winds could be heard above the roar of the waves. Season clenched her hands tightly and curled up in the middle of the bed, while James sat in a chair, talking to her calmly.

"I'd rather be at sea in a storm than on land, ma'am. I never liked to be on land much anyway."

"Tell me about your life, James," she said, trying to find something that would take her mind off the storm.

"I don't remember my ma that much, and I never saw my pa. It was said that me and my ma lived above a blacksmith shop in Boston, but I don't remember that. I was on my own from the time I was seven until the captain found me and took me on board the *Andromeda*."

"Is the captain also from Boston?" Season asked,

thinking she might find a clue to The Raven's identity.

James smiled as if he knew she was trying to trip him up. "The captain likes to say he resembles the foam upon the waves, drifting in and out with the tide, with no permanent home."

At that moment a huge wave slapped against the ship and sent the vessel careening over on her side, spilling Season onto the cabin floor. As the ship pitched and slowly righted itself, James helped Season back to the bed.

"I was ordered to tie you to the bed when the sea got rough. I think the time has come," the lad stated. Withdrawing a length of rope from his pocket, James smiled at Season. "Will you allow me to tie you to the bed, ma'am?"

"Only if you will stay with me as you did before, James. I'm so frightened!"

"I'll stay with you 'til this blow is over," he agreed. After he fastened the rope about her slim waist and secured the other end to the bedpost, James tied another rope about his own waist and then sat beside Season on the bed.

The cabin had become dark since they weren't allowed to light a lantern. Season sought James's hand and felt it tremble so she clutched it tightly. He was no more than a boy, she reminded herself. Although he presented a brave front, she realized he was doing it for her benefit. He was every bit as frightened as she.

Neither of them could sleep because it soon became clear to them that this storm was far worse than the previous one had been. All through the long, horrible night the *Andromeda* rolled and pitched, while Season and James clung to each other for comfort.

When Season could make herself heard above the storm, she talked to James about growing up on Chatsworth, but still the hours seemed to drag. Just before dawn, when the storm seemed to have abated, Season and James closed their eyes in sleep.

During the day Season awoke to the sound of a key grating in the lock, and Briggs entered the cabin. She noticed that he looked worn and haggard, obviously exhausted from his battle with the sea.

"Briggs, thank goodness the sea has calmed," Season said, loosening the rope about her waist and trying not to disturb James.

"The storm is only half over, my lady," Briggs replied, grim-faced. "This calm won't last long. At the moment we are in the eye of the hurricane, but soon we'll have to deal with the backside of it."

Season's eyes were large with fright. "Do you mean we must go through another storm as devastating as the one last night?" she asked in horror.

"I fear so, my lady, but it won't be any worse than the other one. The captain will be at the helm just as he was last night."

Season was irritated now, as well as frightened. She was weary of hearing how well the captain could steer a ship. Did all the men aboard the *Andromeda* think their captain invulnerable? Did they think he alone could battle nature and come out the winner?

She was about to voice her irritation, when James awoke, untied himself, and moved toward the door. "I'm going topside to see the damage," he announced, sleepily trudging toward the door.

"If you are of a mind to, my lady, you could go top-side for a breath of fresh air. There's some broken rigging, but it won't be dangerous to you," Briggs said.

Season lost no time in scooting off the bed. She rushed toward the cabin door so quickly that Briggs had to run to catch up with her.

When Season reached the deck, she took a deep breath. A soft wind ruffled her hair, and the air smelled clean and crisp. It was good to be alive, to relish the feel of the warm sun on her face.

Crewmen scurried about, replacing broken timbers, while the sail master plied his needle to a torn sail. Everyone had a job to do; even James was bailing water out of the longboats and then replacing their canvas covers.

"How is it possible to exist in the center of a storm, Briggs," Season asked as she noted the dark clouds that surrounded the ship. She was astounded by this strange phenomenon of nature.

"Hurricanes ain't all that uncommon this time of year, my lady. The eye of the storm is always calm."

Suddenly Season's eyes were drawn to the helm of the ship. She drew in her breath when she saw the dark, hooded captain with his head bent over a map. It was the first time Season had seen him without his cape. His legs were spread apart in an arrogant stance, and she couldn't help but notice what a dashing, rakish man he was. He wore dark trousers tucked into knee-length black boots, and his white shirt had ruffles at the neck and on the wrists. The Raven exuded energy and power. Season almost felt that there was nothing he couldn't do. She understood why the crew of the

Andromeda placed their faith in him.

Before Season could look away, The Raven raised his masked face, and she could tell he was looking directly at her. She remembered the night they had spent together and her cheeks burned, knowing he was remembering also.

"Briggs," the raspy voice called out. "If the lady has not eaten, now would be the time for her to have something light—nothing heavy since the worst of the storm is yet to come."

"Aye, aye, Captain. Shall I escort the lady below now?" Briggs asked.

With a quickness that surprised Season, the captain made his way down to her. As he drew near, she stood poised, ready for flight. When he leaped over a broken pile of rigging and landed right in front of her, she drew back quickly.

"I'll see to the lady's needs, Briggs," he said in his disturbing, raspy voice.

Briggs nodded and moved away, giving Season a smile. She wanted to call him back as he disappeared from view down the companionway.

"I see you are no worse for the storm, my lady," the captain said in a deep voice. It was unnerving for Season to know that The Raven was staring at her when she couldn't really see his eyes.

"Little you care," she said, turning her back and staring out on a surprisingly calm sea.

"Not so, my lady. Your comfort is always foremost on my mind."

Season could tell by his tone of voice that he was amused. "Why don't you just take me home? I can be of no further use to you now," she said, not bothering to turn in his direction.

"Where would you consider home?"

"You know I am talking about England."

"Am I to gather that you do not want to be set down near your husband-to-be who waits for you in New York?"

Season spun around to face The Raven, and her green eyes seemed to blaze with a slow fire. "You know I can never marry Edmund Kensworthy now. You saw to that!" She became aware that she had raised her voice and had attracted the attention of some of the crew members, so she spoke more quietly. "I don't want to marry any man. I will never allow a man to touch me again."

A heavy hand fell on Season's shoulder as The Raven leaned his head close to hers and spoke in a soft voice so only she could hear. "I am truly sorry for what happened between us the other night. If I could make amends I would do so."

Season was taken by surprise. She had expected anything from him but an apology. "Some things cannot be rectified, as you are aware. If you truly want to make amends you will set me free." She raised her head and stared at the black slits where his eyes should have been. "When will you release me?"

The dark hood dipped. "Unfortunately, at the moment I am unable to comply with your wishes, my lady. The port we make for is a long way from your country or mine."

"Where are we bound?"

"We are on our way to the Barbary States, my lady.

At least we were until this storm blew us off course."

"The Barbary States are a pesthole and a pirate stronghold! I have heard it said that the pirate ships which sail from the Barbary Coast prey on vessels from every country with equal disdain and disrespect."

"So you have heard of the Barbary States?"

"Hasn't everyone? I fear such a place."

The Raven threw back his head and laughed deeply. "You need have no fear for your person, my lady. I would never allow anything to happen to so valuable a cargo as yourself."

"What could happen to me that hasn't already occurred? The only thing that remains is for you to take my life, which I am sure you would do without hesitation should the mood strike you."

Season could feel the captain's anger as he grabbed her arm and half-carried, half-dragged her across the deck. When she tried to put up a struggle, she could see the amusement on the faces of the crew members. As they reached the companionway, The Raven lifted Season into his arms and carried her below. Striding into the cabin, he tossed her onto the bed.

"You have been a trial to me and a thorn in my side ever since I first laid eyes on you," he ground out from between clenched teeth.

Season scrambled to her knees, ready to do battle with the man should the need arise. "I am delighted if I have caused you trouble!" she cried out. "I hope I have also caused you many sleepless nights."

The Raven's hand reached out, and he softly touched Season's face. For the moment she was too stunned to move. "Oh, you have, my lady. Take comfort in the fact that you have danced through my mind day and night."

Before Season could push his hand away, he turned and walked to the door, laughing. At the door he turned to her.

"I meant what I said about eating a light meal. The storm will be at least as strong as the one we had last night. I am sure you wouldn't wish to lose your dinner. Don't forget to tie yourself to the bed as you did before." Without another word The Raven swept out of the room and Season heard the key grate in the lock.

Season stared at the locked door. She wished she dared call him back. For some reason when he had been with her she had forgotten about the impending storm. She lay on the bed, feeling the gentle sway of the *Andromeda,* and she wondered if they would weather the backside of the hurricane as well as they had the front.

It was almost sundown when the sea began to throw its heavy waves against the ship. Season knew this storm would be every bit as devastating as its predecessor, but she was prepared to weather it alone since James hadn't come to her cabin.

She decided she wouldn't lash herself to the bed this time. If the *Andromeda* were going to sink, she didn't want to go to a watery grave tied to a bedpost. It didn't take long for Season to realize her mistake. The second time she was thrown onto the floor, she decided it would be wise to tie herself to the bed.

As she huddled in the darkened cabin, Season realized she had never felt so alone. The waves raged and pounded against the hull of the *Andromeda* until Season felt she was living a nightmare. If the ship were to sink, would the others forget that she was locked below in this cabin? she wondered frantically.

The night seemed endless. She had eaten nothing at all, but still her stomach was heaving. At times, when the ship pitched forward and aft, she was sure they were sinking. The wind blew with a vengeance against the tiny craft and the noise from the storm was deafening.

Season tried to think of something pleasant to take her mind off the danger. She remembered the summer she had turned sixteen and her father had unexpectedly come home to help her celebrate. It had been one of the rare occasions when he had been home for her birthday. That had been the year her father had given her Cinibar. On that occasion he had been in a rare good humor, owing, he had told her, to the fact that he'd seen one of his laws passed in the House of Lords.

Season tried to think of the smell of the honeysuckle that climbed the walls of the summerhouse. Each day in the spring she had walked in the gardens at Chatsworth, taking a book with her so she could curl up in the summerhouse and read.

Against her will, Season's mind seemed to turn to the dark master of the *Andromeda*. Seeing him without his cape, she had noticed that he was tall and muscled, that his shoulders were extremely broad and his waist trim. His legs were long and powerful, and his hands, tanned by the sun, were strong. His body was that of a young man, but what about his face? Would he be ugly and grotesque? She knew he wasn't scarred, because she had felt his face. He'd been clean-shaven and his hair was shoulder length. It was amazing how much she knew about his appearance, and yet she couldn't put a face to him.

Try as she would, Season couldn't seem to get The Raven out of her mind. There were so many things about him that she didn't know—that she might never know.

Suddenly a huge wave crashed against the hull of the *Andromeda,* causing the ship to roll. The sound of splintering wood told Season there had been great damage. She closed her eyes tightly and prayed with all her might. In that moment, she was sure they were sinking!

Would The Raven come to her in her dying moments? she wondered. Would he take her in his arms so they could die together? Season didn't stop to analyze her feelings, she only knew that if she were going to die she wanted to be in the arms of the man who now owned her body.

Season began to cry loudly, but her voice couldn't be heard against the howling of the wind. She wasn't aware that the cabin door had opened until a knife sliced through the rope tied about her waist.

"I knew you would be frightened, so I came to you," said the deep voice of The Raven. He pulled her into his arms, and though his clothing was wet, Season threw her arms about his neck. "The storm is all but over, my lady. Briggs can now handle the ship from here on out."

She buried her face against his broad chest, and he could feel her slight body tremble. "Are you quite sure we are not going to die?" she cried.

"Quite sure, my sweet, sweet lady." His hands were tender as he ran them soothingly up and down her back. "You should have known I would never allow anything as insignificant as a storm to harm you."

His deep voice immediately had a calming effect on Season. She felt her eyelids getting heavy. Wrapped in a feeling of well-being and safety, she buried her face against his neck.

Season was unaware that she was drifting off to sleep. She never knew it when The Raven laid her back on the bed and pulled the covers over her. She didn't hear him when he walked out of the cabin silently, to return to the helm of the ship.

Chapter Eleven

Season awoke to a calm sea. Opening her eyes, she found bright sunlight filtering in through the porthole. It took her a moment to get her bearings. The cabin was in total disarray. Since the maps and logs hadn't been removed from the shelves, they were scattered over the floor.

Her eyes widened in disbelief when she saw the cabin door standing slightly ajar. The door had never before been left open. Season arose on shaky legs and made her way across the cabin. She peeked around the door and saw no one about, so she walked up the companionway.

On deck, the sight that greeted her was a pleasant surprise. They were anchored off the shore of a small island! Season could see white sandy beaches. Behind them palm trees swayed in the warm tropical breeze.

"Morning, ma'am," James greeted her cheerfully.

Season gave the cabin boy an answering smile. "Where are we?"

"This is an uncharted island where we often put in for fresh water and to make needed repairs. The storm damaged the *Andromeda's* mast last night, and it has to be replaced today."

"Will I be allowed to go ashore, James?" Season asked hopefully. She had often read books about the tropics, but she'd never dreamed she would see them for herself. Looking toward shore, she could see that the palm trees ran the length of the island. Seeing pictures of them in a book isn't the same as seeing them in person, she thought. There seemed to be miles and miles of white sandy beach, which she would like very much to explore.

"Me and Briggs remained aboard waiting for you to wake up, ma'am. The captain said we was to allow you to sleep as long as possible and then bring you ashore," James told her excitedly.

"Are there any cannibals or unfriendly natives living on the island?" Season wanted to know.

"No, ma'am, the island is too small and rocky to be inhabited. There ain't nothing but bird life and sea turtles that live there."

"Wait until I change my clothing," Season called as she hurried below. Season quickly slipped into a pink and white candy-striped gown, and twisted her long hair into a knot at the nape of her neck. She frowned at her pink satin slippers, wishing she had a more sensible pair of shoes but knowing these would have to do.

When she reached the deck, she found Briggs and James waiting for her. At Briggs's direction, Season climbed down the rope ladder and into the waiting longboat.

As they approached the island, Season could feel her excitement mounting. How good it felt to be alive! She could hardly wait to feel solid ground beneath her feet.

As the boat touched shore, Briggs climbed into the water and held his arms out to Season. When he saw her hesitate, he smiled. "You wouldn't want to ruin your pretty slippers now, would you, my lady? If you will allow it, I will carry you to shore."

Season nodded and allowed him to lift her into his arms. When he placed her on the sandy beach, her legs felt stiff and she had trouble keeping her balance. Turning around in a circle, she tried to drink in all the beauty of the island. She was sure she had never seen such a blue sky, nor water such a deep aqua color. The palm trees swayed in the gentle trade wind, and the warm sun seemed to kiss her cheeks.

Many of the ship's crew were on the beach mending sails, while others were cutting timber to replace the splintered mast. Off to the left, Season could see two men building an open campfire. Everything seemed so tranquil after last night's storm.

"It's nice ain't it, ma'am," James said, coming up behind Season.

"Perhaps one must experience a near scrape with death to be able to fully appreciate life, James," she said thoughtfully. Season reached down, picked up a handful of white sand, and allowed it to sift through her fingers. "It's just so good to be alive," she whispered.

By now feeling was returning to Season's legs and she wanted to see everything. "Come on, James, let us go exploring!" she cried excitedly as she gathered up

181

the skirt of her gown and ran down the beach. She dodged in and out among the palm trees that grew near the water's edge where the waves lapped the shore.

She was unaware she was being watched by a man who stood on a rise some twenty paces away. He couldn't help thinking how childlike and carefree Season appeared at that moment. He watched as she and James headed for a cove where they would be hidden from the ship's crew.

Season picked up the skirt of her gown and tucked it about her waist. She then removed her sand-filled slippers and tossed them aside. When she grasped James's hand, they both ran laughingly toward the sea.

The man who watched them pulled his leather helm over his head and then made his way down the slope to where his men were working on the mast.

The wind had loosened Season's hair, so she had removed the pins and allowed it to blow free. She was now gathering sea shells and piling them on the beach. James showed her how she could hold the larger shells to her ear and hear the sound of the sea.

Finally, as evening began to fall, she sat down, her back braced against a palm tree. Her bare feet peeped from beneath her gown as she closed her eyes and listened to the soothing sound of the waves lapping at the shore. Season couldn't remember a day in her life when she had enjoyed herself more.

She did not hear the soft footsteps that approached her from behind, and she was unaware that the captain motioned for James to leave.

"I would give a golden doubloon to know what you are thinking, my lady," the raspy voice said.

Season opened her eyes and smiled. "My thoughts have never before brought such a high price."

The Raven eased himself down beside her, removed a coin from his pocket, and tossed it into her lap. "I have paid the price; now you must tell me your thoughts, my lady."

She laughed and picked up the Spanish coin. "You will find you have paid too much, sir. I was merely wishing I could sleep on the beach tonight. I have never before slept beneath the open sky. It would be a great adventure, would it not?"

"Your wish is my command, my lady. I see no reason why you cannot sleep on the beach."

"Are you saying that I may sleep here tonight?" she asked excitedly.

"Indeed I am. If it is your pleasure, I cannot find it in my heart to deny you so simple a request."

"It will not be dangerous, will it?" she asked, wondering why the captain had given in so easily.

"I shall be your watchdog and protector," he said in a deep voice.

"But who will protect me from you, Captain?" she asked, hating how breathless her voice sounded.

"Who will protect me from you, my lady," he countered.

"I have changed my mind," she said. The Raven was sitting much too close for her peace of mind. His proximity recalled the intimacy they had shared. "I don't really want to sleep on the beach."

For the first time, Season noticed that James was nowhere in sight; she and the captain were alone! She started to scramble to her feet, intending to leave, but

The Raven reached out and placed a restraining hand on her arm.

"Abide with me for a moment, my lady. I have brought you a feast such as you have never tasted."

Season watched The Raven with frightened eyes. "What is it?" Season asked, wishing James would quickly return. She noticed for the first time that the captain held something wrapped in palm leaves.

He placed one of the palm leaves on Season's lap, and when she lifted the edge of the leaf, she was greeted by the most delicious aroma.

"This is fish baked the way it was intended to be prepared. The ship's cook, Digger, wrapped it in palm leaves, then covered it with hot coals, allowing it to bake until tender."

Season had forgotten how hungry she was, and her mouth watered at the scent of this delicacy. She picked up a flaky piece of fish and popped it into her mouth. "Mmm, this is wonderful," she declared.

"You are in for another treat, my lady. Have you ever tasted the milk of a coconut?"

"No, but I have read about it in a book."

He chuckled. "It would seem you have read about almost everything in a book. Reading is not the same as experiencing," he said, reaching into a bag and withdrawing a round brownish object. Season watched with interest as he punctured the coconut with his knife and then handed it to her.

"Drink from the hole," he instructed.

Season gave him a doubtful glance. At first she took a small sip, but finding the taste sweet and pleasant, she drank deeply.

The Raven laughed as coconut milk dripped down Season's chin. Reaching out, he wiped the milk away with his finger. "After you have eaten the fish, I will introduce you to the meat of the coconut," he said, and Season could hear the smile in his voice.

Season was surprised to find herself feeling comfortable in his company. She had no fear of him at the moment because he was being pleasant and charming. Taking another bite of the fish, she noticed the captain wasn't eating.

"Are you not hungry, Captain?" she asked, holding a generous slice of fish out to him.

"As much as I would like to dine with you, this helm makes it quite impossible."

She smiled up at him impishly. "You could always take it off," she suggested.

"Alas, my lady, I must decline—that is not possible."

The Raven noticed she had eaten all the fish, so he broke open a coconut and handed her the tender white meat. Season took a bite and found she liked the meat even better than the milk.

After she had eaten her fill, Season stood up and walked down to the water's edge to wash her hands in the salty brine. "How long do we stay on this island?" Season called to the captain who still sat under the palm tree, watching her.

"If all goes well, we should put to sea sometime tomorrow evening."

"Was the *Andromeda* badly damaged by the storm?" she inquired.

"Less so than I feared."

"The storm was very frightening," she said, returning to him and sitting down once more.

The Raven watched her green eyes as she stared out to sea, and he knew she had never had more appeal for him. "Yes, but you and the *Andromeda* both fared well, my lady," he declared in his deep raspy voice.

The Raven reached out, intending to touch a golden curl that nestled against Season's cheek, but when he saw her pull away, he dropped his hand to his side.

Season looked at the setting sun. It appeared to be dropping into the sea as its magnificent dying embers painted the sky a brilliant red. It seemed the sea was afire.

She turned her head to look at the captain, but he was staring out to sea and seemed unaware of her. This gave her the chance to study him up close. His long, boot-clad legs were stretched out in front of him, and his white shirt was unlaced at the throat, revealing the black curly hair on his chest. His sun-browned hand rested lightly on his thigh. Season felt a tightening in her throat. It was as if he were pulling her toward him, yet he hadn't even touched her.

Raising her head, she found he was watching her.

"You are so lovely," he said in a soft voice. "I have seen you with your hair powdered, but I prefer it as it now is. It is much too beautiful to hide under artificial color. Never powder it again," he told her.

"I don't like . . . I usually don't . . ."

She flinched as he reached out and took a golden tress between his thumb and finger, caressing it softly.

"I am in danger, *my* lady—grave danger," he murmured in a soft voice.

Why is it, Season wondered, when he says, my lady,

it sounds as if he is calling her, *his* lady?

"How, and from whom, are you in danger, Captain?" she asked breathlessly.

His hand drifted from her hair to her chin. "The how is you, and the whom is you, my lady," he whispered.

"I don't . . . think . . . I would never—"

"Shh," he whispered, as he placed a finger over her lips. "You are safe enough from me, for I cannot kiss you with this helm on, and I cannot remove it just now."

Season felt a slow-moving fire course through her body, and she tried to think of something to say that would take her mind off the dark captain.

"You said you saw me with my hair powdered. Were you at the ball when I met Edmund?" she asked, hurriedly changing the subject.

He laughed deeply. "You are always full of questions, but if you must know, yes, I saw you at the ball."

Season's green eyes sparkled. "Did I talk to you that night?" she wanted to know.

"I do not think you paid the slightest attention to me that night, my lady. But I, like every other man at the ball, was overcome by your beauty," he said in a voice full of amusement.

"I was never introduced to you, or I would have remembered," she said, trying not to listen to the compliment he had just paid her.

"I believe you are fishing, my lady," he replied good-naturedly. "Would you have me tell you all my secrets?"

Season noticed that it was almost completely dark. There were thousands of stars twinkling in the ebony skies, but she saw that there would be no moon to lighten the dark tonight. She stood up and dusted the sand from her gown.

"Should we not be getting back to the ship?" she asked in an uneasy voice.

He chuckled as he stood to his full height. "No. I promised you could sleep on the beach tonight. Whenever possible, I try to keep my word."

"I hope you don't think I was suggesting that I should sleep here with . . . you!" she said in a horrified voice.

"That is a tempting offer, my lady. You know of course that you have put me out of my cabin. I have been forced to sleep in Briggs's cabin."

"It was not my fault, Captain. If you have been inconvenienced you should place the blame on yourself," she retorted, tossing her golden mane.

Season could almost feel his infectious good humor when he laughed. "Never has the world known anyone like you, my lady. You are not only lovely enough to cause a man to lose his heart, but you are intelligent and witty as well."

Season could think of no reply to his compliment. She felt her heart thumping in her breast and knew she was pleased by his observation. Never before had a man admired her for her intelligence.

"I will send James to you, my lady. He will see to all the necessary comforts."

Season watched The Raven disappear into the darkened shadows, wishing she hadn't been so hasty in her appeal to be allowed to sleep on the beach. He had

188

said he was sending James to her, but it was such a dark night. Would it be safe to sleep on the beach with only a boy as her protector? Already Season could hear strange sounds coming from some unknown birds deep within the island.

She had enjoyed herself today. Even the dark master of the *Andromeda* had been pleasant, and she hadn't felt like his captive. But now that it was dark, wouldn't it be better to return to the ship?

"Ma'am, it's me, James," the young cabin boy called out. He was carrying a torch to light his way, and Season could see that he was also bringing what appeared to be mesh hammocks.

Season began to lose some of her apprehension as she watched James string the beds between palm trees. She had never slept in a hammock before. Laughingly, she sat down in one, then swung her feet up, lay back, and closed her eyes.

"This is wonderful. Do you sleep this way on board ship, James?" She loved the way the hammock swung back and forth with the breeze.

"Yes, ma'am, most of the crew does."

"It is a very pleasant feeling, but do you not become ill from the swaying motion of the ship?"

"You get used to it. Briggs says it's like being rocked to sleep every night.

Season rested her arms behind her head and smiled. The stars seemed so near she felt that she could reach up and pluck them from the sky. She glanced over at James, but couldn't make out his face in the moonless night.

189

"I believe I could spend my life, here, James. Just think about being able to sleep beneath the stars every night."

"Not very practical, my lady," said the deep raspy voice of The Raven. Season had not heard his approach, and she now strained her eyes, trying to make out his form; but he was no more than a shadow.

"One would soon tire of a diet of fish and coconut milk," he told her, placing his hands on either side of her hammock to stop its swaying motion.

"James, are you there," she called out, feeling fear in the very depths of her being.

"James has returned to the ship, my lady."

"Why . . . are you here?" she whispered.

"You did not think I would allow a boy to protect my most valuable cargo, did you? If you will remember, I said I would be your watchdog tonight."

"I . . . thought James would be occupying the other hammock."

"You thought wrong."

"I don't want you to come near me," she said, her voice laced with fear.

"You are assuming I would want to come near you, my lady. It was not my wish to sleep on the beach," he reminded her in an amused voice.

"I didn't mean to imply . . . I was merely—"

"Never mind," he said, moving to the other hammock and lying in it.

Season lay there for a long time, too confused to move. She listened to the lonesome sound of the night birds and was overcome by a feeling of loneliness.

"I have been meaning to speak to you about the

other night, my lady," The Raven interrupted her thoughts.

"Do you mean the night of the storm?"

"No. You know very well the night to which I refer. I owe you an apology. It has never been my habit to force my attentions on an unwilling woman. You have the distinction of being the only one who wasn't willing to come to me. You have my word it will not happen again. So you see there is nothing for you to fear tonight."

She turned her face in his direction. "Is that supposed to make me feel better?"

"I had hoped it would."

"If you are feeling guilty, it is no more than you deserve," Season said, grateful that it was too dark for him to see her face. "I have never harmed you, and I will never know why you felt it necessary to harm me."

The Raven was quiet for a long moment. When he spoke his voice was no more than a raspy whisper. "I think, my lady, I was also harmed by you."

"I don't understand," she said in a confused voice. "I have done nothing to you."

Season felt rather than heard him stand and move to her side. She was startled when he reached out of the darkness to take her hand, and she pulled away from him.

"The night is much too nice to be spent in serious conversation, my lady. Do you know how to swim?"

"Of course, but I would never swim in the presence of a man."

She drew in her breath when he lifted her out of the hammock and carried her toward the waves that lapped at the shore.

"It is a dark night, my lady. I can see you no more than you can see me."

Season bravely reached up her hand and felt his face. The Raven wore no mask to hide his identity!

He knew she was confused, and he laughed.

"The dark night will be my only disguise tonight. It will also protect your modesty. I would suggest you remove your gown if you don't want it ruined."

"I will most certainly do no such a thing," she retorted. Even though she very much wanted to swim in the ocean, she had no desire to be unladylike.

Before Season could protest, he set her on her feet and began unlacing her gown.

"No, stop!" she cried, pushing his hand away.

The Raven only laughed as he pulled the gown over her head. "No one will see you but the fish, my lady. You know you want to swim; why not just admit it?"

Season could now feel the cool waves washing against her feet, and she wanted to submerge her overheated body in the water. "I will not remove my petticoats," she stated modestly.

"Then allow me," he said, deftly pulling yards and yards of frilly white lace over her head. Season felt a thrill go through her body as his hand brushed against her throat.

"I will not allow you to remove any more of my garments," she said in a soft voice.

"I suppose the remaining articles of clothing will not hamper your swimming overmuch." He laughed.

"You had this planned all along, didn't you, Captain? Must I remind you that I am not one of your bar-maids?"

"Actually I didn't plan this. The notion just came to me. As to comparing you to a barmaid, that would be much like comparing a stone to a diamond."

Season became aware that The Raven was removing his own garments, so she quickly waded farther into the water. The waves lapped at her body with a gentle motion, and she was caught up in the excitement of swimming in the sea.

"I am a good swimmer," she called out. "In the summers I swam almost every day at Chatsworth."

"Is it to be a race, then?" he asked, coming up beside her.

By now Season was waist-deep in the water. "As you wish," she called out, diving into a rippling wave. With strong, powerful strokes, she headed out to sea. Season had never swam in the ocean before, and she found the salt water burned her eyes. Ignoring the irritant, she dove beneath the surface, feeling exhilarated. When she surfaced, she was aware that the captain had swum right along with her.

"You are indeed a strong swimmer for a woman," he said turning over on his back and floating beside her.

"For a woman! What do you mean for a woman?" Never in her life had Season wanted anything as badly as she wanted to beat this man. With renewed effort, she lunged forward, taking strong even strokes, assured that she was leaving him behind. She swam until she was exhausted and her arms and legs felt like heavy weights. That was when she realized how foolish she had been. She was too weary to swim another stroke, and she didn't even know in which direction the shore was. It was dark, and she began to panic. What if she were to drown? A new fear came to her: what if there were sharks in the water with her!

In her panic, she began to sink and had to struggle to keep her head above water. When the dark sea closed over her, Season felt as if her lungs would burst from want of air. Just when she thought she was indeed drowning, she felt a strong hand go about her waist and pull her upward.

When Season reached the surface, she coughed and drew a big gulp of air into her lungs.

"My foolish little mermaid," The Raven murmured against her ear. "I concede the race. You won in spirit and courage, and after all that is what really counts."

Season laid her head on his shoulder and allowed him to take them both toward the shore. She didn't know at what point she became aware of him as a man and not merely as her savior. Perhaps it was when her body brushed against his, or perhaps, it was when he turned and his warm breath fanned her cheek. Her arms were about his neck, and she could feel his powerful muscles beneath her fingertips.

"Sweet lady, you will make me forget the promise I made if you don't stop tempting me so," he said, drawing her around in front of him.

Season raised her head and felt his lips against her face. She wanted him to forget the promise he had made. She could think of nothing but the warmth spreading through her body because he was holding her so intimately.

What has come over me? she wondered, as she brazenly turned her face and touched her lips to his. The moment Season's mouth touched The Raven's, he clasped her tightly against him and the water swirled over both their heads. Season felt as if she were floating in a warm world full of feeling.

When The Raven pulled them to the surface, he broke off the kiss. "You do sorely tempt me, my lady. Pray I do not take you up on your invitation."

Season rested her face against his and heard him groan. When she touched his lips with hers the second time, his promise was all but forgotten.

As soon as they reached shallow water, he lifted her into his arms and carried her ashore, laying her down on the sand while he knelt over her.

"You only have to say no, and I will leave you untouched," he whispered.

For her answer, Season twined her hands about his neck and pulled his face down to her parted lips.

"Remember when the morning comes that you asked for this, my lady," he said just before his lips took command of hers in a mind-destroying kiss.

Season didn't want to think about tomorrow. She could only think about his caressing hands running over her body and shaking her to the depths of her soul. Surely she had been created for this moment in time. She was unaware of the rough sand beneath her back as his lips settled on hers.

Incapable of thinking or reasoning, she told herself, this was meant to be, The Raven has become my destiny!

Chapter Twelve

Season trembled as The Raven's hand brushed against the swell of her breast and then moved down to the soft curve of her hips. She gasped as his fingers brushed the length of her inner thigh. Somewhere in the back of her mind a small voice told her this was wrong, but that voice was overpowered by the urgent need The Raven awakened in her. She should be struggling, trying to gain her release, but instead she was twisting and purring, in ecstasy. The growing need in her begged to be eased, the hunger to be assuaged.

The Raven's strong muscled body seemed to absorb Season's soft curves. She pulled his head downward and opened her lips to receive his hot kiss. He didn't hesitate, but settled his body against hers as her fingers explored the broad expanse of his back tentatively.

The Raven pushed Season's chemise off her shoulders and down over her hips. "'Tis wrong," she cried in a moment of sanity. "My soul will be damned to hell for eternity."

"If this be hell, my lady, give me an eternity to spend there with you," his deep, husky voice resounded against her ear.

The sand began to cut into Season's tender skin, and she was surprised when The Raven raised her up and placed her on his shirt. As he lowered his body down on top of her she turned her face to his.

Wild, hot, searing flesh entered Season's body, and she whimpered softly while trying to draw him tighter against her. Their bodies were wet from swimming in the sea, and that seemed to heighten their pleasure. When Season ran her fingers through The Raven's hair, separating the damp strands, he began moving, pulsating deep inside her. His hungry kisses seemed to burn her satiny throat.

Season seemed to have trouble breathing, but she gasped when a new and unexpected feeling shook her body. As The Raven's mouth plundered Season's lips, he mastered her body. She lost count of the times her body shuddered with tremors of passionate fury. Again and again her body answered his masterful manipulation, until at last his body shuddered with an answering fire. Season heard him groan as he relaxed, and she felt his full weight upon her.

Words of love tumbled to Season's lips, wanting to be spoken, but she refused to utter them. This was madness, surely not love. Hadn't Molly once pointed out to her the difference between love and lust. How could a woman love a faceless man? If this be lust, then it is a far more frightening emotion than love, she thought.

"I will say again, my lady, you are damned good. Aside from the fact that you are untested, you are the best I have ever had," he murmured softly in her ear.

The Raven heard her gasp at his cruel words, but he was trying to save himself from surrendering to his feelings for her. He was fighting to keep his freedom. He knew his cruel words had hurt her, but in the long run it was far kinder to do so. The two of them were never meant to be together; they were born enemies. He didn't want to love any woman, especially not this one; and he knew the Lady Season Chatsworth could never love him—not after everything that had passed between them. If she ever discovered his true identity, she would only hate him all the more.

Season cringed at his harsh words. She felt as if he had thrown a dash of cold water into her face, while ripping her heart to shreds. Had he meant to compliment her? she wondered. If that had been his intention, he hadn't succeeded. He had made her feel unclean and tarnished by comparing her to other women with whom he had made love. She lay motionless for a moment. How could she have thought she had any tender feelings for this man? She felt a hurt so deep that she wanted to cry out in pain.

"I hate you. You are a loathsome creature," she whispered through trembling lips. She wished to find words to wound him as he had her.

"I would rather have your hate than most women's love, my lady. I will willingly take any small crumbs you throw my way."

"Crumbs are all you will ever get from me, Raven."

"That will be almost enough," he said, moving off her, "although I feel as if I've had a feast rather than crumbs from you tonight, my lady."

Season felt her throat burn. "What are you going to do with me now?" she asked, as he knelt down beside her. She wished he would just leave her here on this deserted island. She had no wish to ever face him again.

His hand brushed against her breast. "Is that an offer, my lady?"

Season wanted to strike him for what he had implied, but instead she moaned when his finger circled the tip of her breast. His touch seemed to have all the intensity of the raging hurricane that had tossed the *Andromeda* about in its wake.

"Please let me go now," she said in a soft voice. "I can be of no further use to you."

"Suppose I want to keep you as my own?"

She pushed his hand away and sat up. "I am serious, Raven."

"Perhaps I am too."

Season tried to turn away as his hand laced through her tumbled curls. She could feel him lowering her back onto the sand, and she wondered how easily he could make her forget her anger. She wished she had the will to fight him, but when his lips blazed a trail across her face to seek her own, Season groaned in surrender. When he spread her legs apart, she eagerly awaited him.

"I have never known a woman who could set me on fire as you do, my lady. I will have you again if you are willing," he groaned. "I cannot seem to stop myself."

Season didn't answer, and his lips plundered her mouth. When he entered her with a strong forward thrust, she was almost wild with wanton desire.

She gazed up at the star-filled sky, knowing that

whatever the future brought she would always remember that night. It would be burned into her mind for all time.

"My lady, for this moment you belong to me alone," he whispered against her lips. "Other men may possess you in the days to come, but you will always remember I was the first."

"Will other women possess you?" she asked breathlessly.

He turned his cheek and rested it against hers as he started moving slowly inside her. "I have never been possessed . . . until now," he said in a deep voice. "You have entered my blood, and nothing I can do will wipe your memory away."

Season felt her heart soar at his admission. Surely he was as deeply moved by her as she was by him. She wanted to give him something that he would never forget. She wanted to make him think of her every time he took another woman in his arms. Arching her hips upward, she met his forward thrust and set her body motion to match his. Her lips moved over his face to taste the salty sea water that still clung to his skin.

"My lady, my lady, what are you doing to me?" he groaned, as her silken legs twined about his waist.

Season could feel their tempo building faster and faster, and her mind and heart seemed to reach out to The Raven. I will burn a memory into his very soul, she thought as she moved sensuously against his body.

"If I didn't know better I would think you were well trained, my lady," he breathed hotly in her ear. "You set me on fire, Season."

Season moaned as her body reached a passionate

fulfillment. Then she felt The Raven shudder, and he lay limp atop her. When he sprinkled kisses over her face, she twined her fingers through his hair and curled up with her head against his shoulder, feeling almost at peace with the world. It wasn't lust alone she felt for this man. It was also love, she realized. She loved The Raven even though he had no face, and no name!

Her hand strayed to his face, and she traced his profile, trying to imagine what the man she loved looked like. How was it possible that she had found love in the most unlikely source?

"What color are your eyes?" she asked while running her finger softly across his eyelashes.

"What color are the eyes of a raven?" he countered.

Her hand drifted up to his hair. "What color is your hair? Surely you can tell me that much."

He caught her hand and kissed her fingers. "What color are a raven's wings?"

"You have a strong chin, but then I would expect nothing less," she said, tracing the outline of his jaw.

"Your eyes are the most unsettling color of green," he murmured against her ear. "Your hair reminds me of golden corn silk until the sun hits it; then it comes alive as if it were on fire." His hand moved over her face. "Your face is so lovely, that the first time I saw you I couldn't believe my eyes. I have not changed my opinion since then." His hand drifted down to rest against her stomach. "Your body will haunt me until my dying day. You have utterly bewitched me, *my* lady."

She turned her head and tried to see his face. Did he really think her beautiful, or did he say these things to every woman with whom he was intimate?

"I would like to know all about you, but I know you will tell me nothing, Raven."

"Just like a woman," he said, smiling against her face. "You bed one and she wants to know if you put your right boot or your left boot on first."

He could feel her smile. "You know much about me; it's only fair that I know something about you."

"I don't know all that much about you. Would you answer some questions that have been nagging at me?"

Season moved her head against his chest, and the soft curly hair tickled her cheek. "Just like a man, you allow him to make love to you and he thinks that gives him the right to your life story."

She heard laughter rumble within his chest as he hugged her tightly. "I got more than I bargained for in you, my lady. I would wager that nowhere in the world is there a woman to rival you."

"Oh, I don't know. I once saw a picture of Leonardo da Vinci's, *Virgin on the Rocks,* and she might come close," she said flippantly.

"That brings me to what I wanted to ask you," he said, delighted with her wit. "Why is it that gossip says you have been promiscuous with your favors? I found the opposite to be true."

"Oh, that," she smiled. "It is a long story and I wouldn't want to bore you with it."

"I have the time, bore me."

"Well . . . it would be quite amusing if it hadn't made my father so angry with me. If you heard that I was less than pure, you must also have heard that I was betrothed to marry the Earl of Ransford. He was an awful man who was older than my father and a loathsome creature. I begged my father not to make me marry him, but my father wouldn't listen. He kept insisting I marry Lord Ransford. I decided one day that I would take matters into my own hands. My scheme worked better than I had dared hope, although at the time I didn't foresee the far-reaching consequences. I didn't know I would be banished from England to marry a man I had never met."

"What did you do to free yourself that incurred your father's anger?"

"One day Lord Ransford came to visit Chatsworth castle."

"Oh, so the lady lived in a real castle, did she?" he interrupted in an amused voice.

"Of course, what else? Do you want to hear my story or not?"

"Go on, you have my ear."

"Well, as I said, one day Lord Ransford came calling and he brought along two of his friends." Season smiled. "He was a braggart, and I heard him telling his friends he wanted to show off his pure and innocent young bride-to-be."

"Poor fool that he was," The Raven said, smiling.

"You might well say he was a fool. I was in the stable after having ridden Cinibar—"

"Am I to gather that Cinibar is a horse and not a man?" The Raven interrupted again.

"Are you going to interrupt, or do you want to hear the rest?"

"Pray go on."

"Knowing Lord Ransford was a prideful man, I

decided that if I shamed him before his peers he would have to release me from our marriage contract. I waited in the stables until I saw Lord Ransford and his friends coming my way. When they entered the stables, I threw myself against poor Tom, the stableboy, and sent us both tumbling into the hay. You can well imagine the compromising picture Tom and I represented. As you may know Lord Ransford was furious and quickly announced that he would never have me for his wife. What I hadn't bargained for, were the rumors he spread about me in London. I had to deal with a tattered reputation and my father's wrath. The king was so angry with me he demanded that my father have me married off immediately. The rest you know."

The Raven laughed heartily. "Good Lord, you are a minx. You are one of the few women I know who could save themselves in such a circumstance." In that moment The Raven knew he had met the one woman in the world for him. She had a wild spirit to match his own. If only they hadn't been born into two different worlds. They had no common meeting ground. He admired her bravery, and he was sorry that he had added to the lady's troubles.

"So, will you settle for Edward Kensworthy as your husband?" He waited tensely for her answer.

"At the moment I don't seem able to make that decision. I am somewhere on a tropical island and Edmund is somewhere in New York, I suppose."

"When I take you back, it might be a good idea if you were to marry your cousin immediately."

She turned her face away and stared into the night sky. "Why do you say that?"

"Dammit, don't you realize what I have done to you?" he cried out, grabbing her and burying his face in her golden hair. "Are you not aware of the consequences?"

"I know very well what you have done to me. Why should that necessitate my marrying my cousin. I don't think it would be fair to Edmund to have a woman like me as his wife."

"You must realize that I will never offer you marriage." The Raven stood up and pulled Season to her feet. "I can't be expected to offer marriage to every woman I bed. If I did so, I would be a bigamist many times over." His harsh words sliced through Season's heart like a knife.

She fought back her tears and squared her shoulders. "You and I marry one another? Surely you jest," she said, hoping to wound him as he had hurt her. "My position in life would never allow me to marry a commoner, much less a pirate such as yourself."

"I'm glad we know where we stand," he told her in a cold voice.

"I hate and despise you," she cried.

"So you have said," he stated, walking away. "You can wash in the ocean, and I will gather up your clothes and put them on the hammock," he said in an unfeeling voice.

Season ran into the sea and waded out until she was waist-deep in the water. She began to scrub herself all over, thinking she could never wash away the feel of The Raven's hands on her body.

As she came out of the water, she choked down a dry sob. The Raven had taken her body and her heart, and had given her only insults in return. One day she would show him that no man could treat Lady Season Chatsworth with so little respect! She knew she would never again allow him to lay a hand on her. She would be watching for a way to escape, and should she ever be free of this man, she would dearly love to see him swinging from the end of a rope!

Season found her way to the hammock and, feeling around in the dark, pulled her clothing on. She lay down, trying to block out her troubled thoughts. She didn't want to think about the cruel words The Raven had said to her tonight.

Turning over on her side, Season listened to the waves as they gently kissed the shore. She could tell The Raven wasn't asleep because she could almost sense his eyes boring into her. What does he want from me? she wondered.

Her thoughts were so troubled that it was a long time before she slept.

When Season woke, just before dawn, she looked at the empty hammock and knew The Raven had gone.

James sat beside her, a smile on his face. "You'd best eat, ma'am—we sail on the morning tide," he told her.

Chapter Thirteen

The *Andromeda* was under full sail when Briggs spotted another ship off the starboard bow and informed his captain. The Raven gauged the distance between the two vessels and knew that within three hours he would overtake the other craft. They were gaining on the other ship rapidly since the *Andromeda* was the faster of the two.

The *Andromeda*'s canvas sails snapped and crackled when the wind caught them, and the distance between the two ships lessened.

Two hours passed, during which time the crew of the *Andromeda* waited tensely to find out if the ship were friend or foe. It had been over six months since The Raven had taken a prize, and the crew was ready to meet the enemy. Each man aboard The Raven's ship was proud to serve his captain. The men had been hand-picked and were true patriots. They preferred to sail on a privateer vessel rather than serve in the as yet poorly organized United States Navy. In addition, the navy offered its crew eighteen dollars a month while the men of the *Andromeda* received an equal split of any prize taken, and so far the *Andromeda* had taken many prizes. However, The Raven always insisted that any guns and ammunition taken on a captured vessel be turned over to the United States Navy.

"She's a Red Ensign Merchant ship—British," the captain yelled down to his crew. "Load cannon and look sharp," he ordered.

The crew immediately sprung into action, loading and priming the twenty-four eighteen pounders on the upper deck and eight nine pounders on the quarter-deck. A brace of pistols and a cutlass were strapped about each man's waist in anticipation of hand-to-hand combat.

The Raven turned the *Andromeda* leeward and ordered a warning shot fired over the bow of the English merchant ship. "Strike the colors!" he yelled to his crew. Immediately the Stars and Stripes of the United States were hoisted up the flagpole, and the flag caught in the breeze, waving proudly above the *Andromeda*'s mast.

The British ship hoisted her Union Jack and returned a warning shot of her own.

"Look lively, men; we are coming about," The Raven called out. He brought the sails into the wind, coming up almost on the prow of the enemy ship. "Fire guns on the swivel deck!" came the crisp order.

A puff of smoke and the splintering of wood told the crew of the *Andromeda*, they had hit their target.

The Raven ordered the sails lowered as he came up against the hull of the English merchant, which was unable to fire her guns because the *Andromeda* was too near. It wasn't the first time The Raven had taken a prize without being fired upon.

"Do you give quarter?" The Raven yelled across to the captain of the merchant ship.

"I'll see you in hell first!" came the ready reply. Braces were fired from the deck of the *Andromeda,* and they created utter chaos aboard the English ship. The Raven wondered why the British captain had foolishly refused to surrender. The shots that had been fired by the American ship had splintered the enemy's mast, causing it to fall to the deck. Many English crew members were crushed beneath its weight, and others were running about in a frenzy.

"Throw the grappling irons and prepare to board her," The Raven commanded.

The grappling hooks were tossed and caught fast, holding the two ships together. The crew of the American ship swarmed onto the crippled merchant, their pistols aimed and ready to fire. For some strange reason the British crew members made no attempt to defend their ship. Many of them stood with their hands crossed over their chests, while others rushed forward, declaring they were captured American sailors.

"Do you give quarter?" The Raven asked again of the captain, wanting to avoid bloodshed if at all possible.

"Aye, I give quarter," the captain said, tossing his cutlass to the deck. "I am Captain Bruce, at your service. I can tell by your appearance that you are The Raven."

The Raven didn't confirm or deny who he was, but

he turned to his men and ordered them to gather up the firearms and take the prisoners below.

The Raven, in full mask, confronted the defeated British captain. "It was a sorry fight, sir. Why did you not attempt to defend yourself?"

"You were upon us before we could prepare. I had heard The Raven's ship was fleet, but I didn't know the extent of that speed until this day."

"You and your crew are my prisoners, sir."

"So I am to be the prisoner of the infamous Raven? This is a sad day for me."

"Correction, Captain, you are the prisoner of The United States of America," declared the raspy voice.

"It's true then that you fight for that rabble in the Colonies?" the defeated captain of the British ship asked. Captain Bruce was a man in his late fifties, and he stood proud in his blue and white uniform, his brass buttons glistening in the bright sunlight.

"Correction again, Captain. I fight for the patriots against the English tyrant. I am curious though: why did you not put up a better fight? You easily outgun the *Andromeda*.

The captain of the British merchant smiled without humor. "I did not make a fight of it because the crew refused to obey my orders. Being short-handed, we were forced to take on Spanish seamen. They somehow learned that Spain was about to declare war on England, and they became mutinous. I am sure you are aware that others of the crew are Americans who were captured and forced to serve aboard my ship. You have most probably saved my life, and that of my British crew."

The Raven gave a curt bow. "I am at your service, Captain Bruce. If you will show me to your cabin, I will take a cup of wine with you."

Below, Captain Bruce poured The Raven a glass of wine, while he studied his adversary closely. "I have heard many tales of your daring, but I never dreamed the day would come when I would be on the receiving end of your guns. Do they speak the truth when they say you are an English nobleman?"

The Raven raised the wineglass to his lips before answering. "If I were you, I would discount most of the stories that are circulated about me. I am no more than a privateer."

"Hmm, I don't mind telling you that when I saw the figurehead of the spread-winged raven and knew I had a mutinous crew on my hands, I feared you would want my death. You could have created a blood bath, had you wished to."

"I don't know what you have been told about me, but I hope my honor is not in question."

Captain Bruce raised his glass. "I prefer to make my own judgment, Raven. I raise my glass to a man of honor." The English captain took a sip of his wine and then set the glass on his desk. "May I ask what is to be the fate of my ship and crew?"

"Your ship is to be stripped of any valuables, of course. Then a prize crew will be placed aboard her to sail her to Maryland where she will be turned over to the authorities. I would imagine your Spanish crewmembers will be given their freedom, and of course the Americans will be set free. Most probably you and your mates will be held to exchange for our own men who are being held captive by your government."

"A fair judgment. Had I taken you prisoner, instead of the other way around, you would now be bound in chains. There is a high reward on your head."

"I would have expected to be placed in chains, had the battle gone the other way."

Captain Bruce took another sip of wine and stared at the man in the black mask. "I witnessed one of your American privateers being taken but two days ago in these same waters."

"Do you know the ship's name?"

"Yes, she was the *Sea Serpent.*"

The Raven seemed to tense. "Do you know what the *Sea Serpent*'s fate was?"

"No, I know only that she was taken by De Fores, the pirate who sails out of the Barbary States. I saw the battle only from a distance. You can well imagine I wouldn't want to come to the aid of either ship."

"I thank you for this bit of information. The *Sea Serpent*'s captain is a good friend of mine."

"That's a pity, Raven. Who can say what the fate of a prisoner would be at the hands of that black-hearted De Fores. I have heard he is a friend to no country."

The man behind the black leather helm stood up. "I will bid you a fair wind to Maryland. Have no fear, you will be treated with the respect that is due your station."

Captain Bruce smiled and inclined his head. He felt a healthy respect for The Raven. Even if he was the enemy, he had certainly dealt fairly with him.

Lady Season Chatsworth heard the sounds of battle

and climbed up on the chair so she could look out. At first she could see nothing but white puffs of smoke. However, she stayed at her vantage point until the *Andromeda* got under way, and as the ship moved away from the crippled merchant, Season saw the Union Jack lying tattered on her deck!

"Oh, no, it cannot be!" she cried, realizing the ship attacked had been English. In that moment she knew The Raven was indeed an enemy to her country. She clamped a hand over her mouth, thinking she had betrayed her native land by allowing The Raven to make love to her.

The two ships parted company, one following a course to the American coast, the other under full sail for the Barbary States.

The crew of the *Andromeda* had found riches aboard the British merchant and were celebrating with the three kegs of rum their captain had allowed them. The Raven had sent the guns and ammunition to America, hoping they would find their way into General George Washington's hands. The other bounty consisted of gold, silver, rich materials, and jewels. In addition, the merchant ship had carried coffee, tea, rum, and fruit. Each man knew the cargo would bring a fortune once they found a buyer in the Barbary States.

The Raven sat at the desk in the cabin he shared with his first mate, his head bent over a chart. "Briggs, according to my calculations and with a fair wind at our back, we should sight land by tomorrow morning. With a little luck, we should make Tripoli by tomorrow night."

"Aye, Captain," Briggs said, studying the face of the man he admired most in the world.

"I heard some rather disturbing news from Captain Bruce. He informed me that the *Sea Serpent* was taken two days ago by De Fores."

Briggs frowned. "That scurvy pirate! Do you know the fate of Captain Robert Wolf, sir?" Briggs asked, knowing that the *Sea Serpent*'s captain was a friend of The Raven's.

"No, but we will determine that when we go ashore at Tripoli." The Raven tested the tip of his rapier absentmindedly. "I always knew the day would come when I would meet De Fores at the end of a sword. If he has harmed Robert, he will surely pay with his life."

"You will have to be on guard against De Fores, sir. He is underhanded and devious," Briggs warned.

"I have the advantage over him because I know how he thinks. I will deal with him when the time comes."

"Try not to concern yourself about Captain Wolf, sir. He's a tough one."

"Yes. Robert can take care of himself in a fair fight. But to my knowledge De Fores has never been praised for being fair with anyone."

Briggs studied his captain's face. "You have been acting strangely ever since we left the island, sir. I think I know what's bothering you."

The Raven looked up at his longtime friend. "Don't be too sure you can read me, Briggs."

"Correct me if I'm wrong, sir, but you could have put Lady Season on the captured ship and sent her back to America. Why didn't you?"

216

The Raven took a drink of wine and glared at Briggs. "You seem to have all the answers tonight—you tell me," he declared sourly.

"I think you know why. You want to keep the lady for yourself. I haven't ever seen you act this way toward a woman before. Don't you think it's time you sent her back?"

The Raven rose to his feet. "To hell with that!" he said, stalking out of the cabin and slamming the door behind him.

As Season walked the deck beside Briggs, she gazed off into the distance where tiny lights shimmered in the dark night.

"Briggs, can that be land ahead?" she inquired.

"Yes, my lady."

"What land is this? Where are we?"

Briggs cleared his throat. "It's not for me to say, my lady."

"It's Tripoli," said a deep raspy voice behind them.

Season whirled around to face the dark, cloaked figure. "Tripoli is the stronghold for the Barbary Pirates. Are you finally showing your true colors, Captain?"

Briggs seemed to fade into the shadows when the captain stepped up beside Season and stood watching the lights in the distance. "Yes. My colors are the red, white, and blue of the United States, my lady."

"I don't think so. I saw what you did to that English ship. I knew all along you were no more than a pirate. You are common and dishonest!"

His voice suggested that he was smiling. "I warn you, pretty words will never turn my head."

"You claim to be a revolutionary, and I could respect that; but a pirate who would trade on others for their livelihood has my deepest contempt. What did you do with the captain and crew of the English vessel?"

"As it happens, they are in good health and on their way to America. As to my being a pirate, I prefer to be called a privateer, or perhaps a buccaneer," he stated in an amused voice.

"Whatever you call yourself, you are nothing but the lowest form of life. I . . . detest men like you."

"Tell me what you think I am."

"You claim to have an honorable cause only to cover up what you really are."

His deep laughter only served to infuriate Season further. Then, before she could guess his intention, The Raven pulled her into his arms and held her fast.

"Oh, my lady, you do test me sorely."

"Release me this instant," she demanded, pushing against his arms.

"Have you missed me?" he whispered in her ear, refusing to release her.

Season raised her head and stared at his black mask, trying to see his eyes without success. "I would sooner have the lowest creature on earth near me than you. Take your hands off me," came her cold reply.

"Am I to take that as a no?" He laughed.

Season pressed her hand against his chest, and to her surprise, he immediately released her and turned to face the lights of Tripoli. The two of them were silent until Season spoke.

"I recall my father once telling me about the Barbary pirates. He said that Tripoli belonged to the old Ottoman Empire and that the Barbary pirates attacked trading ships, demanding tribute and ransom from all countries. He said they respect no flag. Can that be true?"

"Yes, all that and more. A more loathsome lot you will never meet, my lady."

Season turned to face The Raven. "Somehow I didn't think you would be associated with thieves and cutthroats. Surely you are aware of how ruthless these pirates can be. I have come to know your crew. They do not seem like—"

"Like thieves and cutthroats?" he interrupted.

She nodded. "It isn't too late, Captain. Mend your ways; take me to my father. I know he will reward you handsomely. I will say nothing about being abducted by you. I will merely tell him I asked you to return me to England."

The Raven laughed and touched her face. "I believe the lady is trying to reform me."

"No," she said in a small voice. "I merely want to go home."

He was silent for a moment, and Season could feel his eyes on her face. "Even if it were possible, I could never take you to England, my lady."

"Why? I don't understand. I am merely a woman and have never harmed you, why should you want to continue punishing me?"

His hand went to her face again and he brushed an unruly curl from her cheek. "No, my lady, you are not just a woman," he told her. Season was mesmerized by the tone of his deep voice. Suddenly she wished she could strip the disguise away from his face so she could see the man who held so much power over her. She could tell he was staring at her with such intensity that she felt her knees go weak. She quickly turned away to face the lights in the distance. She needed to think of something to say that would help restore her sanity—anything!

"Do you go ashore tomorrow?" was all she could manage to ask.

"Yes."

"I suppose I will remain aboard ship?"

"No, you will accompany me."

Season turned quickly to face him. "Suppose I should ask someone ashore to help me? What if some kindhearted stranger attempted to rescue me?"

His laughter was deep. "If I were you, I wouldn't look for help among the motley lot you will find in this den of pirates. Believe me, my lady, you are far better off with me."

"What more could happen to me that you have not already done?" she asked in a small voice.

There was a long silence, and then Season heard The Raven's breath coming out in a hiss. "You need not worry, I will not attempt to seduce you again. Briggs has interceded on your behalf and made me see the error of my ways."

Season stiffened, knowing she should feel elated at his admission. Why then did she feel like crying? "Are you saying that you will never try to force me to—"

"Season!" he cried out, using her name for the first time. "I have told you before that I would never have come near you had I known you were untouched. Must you always be reminding me of the deed? When I first took you it was with anger. Later I couldn't seem to stay away from you. It was you who made the first move toward me on the island," he reminded her.

She wanted to deny the truth of his statement, but she knew he was right. Knowing she was treading on dangerous ground, she wanted to blame him for what had happened between them. "No matter what you say or how you try to justify what you did, I will never forgive you."

"I think it is time you went to your cabin, my lady," he said harshly.

"That's right. When you are displeased with me you always send me to my cabin. Can you not stand to hear the truth about yourself?" she dared to say.

"Perhaps you are right."

"I know why you always make me stay in my cabin. You only wear your mask when I am on deck. One day I will see you when you are unmasked, and I will know you immediately. I warn you, I will not hesitate to point you out to General Clinton."

"So you think you would know me if I were unmasked, do you?"

"I . . . yes."

"My hair, what color is it?"

"You implied it was black the other night. All pirate captain's have black hair."

"You read too many books, my lady. What about Barbarossa ?"

"Who?"

"Barbarossa . . . Red Beard. He was a pirate who

lived in the fifteen hundreds."

"I would imagine your eyes are black to match your heart," she said, tossing her golden mane.

"What about a beard?" he asked, amused by her assessment.

"I . . . no. You are clean-shaven."

"Of course, how careless of me. Who would know better than you that I am beardless."

Season's face flamed and she lowered her eyes. "I believe you are right . . . I will go to my cabin."

As she fled down the companionway, Season heard footsteps behind her and knew The Raven was following her. As she neared the cabin, her heart was pounding in her ears. What if he didn't keep his word? Suppose he was displeased with her and wanted to take his anger out on her again?

Her hands were trembling as she entered the cabin. Without turning around, she knew he was standing behind her. She waited tensely for him to speak.

"Good night, my lady," he said, just before he closed the door. Season heard the key grate in the lock, and she knew he had locked her in once more.

She lay down on the bed, fully clothed, and closed her eyes. Why did she feel such an intense loneliness. Why did she regret that The Raven had kept his word and not touched her?

She thought of all the reasons she should hate him, but they amounted to nothing beside her deep feelings for him. How he would laugh at her if he knew she was beginning to love him. She had always believed a woman must respect a man before he could win her heart. That wasn't the case with The Raven. She didn't respect him, but oh, she was beginning to love him.

The Raven entered Briggs' cabin, removed his leather helm, and tossed it on the bed. Lady Season Chatsworth tested his patience to the limit. She fought him at every turn, but at a moment's notice could become soft and loving in his arms. Never had he been so confused where a woman was concerned. Never had he been so in danger of losing his heart.

Chapter Fourteen

When Briggs brought Season's breakfast tray to her, he didn't leave as he usually did, but sat on the chair, watching her silently. Season could sense that he had something on his mind, and she knew he would get around to telling her before long. She had grown very fond of this kindhearted man who always seemed so concerned with her comfort.

She bit into a fresh orange slice and watched the first mate out of the corner of her eye. Gracefully wiping her mouth on the edge of a napkin, she looked him in the face. Briggs was leaning forward, and he looked as if he were about to speak but was having trouble voicing his thoughts.

"You wanted to say something to me, Briggs?" she asked, a smile playing on her lips.

"I have a message for you, my lady."

"From the captain?"

"Yes, ma'am. He wanted me to tell you to dress in an understated manner."

Season suppressed a smile. "Briggs, do you mean he wants me to wear very little clothing?" she asked in mock horror. She couldn't resist teasing the first mate because he was being so serious.

The first mate's face flushed red. "No, no, my lady!" he sputtered. "I believe what the captain meant was that you were to dress in . . . He did mention your green gown."

Season smiled. She knew it was wicked to tease Briggs when he had always been so considerate to her. "I suppose he wants me to look like a pirate's lady. Did he mention whether he wanted me to wear a patch on one eye and strap a cutlass about my waist?"

Briggs laughed aloud. "No. I think he merely wanted you to dress so as not to draw too much attention to yourself—not that everyone wouldn't notice you any-way . . . you being so . . . pretty and all," he stammered.

"Why, Briggs, I believe you just gave me a compliment," she said, her eyes shining mischievously.

He stood up, avoiding her eyes. "If you're done with your tray, my lady, I'll just take it back to the galley."

Season watched the little man pick up the tray and leave the cabin. She then bounded out of bed. Dress in an understated way, indeed. She would show the captain that he couldn't dictate to her what she should wear. She would dress in a manner befitting her station so everyone would know she was a person of some importance. Maybe, just maybe, she would find someone who would be willing to help her escape The Raven!

She only had three gowns with her and two of them

had been worn many times. When they had become soiled Briggs had taken them away and brought them back freshly laundered. One gown she had never worn because it was a ball gown and much too grand to wear on board.

Going down on her knees, Season lifted the lid of the trunk in which her belongings had been placed. Rummaging amont petticoats and undergarments, she found the blue taffeta creation that should be worn only on special occasions.

She smiled to herself as she pulled the gown over her head, finding that of necessity she was becoming very adept at dressing herself. Taking up her hairbrush, she brushed her golden tresses until they crackled. With a spark of mischief in her green eyes, Season picked up the only piece of jewelry she had with her. She smiled to herself as she fastened the emerald and diamond necklace about her neck. Season had no mirror to see her reflection, so she hoped she looked her best. When she finished making her toilet, there was nothing for her to do but sit on the bed and wait for someone to come for her.

Her heart was pounding furiously. Was her rescue near at hand? Would she find someone to help her escape The Raven, someone who would be willing to take her back to England? She was aware that her worst problem would be evading The Raven's watchful eye. She didn't fully understand why he had agreed to take her ashore with him, but she knew she would have to act complacent so as not to arouse his suspicions. Her mind refused to dwell on what The Raven might do should he find out what she had in mind.

Season jumped guiltily when she hard the rap on the door. "If you are ready, my lady, the captain says it's time to disembark." Briggs called out to her.

Season quickly pushed her feet into her satin slippers and rushed to the door. She saw the look of disapproval on Briggs's face when he glanced at her attire. She raised her chin and sailed past him, ready to do battle with him or the captain should either of them make a comment on how she was dressed.

Season gathered up the skirt of her gown and made her way up the companionway. As she crossed the deck, she realized it might have been foolish to defy the captain's orders. Suppose he became angry with her and refused to allow her to accompany him ashore? She hadn't the slightest notion why he had decided to take her in the first place.

It was a hot sultry day, and the morning sun seemed to burn right through Season's skin. The deck of the *Andromeda* seemed to pitch drunkenly in spite of the fact that she was riding at anchor. Briggs took Season's hand to steady her and led her to the ship's railing.

Season drew in her breath as she glanced up at the mast and saw that the flag of the United States had been replaced by the skull and crossbones of the Jolly Roger! She knew that the Jolly Roger owed allegiance to no nation; it was the flag flown by all pirates!

Season felt fear prickle the back of her neck. The Raven had at last shown his true colors. He was indeed the pirate she had often accused him of being.

As Briggs helped Season down the rope ladder, she glanced at the longboat below and saw The Raven looking up at her. Even though his face was hooded, she could feel him staring at her through the slits in his helm and she sensed his displeassure. Wearing his black leather helm and his dark cape that flapped in the wind, The Raven appeared to be the devil himself.

"After the lady has debarked, the rest of you can climb down," he called up in his raspy voice.

Season's hands were shaking as Briggs helped her over the side of the rail. The ship was pitching so badly, she gripped the rope ladder tightly and envisioned herself falling into the sea.

"You will not fall, my lady. If you should, I will catch you," The Raven said.

At that moment Season became aware of her vulnerable position. The skirt of her gown was whipping in the wind and giving the captain a fair view of white petticoats. That thought alone spurred her into action. She hurriedly descended the ladder which swayed beneath her. In no time at all, she felt a strong grip about her waist, and The Raven placed her in the long-boat. He then ordered the others to descend.

By the time they were ready to row for shore, Season counted fifteen crew members in the longboat. She suspected that the remainder of the crew had stayed on board to guard the *Andromeda*.

She looked over at The Raven, but he had his back to her. So far he had made no mention of her gown, but she knew him well enough to guess he wouldn't just allow the matter to drop. Before the day was out, she was sure she would hear about his displeasure.

The heat was oppressive, and Season could feel tiny beads of perspiration running between her breasts. She dabbed at her face with a handkerchief and looked at the ocean longingly. How good it would feel to submerge herself in the cool water. If she was suffering from the heat, she reasoned, the captain must be feeling its effects even more than she since he was draped in black, but he stood at the head of the longboat with his muscular legs spread in an arrogant stance, looking as if he owned the world.

As the longboat neared the shore, Season had a better view of Tripoli. Most of the buildings were either white or soft pink and they were topped by spirals and steeples. As they pulled alongside the wharf, she counted ten other ships riding at anchor. Each flew the Jolly Roger.

The crew of the *Andromeda* was silent as they tied the longboat to the pier and disembarked. Briggs helped Season ashore, and she leaned heavily on him, thinking her legs wouldn't support her weight.

"'Twill take no time at all for you to get your land legs, my lady," he said cheerfully. "It will be no worse than when you came ashore at the island."

The Raven whirled around and faced his first mate. "Dammit, Briggs, while we are in Tripoli, don't ever refer to her as her ladyship! All of you listen to me and heed my words. Lady Season will be known only as Miss Chatsworth, is that understood?" Everyone nodded in agreement.

The Raven reached for Season's arm and pulled her to his side. With long strides he walked across the rotted planks of the pier; Season had to run to keep up with him. Once she stumbled and almost fell, but he braced her with a firm hand about her waist. Even then he didn't slow his stride. He seemed to have no

230

sympathy for Season's predicament, but merely stared straight ahead.

"You will be well advised, my lady, to stay close to my side. There isn't a man in Tripoli who wouldn't slit your pretty throat for those fancy baubles you wear about your neck."

Season shivered at his warning. She was beginning to regret her foolish actions. She saw many strange-looking men giving her a close inspection. Trying to ignore their bold glances, she gazed, wide-eyed, at her surroundings.

By now they had left the pier behind and were entering what she thought must be the heart of the city. The streets were narrow and dusty, and the people they passed looked like none Season had ever seen before. Many of the men wore long flowing robes and turbans. The women also wore robes, and many of them had their faces veiled. Season shivered from fear and tightly clutched The Raven's hand as several of the men seemed to look right through her with their dark, piercing eyes.

There were foul smells coming from the open doorways they passed. The unpleasant odors were reminiscent of rotten food and other things that Season didn't wish to put a name to. Tattered, half-naked children were playing in the streets among the filth and garbage.

Season placed her handkerchief over her nose. The smells were making her nauseous.

As they passed an open door, a lady appeared with a chamber pot in her hand, and Season was abruptly swung aside by The Raven, just as the woman emptied the contents of the pot right in front of them.

231

Season shivered in disgust, but The Raven only laughed heartily. She gave him a heated glance and raised her gown to step over the woman's slop.

As they rounded a corner, the scenery changed abruptly. There were no children on this street, but several brightly-dressed women with painted faces strolling about. One of the women stopped before The Raven to eye him openly and boldly.

"Well, Captain, I surely know who you are," she said, smiling coquettishly. "Everyone has heard that the *Andromeda* has just docked, and you are The Raven, ain't you love?" The woman sidled up to The Raven.

"That's correct, madam," The Raven answered in the irritated tone that Season had heard only too often.

The woman gave Season a quick look, and then her eyes turned back to The Raven. "I know of many who would like to see what you look like behind that mask—myself, I'd like to know all of you," she said, reaching out toward his mask.

The Raven caught the woman's hand in a viselike grip. "Would it be worth your eyesight to gaze upon my face, madam?" he asked in a hard voice. "That's what it would cost you to look upon my face."

Season watched as the woman visibly trembled, and her eyes widened with fear. "I meant no harm, sir. I wanted only to speak to you," the woman said, backing away.

The Raven shoved her none too gently out of his path, and Season watched the frightened creature gather up her skirt and dash into one of the open doorways.

Season had watched the whole exchange with surprise. Never in her life had she seen a woman wearing paint on her cheeks. By the woman's accent Season knew her to be from England's lower classes, and she wondered what the woman was doing in Tripoli.

"How can that woman be so brazen? What is she doing so far from home?" Season asked.

"You might better have asked what you are doing so far from home," The Raven said, taking her arm and leading her forward.

Season had no time to react because the captain pulled her into a huge tavernlike room. So many bodies were pressed into such a limited space that she thought she surely would be crushed. Many men were sitting at tables, drinking rum and laughing with women much like the ones Season had seen outside. The smell of unwashed bodies was almost overpowering, and Season gasped for a breath of fresh air.

Season quickly lowered her head when she noticed a man at one of the tables fondling the bare breasts of a redheaded woman who was giggling with delight.

"Why have you brought me to such a place!" she cried loudly, in order to be heard above the din. "This place is disgusting and degrading!"

She got no answer. Instead the captain led her to a table in the corner where three men were seated. Season watched as The Raven propped his booted foot up on an empty chair. He then tossed a leather pouch on the table, where it landed with a loud clink.

"De Fores, you are just the man I wanted to see," The Raven said in his raspy voice.

As Season watched, two of the men scrambled to their feet, knocking over chairs to get out of the way.

The third man at the table remained seated and smiled lazily up at The Raven. "Sit down, Raven," he invited, nodding to a chair. "I suspected you would show up sooner or later," he said in heavily accented French.

The Raven was toying with the hilt of his sword. "Where is the captain of the *Sea Serpent*, De Fores?"

"He is in a safe place," the Frenchman replied, allowing his gaze to wander to Season for the first time. His eyes widened in surprise and then quickly darkened with admiration.

At the man's bold scrutiny, Season wanted to lower her head, but she forced herself to look him in the eye. He was handsome in a rakish way. His dark hair was shoulder length and was tied back in a queue, and he sported a neatly trimmed beard and mustache. He was dressed in a flamboyant manner, in a green velvet jacket and a gold brocade waistcoat. His plumed hat was of green leather, and when he stood up, Season saw that he wore green leather breeches and boots.

The Frenchman removed his hat and bowed gracefully before Season. "Such a rare jewel. Such loveliness. Can it be that The Raven has finally given his heart to a woman?" he asked in a soft voice, all the while looking Season over from head to toe.

Season clasped The Raven's hand tightly and felt his fingers close reassuringly around hers. "We are not here to discuss my heart, De Fores. I have just given you the money to ransom Captain Robert Wolf."

The Frenchman roared with laughter and sat down.

again. "What makes you think Captain Wolf is to be ransomed? I have grown very fond of him over the past few days. I may decide to keep him."

"You might do well to take the money before I lose interest in the man, De Fores. I might decide to lower the price . . . or not pay it at all," The Raven said in a soft voice that had all the power of a whiplash.

Again De Fores laughed. "It is well known that The Raven and Captain Wolf are good friends, although I never could see why a man with your talents should be interested in a man from the English colonies."

Season became aware that several men were beginning to close in around her and The Raven. She recognized two of the men as the ones who had been sitting at the table with the Frenchman when they had first come in. Looking at The Raven, Season thought he couldn't be aware that they were being hemmed in by De Fores' men.

De Fores smiled and stroked his beard. "I would be less than honest with you, Raven, if I didn't point out the fact that I could get more gold for your head than I can for that of your friend, Robert Wolf. It is said that the British will pay a great price for you . . . dead or alive."

The Raven threw back his head and laughed deeply. "You aren't the first fool who has thought in that vein. The others have long since departed this life."

Season looked about her nervously. Did not The Raven know that he was surrounded by De Fores' men? He appeared to be so arrogantly unafraid that he was either unaware of the impending threat or the bravest man she had ever seen.

De Fores removed his hat and ran the feather through his fingers. "Ah, Raven, the others were not as clever as De Fores, no? At this moment you are surrounded by my men. A nod from me is all it would take to have your throat cut."

The Raven touched the hilt of his sword. "You have foolishly underestimated me, De Fores. Do you really think I would come into your den without benefit of friends? If you will look about you, you will see that you are surrounded, not I."

Season glanced up quickly and saw many familiar faces standing just behind De Fores' men. More than thirty men from the *Andromeda*, swords poised, stood ready to strike. They had come ashore after she and The Raven had left the ship.

The Frenchman hardly had time to react as The Raven smoothly removed his sword and sliced through the air, cutting the feather from De Fores' hat. "As I was asking before . . . where is Captain Robert Wolf?"

De Fores glanced from his men, who had already been disarmed, to the rapier that was being held at his own throat by The Raven. "Surely you recognize a jest when you hear one. I would never turn you over to the British. Do we not belong to the same brotherhood?"

With the point of his rapier, The Raven toyed with the brass buttons on De Fores' waistcoat. "I share no brotherhood with the likes of you, De Fores. I am losing my patience, and you wouldn't like to see that happen. I will ask you only once more . . . where is Captain Wolf?"

De Fores pushed the point of the sword away from his throat and lazily propped his boots on top of the table. "Sit down, Raven. We will drink rum and discuss Captain Wolf," he said as if nothing had happened. Season had to admit that the Frenchman had nerves of iron.

The Raven took Season's arm and seated her at the table; then he sat down himself. Picking up the bag of gold coins, he tossed it at De Fores once more. "I will not play your little game. Take the money and hand my friend over to me at once or I will spill your blood here and now!"

De Fores poured a glass of rum and glanced at Season, winking at her boldly before turning back to The Raven. "He is not with me here. I would be a fool to parade him about the streets of Tripoli, would I not?"

"Where is he?"

"On board my ship, of course. Where else would he be?"

"Send someone for him . . . *NOW.*"

"I will send some of my men to get him, but that will take time. Surely you and the lady will share a drink with me while we wait."

"The lady does not wish to drink with you; however, I will have a mug of rum," The Raven said, reaching for the bottle and pouring a liberal amount into a cup.

"If you will excuse me for a moment, Raven, I will tell my men to bring Wolf here," De Fores said, rising slowly to his feet.

"Sit down, De Fores," The Raven warned. "My men will keep an eye on your crew, while I keep an eye on you. Choose one man of your choice and send him for Captain Wolf. You might tell the man if he tries any tricks, you will be the first to die."

De Fores raised his hands in a hopeless gesture. "Surely you can trust me."

"I do not trust you any more than you trust me. I tire of your little game," The Raven said, rising. Pointing his finger at one of De Fores' men, he motioned for him to come to the table. "Your captain has an errand he wishes you to run," he stated in a quiet voice.

The man stared at The Raven, a sour look on his face, but he said nothing.

Season watched as De Fores instructed his man to bring Captain Wolf to him at once. Obviously De Fores was unafraid of The Raven. A plan began to form in her mind. If she should be presented with the chance to speak to the Frenchman alone, she would tell him she was the Duke of Chatsworth's daughter and implore him to help her. Excitement began to rise in her. De Fores could well be the tool she could use to escape The Raven!

She felt the Frenchman's eyes upon her. She looked up at him and found he was assessing her closely. She smiled at him, thinking to enhance his interest.

"Mademoiselle, I have rarely, if ever, seen a woman with the kind of beauty you possess. De Fores is your most humble servant," he said caressingly.

"Thank you. You are most kind, Captain De Fores," Season said, smiling prettily.

The hooded head of The Raven turned to face her, and even though Season couldn't see his eyes, she could feel anger radiate from him.

"This lady is with me, De Fores. You would be well advised to make your pretty speeches elsewhere," he

238

grated out in a tone of command.

"Surely you do not object if I admire the beauty of your lady. She is so like the pearl among the swine, is she not?" I would trade Robert Wolf for this woman and not quibble over the price."

Season could almost feel The Raven's eyes darken and narrow in on De Fores. "As I said before, the lady is with me, and she stays with me. Where is Captain Wolf's ship and crew?" The Raven demanded, abruptly changing the subject. "I am prepared to ransom the men and ship as well."

De Fores folded his hands together and shrugged his shoulders. "It is most unfortunate that neither the ship nor any of its crew survived. Alas they went to the bottom of the sea," he said regretfully.

"You black-hearted bastard!" The Raven hissed. "I could run you through for this. I know it is your habit to leave no one alive who can bear witness against you. One day you will feel the point of my blade enter your heart and rip it from your body!" The warning hung in the air, and De Fores looked uncomfortable for the first time.

"It is not a bad policy to leave no witnesses, Raven. Had you practiced more caution you would not now have a price on your head. In my view it is a foolish man who does not guard his back."

"A man must always watch his back when you are about, De Fores. More often than not, you will strike a man when he is not looking."

De Fores laughed. "You wound me, Raven. I am but a simple man, trying to make a living in the only way I know how. Surely you cannot condemn me for that?"

Suddenly Season's eyes were drawn to the front of the tavern where several men were being shoved aside by the biggest Nubian she had ever seen. She was amazed to see the man make his way toward their table. When he drew near, he stepped aside and a woman moved forward to stand behind The Raven. Season thought the woman was beautiful in spite of the way she was dressed. She wore black leather breeches and knee boots like a man! Over her white shirt she wore a black vest, and about her waist she wore a rapier and a brace of pistols.

"Raven it's true, you are here!" the woman cried out. "I thought my eyes were deceiving me when I saw the *Andromeda* riding at anchor!"

The Raven stood up and turned to face the newcomer. The woman threw herself into his outstretched arms. Season couldn't hear what they were saying to each other because they had lowered their voices, but it was certain they were glad to see one another. Season felt jealousy burn her heart at seeing the familiar way The Raven hugged the woman. Glancing at De Fores, she saw amusement playing in his eyes. She raised her chin and assumed a look of total indifference.

Now was her chance to talk to De Fores, she thought. Reaching across the table, she motioned for the Frenchman to lean closer to her, and he readily complied.

"You must help me," she whispered frantically. "My name is Lady Season Chatsworth, and I have been kidnapped by The Raven. My father is the Duke of Chatsworth, and if you will help me get back to England, he will reward you handsomely."

She couldn't tell what the Frenchman was thinking as his eyes rested on the neck of her low-cut gown. If only he would believe her she thought frantically.

"Please you must believe—"

"Shh," he whispered, as his eyes darted to The Raven. "Do not worry, mademoiselle, De Fores always stands ready to help a lady in distress."

Season looked back at The Raven and found that he was watching her. Her heart was beating so fast she could hardly breathe, and she knew her cheeks were flushed. Do I look guilty? she wondered. She prayed silently that he wouldn't guess that she had been trying to enlist De Fores' help.

The Raven motioned for his crew to escort De Fores' men back to their ship. As soon as they had departed, he returned to the table, leading the lady dressed in black. When he pulled the lady onto his lap, Season felt as if someone had just delivered a mortal blow to the pit of her stomach. No, that was foolishness; she couldn't be feeling jealous over a man who had kidnapped her and held her against her will! That was impossible.

"Who is this person?" The woman asked, nodding at Season. Her voice was unmistakably American.

"No one you need concern yourself with, Maude. She is merely a business venture of mine."

Stung by his insult, Season tossed her golden mane in defiance. She was further insulted when the woman called Maude stood up and walked around the table, assessing Season closely.

When Maude drew even with Season, she flicked the sleeve of her gown. "Such fancy packaging. I've never known you to take a woman on board the *Andromeda* before now." Season watched as jealousy leaped into the woman's eyes. "Where do you come from?" Maude asked her directly.

"It is none of your affair. I have nothing to say to you," Season said haughtily.

Before Season had time to think, Maude had unsheathed her sword and held the point against her breast. "You have a sharp tongue . . . shall I carve it out for you?" Maude asked in a menacing voice.

Never had Season felt so near death. She knew one wrong move from her, and she would breathe her last. Pride was the only weapon she had to use against the woman, so she raised her head and her icy green eyes locked with Maude's blue ones.

"Take yourself away from me. I am not afraid of you." Season pushed the blade away from her breasts, surprised at how calm her voice sounded.

Tense moments passed as the two women glared into each other's eyes. Then Season rose slowly to her feet and placed her hands on her hips. "Do you think I am afraid of a woman in men's breeches?" she asked in a clear voice.

Maude sliced her blade through the air and rested the point just above Season's heart. Season would never know what might have happened had The Raven not stepped between them. He casually reached up and pushed Maude's blade away from Season's chest.

"I'm afraid I cannot allow you to damage so valuable a cargo, Maude," he said in his raspy voice that Season knew was laced with humor.

"She tests me," Maude said in an angry voice.

"She tests me as well, Maude, but she is of no consequence. Come, have a cup of rum with me," The Raven drawled.

Season could feel the sting of his words in the very depth of her heart. He was treating her as if nothing had ever passed between the two of them. She could feel her anger mounting. How dare he flaunt his mistress in her face. How dare he treat her as if she were a nobody!

Season looked across the table at De Fores, and he gave her a guarded smile. It was as if he were telling her to bide her time. She was almost sure he was going to help her. She would find her satisfaction for today's insults by freeing herself from The Raven.

Maude sheathed her sword and straddled a chair. "I suppose you are right, Raven; this woman is of no consequence."

All at once the table was surrounded by several other sea captains, and they all seemed genuinely glad to see The Raven. Season had never seen so many people from so many different walks of life. There were sea captains with turbans wrapped about their heads. Some spoke Italian while others spoke Spanish and Portuguese. It gave Season pause to wonder how this pesthole could exist. Where were the authorities? Was there no one to bring law and order to this part of the world?

Season was receiving her share of curious glances, but no one dared to approach her. Suddenly she became weary. There were so many people pressed into such a small space, and the noise was deafening. She took a deep breath, wishing she could leave this filthy place.

At that moment, Season heard Briggs's voice, and she watched the little man approach the table. "We put Captain Wolf on board the *Andromeda,* sir." He was addressing The Raven.

"How is Robert's health?" The Raven asked, watching De Fores' face closely.

Briggs shot the Frenchman a disgusted glance. "He's been ill-treated, sir. He's got wounds that haven't been seen to, and it looks like he ain't had a decent meal in days. He's got dysentery."

The Raven stood up slowly. "We will meet again, De Fores. Next time you may not be so fortunate as to escape with your life."

De Fores smiled and looked at Season. "Yes, it is preordained that we shall meet again . . . never fear." It was almost as if he were telling Season he would see her again. She quickly glanced at The Raven, but he didn't seem to catch the hidden meaning behind De Fores' words.

Season was overcome with relief when The Raven took her arm and led her out of the tavern. Once outside, she took a deep breath of fresh air and let it out slowly. As they crossed the dusty streets, Season noticed that Maude and her Nubian were following them. Briggs and several of the *Andromeda*'s crew members were just a few paces behind Maude.

When they rounded a corner, Maude came up beside them and slipped her arm through The Raven's. "Where do you go from here, Raven? I hope you will be here longer than you were last time," the woman said, giving Season a poisonous glance.

"I cannot tell you where we are going, Maude. My

crew is now taking on stores and supplies. I fear we must sail in two days' time."

"So soon?" she asked regretfully. "I was hoping you would stay a few days with me." Season noticed that she smiled boldly up at the captain.

He laughed deeply. "Time and tide are always against us, Maude."

"I am surprised you allowed De Fores to live, Raven. You would have done the world a favor if you had cut his black heart out," the woman said, changing the subject.

"I am not finished with De Fores yet, Maude. He knows it, and I know it."

"I don't trust him, Raven. He's a devil. You made him look bad today; he will not forget it."

Season was not listening. She was lost in her own thoughts. Her heart seemed to burn with a need to escape The Raven. Today she had been humiliated and made to look the fool. Even now, The Raven paraded his mistress before her. What better way to strike out at him than to escape with the help of his most-hated enemy. She hoped that De Fores would come to her rescue. Surely he had believed her story.

Suddenly The Raven's words penetrated Season's thoughts. "Maude, I wonder if you would mind keeping an eye on my . . . prisoner for me."

Season would have voiced her objections, but Maude spoke up first. "You can't ask me to keep this fancy piece. I'd sooner cut her throat."

"She isn't so bad once you get to know her." The Raven laughed. "Do this for me, Maude. I have never asked a favor of you, but I'm asking now."

"Aye, 'tis true. You never have asked anything of me, but you have helped me often. How can I deny you this one thing? I will do it."

"I will not go with her," Season spoke up. "I don't like this woman."

The Raven took Season's arm. "You will do as you are told, because you have no choice." He glanced up at the other woman. "Keep a wary eye on her, Maude. I don't like all the attention she attracted at the tavern. Don't trust her for a moment; she is very clever."

The Raven moved over to Maude and they talked in hushed tones so Season couldn't hear what was being said, but out of the corner of her eye, she saw a shadow moving across the street, and she realized it was De Fores. The Raven was unaware that the Frenchman was following them. Perhaps it would be best to go with Maude, Season thought. If De Fores were going to help her escape, would it not be better for her to be with Maude than aboard the *Andromeda?*

Season hid her rising excitement. Soon she would be free of The Raven. Before long she would be on her way back to England!

Chapter Fifteen

Season looked out the bedroom window at the street below. The windows had bars on them, and they were much too high. She wouldn't be able to escape through them. The door was made of heavy oak, and it, too, seemed to be impregnable. She had been locked in by the huge Nubian hours ago. The Raven had escorted them to Maude's house and had left them at the door without a word to her.

Season had been given neither food nor water, and she now found that she was both hungry and thirsty.

She walked about the bedroom, noticing how feminine everything was. The bed covering was pink lace, and the rug on the floor had a red and yellow floral pattern. Maude might dress like a man, but evidently she enjoyed having womanly frills in her bedroom.

Season paced back and forth as the clock on the dressing table ticked off the minutes. She began to wonder if The Raven had ever been in this room. Yes, most probably he had. She could tell by the way Maude had reacted to him, that they had been lovers; perhaps they still were. Season didn't stop to wonder why thinking of The Raven making love to Maude was so painful to her. She had been deeply hurt by The Raven's treatment of her that day, and she wanted to strike out at him and hurt him.

When is this horror ever going to end? she wondered. She loathed and detested the arrogant, hooded man everyone called The Raven. What mystery did he hide behind his black mask? What power did he have over her that he could make her love him?

She walked over to the window once more and glanced out, hoping to catch a glimpse of De Fores. Had she been mistaken to think the Frenchman would come to her rescue? No, she had seen the glint in his eyes when she had told him her father would pay him well for her return. Besides, she sensed a deeper reason why he would help her. De Fores hated The Raven; he would be only too glad to take something away from the captain of the *Andromeda*.

Season heard footsteps outside the bedroom door and then a key grating in the lock. She wondered if she was going to spend the rest of her life behind locked doors.

Maude entered the room, carrying a tray of food. She gave Season a poisonous glance as she set the tray on the dressing table and motioned for Season to eat.

Season was hungry, but she walked reluctantly over to the tray. Eying the food, she discovered it didn't look too bad. She noted a generous slice of meat, buttered bread, and slices of an unknown fruit.

"Does this meet your majesty's approval?" Maude asked, a sneer on her lips and a gleam in her pale blue eyes. "I surely wouldn't want to offend your majesty with my humble offerings."

"It looks good," Season replied, refusing to be baited by this woman.

"What's your name?" Maude demanded, propping her booted foot on a chair and looking Season over.

"I am known as Lady Season Chatsworth in England. My friends call me Season . . . you may call me Lady Season," she stated, biting into the meat and finding it was delicious.

"La-di-da, Lady Season Chatsworth," Maude said sarcastically. "Ain't you the grand one though," the woman taunted, with a vicious curl of her lip.

"What kind of fruit is this?" Season asked, refusing to be baited once more.

"It's a banana," Maude answered sourly.

"I find it to be quite tasty."

"What are you doing with The Raven?" Maude asked, sitting down in the chair.

Season took another bite of the banana and swallowed it before answering. "I am not with him by choice. I was kidnapped by the man you think so highly of."

"I'm certain he didn't abduct you because he was partial to your sweet nature," Maude observed.

Season looked into Maude's eyes. "I wonder how you would behave in like circumstances. How would you feel about a man you didn't even know who stole you away in the dead of night and held you captive?"

"I don't know," Maude answered speculatively. "My

own father sold me to a man who was three times my age when I was but fourteen. He said if I was nice to the man I would become his wife and be provided with a decent home. Less than a year later, I found myself on the slave block in Madagascar. I was bought by a Moor, and was forced to live with him as his woman. He was a pirate and as mean as they come. I could tell you things that would curdle that blue blood of yours. I would still be his woman had not The Raven attacked Ajon's ship one day and freed me."

Season was horrified by Maude's confession. "Why did The Raven rescue you?" she asked.

"Oh, he didn't attack Ajon to save me. He didn't even know of my existence at that time. Ajon had foolishly shanghaied several of The Raven's men, and he was merely taking them back. Ajon lived to rue the day he tangled with The Raven."

"What did you do once you were free? Surely you could have returned to America."

Maude's eyes seemed to turn sad. "What was I to do, return to my loving father? I had sunk as low as a human being could go, and many times I wanted to die; yet I lived. I had nowhere to go and no friends or money."

"So you came here to live." Season couldn't disguise the horror in her voice. She now felt pity for this woman who had been so badly treated. She couldn't help but see the similarities between her life and Maude's.

"No. I didn't come to Tripoli right away," Maude continued. "I begged The Raven to give me Ajon's ship, the *Albatross,* and he agreed. That is how I became what I am today. No man puts his hands on me unless I say so. I have gained a certain amount of respect, and I do live well."

"You are a . . . pirate?"

"Yes, and a damned good one, too."

Season shook her head in disbelief. She began to admire this woman for standing up for herself. "I could never be as brave as you are. I admire your courage."

Maude frowned. She did not know whether this grand lady was making fun of her or whether she was being sincere. The light in the other woman's eyes led her to believe she was speaking the truth. "It's a hard life. The hardest part is dealing with men and trying to convince them I am their equal. I have managed to succeed quite well."

"Are you never frightened? Do you never wish for another kind of life?"

"I am often frightened, but I can't allow it to show," Maude confessed. "As for wanting another life—the sea is in my blood. I suppose I will sail the world until I die. I wouldn't trade places with any female I know."

On a sudden impulse Season reached over and placed her hand on Maude's. "My life has been not unlike yours. I was offered in marriage to a man who was older than my father. When I objected, my father sent me to America to wed a man I had never met. Before the wedding could take place, I was abducted by The Raven. It seems both you and I have had very little control over our lives."

Maude blinked her eyes. Against her will, she was beginning to like this young woman. There was no doubt in her mind that Season spoke the truth.

"Aye, it would seem we were both ill-used by men."

Both women lapsed into silence, then Season spoke. "Are you in love with The Raven?"

Maude's pale blue eyes seemed to soften. "There are many women who love the elusive Raven, but no woman has ever clipped his wings. I have known many men, but not a one who can compare with him. He is very compassionate, loyal, and fearless. Yes, I love him, but to love him and try to hold onto him is like trying to catch the wind . . . or tame the wild raven. His mistress is the sea."

Season sighed heavily and stood up. "I fear I do not see him as you do. Perhaps you have seen a side of him that has not been revealed to me. I picture him as an abductor of innocent women, a looter, and a pirate."

Maude walked over to the bed and lay down, propping her head up on a pink satin pillow. "If The Raven abducted you, he must have had a good reason. Do you know what it is?"

"I have been told that he was holding me hostage until a man named Silas Dunsberry could be exchanged for my release. It is said the man was executed; still I remain The Raven's prisoner."

Maude made a whistling noise through her teeth. "You're in a hell of a fix, ain't you?"

"Maude, could you help me escape," Season asked hopefully. "If you would take me to England, my father would pay you well, I promise."

"No, I would never go against The Raven. He knows he can trust me. Even if I agreed to take you to your father, The Raven would catch up with us and there would be all hell to pay."

Though Season had known what Maude's answer would be before she asked the question, she was desperate and could leave no avenue of escape untried. Sitting down on the edge of the bed, she looked into Maude's blue eyes.

"Have you ever seen The Raven unmasked? Do you know what he looks like?"

Maude laughed aloud. "I have been with him when he was unmasked, but I didn't actually see his face, if that's what you are asking."

Season knew only too well what Maude was implying. She was saying The Raven had made love to her in a darkened room. Season flushed and lowered her eyes.

"Why do you think he wears a mask?" she asked hurriedly.

"Everyone has a theory about that. Some people say he is horribly deformed, but I know that to be false. Others say he is an English nobleman. Me, I have my suspicions as to why he keeps his identity a secret, but I ain't telling no one what I think."

"I know he doesn't wear his disguise aboard the *Andromeda.* I believe his crew know who he is."

"That may well be, but not a one among his crew would ever betray him. He has a way of inspiring loyalty in men as well as women."

"I suppose," Season sighed.

Maude reached over, took Season's chin, and tilted her face up so the dying rays of the sun hit her. "I wonder why The Raven hasn't sent you back. Why does he continue to hold you hostage?"

"Season shook her head. "I wish I knew the answer to that myself. I would give anything to be free of that man. It seems a lifetime since I was first abducted."

Maude moved off the bed. "You are very lovely; could it be that he has at last found a woman who has a claim on his heart?"

"No. I hate him and he always tries to humiliate me. I suspect he will be almost as glad to see the last of me as I will be when I am free of him."

"I wonder?" Maude speculated; then she smiled. "The Raven will be here tonight and I want to look my best." Maude walked over to a trunk and removed a bright red satin gown and held it out for inspection. "I have been keeping this for just such an occasion."

Season turned away and stared out the window as Maude began dressing. Why did she feel such an empty ache deep inside? she wondered. She would have to be crazed to feel jealous of The Raven.

"Fasten me up the back, will you?" Maude asked. Season performed the task and then watched as the woman brushed her wheat-colored hair. When she had finished, Season noted that the woman was not unattractive.

"I may not be as beautiful as you, lady what-ever-your-name-is, but I'll wager I'm more woman than you will ever be. I have pleased The Raven in the past; I shall please him again tonight. Your beauty will not help you, for you will sleep alone while I enjoy the company of The Raven. Something tells me that thought bothers you."

Season watched, speechless, as Maude moved to the door and swept out of the room, turning the key in the lock once she was outside. Wild, jealous feelings coursed through Season's veins.

"I hate The Raven!" she shouted, picking up a pink pillow and throwing it against the door. Then, hearing Maude's muffled laughter, she sank down on the bed.

The time passed slowly as day gave way to night, and Season again began to pace the room. She wondered if The Raven and Maude were locked in a passionate embrace. Would he kiss Maude as he had her? Season threw herself on the bed and pounded the pillow with her fist. "Just you wait," she cried. "I will make you pay, Raven."

The day's events had tired Season, and when she noticed the clock marked the midnight hour, she felt sure if De Fores intended to rescue her, he would already have come. No. Perhaps he would wait until The Raven left. She closed her eyes, no longer fighting sleep. Why should she care what The Raven and Maude were doing? Neither of them meant anything to her. She hoped De Fores knew that The Raven would be sailing in two days. If he were going to rescue her, it would have to be soon.

She yawned and closed her eyelids, drifting off to sleep.

The Raven stood at the railing of the *Andromeda,* staring at the lights of Tripoli. Perhaps it had been a mistake to leave Season with Maude. He had grown accustomed to having her aboard his ship and it seemed lonesome without her.

"It don't seem the same without the little lady, does it, Captain?" Briggs said, as if he had been reading The Raven's mind.

"No, it doesn't, Briggs. I was just wondering if I made a mistake in leaving her with Maude."

"You always visit Maude when we are in Tripoli—will you be going to her house tonight, sir?"

The Raven watched the distant lights play on the water. "No. I don't seem to want to, Briggs."

"The little lady really got under your skin, didn't she, Captain? I've never known you to turn down an invitation from Maude."

"Well, you are seeing it now, Briggs," The Raven said sourly. "Don't you have someone else's business to tend to besides mine?"

"I was just thinking, Captain. De Fores seemed to show a lot of interest in Lady Season today. Suppose he finds out she is staying with Maude?"

The Raven's hands gripped the rail. "My God, I didn't even think about that, Briggs. Maude would be no match for De Fores and his crew. Take a handful of men and go make sure everything is all right. As a matter of fact, I would feel better if you brought Season back to the *Andromeda*. I would go myself, but I dare not leave Robert since he is so ill."

The first mate nodded his head and rushed off to gather some men together. The Raven continued to stare toward Tripoli. He was just being foolish; Season probably wasn't in any danger from De Fores. The man wouldn't dare lay a hand on her. Still, a nagging fear seemed to eat at the pit of his stomach. Season had become as necessary to him as the air he breathed. He couldn't bear the thought of De Fores—or any other man—touching her either, for that matter.

He watched as Briggs and four other crew members

256

went over the side of the ship and dropped into the longboat. He knew he would breathe a lot easier when Briggs returned with Season.

Season awoke when she felt a hand clamped over her mouth. She could see the shape of the man who bent over her, and she knew he was De Fores!

"Do not make a sound, my lady. It is me, De Fores, and I have come to rescue you."

Season nodded her head in understanding, and he removed his hand from her mouth. Her heart was pounding with excitement as he took her hand and led her across the room. She could hardly believe she was about to be free! Season couldn't help but think how angry The Raven would be when he found his captive had been spirited away in the dead of night.

"Dress quickly; we do not have much time," De Fores ordered. "I want to catch the morning tide."

Season hastily slipped her gown over her head, so anxious to be gone that her hands trembled excitedly. When she had completed dressing, she followed De Fores out of the room and then cautiously descended the stairs. When they reached the front door, Season tripped over something and lost her footing, falling to the floor. She almost screamed out when she saw that it was Maude's Nubian slave, a knife sticking out of his back.

As De Fores jerked her to her feet, Season stifled a sob. She hadn't meant him to kill anyone while trying to rescue her. She was horrified that a man was dead because of her.

"Come along, my lady. It will not be long before the dead bodies are discovered and I want to be far from here when that happens."

Season jerked her hand free. "You cannot mean that you have killed others!"

"What did you expect? Did you think I could just walk in and say excuse me but would you hand Lady Season Chatsworth over to me?" He took her arm and led her forward. Season was confused. She hesitated. Hadn't she asked this man to help her? Why did she feel so heavy-hearted now?

De Fores led her out into the street where several men awaited them. It was a bright moonlit night, and the streets of Tripoli were deserted as they made their way down to the sea. Keeping well into the shadows, they finally reached the pier. Season was afraid that any moment they would be discovered and she would be recaptured by The Raven, the man she detested.

When De Fores lifted her into the longboat, Season became more confident. De Fores' men began to row out to sea, and she relaxed. Before too many minutes passed, Season saw De Fores' ship looming up out of the darkness. She couldn't help but look to the far right where the *Andromeda* rode at anchor. She could easily make out the figurehead, the raven in flight. How good it felt to be free of her dark master's dominance.

De Fores helped Season aboard the ship, and she was shown below by a silent and brooding crew member who seemed to view her with angry eyes.

"Will you send your captain to me as soon as possible?" she asked, turning to the man. "I want to discuss some important matters with him."

"The captain ain't got no time for you now. He's got to get the ship under way. You'll have to wait until it's convenient for him to come to you," the man answered suggestively.

"I do not think my request is unreasonable. Tell him I want to see him at once!" she demanded.

"I ain't working for you. It's because of you that we will soon have The Raven down on us. If the captain had listened to me, he would never have got mixed up with The Raven's lady. That man ain't nobody to fool around with. I fear we'll all live to rue this night."

Season wanted to protest, but the man turned away and stalked out of the cabin. She soon heard the old familiar sound of a key grating in the lock. She might be locked in a ship's cabin again, but she was free, she told herself. No longer would she be the prisoner of the dark lord of the sea. Her only wish was that she could see The Raven's face when he finally discovered she was missing.

The Raven stood beside the bed where his friend, Robert Wolf, lay. He noticed that Robert's face showed the agony he was suffering. Wolf had a festered wound on his leg, and his wrists were rubbed raw from being chained. Touching Robert's forehead, Raven discovered he was running a high fever and appeared to be unconscious.

Maxwell, the ship's doctor, had treated Wolf's wounds, and then had shaken his head as he'd looked at his captain. "He's been terribly mistreated, Captain. He needs liquids and rest. I'll have to keep a close eye on his wounds to make sure gangrene doesn't set in."

"Do what you can for him, Maxwell," The Raven

said grimly. "I must go topside and watch for Briggs. He should have returned by now."

It was almost dawn, and The Raven hadn't slept in the last two nights. He leaned against the railing as he watched a ship weigh anchor and put out to sea. She was the *Blue Dolphin,* De Fores' ship. The morning breeze caught at her canvas as she moved silently out to sea.

James joined his captain and they both watched the *Blue Dolphin* leave port. "He'll be off to practice his mischief on some poor, unsuspecting ship, Captain," the cabin boy observed.

"Yes, and it's just as well. If he stayed around, I would probably run him through for the way he treated Robert," The Raven answered, feeling almost relieved that De Fores was leaving. That must mean that De Fores hadn't gone to Maude's house, as he had feared.

"The doctor says Captain Wolf has a good chance of making it, sir." James watched his captain's face. "When do we sail, sir?"

"I have received a message from John Paul Jones; he is in France and has asked me to join him there. I have decided to leave at once. We will sail immediately upon Briggs's return. Have the men make the ship ready."

"France ain't too far from England. Will you set the lady free when we reach there?"

"Just do as you are told," The Raven snapped, turning his back and watching the sun rise on the fading sails of the *Blue Dolphin.*

The Raven was sitting beside Robert Wolf's bedside

when Briggs came bursting into the cabin. "Captain, sir, Lady Season has disappeared. I didn't see hide nor hair of her at Maude's house!"

The Raven stood up slowly. "What are you saying, Briggs?"

"I found Maude unconscious, and that Nubian of hers was dead, stabbed. There was no sign of Lady Season and when Maude regained consciousness, she didn't know what had happened to her either."

The Raven ran his hand through his hair. "Did you search the house thoroughly?"

"Yes, sir," Briggs replied in a distressed voice. "There was no sign of a struggle; she's just gone. I found her necklace lying on the floor."

The Raven took the necklace and watched the diamonds and emeralds shimmer in the light. "My God! De Fores has Season!" he cried, as he ran from the cabin.

"All hands on deck!" he yelled. "De Fores has taken Lady Season! We get under way immediately." He took the helm and his hands gripped the wheel tightly. His eyes stared at the distant horizon where the *Blue Dolphin* had disappeared. "I'll see you dead for this, De Fores," he said aloud. "If you harm one hair on her head, your death will be horrible to behold!"

Season walked about the cabin impatiently. She vowed that when she was safely back with her father, she would never again be behind a locked door. This certainly wasn't what she had had in mind when she'd asked De Fores for his help. She noticed the cabin was

261

in disarray and wrinkled her nose. It wasn't very clean. The covers on the bed were filthy and rumpled. Indeed, these quarters smelled of perspiration and unwashed bodies. Never mind, she told herself. Soon I will be back in England and this will be a nightmare I have left behind. In no time at all The Raven will be nothing more than a bitter memory.

The door opened suddenly and De Fores entered the cabin. He smiled at Season and unbuckled his sword, letting it clatter to the floor.

"We have made it, my lady. I always knew the captain of the *Andromeda* was no match for me. Once again I have plucked The Raven's tail feathers, no?"

"Is there no fear he will pursue us?"

"Oh, he will try, but there is no way he can catch us now. By the time he realizes I have stolen his lady, he will not be able to find us. There is no one to tell him that you are with me; after all, Maude and her servant are both dead."

Season felt her stomach churn. "You cannot mean that you killed Maude!" she cried, horrified. "I didn't expect you would harm anyone."

De Fores shrugged his shoulders. "I did what I thought was necessary."

Season felt sick. She remembered that Maude had not been unkind on the preceding evening. Maude's death lay heavily on her shoulders; but she set her grief aside and faced De Fores.

"Have you set a course for England?"

He laughed, and his white teeth gleamed brightly. "I am De Fores, the pirate. I cannot sail leisurely up to the English shores. The *Blue Dolphin* would be sunk before we ever sighted Dover."

"What do you plan to do then?"

"We will talk about that later," he said, stripping off his jacket. "Right now I am hungry—how about you?"

"No, not very," she answered, beginning to pace the floor again. "One other thing I want to talk to you about," she said, stopping in front of him. "I insist that I not be locked in this cabin. I have an aversion to being locked up."

De Fores' eyebrow quirked. "Excuse me, my lady, but you must trust me to do what is best for your safety. If I left the cabin door unlocked, you would be ravished by one or several members of my crew."

Season's cheeks stained crimson. "Surely not. I was never in that kind of danger aboard the *Andromeda.*"

"Ah, yes, The Raven's crew. They may have had thoughts in that direction, but they would never exercise them. I believe they are referred to in Tripoli as the gentlemen of the sea," he said in a contemptuous voice.

"Are you quite sure The Raven cannot catch up with us, Captain De Fores?"

He smiled as his eyes ran the length of her body. "Have I not said you have nothing to fear from him?" He sat down on the edge of the desk, looking deeply into Season's green eyes. "Tell me about yourself and how you came to be on board the *Andromeda?*"

Something about De Fores' attitude bothered Season. She didn't think it was any of his business how she came to be on the *Andromeda*. "I was taken from my bedroom one night and held for a prisoner exchange."

"I see," the man said, stroking his beard thoughtfully. "Did the good captain leave you untouched? I have been told that he once rescued a Spanish ship in distress. There were five females on board and The Raven set them down on Spanish soil unmolested."

Again Season felt her face flush. She lowered her head. "We are not here to discuss me or The Raven. All I want to know from you is how soon you can get me back to my father. You said you couldn't sail into an English port, but you could set me down in France and I could find my own way home from there."

Season turned away because she didn't like the way the man was watching her. She didn't realize he had come up behind her until she felt his hand on her hair.

"Alas, my lady. My countrymen would be more inclined to hang me than your British countrymen."

"What do you intend to do then? Have you no plan in mind?"

He merely laughed and ran his hand down her hair. "I have never seen hair the color of yours, my lady. It is the color of gold with the color of red flames mixed in. I knew it would feel like silk in my fingers."

She turned to him quickly, her green eyes blazing like fire. "Do not dare ever lay your hand on my person again. You will be well paid when you see that I get back to my father. Until that time, I will ask you to keep a respectable distance from me."

De Fores' white teeth flashed and he grinned widely. "Did my friend, The Raven, also keep his distance? Would your father pay any less for your return should you be . . . let us say not quite pure?"

"How dare you, sir! You are insulting and disgusting," she said, beginning to feel more uneasy by the moment.

De Fores smiled, apparently undaunted by her outburst. "If you want my help, you must pay for it," he said, as his hand settled on her arm. When Season tried to move away, his grip tightened.

"I have told you that my father will pay you when I am safely returned to him. He is a very powerful man and will see that you are greatly rewarded," she said, choosing to misunderstand his meaning.

His eyes opened wide in amusement as his hand trailed across her shoulder then down across her heaving breasts. Season shuddered in disgust. A scream formed in her throat, but she held it back, knowing no one aboard the *Blue Dolphin* would come to her aid. De Fores smelled of stale rum and body sweat. She pushed against him and stepped back a pace, only to find herself against the bed.

"If you touch me, The Raven will kill you," she whispered through trembling lips, knowing deep down that it was the truth. She knew she would rather die than have this man put his hands on her again. Season now realized she had been very foolish to ask a man like De Fores to help her.

She couldn't bear to look into his leering face another moment, so she closed her eyes. As he slowly advanced toward her, Season prayed for death. Anything would be preferable to what this man had in mind for her. The Raven had been so different from De Fores. While he had often frightened her, she had never felt disgusted by him. In that moment she wished that The Raven would come for her. She had very little doubt that The Raven would try to find her, if for no other reason than to show De Fores that he couldn't take something away from him . . . but he wouldn't know where to search for her.

"You have nothing to fear, my lady. De Fores knows how to please a lady," he said, pushing her back on the bed.

Season scrambled off and ran for the door. "Don't come near me!" she screamed.

De Fores was across the cabin before she could reach the door. He gathered her up in his arms, threw her onto the filthy bed, and dropped down on top of her, pinning her onto the mattress. Season tried to struggle, but the Frenchman was too strong for her. His evil laugh made her want to hit him, but he caught her hands in one of his and grabbed the neck of her gown with the other. She heard the material rip, and she cried out.

Season realized the hopelessness of her situation when he straddled her and let his hand drift down to her exposed breasts.

"Don't touch me, you are filthy!" she screamed. "I don't like you!"

A frightening gleam came into the Frenchman's eyes as he stared down at her. "You are so lovely," he said in a harsh voice. "I will soon have you. I knew it the first time I saw you with The Raven. You made it easy for me to spirit you away from him."

Season struggled as his hand clamped down on her breast. Kicking her legs and twisting her body, she managed to catch him off balance, and she wriggled out from under him and off the bed. Loud sobs were

coming from her throat as she looked about for somewhere to run. Realizing the door wouldn't be locked,
she ran in that direction. If she could only make it topside, she would throw herself over the side before she
would submit to this awful man!

Sinister laughter issued from De Fores' lips as he
leaped across the room and, grabbing Season by her
hair, yanked her back against him. "I like women with
spirit, although I do not understand why you are fighting me when you have obviously been violated by The
Raven."

A calm seemed to descend upon Season and she
raised her head as she felt her courage returning. She
knew the captain of the *Andromeda* would face danger
bravely, and that thought gave her the courage she
needed.

"You are unfit to speak The Raven's name, De
Fores. He is twice the man you will ever be," she said,
tossing her head defiantly.

She watched as her words struck home and De
Fores' face became distorted with anger. "I will show
you who is the better man," he said between clenched
teeth.

Season's head reeled as he struck her several times
across the face. Then her body seemed to fly through
the air as he shoved her toward the bed. As her head hit
the bedpost and she slid to the floor, a dark cloud
descended upon her. She tried to force it aside. Raising
her hand to her mouth, she found it was bleeding. Season tried to rise as De Fores advanced on her but she no
longer had the strength to fight him.

"Captain, come quick!"

Season heard the excited voice through a haze of pain.

"There are sails off the horizon and she's closing fast. As well as I can make out, she looks like the *Andromeda,* sir!"

De Fores muttered a strangled oath and reached down, jerking Season to her feet. "We will settle this later, after I have disposed of your lover," he ground out, striking Season again and sending her reeling against the wall and onto the floor.

As Season looked up the cabin seemed to tilt. Her head was in a fog, but her heart was lighter. Hearing the door being locked, she crumpled into a heap.

"He has come!" she cried. "The Raven has come for me!" Crawling on her hands and knees Season made it to the porthole. It was not as high as the one on the *Andromeda* so she pulled herself up to look out.

Tears and blood mingled on her face as she caught sight of the *Andromeda,* white sails unfurled and waving proudly in the wind. She knew her dark lord would be standing at the helm, and soon he and De Fores would be in a life and death struggle. The battle between the two men wouldn't end until one of them was dead!

Never had anything looked so beautiful to Season as the *Andromeda* striking her colors and raising the Stars and Stripes to wave magnificently in the breeze. It was strange, but she no longer thought of The Raven as her enemy. He had found out she was in trouble and had come to save her. She wouldn't allow herself to think of what would happen if De Fores won. She was sure no one could come up against The Raven and win.

Season watched as the *Andromeda* changed course several times to catch the wind, each time gaining on the *Blue Dolphin,* and she held her breath as a white puff of smoke bilged from the *Andromeda*. Moments later the *Blue Dolphin* wavered under the impact of a direct hit.

Season could hear men scurrying about, and loud screams announced that the shot had taken its toll. At that moment Season felt pure joy. It didn't matter to her that The Raven might have sunk the *Blue Dolphin* and she end up at the bottom of the sea with the crippled vessel. All that mattered was that The Raven had come for her! Even if she died, she would take with her the thought that he had cared enough to come after her. No! She couldn't delude herself into thinking he had any tender feelings for her; she was merely his possession and he would never allow anyone to take from him what he considered his own.

Season's eyes filled with tears as she watched the *Andromeda* pass the porthole to be lost from her sight. She knew now that she loved the dark lord of the sea. He had made her a woman and had stolen her heart.

He might deny it, but she *was* The Raven's lady!

Chapter Sixteen

The Raven's eyes narrowed as he made a pass at De Fores' ship. He saw that the shot he had fired had caused considerable damage. He would come at the *Blue Dolphin* from the port side. Knowing De Fores would have taken Season to his cabin, he didn't want to risk injuring her in any way.

He muttered an oath as he slipped his leather helm over his head and steered the *Andromeda* directly for the crippled ship. As he watched the *Blue Dolphin* change course, a laugh escaped his lips. De Fores would use every trick to escape, but this was one time he wouldn't get away.

The Raven wouldn't allow himself to dwell on Season's fate, because if he did, he knew he might lose his nerve and make some fatal mistake.

"Keep her into the wind, Briggs. Steady as you go," he called out.

By now the Frenchman had swung his ship around and fired his bulwark guns. Three of his shots went wild, but the fourth hit the *Andromeda,* and splintering wood flew into the air.

The Raven made a quick assessment of his ship. Several men lay on the deck, and the mast had begun to sway as though it might come down.

"Ease the helm down, Briggs. You men there clear the deck of rubble, and prime for firing." At the captain's command the crew sprang into action. Some of them threw splintered planks overboard while others loaded and primed the nine pounders on the quarterdeck.

The Raven took the helm and sent Briggs to direct the firing of the cannon. He turned the *Andromeda* into the wind and brought her about broadside across the *Blue Dolphin*'s helm.

"Steady, steady, blast her as she comes by, Briggs," came the loud command from the captain.

The noise was deafening as the cannon let loose. Not one of the five shots fired missed their target. The hull of the *Blue Dolphin* was shattered, her mast was hanging over the forward deck—she was crippled. As the *Andromeda* made a forward pass, The Raven watched as utter pandemonium broke out on the *Blue Dolphin*'s deck. Men were jumping over the sides, and a fire had broken out below.

Bringing the *Andromeda* about, her captain sailed her alongside De Fores' ship.

"Quarter, quarter," many crew members on the Frenchman's ship cried as the men of the *Andromeda* threw their grappling irons over the side to hold the two ships together.

"Where is your captain?" The Raven yelled.

"I am here, Raven," De Fores called. He stood on deck, holding Season in front of him. "If you value your lady's life, you will remove your hooks and sail away."

The Raven tensed. He could see the blood on Season's face, and his anger overruled his good judgment. He watched as she struggled to cover her nakedness by pulling her torn gown together.

"If you have harmed the lady, De Fores, I will kill you." The threat was softly spoken.

"She will be unharmed if you sail away," the Frenchman called out.

Season raised her eyes to where The Raven stood. She could tell he was rigid and undecided. She sent him a silent message, begging him not to leave her.

Everyone suddenly fell silent, waiting for The Raven to speak. Season feared he would do as De Fores asked and leave, so she took matters into her own hands. De Fores was holding her about the waist, a knife blade at her throat, but with a sudden move, she stomped down on his foot as hard as she could and simultaneously jabbed her elbow into his stomach. She caught the Frenchman by surprise, and he loosened his grip on her long enough for her to slip away from him. Season's legs flew as she ran across the deck toward the *Andromeda* and safety.

She didn't see the dark lord of the *Andromeda* grab a rope and swing himself onto the deck of the *Blue Dolphin.* His crew quickly followed suit, and the clash of metal could be heard as both sides came together.

Season was bumped and jostled about, all but forgotten in the heat of battle. When she felt a hand on her shoulder, she swung about to see James's smiling face.

"Come with me, ma'am, it ain't safe here," he said, pulling her forward. The two of them ran across the deck and climbed quickly aboard the *Andromeda* as sounds of pain and death echoed across the water.

When James tried to lead Season below, she jerked free and climbed up to the quarter-deck for a better view of the battle. She had to know if The Raven was safe; it was hard to judge which crew had the advantage. She sought The Raven in the melee and finally found him. He and De Fores had drawn swords and were crossing blades.

She clutched her hands tightly together and watched as The Raven's powerful forward thrust caught De Fores in the forearm and laid the flesh open. The Frenchman went down on his knees, begging for mercy. When Season saw The Raven raise his sword, she turned quickly away, not wanting to witness De Fores' cowardice or his death.

Clamping her hand over her mouth to stifle a cry, she at last allowed James to lead her below. Her legs felt so weak she was sure she would never make it down the companionway, but the horrible sounds of battle followed her to the captain's quarters. Season lay on the bed and buried her head under a pillow, hoping to drown out the sounds of the dying. She felt it was her fault that men would die this day. If she had not enlisted De Fores' help to get away from The Raven, none of this would have taken place.

"If you are all right, ma'am, I'll just go topside," James said, patting her awkwardly on the shoulder.

Season was too sick to answer. Tears stung her eyes,

and she felt as if this were the end of the world. Soon the battle would be over and when The Raven would come to her—she did not doubt that he would be the winner—she would have to tell him it was her fault that so many men had died. She thought about Maude's death and felt worse than ever.

The fight aboard the *Blue Dolphin* ended as soon as her crew realized their captain was dead. The Raven's men stripped the burning ship of her valuables, and put her crew to sea in longboats, giving them enough food and water to see them safely back to Tripoli.

The grappling irons were removed and the *Andromeda* sailed a short distance away and aimed her guns at the dead Frenchman's crippled vessel, which took three direct hits and quickly sank, taking her dead captain to the bottom of the sea with her. The only evidence that the *Blue Dolphin* had existed was the yellow sulfur cloud that hovered over the water where she had sunk.

Season had been so exhausted she had fallen asleep. When she awoke, she could tell they were under sail by the gentle swaying of the ship. The cabin was in total darkness, and she sat up, thinking how wonderful it was to be free!

She moved off the bed and groped her way toward the desk where she knew she would find the lantern. When light filled the cabin, she looked about her as if she had come home. How fresh and clean the quarters were. Tears of hopelessness washed down her cheeks.

How foolish she had been to think she could ever

escape The Raven. He would have gone to the ends of the earth to get her back, and she knew now that she didn't ever want to be parted from him again. As surely as she lived and breathed, she belonged to him heart and soul. Probably he would soon tire of her and set her free, but until that time she would relish his nearness and what little affection he showed her.

Season saw the tub of fresh water that awaited her, and she silently blessed Briggs for looking after her comfort. Opening the trunk, Season removed her white nightgown and laid it across the foot of the bed. Undressing, she lowered herself into the tub and almost groaned when the soothing water caressed her battered and bruised body. She lathered her hair with the sweet-smelling soap and leaned back, closing her eyes and enjoying the cool cleansing water. At last she rinsed her hair and washed the blood from her face. Then she scrubbed every part of her body that De Fores had touched. She wasn't sorry he was dead. The world is a far better place without men like him, she thought. Indeed, she doubted that anyone would mourn his passing.

At last feeling clean, she stepped out of the tub, dried herself thoroughly, and slipped into her nightgown. She then climbed into the middle of the bed and began to brush the tangles from her golden hair.

She sat there a long time, not thinking or feeling anything, just overjoyed to be alive. When she began to feel hungry, she climbed off the bed and made her way to the cabin door. Turning the handle, she found it to be locked as she had known it would be.

Season was in the process of returning to the bed

when she heard a sound at the door. Turning, she came face to face with The Raven!

He just stood there, staring at her through the slits in his helm, and she could sense his anger. Season wanted to run and throw herself into his arms, but she didn't think he would welcome such a gesture at the moment.

She noticed for the first time that he was carrying a tray of food when he motioned that she should be seated. He kicked the door shut and followed her across the room. When she was settled on the bed, he placed the tray on her lap.

"Have you taken on Briggs's chores?" she asked, unable to think of anything else to say. She watched him closely and could feel his displeasure. She felt that she deserved his contempt. He had every right to be angry with her.

He said nothing, merely sat down on a chair and continued to stare at her. Season's throat became dry, and she nervously clasped and unclasped her hands. It was most unsettling to be observed so closely by someone at whom you couldn't stare back. She realized how The Raven's enemies must feel when they were on the receiving end of his anger.

Season could not stand the silence. "I have observed that when you go into battle, you wear the leather helm, Raven. On all other occasions you use the soft leather hood."

He didn't answer, just sat and stared at her, but when she thought she could stand his scrutiny no longer, he spoke. "Just tell me one thing, Season, did you enlist De Fores' help at the tavern when I wasn't listening?"

"Y-yes."

"Are you aware that because of you two of my men are dead and three more may not last the night?"

Season's mouth flew open in horror. "I am so sorry, I never meant this to happen. I merely wanted to go back to my father."

"I warn you that in the future, Season, I will not tolerate disobedience, is that clear?"

Some of her old fire returned. "I am not a child. I have never had to obey anyone except my teachers and my father. What gives you the right to tell me what to do?"

"You are fortunate to be alive." His voice trailed off and he reached out to touch her bruised cheek, but she flinched at his soft touch.

"Damn De Fores," he swore. "He has hurt you. Your face is puffy and your lip is cut."

"It is nothing . . . no more than a few bruises," she said, not knowing how to deal with this sudden shift to tenderness. She could feel a tenseness in him and knew instinctively that he was worried about more than a few bruises.

His finger tenderly touched her swollen lip. "Did he touch you in any other way?" It seemed as if he had to force himself to ask her the question that had been haunting him.

Season swallowed a lump that had come to her throat. "No, but he would have if you hadn't come when you did."

"Did you wish to be free of me so badly that you would enlist the help of someone like De Fores? Didn't you know what he would be like?"

Season shook her head. "I didn't think. All I knew

was that I had to get away and he was the only one who seemed willing to help me."

He withdrew his hand. "I have come to realize how greatly you have suffered at my hands. I abducted you out of anger, but I kept you for a reason that, until now, I wouldn't even admit to myself. You were nothing more than an innocent young girl when I took you. I am in a repentant mood tonight, and you have my word that you will not have to suffer my presence any longer than is necessary."

"Are you taking me home?" she asked with a sinking heart. Where only days ago she had wanted only to escape from him, now she realized she would be heart-broken should he cast her aside.

"I regret to say I have pressing business in France or I would take you back now. Once my business is completed, we shall talk again."

"Are we now on our way to France?"

"Yes. Depending on the weather, we should be in France within two weeks' time.

The Raven stood up and stared down at her. "Will you ever find it within your heart to forgive me, Season?" he asked in a strange voice.

"I don't know," she said, tears sparkling in her green eyes. She was feeling very like the young girl he had earlier accused her of being. "Perhaps it is I who should ask your pardon. Because of me, Maude is dead. I know how you felt about her."

"Do you, Season?"

"Yes, I think so."

"I doubt that you do, but set your mind at rest. Maude still lives."

Season felt as if a weight had been lifted from her shoulders. She smiled brightly. "I cannot believe I am saying this, but I liked Maude. I am glad she is alive so she can sail aboard her pirate ship and command her raids on unsuspecting merchant ships."

The Raven laughed deeply. "That she will. Maude will never allow anyone or anything to get her down." He turned abruptly and left without another word.

Season stared down at the tray of food in her lap, feeling dejected. The Raven didn't want her any longer. He was sending her away. She bit her trembling lip as her eyes filled with tears. What kind of life would she be going back to? How would she get through the years to come?

As the days swiftly passed, Season began to wish time would stand still. She knew once they reached France it would be only a matter of time until The Raven kept his word and allowed her to go free. She was in agony at the thought of never seeing him again. He never came near her anymore, and she missed him desperately. Sometimes she would see him when Briggs took her out for a stroll, but he never paid the slightest attention to her. Season began to wonder if somewhere there was a woman to whom he always returned. She couldn't help but wish she were that woman.

One day Briggs brought Captain Robert Wolf to the cabin and introduced him to Season who liked him immediately. He had sun-bleached blond hair and soft gray eyes. Although he walked with a slight limp, he assured Season that when the wound was healed he would be as good as new. The two of them soon became fast friends. Season found it easty to talk to Robert, and she liked his boyish charm. She learned that he was five years her senior and a privateer like The Raven. From a slip Robert made Season also learned that they were on the way to France to meet with an American naval officer called John Paul Jones.

Each day now, Season and Robert walked on deck in the bright sunlight, and she found that Robert often made her laugh. He was not only witty, he was charming, gentlemanly, and polite. Though he was loyal to the Colonies while her loyalties lay with England, they never spoke of their differences.

One evening as they walked on deck just at sunset, Season paused at the railing to watch the waves lapping at the side of the ship.

"Robert, what do you know about The Raven?"

He cocked his curly head and smiled at her. "More than most people and less than some."

"Which is no answer at all, except a polite way of telling me to mind my own affairs," she said, smiling.

"Call it the creed of the sea, loyalty among friends, or if you like . . . I owe him my life."

"I know next to nothing about The Raven," she said, sighing. "Where does he come from? Does he have a family? What does he call home when he isn't at sea?"

"The only family I can tell you about is his uncle, a man named Silas Dunsberry. I can only tell you this because Silas is dead; therefore, no one would be able to trace The Raven through him. Few people knew that The Raven and Silas were related, and those who did, never discussed it."

Season searched Robert's face. She tried to speak but her throat was dry. Her tear-filled eyes turned out to sea as she remembered why The Raven had come to her in anger on the night he had learned of Silas Dunsberry's death. The man who was to be exchanged for her but who had been executed instead had been The Raven's uncle!

"Was he very close to his uncle?" she managed to ask at last.

"Yes. They were very fond of one another, Season. It was a great blow to The Raven when he learned of his Uncle Silas' death."

Silence hung heavily between them until Robert spoke. "Have you ever been to France?" he asked in a lighter tone.

"No. I had done very little traveling until I sailed for the Colonies. I can speak French, however." Then Season, too, changed the subject. "Tell me, Robert, what will you do when you get back to America?"

He gazed out to sea. "The first thing I must do is report to Congress. The Raven and I agree that the pirate stronghold in the Barbary States must be wiped out. It has become a hazard to every seagoing vessel. The Raven doubts that Congress will have the time or the inclination to deal with the pirates at this time, but it's worth a try."

Season smiled. "How would you define the difference between a privateer and a pirate?"

"One of them fights for a cause and the other doesn't. Since you have met both kinds in The Raven and De Fores, I will leave you to judge which is which."

"I see what you mean," she said thoughtfully. "What

282

will you do after you have made a report to your Congress, Robert?"

"Well, to be honest, I will pay a call on a young lady whom I haven't seen in a very long time. When I thought I was going to die, the thought of her black hair and soft brown eyes gave me the will to live. I didn't want to die until I told her how I felt about her. When I left home, she was much too young for me to declare my feelings to her. I pray she has not looked elsewhere for a husband while I have been at sea."

"Tell me about her."

Robert smiled. "Her hair is as black as a midnight sky, and her eyes defy description. I always called her funny face when she was small, but her face is anything but funny. I have known her since she took her first step, and I placed her on her first horse. I believe I have always loved her and have merely been waiting for her to grow up so I could declare myself to her."

Season touched Robert's hand. "You are so fortunate to know love, and the woman you love is fortunate also. Tell her about your feelings soon, Robert. I believe love is too precious to waste."

He clasped her hand and looked deeply into the depths of her green eyes. "Lady Season Chatsworth, you are the fairest of the fair. I believe I shall always envy the man you will one day marry."

She smiled brightly. "You don't mean that, and you know it. Your heart is already spoken for, by a young girl who has hair as dark as midnight. I will always hope that you find happiness, Robert."

"And I will hope that you, too, one day find your heart's desire, Season.

Season looked away from him and her eyes fell on the dark lord of the *Andromeda*. "I fear happiness and I are strangers, Robert. I fear it will always be so with me."

"Such a touching scene," The Raven rasped in his deep voice. "Have I interrupted a little tête-à-tête?"

Robert released Season's hand and stepped back a pace. "No. You saw nothing more than two good friends wishing each other well."

"How touching," The Raven said in a biting tone. "Don't you have somewhere else to be, Robert?"

Robert smiled at Season. "You may not be as much a stranger to what we were discussing as you think, my lady." He laughed and bowed slightly before moving away.

"I will not tolerate you flaunting yourself before other men, Season. I would have thought you had learned a lesson with De Fores. Dammit, don't you know all the men aboard this ship are half in love with you."

Season turned to him and tossed her hair as she always did when she was angry. He knew all her endearing habits by now. Her green eyes sparkled when she was angry. She clutched her hands when she was nervous. When she was frightened her green eyes opened wide, and when she was deeply moved by something, those same eyes flamed like green fire.

"I was not flaunting myself as you suggested. I like Robert; we are good friends."

His hand shot out and captured her chin. "Just how good a friend is Robert to you?"

"I don't know what you mean."

"Don't you?"

She moved his hand away. "Don't judge Robert by your standards, Raven. He has always been kind and respectful, which is more than I can say for you."

He was silent for a moment, and when he spoke his voice was no more than a whisper. "You do wound me sorely, my lady."

"If I had been handed the chance De Fores was offered, I would have run you through," she said, stomping her foot in anger.

He laughed, and Season knew his good humor had returned. Taking her by the arm, he guided her down the companionway. "I have no doubt that had you been in De Fores' boots, you would have done just that," he said, obviously amused.

Season pulled her arm away and rushed ahead of him. When she reached the cabin door, she knew he was close behind her. As she entered the cabin, she expected him to follow her, but instead she heard the key grate in the lock. She was locked in, alone.

Season's anger abated after she stood in the middle of the cabin and allowed tears of helpless fury to wash down her cheeks. How much more of this torture could she take? she wondered. When would all this end?

When The Raven returned to the deck, he found Robert waiting for him. Removing his leather helm and tossing it aside, he glared at his friend.

"Weren't you a little rough on Lady Season, Raven?" Robert asked daringly.

"What I do with Season is no concern of yours. I will not have you making calf eyes at a woman who is under my protection. That goes for you or any other member of this ship," The Raven said, raising his voice so everyone within earshot could hear.

Robert raised his eyebrows. "You always were a hot head, but I have never before seen you make such a fool of yourself over a woman."

"And you were always a romantic and a fool, Robert. You are talking nonsense as always."

"I may be a fool, but I would guess you are in love with the lady and you are jealous of anyone who comes near her. Dammit, you are going to be hard to get along with for the rest of this voyage."

"You are crazed, Robert," The Raven said sourly.

"Am I? I don't think so. You had best put her from your mind, Raven. You must take her back to her people, you know."

"I will take her back when I decide to do so, Robert. You are getting to be as bad as Briggs, always hounding me about her. Dammit, I am the captain of this ship, and I'll give the orders around here."

Robert smiled patiently. "Lord, you must be in love. You are bellowing like a denied bull."

Suddenly all the fire seemed to go out of The Raven. He leaned against the ship's railing and stared out to sea. "I have wronged her, Robert. God, I must be out of my mind; I don't want to take her back. She can hardly stand the sight of me, flinches every time I come near her. I know I will have to do the right thing and return her to her father, but it is ripping my heart apart."

"I wouldn't worry overmuch about that. Perhaps you will be able to win her over as your other self. She doesn't know who you are."

"That can never be now. If she ever found out who I

really am, she would hate me all the more."

"Where will you take her? You cannot set her down on English soil, and you can't very well go sailing into New York harbor either, Raven."

"I don't know. I had thought perhaps I would take her to Lucas Carrington's plantation in Virginia. As you know, he's a friend of the English and he will see her safely returned to New York."

Robert's mouth gaped open. "Good Lord, you cannot be serious. How will you arrange it?"

"It won't be as hard as you might suppose, Robert."

"I don't want to be a party to this. That will be like handing Season from one captor to another."

The Raven turned his gaze on his friend. "I have no choice, Robert. Lucas Carrington will see that she is safely returned to New York."

Robert smiled. "Can you trust him to do the right thing?"

"You know him better than I do, Robert. What do you think?"

Robert looked out to sea and frowned. "I think only time will tell, my friend. I wouldn't want to be in your boots for all the gold in the world."

"Why?"

"For the obvious reason—Lady Season Chatsworth!"

Chapter Seventeen

The wind dropped and a flat calm prevailed soon after the *Andromeda* reached the port of Lorient and anchored in thirty fathoms of water. The French coast gleamed brightly in the noonday sun, but The Raven's crew lowered the canvas and immediately set to work on repairs under Briggs's direction.

Off to the right of the *Andromeda*'s bow, John Paul Jones's ship the *Bonhomme Richard* was anchored. Captain Jones had named her for Benjamin Franklin's *Poor Richard's Almanac*. She was a sleek vessel, and the Stars and Stripes waved proudly from one of her masts. John Paul Jones walked her deck, hands clasped behind his back and eyes trained on The Raven's ship, taking in the damage.

"So The Raven did answer my summons," he said to his first mate. "I half feared we would sail before he arrived."

"Will he come directly to us, sir?" his mate wanted to know.

John Paul looked at the position of the sun to gauge the hour. "No, he will wait for the cloak of darkness. I calculate he will not come to me for at least another seven hours."

"Could you not go to him, sir?"

"No. He has come this far to see me; another few hours cannot make that much difference. I wish some of our naval officers were as dependable as The Raven. Perhaps if they were, we would have won this war long ago," John Paul speculated.

"The *Andromeda* is a sleek vessel, Captain. I have heard she is one of the fastest afloat."

"You heard right. There is no ship faster than The *Andromeda.*" John Paul's hazel eyes scanned the French coast, and he sighed in exasperation. He had cooled his heels in France for months, waiting to put out to sea once more. He blamed mismanagement and slow correspondence from Congress for the delay.

The bright sunlight reflected off the metal buttons on Captain Jones's blue officer's jacket. His white waistcoat and breeches were spotlessly clean. He presented an imposing figure as he stared at the cloudless sky and reflected that he had always thought of himself as a patient man, but lately he had been tested to the limit. He felt that he was surrounded by incompetence. His hands had been tied by his superiors. John Paul thought that perhaps, with the help of The Raven and other privateers like him, he could achieve naval superiority over the British.

The deck of the *Bonhomme Richard* was deserted

but for one lone sentry as The Raven climbed over the rope ladder behind the sailor Captain Jones had sent to fetch him. The man on guard did not seem surprised to see the dark, hooded figure crossing the deck, nor was The Raven challenged when he descended the companionway to meet with the ship's captain.

Silently The Raven was led to a cabin, and then his guide departed. He rapped on the door and it was immediately opened by the man who was already a legend of the sea—Captain John Paul Jones.

The captain motioned for The Raven to enter, and then he shut the door and shot the bolt home. The two captains were alone, so The Raven slowly removed his leather hood and tossed it aside.

The men looked at each other for a moment without speaking, for each greatly admired the other. John Paul had a keen eye, high cheek bones, and a sharp nose. His chin was strong and stubborn, and his neatly dressed hair was tied back in a queue. His was a passionate face that had the look of a man who was not at peace with himself. Suddenly Jones's spare, taut body seemed to relax, and his mouth, which could easily curl up in scorn, eased into a warm smile as he extended his hand to The Raven.

"You are about a week late, Raven. It is only due to providence that I am still here to greet you at all," he said, shaking The Raven's hand vigorously.

"I regret the delay, but it was also due to providence," he answered, smiling.

"Oh?" John Paul said, raising his brow quizzically. "I saw that your crew were making repairs. Did you perhaps have a run-in with another ship?"

"Yes. I had a little run-in with De Fores."

"And?"

"The *Blue Dolphin* was sunk and her captain went to the bottom of the sea with her."

John Paul's hazel eyes lit up. "In that case, I will forgive your tardiness. You have done the world a great service by relieving us of that scourge. Come, take a seat—we have much to discuss and so little time to do it."

The Raven sat down and leaned his head back. "What's the news from home, John Paul?"

Captain Jones smiled slightly and looked sharply at his guest. "It is said that a pirate by the name of The Raven has sailed boldly into New York harbor and kidnapped the Duke of Chatsworth's daughter. It is also said that her father and King George are most anxious to have her safely returned to England."

"Actually," The Raven drawled, "I sailed into New Jersey. I am not a complete fool."

"When I inferred you might consider taking a hostage of some importance, I didn't mean that important. Nor did I intend that you should take a woman. There is a great outcry over the incident, even from our own Congress."

"Circumstances dictated that I act with all possible haste. I didn't have time to search for a hostage. I took the first one at hand, which just happened to be Lady Season Chatsworth."

"Yes, I know. I heard about your Uncle Silas. He was a gentleman and a patriot; we shall all miss him."

"We are agreed on that."

John Paul stood up and avoided The Raven's eyes.

"Since you already have Lady Season Chatsworth, there is no reason we can't use her to our best advantage. Hell, with her to bargain with, we could gain the release of all our men rotting on English prison ships."

The Raven crossed his long legs and looked at his friend through lowered lashes. "No, I will not allow you to use the lady in that capacity. As soon as our business is concluded, I am taking her back to America."

John Paul's face clouded over and his eyes blazed. "You are not very wise, Raven. I could take her from you now, and no one would fault me for it. In fact, there are those on both sides who would be most anxious to see her returned to her father."

The Raven laughed. "You are much too wise to attempt anything so foolhardy. I would never give her up to you without a fight, and you and I are friends. Have you forgotten we fight for the same side? I have no desire to train the *Andromeda*'s guns on you, John Paul, but I will not allow you to take Season from me."

Slowly John Paul's mouth eased into a smile. "You are right. We have more important battles to wage. I would never raise a sword or aim cannon at you anyway. You are much too valuable to the cause."

The Raven nodded. "I assume you had something important on your mind or you wouldn't have sent for me."

John Paul sat down and looked long and hard into the unmasked face of The Raven. "First of all, I would like to commend you on a job well done. Without your intelligence gathering, we could not always strike when the enemy is most vulnerable. I envy you your freedom to come and go as you wish. I often feel that my hands are tied. It is a stone around my neck that I must wait for the approval of Congress before I can put out to sea. If I had chosen the path of a privateer as you did, I would have no one to answer to but myself."

The Raven nodded his head. "I could never last through the petty quarrels that come out of Philadelphia. I suppose I am too stubborn to take orders from a body of men who wouldn't know the first thing about sailing a ship."

"I'll drink to that," John Paul said, uncorking a bottle of wine, pouring some of the contents into two glasses, and handing one to The Raven.

"I heard about your victory against the British ship *Serapis*. You are to be congratulated, John Paul."

"Did you also hear that King George knighted the captain whom I defeated in that battle. Hell, if they will send him to me again, I will defeat him, and the king can make a damned duke out of him!"

The Raven laughed deeply. "Who knows, perhaps the English find it an honor to be defeated by the renowned Captain John Paul Jones."

John Paul's laughter joined his. "Who knows, if the English captain were to meet and be bested by The Raven, King George might very well step down and make him king in his stead." Both men laughed, light-heartedly enjoying a joke at the expense of the English.

"Raven, I heard you took a fine prize off America's coast. I'll be damned if you aren't the bold one."

"She was a good prize. I sent her to Philadelphia, hoping our navy could use her."

"I half wish you had sent her to me. I am sick of the

delays I have encountered lately. I have had problems finding a crew, and I have Congress and Richard Henry Lee to deal with."

"What has Lee done now?"

A contemptuous look came over John Paul's face. "It would seem the honorable Mr. Lee had a carriage built here in France and he wants it transported to America. You are aware of how badly General Washington needs supplies, uniforms, guns, and ammunition?"

The Raven nodded.

"Henry Lee wanted to have the cargo destined for Washington's troops unloaded to accommodate his damned carriage!" John Paul said in a strangled voice.

"Did he succeed?"

"I don't know yet," John Paul said, shrugging his shoulders. "Most probably he will."

The Raven took a sip of wine and looked at his friend. "The hour grows late, so you had better tell me why you sent for me, although I already suspect what you want."

Captain Jones took in a deep breath. "I have repeatedly asked Congress to send a naval expedition to the west coast of Africa to destroy the English-African trade. I wanted to occupy St. Helena to intercept the British East Indiamen which put in there on their passage home, but Congress refused me permission. What I want to know from you is, do you think you can do anything to bring this about?"

"As you must know, I don't have Congress' ear. I can never approach them as you could. I don't see how I can be of help to you in this."

"Raven, you should be decorated for all you have done to help our cause. Yet your exploits go unheralded. I would wager that you have taken or sunk more English vessels than the rest of us combined."

"I thank you for your praise, but I have no wish for glory. I want nothing more than to serve my country to the best of my ability."

"I knew you would feel that way; that's why I asked you here. I also know how the other privateers respect you. Do you think you could pull all the others together and take St. Helena?"

The Raven shook his head. "You must understand, John Paul, unlike our navy, the privateers are not banded together, but act as individuals. There is no way I can bring them together. All I can promise you is that I will continue to strike at the enemy in the way I have in the past."

"I was afraid that would be your answer, but I had to try all the same."

"I have heard rumors that France has declared war on the English, and that Spain is considering doing the same. Is there any truth to the rumors?"

"I pray that will come about. The British are a terrible foe, and masters of the sea. I admit to having a goodly amount of respect for their ability, but even they cannot hold out if the whole world declares war on them."

John Paul stood up and extended his hand to The Raven. "It is almost daylight, and you must return to your ship. While the French are our allies, it would still be wise for you to leave on the morning tide."

The Raven gripped his friend's hand. "I am sorry

that I couldn't help you carry through with your plan."

"It is but another setback for me. I grow used to them by now. You realize that this meeting between us never took place. If you are ever asked if you spoke to me, I will expect you to deny it."

The Raven laughed deeply. "What meeting?"

He replaced his leather helm and then walked to the door. As he shot the bolt, John Paul's voice stopped him.

"Is she as beautiful as they say, Raven?"

"Who?"

"Lady Season Chatsworth."

"Yes, extremely beautiful."

John Paul smiled and nodded his head. "God's speed, Raven. I know not when or if we will ever meet again. Keep a fair wind to your back."

The Raven departed as silently as he had come. John Paul seated himself again and reflected on his visit with the captain of the *Andromeda*. He envied The Raven his freedom. Unlike the privateer, Captain Jones had too many people—all with different points of view—telling him what he was to do.

Just before sunrise, the *Andromeda* spread her sails and moved away from the French coast, heading west toward the Americas. The weather was fair, and the breeze strong, as The Raven's ship began her homeward journey. Many of her crew members had not seen their families in over two years; so their hearts were light as they anticipated seeing their loved ones. There was one man on board, however, who did not share the

297

others' joy. The Raven was in no hurry to reach the American coast, for then he would have to take Lady Season Chatsworth ashore and turn her over to Lucas Carrington. He didn't yet know how that would be accomplished.

Season was painfully aware of the passing days. Deep in her heart she feared that when The Raven returned her to America, she would never see him again. With each passing hour her heart seemed to grow heavier. She hadn't even seen The Raven since they had reached the French shore.

Her only companions had been James and Briggs. For some reason that Season couldn't understand, Robert Wolf was avoiding her, and she missed his company. He had always made her laugh, and right now she could find nothing to be happy about.

Each day in the cool of the evening, Season and James walked the deck. At those times, her eyes searched the ship for The Raven, but he was never there. She felt as if she were living in a void with no past and no future, but sometimes she found herself wishing she could sail throughout eternity aboard the *Andromeda*.

Season was lying on the bed, looking over a map. She had studied the maps so often they had begun to make more sense to her. When she heard the key in the lock, she sat up. Her heart leaped into her throat when The Raven entered the cabin.

"I have something I want to show you, my lady," he said in his raspy voice.

Feeling neglected by him, Season was in no mood to be forgiving. "I don't want to see anything you would show me," she answered, a pout on her lips.

The Raven laughed, thinking how lovely she looked with her golden hair streaming down her back. "I think you will want to see this. Few human beings have ever been fortunate enough to witness what I want to show you."

Season slid off the bed. "What is it?" she asked, her interest piqued.

"Come and I will show you," he said, holding his hand out to her.

Season placed her hand in his and allowed him to lead her out of the cabin and up the companionway.

When they reached the deck The Raven led her to the railing and pointed out to sea. Season watched as several large fish weaved their way through the water.

"I wanted you to see this. As I told you, few men have been privileged to watch this phenomenon of nature."

"Those are whales are they not, Raven?" Season asked with interest.

"Yes, and if you will look closely you will see that there are five of them swimming together. The one in the middle is very old and the two on either side of him are what we call pilot whales."

"Why do they swim so near the ship?" Season wanted to know.

"No one knows for sure. The one in the middle has come to die, and the others are keeping him company. They will stay with him until he is dead; then they will disappear and swim out to sea."

"I never realized a fish could have feelings. It is as if the one who is ill is their grandfather, and the others want to bring him comfort in his last hours. How very sad it all is."

"Whales do have feelings, Season. For some strange reason, they seem to like and trust man, which is a pity. The whale has no natural enemies other than man, my lady. They have never been known to attack one another, and regardless of what you have heard, they will not attack a ship unless they have been wounded by man and are fighting to survive."

Season watched as the old whale came to the surface very near the ship. It seemed to be having trouble staying afloat and she realized it was suffering. "It's almost as if the pilot whales were asking us to help the old whale, is it not?"

"That's what it seems like, Season."

"Can you not do something to put the poor creature out of its misery?" she asked, tears in her eyes.

"No, it is best not to intervene in any way. The pilot whales will take care of their . . . grandfather as you put it. I do not believe we should interfere."

Season looked up at the black slits in The Raven's mask. "I think it is very sad," she said. "I no longer want to watch."

He took her hand. "Season, I didn't ask you to watch this to make you sad. I do not look at it in the same way you do. To me it is rare and beautiful to watch how nature's children take care of their own. I thought you might be able to see the humane side of the death of the whale."

Season smiled weakly. "Yes, I suppose you are right. It is admirable that the whales look after their old. I fear our society is not always so thoughtful."

"You may stay and watch if you wish," The Raven

said. "I must return to the helm."

Season's gaze followed his retreating form and she wanted to call him back. She could sense something in him that she had never felt before. What was it? Sadness? She turned for one last look at the huge fish and saw that one of the pilot whales was very near the ship. She looked directly into the animal's eyes and shivered. She was almost sure the whale wanted the help of the men on board this ship. She wasn't sure whether the pilot whales wanted the sick animal put out of its misery or whether they thought the men might be able to make it well.

She turned away and rushed down the companion-way to her cabin. Nature was sometimes cruel. Living and dying, love and hate, they all came together in the end. Season stretched out on the bed and rested her head on her arms. Had she not once hated The Raven? Now she would love the faceless man until the day she died.

Two weeks had passed since the day The Raven had shown Season the whales. Once again it seemed he had forgotten her. Twice while strolling on deck, she had seen him, but he had paid her no heed.

Now, as she lay abed, Season was dreaming, and in her dream she could feel The Raven's hands move over her body. She could feel the softness of his caress and the magic of his kiss.

A noise roused her from her dream and she sat up. She could feel the difference in the way the *Andromeda* rode the water. Instinctively, she knew the noise that had awakened her was the lowering of the anchor.

Scrambling off the bed, she raced to the porthole and climbed upon the chair to peer out. Seeing land in the distance, she realized that they had reached their destination. Sandy beaches led to dense forest. They were off the coast of America.

Season stepped off the chair and closed her eyes, willing herself not to cry. She was being abandoned by the man she loved, and he hadn't even had the decency to tell her why he was casting her aside.

She heard the key in the lock and raised her head proudly. She knew it would be The Raven before he entered, and she wasn't about to let him see how much she was hurting.

When he entered, Season realized she was wearing nothing but her thin white nightgown and she pulled the spread off the bed and held it in front of her.

"Wouldn't it behoove you to knock before you enter a lady's room? Suppose I had been undressed," she scolded, using her anger to cover her hurt.

He merely shrugged his shoulders. "I have felt every inch of your body and can well imagine how you would look undressed. There is no reason to pretend maidenly modesty with me, my lady," he said in his deep voice.

"You have left me with nothing. No gentleman will ever want me for his wife. You have reduced me to nothing better than a street woman."

His shoulders shook with silent laughter. "The thought of you plodding the streets selling your . . . charms is highly unlikely. Fear not, my lady, you will find some poor misguided fool who will offer you marriage and make an honest matron of you. I am sure Edmund Kensworthy will more than likely vie for that role in your life."

"You are a horrid beast and a libertine. How dare you laugh at me and make light of my virtue!" she shouted, picking up the book which lay on the desk and throwing it in his direction.

He artfully dodged the missile, and it landed with a thud against the door. "Tsk, tsk, the lady does have a temper," he said in amusement.

Season was stunned by his cruelty. He had never before mocked her so. It almost seemed that he wanted her to hate him. Her anger at its peak, she ran across the room and grabbed his hood, but the captain seemed undaunted by her action. He merely took her hands and held them fast, laughing all the while.

"You are a regular little wildcat. I thought I had partly tamed you . . . apparently I was mistaken."

"You beast! I look forward to the day when I can watch you hang for what you have done to me!" Season cried, trying to jerk her wrists from his grip.

"I would do many things to please you, my lady, but forgive me if I don't hasten to dance at the end of a rope for your amusement."

"I *will* see you dead, Raven, upon my word I will," she said softly.

"That may very well be, my lady, but you will have to wait your turn. There are many who would like to see the end of The Raven."

"How many other women have you had at your mercy? Should we all form a line to watch you get what you so justly deserve, Raven?"

Again his shoulders shook with mirth, and he released her hands. "I have never found it necessary to force a lady to my bed. Perhaps they line up to get into my bed."

"Oh, yes. I'm sure of that. Why didn't you take one of them instead of me? I detest you!"

There was silence from behind the dark mask for a moment; then he spoke softly. "I never did require that you hold me in high esteem. It is hoped that when you look back on the time we spent together, you will think a little more kindly of me."

"Are you sending me ashore here, or am I required to swim?" she asked, feeling defeated as she always did when she came up against The Raven.

"Unless you are a stronger swimmer than I recall, I would suggest you stay with us for a while longer."

"What land did I see from the porthole?"

"That would be Virginia, my lady."

Season felt confused. "Why have you brought me here? I don't understand."

"I have come to you now with the express purpose of telling you what is to occur. "I have heard you speak of Lucas Carrington in glowing terms. Since he is a relative of Edmund Kensworthy, I will place you in his care and trust him to see that you are safely returned to your intended bridegroom."

In that moment Season called on all her inner strength. Her heart was breaking because The Raven was abandoning her, but she couldn't allow him to see that. He would merely make sport of her if he knew of her love for him.

"Am I to be cast aside like so much excess baggage now that you no longer have a use for me?" she asked, raising her head proudly. Her cheeks were flushed and her green eyes were blazing brightly.

"I thought it was your wish to be released," he said, hardly above a whisper.

"It is, of course," Season said, trying to cover up for her hurt and resentment, "but I would rather you had taken me back to New York, or better still England."

"I have already sent word to Carrington's plantation, asking him to meet me on the beach with a carriage tonight. If he is in residence, he will be there . . . if not, I will consider taking you to New York, but never England."

"Will you personally hand me over to Lucas Carrington?" she asked, hardly able to bear the thought of never seeing him again.

"Of course, my lady. I would never allow another to finish what I started. It was I who abducted you in the first place, it is I who will see that you are in safe hands."

"I never want to see you again. I will be glad to be rid of you," Season said softly.

"I am pained that you should say so, my lady. I will be sorry to be parted from you." Not allowing her time to reflect on his words, The Raven swept out of the cabin and locked the door behind him.

Season wiped the tears from her eyes and went about the cabin gathering up her meager belongings and try-tying them into a bundle. Soon the captain's cabin would show no trace that she had ever been its occupant, she thought sadly. She would be swept from The Raven's life and erased from his mind forever, but she knew she would never forget him.

Season knew deep in her heart that the man who had no name and no face would always be her one true love.

Chapter Eighteen

It was not yet dark when Season walked across the deck of the *Andromeda* for the last time. She saw The Raven waiting for her at the railing, and her heart seemed to rise into her throat. There seemed to be a tenseness about him, as if he couldn't wait to be rid of her.

Lady Season Chatsworth was proud, and she was determined she wouldn't let The Raven know that her heart was breaking. Although she wanted to beg him not to send her away, her feelings didn't show on her beautiful face. She had decided that if he didn't return her love she would be better off without him.

The only ones who seemed sorry to see her go were Briggs and James. She reached out her hand and James placed his in it. Pulling him into her arms, she felt tears run down her cheeks.

"Take care of yourself, James. I will miss you and all the wonderful times we spent together."

James raised sad eyes to her. "Nothing will be the

same without you, ma'am."

"I will think of you growing straight and tall, James, perhaps one day you will have your own ship."

Tears brightened James's eyes and he looked down at his feet. He sniffled and then muttered, "Goodbye, ma'am."

She gave him a smile and turned to Briggs. "I will miss you, Briggs, and the tender care you took of me. If you ever decide to give up the sea, I could always find a place for you in my service."

"If I ever gave up the sea, my lady, there is no one I'd rather serve than you."

On impulse she threw her arms about Briggs and gave him a kiss on the cheek. The first mate beamed brightly and cleared his throat. "The *Andromeda* just won't seem the same without you, my lady. The crew wonder if you would accept a small remembrance from them?"

Season looked up and saw that all the crew members had lined up behind the first mate. "What is it, Briggs?"

Briggs reached into a pouch, withdrew something, and held it out to her. "It's a wooden model of the *Andromeda,* my lady. We all sort of took turns at carving it."

Season took the beautiful carved likeness of the *Andromeda* and ran her hands lovingly over the figure-head of the raven in flight. "Thank you all so much," she said, as tears gathered in her eyes. "I will treasure this always. Whenever I look at this, I shall remember each and every one of you, and all your kindnesses to me."

Season knew if she didn't leave soon she could not

hold back her tears, and when she looked upon the faces of the crew members who had gathered about, she saw sadness in their eyes as well. She had come to know many of them so well, and they had always treated her with kindness and respect.

"I don't see Robert Wolf, Briggs. Tell him for me that I wish him well."

"I will do that right away, my lady," Briggs said in a strangled voice.

Season looked at the dark captain and could tell he was impatient to be off. With a nod of his head, he leaped over the side of the ship and descended into the longboat so he could assist her. Briggs helped her over the side and then she felt The Raven's hands about her waist. He seemed to suspend her in the air for a moment before he placed her in the boat.

Several crew members then scrambled down the rope ladder and soon began paddling toward the shore of Virginia.

Season watched the dense tree-lined forest draw closer with each wave that washed them toward the shore, and the nearer she got to land the heavier her heart became.

The Raven stood at the helm of the boat, looking at the coastline as if he were alert for trouble. Season realized the danger he was in should he be spotted by the enemy.

The evening breeze picked up his dark cloak and whipped it out behind him. Is he thinking about me? Season wondered. Could he be experiencing just the smallest regret at sending her away?

Sadly, Season looked back at the *Andromeda* when

the longboat scraped against the sand. The crew quickly secured the line, and The Raven stepped ashore and lifted Season into his arms.

When he set her on her feet, Season turned to him. He stood with his arms folded across his chest, silently observing her. She watched him turn to look down the beach and then at the distant forest. She knew he was wary of being caught on the shore.

The other crew members remained near the longboat while The Raven took Season's hand and led her farther up the sandy beach. When he released her hand he moved a few paces away from her.

Season closed her eyes, willing him to come to her and declare that he loved her. Surely he must feel something for her. It wasn't too late; he still had time to take her back to the *Andromeda*. Season heard him move, and in two long strides he was beside her.

"Someone is coming, my lady, I hear the sound of a horse and buggy," he said in his raspy voice.

She reached out her hand and placed it on his shoulder. "It isn't too late, Raven. You can still take me back to the ship with you," she said, forgetting her determination not to beg him.

"My lady, we said our goodbyes already. Do not make this harder than it has to be."

Season swallowed a sob. He could hardly wait to turn her over to Lucas Carrington. She could feel his haste to be gone. So be it, she thought. If he didn't want her, she could easily do without him.

Season heard the sound of horses' hooves, and a carriage came into sight on the rise just above them. She watched as the carriage door opened and a man stepped to the ground. As the newcomer drew near, she could see that it was indeed Lucas Carrington.

He seemed to ignore The Raven and walked hurriedly up to Season. "Are you hurt in any way, my lady?" he asked, his golden eyes full of concern.

Lucas Carrington was just as she remembered him, but perhaps not as arrogant as before. "I am well," she answered, feeling as if her heart had been ripped to shreds.

For the first time Lucas looked at The Raven, and Season could see the anger in his eyes. "Please take me away from here," she said in a pleading voice, fearing there would be trouble between the two men.

Lucas' golden eyes swept her face for just a moment before he turned back to the hooded man. "You will pay for this, Raven. There is nowhere you can hide from the hangman's noose," Lucas said in a low, menacing voice.

The Raven merely laughed. "It will take a better man than you to catch me, Carrington."

Season watched the man she loved walk away without a backward glance. When he reached his men, he bowed gracefully to Season and leaped into the longboat. "Goodbye, my lady. God be with you," he called out, as the boat caught the waves and headed back to the *Andromeda*.

Season felt a burning behind her eyes and turned her back. No one would ever know that she had just died a little inside.

Lucas Carrington took her arm and led her toward the waiting carriage. "Let's get you home, my lady. My sister is most anxious to welcome you."

Season turned her head for one last look at the long-boat which was already halfway to the *Andromeda*. She could hardly make out the dark, cloaked figure that stood at the helm. He was leaving her life as suddenly as he had entered it, and she had the feeling that she would never see him again.

Lucas assisted her into the coach, and Season sank down on the red Moroccan leather seat. A hasty order was given to the coachman, and they started off, the wheels of the coach spraying the loose powdery sand in its wake.

Season folded her hands in her lap and gazed up at Lucas to find that he was watching her with his disturbing golden eyes.

"I am sorry to be an inconvenience to you, Mr. Carrington, but I had very little say in this matter."

Lucas could see that Lady Season Chatsworth was very different from the young girl he had met at the ball in New York. Where once her skin had been white and creamy, it now had taken on a golden hue. There was also a new sadness about her that tugged at his heart.

"I can assure you, my lady, that you are most welcome in my home. My sister and myself are only too happy to place ourselves at your disposal. Should there be any way I can be of service to you, you have only to ask."

"You are most kind, sir."

"Not at all. I know you have been through a long ordeal, but I wonder if you feel up to answering a few questions for me? It would be best to answer while the incident is still fresh in your mind."

"I . . . am fine, but I don't know what I can tell you

312

that would be of any help," she answered, knowing he wanted her to tell him about The Raven.

"But surely you will be able to help us, my lady. You have been a captive of The Raven for over three months. We will be anxious for you to tell us anything that might help us find him."

Season hesitated. She knew she had no reason to be loyal to The Raven or his crew. He was an enemy of her people, and yet she couldn't bring herself to speak against him. "I am afraid I can be of little help to you. For the most part I was confined to a cabin."

"You must have some clue to The Raven's identity. I wouldn't press you this way, but time is of the essence."

"No, I never saw him unmasked. Sometimes he wore a leather hood and at other times he wore a leather helm. I haven't the slightest notion who he could be."

"What about the crew? Surely you could give me some of their names. Anything would be of help."

Season thought of Briggs and James. She couldn't bring herself to betray their identities. She would never forgive herself if anything she said to Lucas Carrington helped the authorities to establish their identities.

"I am truly sorry, Mr. Carrington. I can tell you nothing at all."

"Perhaps you would be willing to tell General Clinton what you observed," he suggested.

"I will be able to tell him nothing more than I have told you. Forgive me, Mr. Carrington."

He smiled kindly. "I must be a brute to grill you this way. You are tired now. Perhaps when you have had time to rest you will begin to remember something that will help us."

Oh, yes. I am tired, Season thought as she leaned her head back and closed her eyes. She hadn't realized how exhausted she was until Mr. Carrington had mentioned that she had been aboard the *Andromeda* for three months. Time hadn't existed for her while she had been at sea. She reflected on how strange it was that in such a short period she had become an entirely different person. Right now nothing seemed important to her. Perhaps one day she would begin to feel alive again, but not now. The hurt was still too new.

Season opened her eyes and found Lucas Carrington staring at her. His probing golden eyes disturbed her so she gazed out the window. Most probably he was wondering, as everyone else surely would, whether she had been ravished by The Raven.

She searched for something to say to him that would end the uncomfortable silence between them. "You once told me Virginia was lovely, Mr. Carrington. I never expected I would be seeing it for myself."

"Did I exaggerate?"

Season looked out the window of the coach at the lovely tree-lined roadside. In the green meadows they were passing, wild flowers of every color and description were in full bloom. She felt a pang of homesickness for Chatsworth.

"No, you most certainly didn't exaggerate, Mr. Carrington. Your Virginia is very much like the part of England which I call home."

"If you will look to your left, my lady, you will see our destination."

Suddenly the trees thinned and Season saw a village in the distance. The carriage turned up a lane that led in that direction. "I thought you told me you lived on a plantation, Mr. Carrington."

"And so I do. Our American plantations are very like small villages, my lady. They are self-sustaining. We have our own blacksmith shop, storehouse, barns, and stables. To your right you will see the weaver's house, and to your left are the slave quarters. As you can see, we are pretty much cut off from the rest of the world, so we have to be self-sufficient."

"Are there no nearby towns or villages?"

"The closest would be Williamsburg. It is a good two-day ride."

Season turned back to Lucas. "Again I would like to apologize for being inflicted on you. If I can get in touch with my cousin, Edmund, I will not long test your hospitality."

His golden eyes rested on her face. "I can assure you that you will be most welcome. In fact my sister, Rebecca, will be overjoyed to have you stay with us. She is about your age and is starved for female companionship."

"You are very kind, sir."

Lucas saw tears in Season's emerald-colored eyes before she quickly looked away. "Why do you cry, my lady?" he asked softly.

"Forgive me, but you are so kind. I hate women who cry, don't you?" she asked, dabbing at her eyes. "It is not habitual with me, I promise you."

Lucas reached out with his gloved hand and pushed a golden curl from her face. "Have you suffered a great deal?"

Season smiled through her tears, warming to the

concern she heard in his voice. "I wouldn't want you to think I have been beaten or abused. I was not treated unkindly. I suppose I just have to make an adjustment. For so long I have been confined to a small cabin, but now, suddenly, I can have all the space I want. I can tell you one thing, no one will ever lock me in a room again. I detest being locked up."

"You have changed, my lady."

"I suppose I have grown up a great deal in the last three months."

He smiled. "I cannot see that you have aged a day since I saw you last."

Season could feel herself beginning to relax. Lucas Carrington was easy to talk to, and she could tell he was trying to make her feel at home.

"If you will look off to your right, my lady, you will see Rosemont."

Season looked out the window and saw a majestic brick colonial mansion sitting atop a gentle sloping hill. At one time the bricks must have been red, but over the years they had mellowed to a soft pink color. At the bottom of the hill there was a river, and behind it a heavily wooded area. There were plowed fields, and several blooded horses frolicked in green meadows.

Season looked at Lucas. "I have the feeling that this was untamed land which has been carved out of the wilderness. The soil is new and the very air we are breathing is young. I have the strangest feeling that this land will one day be a great country. How could it help but be, for there are unlimited resources here. Someday this land will be a country apart from England. For the first time I begin to realize what the colonists have been fighting for."

Lucas gave her a quizzical glance. "Careful, my lady, you speak treason," he said, smiling slightly.

"Perhaps I am beginning to see what The Raven was trying to tell me. This land shouldn't belong to England. It should belong to the ones who were born here—those who have cleared and worked the land, and those whose mothers and fathers are buried here."

"Are these the views of The Raven?"

"He never actually said this to me, but I know that is what he is fighting for."

Season didn't realize the carriage had come to a halt until Lucas reached over and opened the door. "I think it would not be well for you to voice your newly formed opinions too freely, my lady. There are those who will not understand what you are saying."

"Do you understand, Mr. Carrington?"

He got out of the carriage and helped Season alight before he answered her.

"I understand, my lady, but I don't altogether agree with you."

"Strange, isn't it, that I am taking the stand you should be taking, Mr. Carrington, while you are defending England as I should be doing?"

Lucas smiled, "It's a strange world we live in." He took her hand and helped her up the steps. "Welcome to Rosemont, my lady."

Before they reached the entrance, a young woman rushed out the front door. She hesitated for a moment and then rushed forward to embrace Season.

"I am glad you are here. Since Lucas and I found out you were coming, I have been watching the road." She looked a little uneasy, and Season could tell she was thinking she had been too forward. "I suppose I should call you, your ladyship, shouldn't I?"

"My lady, this impulsive young woman is my sister, Rebecca. Rebecca, Lady Season Chatsworth."

Season smiled warmly. The girl was so lovely. She had the same black hair as her brother, but where as his eyes were golden in color, the girl's were a soft brown. "I am delighted to meet you, Rebecca. I hope you will feel you can call me Season."

"Oh, I could never call you by your name. I don't think Lucas would approve."

Season laughed delightedly. "The permission is mine to give, and I insist you call me Season."

Rebecca looked doubtfully at her brother and then smiled. "All right, Season," she said, linking her arm through her new friend's. "Are you tired, hungry, thirsty?"

Season smiled. "Yes, all of those."

Rebecca led her into the house. "The first thing we must do is to get you settled. Follow me upstairs and I will show you to your room. I think you will like it since it faces the back of the house which is much quieter and you will have a good view of the river. Did you bring any trunks? No. How foolish of me, of course you didn't," Rebecca said, flushing slightly. "Lucas said I wasn't to say anything about your being kidnapped, and you are hardly here a minute and I have already made a fool of myself."

"It's all right, Rebecca, don't concern yourself. I think you are very charming."

"I am rambling like a magpie . . . it's just that I am so

318

happy you are going to be staying at Rosemont."

Lucas smiled at his sister indulgently. "You will have to excuse Rebecca, my lady. I warned you she would be glad to see you."

He handed Season's bundle of clothing to his sister and bowed slightly. "I will leave the two of you to get acquainted. I have an errand to run. Don't expect me back until the dinner hour."

"Don't be late, Lucas. Ruthy is preparing chicken and dumplings," his sister called after him.

Rebecca showed Season to the lovely room she would be staying in. There was a soft blue rug on the floor and the big fourposter bed had cream and blue bed coverings. The walls were covered in cream-colored silk; the soft curtains at the window were ice blue. Season was surprised to find such luxury in this yet undeveloped land. Yet all the rooms she had seen had been elegantly furnished, and the house had a warm feeling.

"Would you like to lie down and rest awhile?" Rebecca asked.

"No, but I would like something cool to drink," Season told her.

Rebecca directed the maid to put away Season's few belongings and she led the way downstairs.

Season and Rebecca sat on the veranda where the cool May breeze stirred the leaves of the budding dog-wood trees. They found many things to talk about. They spoke of fashion and travel. Rebecca wanted to know all about Season's home in England and what it was like growing up in a castle. Season was beginning to like Rebecca very much.

It soon became apparent that Rebecca had purposely not brought up the matter of her kidnapping, but Season, who had never had a friend, felt the need to talk to someone about her ordeal.

"Rebecca, there is no reason to avoid discussing my kidnapping. In fact I think it might help if you would allow me to talk about it."

Rebecca reached out and took Season's hand. "I wouldn't want to do anything that would upset you. Lucas would be angry with me if I were to ply you with questions."

"I believe you and I are friends, Rebecca. Please don't feel that you have to watch what you say around me."

"Was it very bad for you, being The Raven's captive?" Rebecca asked, her soft brown eyes shining with sympathy.

"At first I was very frightened, but three months is a long time—in my case it seemed like a lifetime. After a while, I came to love the sea."

"It must have been just awful. In your place I would have been terrified."

"At times it was very bad. During a horrible storm, I feared the ship would sink."

"I hate storms and I would hate them even more at sea."

"It wasn't a pleasant experience."

"Season, when the man—The Raven's first mate—came to our door to tell Lucas and I The Raven was turning you over to us, he said he had a message from

Robert Wolf. Is it true that Robert is alive? Did you see him on the *Andromeda?*"

"Yes, I did. I wasn't aware that you knew Robert."

"He is a neighbor of ours. I have been worried sick about him. His family hasn't heard from him in over a year. It has been longer than that since I heard from him."

"I talked to Captain Wolf many times. He was held captive by a pirate named De Fores until The Raven rescued him. He was ill for a time, but when last I saw him he had recovered very nicely."

Rebecca's eyes grew misty with tears. "Are you sure Robert is all right? I have been half out of my mind with worry over him."

"Yes, I promise you he is well. You seem to be very fond of him."

"I have known Robert all my life. I cannot remember a time when I didn't love him."

Season looked at Rebecca's midnight black hair and knew that she was the one Robert had spoken of with such feeling. She smiled. "Robert spoke of you—yes. You are the young woman he told me about aboard the *Andromeda.* Did Robert ever call you funny face?"

"That was always his nickname for me. What did he say about me?" Rebecca asked eagerly.

"I don't think it would be fair to him if I repeated what he said, do you?" Season teased.

"Oh, please tell me, Season. Did he say he liked me or did he call me a pest as he always did to my face?"

"I think I will tell you. After all, it's only right that we females stick together."

"Don't tease me, Season. Tell me what Robert said,"

she begged.

"I want to get this straight now," Season said thoughtfully. "He said when he thought he was going to die and it was too painful to go on, he thought of dark hair and soft brown eyes. He said he thought of his love, knowing he couldn't die until he told her he loved her. He said he had watched her bloom and grow."

Rebecca placed her hands to her flushed cheeks. "Could it be me he spoke of? Suppose he spoke of another. I have waited all my life for him to love me. Yes, he spoke of me, because he once told me that he had watched me bloom and grow. Season, Robert loves me! Why has he never told me?"

"I should not have told you, Rebecca. He will want to tell you himself."

"No, I'm glad you did. Now I can be ready for him when he comes home. You said he was ill. Are you quite sure he has recovered?"

"Yes, Rebecca, I would not have told you that if it weren't true."

"When will he be home? When can I see him? His note told me only that he would see me soon."

"He told me he had to report to your Congress before he came home."

"I am deliriously happy. Surely it won't be too long until I see him." Suddenly Rebecca's face whitened. "He isn't being held prisoner by that awful Raven, is he?"

"No. From what I understand Robert and The Raven are good friends."

"Many people whisper about The Raven. Some say he is a patriot, and others claim he is a pirate. I am appalled by what he did to you. I would be frightened to meet him in the flesh, but I will always be grateful to him for rescuing Robert for me."

"Grateful to whom, funny face? Did I just hear my name mentioned?"

Season watched Rebecca's cheeks redden when Robert Wolf walked up the steps to the veranda. Seeing the hunger in his eyes when he looked at the young girl, Season excused herself and went into the house so the two of them could be alone. She doubted that either of them were aware that she had left.

"Robert, you are safe. You are here!" Rebecca cried, taking a timid step in his direction.

"Are you glad to see me?" he asked in a deep voice.

"I shouldn't admit it, but yes, yes, Robert, I am very glad you are here."

He took her hand and pulled her into his arms. "I made myself a promise some time back that if I were ever fortunate enough to see you again, I wouldn't rest until you became my wife, funny face."

Rebecca raised her face to Robert's and he kissed her softly. He quickly broke off the kiss and smiled down at her. "I am glad to see you, funny face," he said softly.

"I have waited a long time for you to admit that you love me, Robert. You just asked me to marry you, but I didn't hear you say anything about love."

He lightly thumped her nose. "I love you, funny face. Yours is the first face I want to see when I get up in the morning and the last I want to see at night. Will you marry me, Rebecca?"

Her dark eyes lit with happiness. "We will have to get Lucas' approval."

Robert kissed the tip of her nose. "You just leave your brother to me. He will probably think I am doing him a favor by taking you off his hands."

She giggled delightedly. "That may very well be, but you are never going to get me off your hands."

He drew her tightly against him. "As if I would want to. Even now I am anxious to have you tied to me by marriage. I will ask Lucas for your hand as soon as possible."

The enamored pair kissed, both glorying in their newly confessed love.

Season saw that the door to the library was ajar, so she wandered into the room. There were bookshelves all the way to the ceiling, so she walked along a wall, looking at book titles. The afternoon had turned quite chilly, and she noticed there was a warm fire burning in the marble fireplace. It made the room warm and inviting.

"Do you perhaps read, my lady?"

Season jumped guiltily as if she had been caught doing something wrong. "I . . . yes. I know it isn't considered fashionable for a woman to read, but my brain would go stale if I were denied the privilege of reading."

She looked into Lucas Carrington's golden eyes and saw amusement there. She didn't think what she had said was particularly amusing. "I apologize for coming into your sanctuary uninvited. When my father was home, I was never permitted in the library unless he summoned me."

"That rule does not hold true here at Rosemont, my lady. You are welcome in this room, or in any other room you choose to enter."

"I find myself in your debt, Mr. Carrington."

"Not at all, my lady," he said, bowing gallantly.

"There is yet another favor I would ask of you, sir. You and your sister have been so kind to me, would you think it unseemly if we were to be on a first-name basis? I would hope that you might call me Season. 'My lady' seems so stuffy and formal." In truth, when Lucas Carrington called her "my lady," it reminded her too much of The Raven.

Amusement laced his golden gaze. "Done, Season. Now I would ask a boon of you."

She smiled prettily, as if she knew what was on his mind. "Yes, Mr. Carrington?"

"I would deem it an honor if you would call me Lucas. Dare I hope that you will do that."

"Done, Lucas."

"What kind of books do you prefer to read, Season?"

"I find I have an insatiable appetite for almost any reading matter, although I admit to being a romantic at heart. Your library is quite extensive. It's much larger than the one at Chatsworth."

"Do you still miss your home? I remember when we talked at the ball, you were homesick."

"I . . . so much has happened since then, Mr.— Lucas. I don't really know where my home is."

His brilliant eyes glinted. "I hope you will think of Rosemont as your home."

"It is a very lovely home. You live very graciously, Lucas, but I do not belong here. What will become of me?"

Lucas took her hand and led her over to the sofa. "You have but to tell me what your wish is, and I will try to fulfill it, Season. Should you wish to return to England, I will arrange it. Should you prefer to return to New York, I will immediately send word to Edmund that you are staying with me. I feel sure he would come to Rosemont as soon as he could get away."

Season shook her head. "Poor Edmund, I had almost forgotten about him."

Lucas took her hand. "If it is your wish, you are welcome to remain at Rosemont until you are stronger and can decide what you want to do."

"Why are you being so kind to me, Lucas?"

He was quiet for a moment, as if trying to decide how to answer her. "Perhaps I feel responsible for you. Let's say that I would like to make up to you for what a fellow countryman has caused you to suffer."

"I don't know how you can say that. I most certainly do not hold you responsible for what has happened to me. I hold no one to blame."

"Not even The Raven?"

"Him least of all."

Lucas' eyes narrowed. "You have every reason to hate that man, and yet I get the feeling you do not. You must be a very forgiving woman, Season."

"Hate is a very strong emotion. There are those who say love and hate are but a hair's-breadth apart. I think

326

they may be right."

"I am not sure I understand you."

Season smiled and stood up. "I have taken up enough of your time. I thank you for the offer to stay at Rosemont. I believe I would like to remain here for a time. I don't really want to see anybody right now."

"Does that include my cousin, Edmund?"

"Especially Edmund. I don't expect you to understand, but I don't want to face him for a while."

"Some things do not have to be explained, Season. I will see that your wishes are honored . . . if I can. Edmund can be very insistent at times."

"I will leave you in peace," she said, smiling. Somehow his kindness made her want to cry.

Lucas watched her leave, and then he sat down at his desk and began shuffling through the mounds of paperwork that needed his attention. After a while he pushed the papers aside, realizing he couldn't concentrate on them.

The Lady Season Chatsworth seemed to be weaving a spell about him. He envisioned her sad green eyes, and he wished he could make them light up with happiness. Would it be possibloe for him to make her smile? Lucas thought of his cousin, Edmund, and knew he would be coming to Rosemont as soon as he discovered where Lady Season was.

"Damn," he said, standing up and stalking out of the room. He had many things to attend to, and he couldn't afford to have a woman stand in the way of his plans.

As Season walked out onto the veranda and gazed

into the distance, a feeling of peace descended on her. This was a lovely land, and there was excitement in the air here.

Perhaps in this new land she would be able to find herself. Perhaps she would be revived and reborn here in this Virginia.

Chapter Nineteen

As Season hooked the neck of her green gown, she wished she had something else to wear. She had worn her three gowns so often that they were all badly faded. She longed for her diamond and emerald necklace—it would at least brighten her appearance—but she knew she had left it in Maude's bedroom the night De Fores had come for her.

Sweeping her hair to the top of her head, Season secured her golden curls with two ivory combs. Standing back, she observed her image in the mirror, not at all pleased with her shabby appearance.

When Season entered the sitting room to join the Carringtons, she found Rebecca kneeling in front of her brother with her arms around his neck. When they saw Season, they both stood, and Rebecca ran to Season.

"You will never believe what has happened, Season. Robert has asked for my hand in marriage and my brother has given his consent!"

Season laughed delightedly and hugged the young girl. "Somehow I am not in the least surprised. I am so happy for you. Where is Robert? I would like to congratulate him. I believe he is getting a jewel for a wife."

"He had to leave for Philadelphia, but he promised to return to me very soon."

Lucas draped his arm about his sister's shoulders and hugged her to him. "I will be glad when Robert takes you of my hands, minx. I have little doubt you will lead poor old Robert a merry chase."

Rebecca laid her head against her brother's shoulder and smiled up at him. "You will miss me and you know it. Who but I would put up with you?"

"You are right," he said, kissing her cheek. "I shall miss you sorely even though you will be living only a short distance away."

Season felt warmed by the love brother and sister had for each other. She wondered, had her own brother lived, if he and she would have been as close as Lucas and Rebecca Carrington.

"Please come and sit beside me, Season," Rebecca said, steering her to the sofa. "Dinner will be ready in half an hour."

When Season was seated, she looked at Lucas, who was leaning against the mantel. His eyes rested on her, and something in their golden depths disturbed her. She was relieved when Rebecca drew her attention away from her brother.

"I do wish Robert could have stayed for dinner tonight. I hope he will not be away long," Rebecca stated.

"Robert will envy me for having the two most beautiful women in the Colonies to myself tonight," Lucas said, seating himself on a chair.

"Not the Colonies, Lucas. The United States of America." Rebecca corrected him.

Lucas shrugged his shoulders. "What's in a name, my dear sister?"

Rebecca turned to Season. "You see before you a house divided. "I am a staunch supporter of Congress and General Washington, while my brother leans more to the side of your King George. But our differences have not affected our relationship, Season, and I hope politics won't come between you and I."

Season laughed. "If you can suffer the presence of one of King George's subjects under your roof as well as you tolerate your brother's politics, I will be glad to be your friend."

Rebecca laughed delightedly. "I just knew we would be friends the moment I saw you."

Season looked at Lucas and found he was still watching her. "I am aware that Robert is a patriot, Lucas, and yet the two of you are friends. How can that be?"

Lucas looked deeply into Season's eyes. "My friendship with Robert spans many years. We try never to discuss our politics because we learned years ago that we didn't agree on the subject. You may have already learned that my sister has no sympathy for my convictions. She is a true patriot—she and I never discuss politics either."

"What a strange country. A Tory can live in harmony beside the Whig, and in your case under the same roof," Season observed. "I wonder if this could happen anywhere else in the world?"

"Our countrymen do not always get along, and there has been much bloodshed between the two parties, but you will have to remember, be we Tory or Whig, we are all Americans first. My brother thinks the English are the best hope for the future of our country, while I feel the opposite is true. I certainly do not mean to offend you; I simply do not think of you as English, but as my friend."

"Rebecca, you might be surprised to learn that our guest shares many of your own views about the Colonies. Only today I heard her voice opinions much like your own," Lucas said lazily. He smiled at Season.

"Is that true, Season?" the young girl asked.

"Don't misunderstand me. Like you, my first loyalty will always be to my country. I just happen to think the Colonies should have the freedom to govern themselves. I find this a new and exciting land. I sincerely believe America is headed for greatness."

Lucas said nothing, but his eyes seemed to soften as they rested on Season's face.

Rebecca stood up and clapped her hands together. "We think very much alike, Season. Now if we could only convert my brother to our side."

Season smiled at Lucas. "I think perhaps your brother will never allow a woman's opinion to sway him."

Lucas lowered his lashes. "I don't know, my lady. Perhaps you could." Before Season had time to reply, Lucas rose and extended his arms to both ladies. "Quinton just gave the signal that dinner is ready. Poor Robert, having to rush off to Philadelphia while I entertain a Tory and a Whig at my dinner table," he said in an amused voice.

The conversation seemed to flow at dinner. The surroundings were elegant and the food was well prepared. It was quite apparent to Season that the Carringtons were a very wealthy family.

Season learned that Rebecca's and Lucas' mother and father had died ten years ago from a yellow fever epidemic that had swept the valley where Rosemont was situated. At a very early age Lucas had taken over the running of the huge plantation, and he had obviously made it prosper.

During dinner, Season was often aware that Lucas was watching her, and she felt uncomfortable under his golden gaze. She remembered the first time she had met him; at that time she had experienced the same reaction to him. He was a very handsome man, and she did not doubt that he knew it. He had most probably been spoiled by the attention he received from eager young women. She was surprised that he had not already taken a wife, but she thought that perhaps he did have someone in mind to be mistress to Rosemont.

After dinner they adjourned to the sitting room. At first Lucas and Season listened while Rebecca played the spinet, but soon they joined in and raised their voices in song. As Lucas and Season sang an old Irish ballad, their voices blended sweetly. Season was a soprano, while Lucas' voice was deep and clear.

Green is the color of my true love's eyes.
Green are the hills where my sweet love lies.
Dark is the ship that will carry me away.

Blue will be the sky on our wedding day.

As the last haunting note of the ballad vibrated in the air, a lump rose in Season's throat. She found she couldn't look into Lucas' eyes because she knew he would be watching her closely. Some current flowed between them. She didn't know what it was, but she knew that Lucas was aware of it also. Whatever it was, it made her feel uneasy, for she couldn't put a name to the feeling.

So beautifully had Season's and Lucas' voices blended that Rebecca felt tears in her eyes. "That was so very lovely. It was as if the two of you were meant to sing together," Rebecca said, wiping her eyes. "Never have I heard anything sound so beautiful."

Lucas then did something that startled and troubled Season. He touched her face softly and tilted her chin up. "Were we meant to . . . sing together, my lady?"

"I have never sung with anyone before. I found it a pleasant . . . experience."

Lucas laughed and moved to the sofa. When he sat down, Rebecca seated herself beside him, leaning her head against his shoulder.

Once more Season could feel the love in this house and the closeness between brother and sister. Love was something she knew very little about. Her first experience with man-woman love had ended in heartbreak. Somewhere upon the sea, the *Andromeda* sailed with her dark master at the helm. Did he think of her? Did he miss her just a little? She doubted that he gave her more than a passing thought.

"I want to inform you ladies that I will be leaving

first thing in the morning," Lucas said. "I am going to New York, Season. While there I will speak to Edmund about you and tell him it is your wish to remain at Rosemont for a time."

Season frowned, wishing Edmund did not have to be informed of her whereabouts. She had no desire to return to New York, nor did she want to think about getting married. She wanted to be given time to heal from her hurts.

"Season, have you a message you would like me to pass on to Edmund?" Lucas asked.

"N-no, as you are aware I hardly know Edmund. I would, however, like to ask a favor of you, if you won't find it too inconvenient."

"I am at your command. You have only to ask," Lucas said in a deep voice.

"I would like very much to remain here at Rosemont for a time, as you suggested I might."

"As I told you earlier, you are welcome to stay as long as you like," Lucas replied. "You will be glad for Season's company, won't you, minx?"

"Yes, please stay with me," Rebecca added. "I will love having you with me. You can help me plan my wedding. Lucas says I am to spare no expense on my trousseau, and I would welcome your advice."

"I can hardly say no to such a charming offer. I think it will be fun to help you with your wedding." Season lapsed into silence, remembering the time at Chatsworth when she had been forced to plan her own wedding to Lord Ransford.

"There is something else on your mind," Lucas observed.

Season stood up and leaned against the spinet. "Yes, would you mind? . . . I hardly know how to ask this because you may think it very forward of me."

"Nothing you could ask of me would be too forward, my lady," Lucas told her gallantly.

"Thank you," she said in a small voice. "My maid, Molly, is staying with the Tibbs, I know she will be half out of her mind with worry. Would it be possible for her to . . . would you mind if she came to Rosemont?"

Lucas rose to his feet and went to Season's side. "I will see to her travel arrangements personally," he answered. Taking her hand he raised it to his lips, and Season felt a tremor shake her body. She was bewildered. Why did she feel drawn to Lucas Carrington? What would happen to her if she became drawn to every handsome man she met? She remembered Molly once telling her about women who handed their favors out to every available man. Was she like that? She wouldn't allow herself to look at Lucas, fearing he would read her thoughts. She stared at his long lean fingers and wondered what it would feel like to be caressed by him.

Season swallowed deeply and freed her hand from his. "If you will excuse me, I will wish you a good-night and a safe journey."

Lucas watched Season rush from the room, knowing he was drawn to her. It was more than her beauty and kindness that touched his heart. Obviously she had been deeply affected by her capture, and he wanted to help her heal.

Rebecca came up beside her brother and looked into his face. "I just love Season, Lucas. Tonight I realized you like her too. Wouldn't it be wonderful if you and she—"

"Don't be a fool, Rebecca," Lucas broke in. "The Lady Season Chatsworth was not meant for a Virginia planter. She was born to grace a wealthy man's castle."

"Edmund is not wealthy, nor does he have a castle," she reminded him.

"She will never marry Edmund," Lucas whispered, a faraway look in his eyes.

The weeks passed quickly as Season and Rebecca became better acquainted. Season had never before had a close friend, and at first, it had been difficult for her to talk about herself to Rebecca. But Rebecca's sunny disposition and her kindness soon drew Season out.

Sometimes they would ride across the plantation and take a picnic lunch to eat beneath a tree. At others they would take long walks and talk about the nonsensical things that interest very young women. And, of course, the two of them spent hours with the dressmaker who was making Rebecca's trousseau.

At Rebecca's insistence, the dressmaker had also made Season several gowns and a riding habit. One of the gowns was a plain gray cotton with black lace at the hem of the skirt and the edges of the puffed sleeves. Another was a green satin with a lace overskirt, for evening wear. Season had insisted on paying for her own gowns. She had paid the seamstress with the gold piece The Raven had given her that day on the beach when he'd said he wanted to buy her thoughts.

Meanwhile Season was growing to love Rosemont. Rebecca had told her that Lucas' grandfather and grandmother had settled here, cleared the land, and built the house after moving to Virginia from England. Now, even though there was a war going on, Virginia seemed to thrive. Rosemont's fields were planted with cotton, tobacco, and corn; and each day Season could hear the field hands singing on their way to work. Rebecca had mentioned that a very able overseer looked after the plantation since Lucas was gone so much of the time.

As time passed Season found she could tell Rebecca many things about her capture, but she couldn't bring herself to tell her about The Raven or that she loved him.

One evening Rebecca walked into Season's bedroom, pulling on her lace gloves. Season was wearing her new green evening gown and she turned around, presenting herself for Rebecca's inspection.

"My, but you do look beautiful. All the men at the ball are going to swarm around you tonight." Rebecca beamed.

"Pity Robert cannot see you, Rebecca. You are simply breathtaking."

Rebecca sat down on the edge of the bed and watched her maid, Drucilla, arrange Season's hair. "Season, my brother told me before he left that it might be wise to introduce you to everyone as Mistress Season Chatsworth without revealing the fact that your father is a duke. He thought it might save you the trouble of having to answer a lot of questions. Would you have any objections?"

"No. The reasoning is sound. Tell me, what are your neighbors like?"

"The host and hostess are the Bartletts. They have a son who is Lucas' age, but he may not be home since he is in the army. He is an aide to General Washington. Their daughter, Marlana Bartlett, is blond and pretty. She has had her eye on Lucas for a long time. Mrs. Bartlett would like nothing better than to see her become the mistress of Rosemont. She is very sure that will come about one day. Aside from that, tonight should be fun, and I hope you enjoy yourself, Season."

"The only gala I have been to since I came to America is the ball I attended in New York."

"You will find tonight quite different, I'm sure. After all, this is a country affair. Still, people will be dressed in a very grand manner, and most of them will even have their hair powdered. I don't ever powder my hair; Lucas doesn't like it."

Season remembered The Raven once asking her never to powder her hair. She looked at the box of powder that Drucilla held in her hand, and shook her head. "I find having my hair powdered very tedious. I do not want it powdered tonight, Drucilla."

"Oh dear, look at the time. We are going to be late!" Rebecca cried, rising from the bed.

Rebecca introduced Season to many of her neighbors, and Season found them to be very gracious. She danced the minuet with several young American officers and wondered why she felt years older than them.

The dining room table was laden with food, but Season took only a few bites of the meat and none of the vegetables. When desert was served, she declined it altogether. Rebecca spent a good deal of time with Season because she realized her friend was alone in a strange land.

She realized that the music and laughter didn't seem to reach Season who seemed to be standing apart from the festivities—an onlooker. She was always polite when spoken to, but rarely contributed to the conversation.

While Season and Rebecca were watching the dancers, having both just declined to dance, Marlana Bartlett came up beside them and looked Season over from head to toe. Season smiled at the girl, thinking she was very pretty, but she got no answering smile in return.

"Tell me, Miss Chatsworth," Marlana asked, "why is it that you are visiting Virginia?"

Rebecca quickly intervened. "Season is a friend of the family, and Lucas and I urged her to spend some time with us at Rosemont."

Marlana's crystal blue eyes took on a guarded look. "I was not aware that you were acquainted with anyone from England, Rebecca. I know your brother's friends are mostly English, but I thought you were against the British, as are most of us in this room."

Season gasped at the underhanded insult that had just been dealt her, and she looked to Rebecca for guidance. Before Rebecca could reply, Marlana's mother joined the conversation.

"I was certainly not aware that you were from

England, Mistress Chatsworth."

"La, Mother, how could you miss it? Have you not listened to the fancy way she speaks? If she doesn't come from England, it's a safe bet that she was educated in England."

"You have a good ear, Mistress Bartlett, and you are quite right. I have only recently come from England," Season put in. "I find I like your lovely country very much." She had seen the fire in Rebecca's eyes and had realized that her friend was ready to do battle on her behalf. But Season didn't want to be the cause of Rebecca having trouble with her neighbors.

"*My* country!" Marlana said sarcastically. "You English are determined that the United States will remain under *your* domination."

Season's face whitened, and she saw the satisfied smile on Marlana's mother's face. Not knowing what to say, she turned to Rebecca.

"If you insult my friend, Marlana, then you insult my brother and me as well," Rebecca warned.

"Just how good a friend is she, Rebecca?" Marlana wanted to know. "Is she your friend or your brother's?"

Rebecca realized that the angry glint in Marlana's eyes indicated jealousy, and she was about to voice that opinion when a deep voice spoke up from behind her.

"Season happens to be a friend to us both," Lucas Carrington drawled.

Four pair of eyes fastened on Lucas as he slipped his arm about his sister's waist and took Season's hand in his. His eyes sought Marlana's.

"It is very kind of you, Marlana, to make our guest feel so at home," he said, raising an eyebrow.

Marlana lowered her lashes, mortified because Lucas had overheard the conversation, but she managed to recover quickly.

"Lucas, you awful man, I am so happy to see you, even though you have neglected me shamefully." With a pout on her pretty mouth, she moved to his side, stood on her tiptoes, and kissed him boldly on the lips.

Lucas smiled. "I find it amazing that you are still single, Marlana. How can it be that some young gentleman hasn't already made you his wife? You are far too beautiful to remain unmarried for so long."

"She's waiting for you," Rebecca mumbled under her breath, so only her brother could hear. Lucas arched an eyebrow at his sister and a slight smile touched his lips as his hand tightened on Season's.

Marlana pulled on Lucas' arm, forcing him to release Season's hand. "Come and dance with me, Lucas. It's been simply ages since we danced together."

"How remiss of me, Marlana," he said, leading her to the dance floor.

"Don't they look well suited?" Mrs. Bartlett said, glancing pointedly at Season.

"Indeed they do, ma'am," Season agreed, and Mrs. Bartlett walked away with a satisfied smile on her face.

"If Lucas isn't careful, that witch will get her claws into him," Rebecca observed.

"I had the mistaken impression that you and Mistress Bartlett were friends, Rebecca."

"No, she has never been a friend of mine. All she ever wants is to get Lucas to propose to her so she can get her hands on Rosemont."

Season looked at Lucas Carrington. He seemed to

stand out from all the other men. Like many of the other gentlemen in the room, he didn't wear knee breeches, but was dressed in gray pantaloons tucked into black boots. His matching jacket was unbuttoned, revealing the white lawn shirt beneath, and his black hair was neatly tied back in a queue. He was tall, handsome, and very male.

"A woman would have to be blind to want to marry your brother only to get her hands on your plantation. No. I do not believe for one moment that Mistress Bartlett could only be thinking of Rosemont, Rebecca."

"I want to apologize to you for her shameful behavior. She is just jealous. She thinks Lucas is interested in you. I hope Lucas doesn't tell her that you are engaged to marry cousin Edmund. I would enjoy watching her suffer."

"She is very lovely. Do you think Lucas is interested in her?"

"Who can say with Lucas? As far back as I can remember he has had women chasing after him, but I do not believe his heart has ever been engaged by any of them. I cannot say how he feels about Marlana, but if she had her way they would be married tomorrow."

Season sighed. "One thing is certain; Mistress Bartlett and her mother are not overly fond of me."

"Of course not. You are beautiful, and they are afraid that Lucas is interested in you."

"Oh, surely you are mistaken. They couldn't think that. I hope you will set them straight on that point," Season said, feeling distressed.

Rebecca laughed delightedly. "No, I don't think I will. It would be much nicer to see them both squirm a bit. I have no fondness for either of them."

"You are a minx, just as your brother says. I wonder if Robert knows what he's getting himself into with you."

"I would be a fool to let him know my true self until I have him hooked good and proper." Rebecca laughed.

Season laughed too, and both girls turned to watch Lucas lead Marlana off the dance floor and over to the punch bowl. Season watched Lucas smile as Marlana Bartlett placed a hand on his shoulder. It seemed to Season that he liked the woman a great deal. She wondered why that thought bothered her.

A short time later Lucas excused himself from Marlana and crossed the room to Season and his sister. Taking Season's hand, he bowed to her.

"I have done my duty by dancing with the hostess' daughter. Now I wonder if you would honor me with the next dance?"

"Are you not concerned that Mistress Bartlett will take exception if you dance with me?" she asked, a devilish twinkle in her green eyes.

He offered her his arm. "Let's test her and see."

Season laughed, suddenly feeling light-hearted. Lucas realized it was the first time he had seen her really laugh, and laughing made her more beautiful than ever.

"Who am I to say no, if you want to use me to make your lady love jealous?"

"How can you be sure I wasn't using her to make you jealous?" he said, lowering his lashes and staring at her lips.

Before Season had time to think about his statement,

he bowed and she curtsied; then they circled and turned to the next partner. Season was led around the room and then returned to Lucas.

"I apologize if I have created trouble for you. Had I realized how the Bartletts felt about the English, I would never have come tonight."

"Nonsense. It isn't for you to apologize. Marlana was being herself. It would not have mattered where you came from. I would wager her anger stems more from the fact that you are the most beautiful woman here."

Season caught her breath and quickly lowered her lashes, pleased by his compliment until she reminded herself that he probably spoke glowing words to every woman with whom he came in contact.

"Tell me, Lucas, did you see Edmund? Did you tell him I was staying at Rosemont?"

"You ask me two questions, and I'll answer them both with a yes. I must confess Edmund wasn't at all pleased that you were staying with me. He would have come to Virginia to get you, but for one small problem."

The dance had ended and Lucas led her from the floor. "What problem?"

"It's very simple. As a British officer, he couldn't very well come to Virginia since he would be shot on sight. If he were to choose to remove his uniform and come to Virginia, he would then be tried and shot as a spy. You can see the dilemma he faces."

Season nodded, not in the least sorry Edmund couldn't come to Rosemont. She wasn't ready to face him just yet. "Lucas, I wonder if my father has been notified that I am safe? I thought of writing to him, but Rebecca told me they would never allow a letter from Virginia to reach England."

"I myself tended to it when I was in New York. Your father will soon know of your safe return. I can also arrange for you and your father to correspond if you would like, and I have brought someone back from New York, someone I believe you will be pleased to see."

"Molly?"

"Yes, Molly, and all your belongings. Your maid was only too eager to accept my offer to bring her to you."

"Again I am in your debt, Lucas. How will I ever be able to thank you for all your kindnesses?"

He looked deeply into her eyes. "One day I may ask you to pay."

Season had no time to reply to his strange statement because Marlana appeared at his side. "Lucas, I would like you to come into the garden with me. Mama has planted some new rose bushes, and they are a most unusual shade of red."

"If you will excuse us, Season," Lucas said, before Marlana took his arm and led him away.

Season thought the ball would go on forever. She was weary of dancing with so many different gentlemen, and she was tired of having to keep a pasted smile on her face. What is the matter with me? she wondered. Not long ago she would have been delighted to attend a ball. Now, she was grateful when Rebecca came up to her and announced that Lucas was ready to go home.

Marlana accompanied them to the coach and made Lucas promise he would come to tea the next day, and when the carriage pulled away, Rebecca broke into laughter.

"You had better watch out, my brother. Marlana has her eye on you as husband material." Rebecca batted her eyes and tried to imitate Marlana's voice. "Lucas dear, I will simply die if you don't come to tea tomorrow at four."

Lucas couldn't help but laugh, and Season clamped a hand over her mouth so as not to show her mirth. "You minx, do you never tire of badgering me. If I recall correctly, you have said the same thing about a number of other young ladies in the past."

"When I'm married, I will no longer be able to point out the pitfalls and traps overzealous ladies are setting for you, and chances are you will fall into one of them. You may or may not have noticed, but Season and I were not invited to Marlana's tea tomorrow."

"I'm not sure you are being fair to Mistress Bartlett, Rebecca; she is a very pretty woman," Season said.

"Be that as it may," Lucas spoke up, "but she has her mother's temperament."

"Well, if you have noticed that, there may yet be hope for you, Lucas," his sister declared. "I'm glad you are home," she added, linking her arm through his. "How long can you stay this time?"

"I must leave first thing Monday morning."

"I wish you didn't always have to run off to New York," she added wistfully.

Lucas leaned his head back and crossed his long legs. "I know, Rebecca, but this war cannot last much longer. Soon it will be over and I will have to make no more trips."

When the carriage pulled up to Rosemont, Season saw Molly standing on the steps. Without waiting for Lucas to help her from the carriage, she ran to her maid and enfolded Molly in her arms.

"My, lady, my lady, you are safe!" the maid cried. "I thought I would never see you again."

"It's wonderful that you are here, Molly. Please don't cry. As you can see, I am enjoying good health."

"Was it awful for you?" Molly wanted to know, looking Season over carefully.

"We will talk about it later. Right now all I want to do is go to bed."

"I have emptied all your trunks and put your belongings away. Your nightgown is laid out for you. Oh, my lady, I thought you were lost forever."

Season took Molly's hand and turned her to face Lucas' sister. "Rebecca, I would like you to meet Molly. She has looked after me ever since I was a child."

"Pleased to meet you, ma'am," Molly said, bobbing a curtsy.

"Welcome to Rosemont, Molly. If there is anything you require, just ask Drucilla, and she will assist you."

Season bid Lucas and Rebecca good-night and walked up the stairs to her bedroom. How good it was to have Molly with her, she thought. Would she ever be able to repay Lucas and Rebecca for their kindness to her?

Chapter Twenty

It was the beginning of August when Season began to suspect she was carrying The Raven's child. Each morning she would awaken feeling nauseous. Until then, it had never occurred to her that she had yet another price to pay for loving The Raven. She began to watch and pray for a sign that she wasn't carrying a child. But with the passing of time, she could no longer lie to herself.

Rebecca was aware that Season had become withdrawn and silent, and for the last week had stayed mostly in her room. Rebecca had instructed the cook to prepare meals she knew Season would like, but they went uneaten. Rebecca even suggested a trip to Williamsburg, hoping it would cheer her friend, but Season refused to go. Nothing Rebecca could do seemed to draw Season out of her dark mood.

Season continued to brood in her room, and she was beginning to look pale and drawn. Beside herself with worry, Molly kept a watchful eye on her charge.

Season was in torment. She cried a lot and never went out of the house. Each time Rebecca suggested contacting the doctor, Season dissolved into tears.

Most of the time Season sat by the window and stared down at the woods at the back of the house. She knew she would have to make a decision before too long; soon she must leave Rosemont. But she couldn't bear the thought of Rebecca finding out about her condition, and she knew she could never face Lucas when the truth became known.

Often she would curse the man who had got her with child and then abandoned her. At one moment she was sure she hated The Raven, and in the next she silently begged him to come back for her.

It was the last week in August when a carriage pulled up in front of Rosemont house. Rebecca, seeing her brother disembark, flew out the door and down the steps to meet him.

"Lucas, thank goodness you are home! Season is very ill and I don't know what to do. She refuses to see the doctor. I am at my wits end with worry."

Lucas turned to the distinguished gentleman who climbed out of the coach. "Did you hear what my sister has said, Your Grace?"

The duke looked grim. "Did you say my daughter refused to see a doctor, young lady?"

"Yes, Your Grace," Rebecca said, bobbing a quick curtsy and staring in awe at Season's father. "I am so glad you are here; perhaps you can make her see the doctor."

"Show me to my daughter's room immediately," the duke commanded, his voice authoritative.

Season plucked at the lace on her nightgown. It wasn't like her to just give up. She had always been a fighter, but lately all the fight seemed to have gone out of her. She was frightened and unsure about her future; and she felt there was no one she could trust with her guilty secret.

Molly watched her lady, a frown on her face. She had tried everything to make Season smile, but so far nothing had helped. The maid feared that if Season didn't begin to eat some solid meals soon she was just going to waste away to skin and bones.

When the door was suddenly pushed open, Molly's face lit up. She quickly dipped into a deep curtsy. "Your Grace, thank God you've come!" she cried.

When Season saw her father, a sob escaped her lips. "Papa, oh, Papa," she cried. "I needed you and you came." She held out her trembling hand to her father.

The duke stood over his daughter, taking in her paleness and noticing how frail she looked. He had never known her to have a sick day in her life. Since he had first received word of her kidnapping, he had been out of his mind with grief. At last he had come to realize she was all he had left in the world. He blamed himself for sending her to America, and he knew that if anything happened to her he would have nothing left.

Taking her limp hand in his, he sat down on the edge of the bed and pushed a tumbled curl away from Season's face. The Duke of Chatsworth looked into green eyes that had lost their luster. He couldn't help but think how ironic it would be if, now that he had come to realize how precious his daughter was to him, he might lose her. How like her mother she looked, lying against the pillow which was only a shade whiter than her face.

"Season my dear, dear child," he said in a voice that shook with emotion.

"Papa, I am so glad you have come!" she cried. "Do not abandon me now."

"I will never leave you again, child. When you are well enough, I will take you back to Chatsworth, and you will never have to marry anyone if that is your wish. I have already said as much to Edmund Kensworthy."

Tears streamed down Season's face. Could this be her father, so kind and loving? What would he say when he learned she was with child? That thought only made her cry all the more. How could she ever tell him her guilty secret?

"I am going to send for the doctor right away, and you will soon be on the mend," he said, tenderly touching her tear-wet cheek.

Season buried her face against her father's shoulder, knowing she had to tell him the truth even if he hated her for it. Raising her face, she looked into his eyes. "I do not need a doctor to tell me what is wrong with me, Papa. I already know what it is."

He smiled at her. "I was not aware that you could practice medicine, my dear."

She looked into his clear green eyes, hating what she must tell him. He was such a proud man, she knew it would rip his heart to shreds. "Papa, I am . . . with . . . child," she whispered hesitantly, as fresh tears washed down her face.

Mason Chatsworth looked thunderstruck for a moment, and he felt his daughter's hand tremble. "That devil! I had hoped that he had not . . ." He stood up and turned his back. "If it's the last thing I ever do, I will see that The Raven hangs for this. How dare he take a young girl and . . ." He turned back to Season. "My poor child, how you must have suffered. I blame myself for this."

"No, Papa, no, it isn't your fault. I am to blame." Season knew she had to tell him the truth. She couldn't have him think that he was at fault in any way.

"Papa, please sit beside me. I will not have you blaming yourself. I want you to know the truth."

He sat down and took her hand in his. "I know you are about to be forgiving, Season, but it is my fault. I promise to make this all up to you somehow."

"Papa, listen to me. I have never lied to you, and I will not start now. He . . . The Raven . . . didn't force himself on me. I am not the innocent you may think."

He shook his head. "You are little more than an innocent child. How would you have known how to handle a man like that. No, my dear, you are not to blame. Never again say that you are at fault."

She laid her cheek against his. "If you won't blame yourself, then I won't blame myself either. Do we strike a bargain?"

He laughed. "That's the spirit I want to see. Together we will fight the world, my dear child. We are from a proud and noble family. When the Chatsworths have banded together, they have never been defeated."

"Papa, I cannot go back to Chatsworth with you. Already your friends believe the worst about me. Before it was untrue; now I'm not so sure."

"That's where you are wrong, my dear. When Ransford heard you had been kidnapped, he and I had a long talk. I explained the trick you had played on him, and he even laughed. He went to the king and retracted all he had said about you. You can only guess how many people have come up to me and said that it is a pity you were unjustly accused."

"I'm glad for you, Papa, but that won't help either one of us now."

"I have a plan, Season. I have been thinking about giving up my public life. You and I will return to Chatsworth and raise your child. I suppose we can make up some story about your being married here in the Colonies."

Season had never seen her father behave in this way. She knew how much his seat in The House of Lords meant to him, and she certainly would not allow him to give it up on her account.

"If it is your wish, Papa, I will go home with you, but only if you promise me you won't give up your office. I have enough guilt, do not add more to it."

"You are such a dear child. It's a pity it took a near tragedy to make me see that." He patted her hand. "We shall talk on this more later. Right now I want you to rest."

"Papa, I suppose if Edmund were still willing to marry me when he finds out the truth about me and the baby, I could . . . marry him."

"No, I will never ask that of you again. If some day you find a man you want to marry, then you will have my blessing. Until that time, put the thought out of your mind. Perhaps it would be best for all concerned if, when the child is born, we give it to someone who will care for it."

"No, Papa, I could never give this child away. No matter who his father was, he will be a Chatsworth."

Her father's eyes became sad. "If that is your wish, we will keep the child." He bent forward and kissed Season on the cheek. "You rest now."

Season watched her father leave the room. Her heart was breaking for the pain she had caused him. There was no joy in her heart at the thought of going back to Chatsworth, just as there were no tender feelings inside her for the child she carried. But she would have her baby and take it to Chatsworth. Perhaps in time she would be able to forget about the child's father.

The Duke of Chatsworth sipped his claret while studying Lucas Carrington's face. He had begun to respect this young man when he met him in New York, and he had learned, on the trip to Virginia, that they shared many common interests. Lucas was obviously a man with a great deal of common sense, and his plantation proved him to be a shrewd businessman. The duke thought that if his own son had lived, he would not have wanted him to be any different from Lucas Carrington.

"Rebecca has told me, sir, that your daughter is feeling much better since your visit with her."

The Duke of Chatsworth took a deep drink of his claret and set the glass down. He hesitated to answer, not knowing what to say. Soon all the world would know that his daughter was going to have a baby without benefit of marriage. He made a quick decision that he would confide in Lucas Carrington, somehow sensing he could trust the young man.

"First of all, let me start by saying how grateful I am that you took my daughter in. You will find that I am a very generous man where my daughter is concerned. I would like to repay you."

"Your generosity verges on being an insult, sir. I would never take money in exchange for my hospitality."

The duke smiled. "I thought that might be your attitude, my boy. Forget I brought it up. In any case, I won't have to encroach on your generosity much longer. I will be taking my daughter back to Chatsworth Castle as soon as her health permits."

Lucas studied the older man's face. "I would be sorry to see you rush her recovery."

Mason Chatsworth was quiet for a moment, and then he cleared his throat. "I have just learned some very grave news, Lucas. You will understand my reluctance to speak of it, and I will ask you to keep what I am about to tell you in the strictest confidence."

Lucas' face whitened. "Your daughter isn't worse is she, sir?"

Lord Chatsworth took a deep breath. "Not in the way you mean. Season is with . . . child!"

Lucas felt as if someone had just dealt him a heavy blow to the midsection. He gripped the arms of the chair he was sitting on so tightly that his fingers whitened. "Is it a certainty, sir?"

"My daughter seems to think it is. It would seem that black-hearted pirate had his way with her. I would kill him with my bare hands if I knew where to find him," the duke said, tossing down the rest of his drink.

"Is that what your daughter said?"

"You may not believe this, but my daughter tried to defend the man. That is the way Season is. I don't mind telling you, I have been a failure as a father, but I intend to make it up to her now. I allowed her to grow up alone at Chatsworth, with no one to see to her well-being except the servants. She was always a sweet child though, and she never complained when I was too busy to spend Christmas with her or when I forgot about her birthday."

"You don't have to tell me this, sir."

The duke's eyes became sad. "It needs to be said, but I suppose the one I should be addressing is Season. You should have seen her eyes light up every time I came home. She has always been so much like her mother, lovely and kind. Unlike her mother, however, Season has the devil's own temper when she becomes angry. Did Season ever tell you her mother was the daughter of a Scottish laird?"

"No, I never knew that."

"Her mother was sometimes wild and unpredictable, but never in all our life together did I have one boring day. After she died, I never found a woman who could compare with her, so I never remarried."

Lucas was having a hard time following the duke's conversation. All he could think about was Season and what she must be going through. "Your Grace, I hope you won't think me impertinent, but I would deem it a great honor if you would allow your daughter to marry me."

The duke let out his breath. "No, it's impossible. You are a fine young man and I admire you, but Season is, after all, of noble blood."

"I understand that, Your Grace, but you have my word that I would make her a good husband. I would treat the child she is carrying as if it were my own."

"You would be willing to marry Season, knowing that she carries another man's child?"

"I would be honored to be her husband."

"What are your feelings for Season?"

Lucas looked the duke straight in the eye. "I feel very much about your daughter as you must have felt about your wife. I believe that if I were married to her I would never know a boring day. Long ago I recognized the qualities in your daughter that you just spoke of. I will be honest with you and admit that I am not worthy of her. There are things about my life that I cannot tell you, and I have known many women in my time; but if your daughter were my wife, you have my solemn vow that I would make her a true and faithful husband."

Mason Chatsworth was thoughtful for a moment. While Lucas Carrington was not of the nobility, he was a gentleman and loyal to England; and he was apparently well fixed, judging by the prosperous appearance of Rosemont. Season would never want for anything.

"Your offer is an honorable one, my boy, but I promised Season I would never force her to marry against her will. I intend to keep that promise."

"What would be your objection, sir, if I could convince your daughter to accept me as her husband?"

The duke was thoughtful. If Lucas were to marry Season, he would give her child a name, and he realized that from a woman's point of view Lucas Carrington would be considered a handsome devil. No. He could find no objection other than the fact that Lucas had no title. However, here in the Colonies such things didn't seem nearly as important as they were in England.

The duke ran his finger around the rim of his glass. "If you could convince my daughter of your good intentions . . . and if she were to give her consent, I can think of no valid objection. I warn you, she has always said no to her suitors in the past, and most probably she will give you the same answer. You are not to pressure her. If she says no, you are to consider the matter dropped."

Lucas stood up and filled both their glasses. He then raised his in a toast. "To my success with your daughter, Your Grace."

The room suddenly became silent. Each man was thinking about the girl who lay upstairs. Both men loved her, each in his own way.

Season walked to her bedroom window and looked down on the forest. Her heart somehow felt heavy at the thought of leaving Rosemont. She had not been unhappy here. Rebecca was the only friend she had ever had, and she liked Lucas, and was grateful to him for his kindness to her.

She walked over to the side table and sat down.

Picking up the fork, she tasted the chicken Molly had brought her earlier. She remembered the time aboard the *Andromeda* when The Raven had forced her to eat turkey. How long ago that seemed now.

She wondered what The Raven would say if he knew she was carrying his child. If he would come for her, she knew she would not hesitate to go with him.

Sighing heavily, she stood up and walked over to the mirror. Her stomach was still flat and her waist was still trim. Raising her face upward, she closed her eyes. What would Lucas Carrington think of her if he knew her guilty secret? For some reason, that bothered her more than anything else at the moment.

Season thought back to her first meeting with Lucas. At that time she had thought he was the answer to every young girl's dream. Now that she had come to know him, she hadn't changed her mind.

She opened the lid of the trunk which contained some of her personal belongings and removed something wrapped in a silk scarf. Unfolding the scarf, she stared down at the wooden model of the *Andromeda* that Briggs had given her. Tears fell on the tiny ship as Season cursed herself for caring about a man who had forgotten her very existence. She knew she would always be reminded of The Raven by the child she was carrying within her body.

Chapter Twenty-One

The Duke of Chatsworth had been at Rosemont Plantation for three weeks. He knew Lucas would soon ask his daughter to marry him, and he found himself hoping Season would accept. The more he came to know Lucas, the more he respected him. He knew Season could do far worse than becoming the mistress of Rosemont. In the past weeks he had spent a great deal of time with his daughter, and each day she seemed to grow stronger. There was now color in her cheeks, she laughed more often, and she no longer kept to her room. Season enjoyed sitting on the veranda and listening to the slaves singing their age-old song as they returned from the fields.

The forest that surrounded Rosemont was awash with brilliant autumn colors, and here in this beautiful Virginia valley she almost felt at peace with herself.

Robert Wolf was supposed to return anytime now, for Rebecca was to be wed in two more days. Season had watched her friend make plans for the wedding, and she felt a bit envious of Rebecca's happiness.

Lately Season would find Lucas staring at her, and she wondered if he suspected that she was hiding a guilty secret. That morning Lucas and her father had ridden into the fields because her father had wanted to see how cotton was picked. Now Season found herself watching the road for their return. She knew she was not well enough to travel yet, but sometime that day she intended to speak to her father about leaving for England.

Hearing a rider gallop up the driveway, Season glanced over to see Lucas dismount. He slapped his horse on the rump and sent the animal running toward the stables. When he saw Season sitting on the veranda, he smiled and waved.

Season watched him approach. He wore buff-colored trousers tucked into brown riding boots, and his frocked jacket was thrown carelessly across his shoulders. She noted that his black hair glistened in the bright sunlight.

Lucas' boots made a crunching sound as they struck the pebble-strewn walk, and when he climbed the steps to the veranda, Season noticed he was watching her closely.

"It's good to see you up and about, Season. It has always been a belief of mine that fresh air is a great healer," he said, sitting on the chair across from Season and stretching his long legs out in front of him.

"I was told that you went riding with my father," she said, for want of something better to say. "Why did he not return with you?"

"Your father became so engrossed in watching the

fall planting, he stayed behind with my overseer, Walls, to watch. He should be along directly."

"I think I will go in now," Season said, starting to rise, but Lucas gripped her shoulder, forestalling her movement.

"Stay with me for just awhile longer, Season. I have been wanting to speak to you for over three weeks, but could never find the right time."

She leaned back in the chair but didn't relax because she was wondering what he could possibly want to talk to her about.

"I understand you are feeling stronger, Season. I can see there is more color in your cheeks."

"Yes. I am well enough to travel now."

"Has your father mentioned the conversation he and I had about you?"

"No," she answered, wondering if her father had told Lucas about the baby she was carrying. For some strange reason Lucas seemed nervous and she wondered what was on his mind.

"Lately, I have come to believe I need a wife. When Rebecca marries Robert, Rosemont will be without a mistress."

Season felt as if a fist had just tightened on her heart. For some unknown reason, she didn't want to think about Lucas being married. Perhaps he was telling her that he wished her to depart Rosemont before he brought a new wife home.

"As I just told you, I am now well enough to travel. In fact, I was just thinking I would talk to my father today about leaving for England. I can understand why you wouldn't want a guest in your home if you are intending to bring a new bride to Rosemont."

Lucas sighed in exasperation, knowing Season had missed his point. "What I am trying to tell you, Season, is that when Rebecca leaves, I will be completely without female companionship."

"Lucas, I think I should advise you that when you propose to Mistress Bartlett, you must not make it sound as if she will be replacing your sister. Surely you can be more romantic than that. A woman likes to hear pretty words from her intended husband."

Lucas swore under his breath. He was making a muddle of his proposal, but dammit, he had never asked a woman to marry him before. How was he to know the right approach to a woman's heart?

"Season, I don't want a wife to replace Rebecca, and I don't want to marry Marlana Bartlett. My God, don't you recognize a marriage proposal when you hear one?"

Season froze. "Surely you are not proposing to . . . me! No, that would be quite impossible."

Lucas studied her face lazily. "I realize you are from English gentry and I am merely a planter from Virginia, but I believe you and I could get along quite well together."

Season's face paled. "Did my father put you up to this, Lucas? How much did he offer to pay you if you would make a respectable woman of me?"

"Asking you to be my wife was entirely my idea, although I did ask your father's permission before I spoke to you. You don't know me very well, Season, if you think money could induce me to marry a woman I did not choose."

Season suddenly felt sick inside. Lucas knew about the baby, and he was offering her the protection of his name. He didn't love her; he pitied her. "You go too far, Lucas. How dare you ask such a thing of me! Did you really think I would say yes to such a preposterous notion?"

"I find I like the idea of you being my wife. Does marrying me sound preposterous to you?"

"Indeed it does," she said, her green eyes flashing. "I never took you for a fool until now, Lucas. I never thought your kindness toward me would one day turn to insult."

"Can I ask you to explain that statement?" he asked, as his golden eyes took on a guarded look.

"I know you are only feeling pity for me. Well, spare me your pity. I will not marry you or any other man just to give my baby a name. I will have no man for my husband. At the moment I have very little regard for your gender. You are all selfish and think only of your own needs. I can very well do without all of you."

"Did he hurt you so badly?" Lucas asked softly.

Season didn't pretend to misunderstand, and she hated the fact that tears gathered in her eyes. "The Raven killed my heart!" she cried.

Lucas went down on his knees and gathered Season into his arms. While he gently stroked her hair, she cried out her misery. Lucas waited until her tears were spent before he spoke. "If you allow me, Season, I will prove to you that not all men are selfish. Say you will marry me, and I will strive to replace your faith in life as well as men."

A shudder shook Season's slight body. How easy it

would be to say yes to Lucas. She knew she had some deep unexplored feeling for this man. Suddenly she decided she had to tell him the truth about herself. Perhaps then he would turn away in disgust and withdraw his marriage proposal.

Gathering up all her courage, Season looked into Lucas' soft golden eyes. Her own eyes were stinging, and at the moment it seemed that her throat had closed. Moving away from him, she realized the hardest thing she would ever have to do would be to be truthful with him about The Raven.

"Lucas, I am going to be honest with you, no matter how much it hurts. I will understand if you never want to see me again after I tell you about myself. I was not ravished by The Raven as you might think. I gave myself to him. I don't expect you to understand this, but I love him. Forget about me, for I am not worthy of you. Go to Marlana, who is fresh and clean, and offer her your name. You deserve much better than I. With Marlana you would have a wife who loves you, who can give you your own children. With me, you would have a woman who loves the father of the child she is carrying."

Season saw Lucas' throat work convulsively, and she realized he was deeply affected by what she had just told him. "How can you love such a man, Season? You say you gave yourself to him willingly, but I feel you would never have done so if he hadn't used his experience with women against you. I had heard there was some kind of scandal about you in England, was that also true?"

"There is no reason you should believe me after what

I have just told you about myself, but The Raven is the only man I have ever been with. If it were possible, I would tear him from my heart, but I just cannot seem to forget him. Believe me, Lucas, I am not the woman for you."

"I think you are wrong. None of what you have told me matters. If you will give me a chance, I can prove to you that not all men are like The Raven. I have never wanted to marry a woman before. Please, take what I offer you, Season."

"Lucas, you don't understand. If The Raven were to come to me at this moment and ask me to go away with him . . . I would go. That's the kind of woman I have become."

"You must have seen his face then, or you could not love him."

"No, I cannot even offer that as an excuse. I know you will find it hard to understand that I could love a man whose face I have never seen. But I believe I would recognize him if I ever saw him unmasked. I will never forget the sound of his voice."

Lucas traced a pattern across the arm of the chair he was sitting in. "Suppose, after all you have told me, I still want you for my wife?"

"Then I would think you mad. You can have any woman you want for your wife. Have you forgotten about the child I carry?"

He ran his open palm down the leg of his trousers as if he was nervous—the one emotion Season would never have associated with Lucas Carrington. "No. I could hardly forget the child. You have my word that if you become my wife, I will raise this child the same as any other child you would give me. Think about that, Season."

"Why, Lucas? I don't understand."

He looked into her eyes. "Suppose I told you I have been unable to get you out of my mind since that first night you swept into my life? Suppose I said I am hopelessly in love with you and will find no peace until you belong to me? Would you believe me if I say you are the only woman I have ever loved?"

"No. I would say you speak a lie."

He smiled. "All right. What if I should tell you that I would like to have a wife who is beautiful and kind and carries a title?"

"Then I would believe you."

"Will you say yes, then?"

"No."

"Have you thought of the child?"

"I try not to."

"I think you should consider the child's future. You know what a child is branded if it is born without a father. The word is bastard, Season. Do you want that stigma to be attached to your child?"

Her eyes filled with tears again, and she despised herself for crying. "No, I wouldn't want that for this child. I try to think I don't care about this baby, but I find I am developing a true mother's heart."

"There is no reason for you to agonize over the baby's future. When the child is born he will have the Carrington name if you say yes to me."

Season thought of the other reasons why she should say yes to Lucas' proposal: she was more than a little drawn to him, and he lived a long way from London—

she had to consider her father's good name in England. Still she was a little frightened of Lucas, not because she thought he would harm her but because he seemed bigger than life and was so overpowering.

"I could never make you happy, Lucas."

"That is not a requirement, Season, but I would do all in my power to make you a good husband and to give you happy days."

She smiled slightly. "Would that include giving up all your lady friends?"

For a moment his golden eyes blazed and his voice was passionate. "If you belonged to me, I would never want another woman. This I solemnly vow to you before God."

Season placed her fingertips to her throbbing temples. "I don't know, Lucas. You have taken me completely by surprise. I never expected you would want to marry me."

"Say yes, Season," he urged.

"If I did accept your proposal, you might live to regret it, Lucas."

"Not in a million years."

"I am not even sure I could ever be a proper wife to you."

Suddenly his golden eyes danced, for he could see that she was weakening. "Let us strike a bargain, my lady. If you marry me, I will not force my attentions on you . . . neither will I adopt a hands-off policy. Perhaps with patience on my part, you will one day come to me willingly."

She bit her lower lip and then smiled. "I cannot for the life of me, understand why you would want me.

There are so many other young ladies, without my problem, who would leap at the chance to be the wife of Lucas Carrington."

"It's all very simple, Season. When I see something I want, I never give up until I acquire it—I want you." He took her hand, raised it to his lips, and kissed it softly. "Do we strike a bargain, my lady?"

Suddenly Season knew she was going to say yes. She couldn't understand why, but for some reason her heart was pounding and she could hardly breathe. "I will say yes, if you are sure this is what you want. I must warn you though, the day may come when you will regret the deal we struck today. If you ever begin to have second thoughts, remember the warning I give you today."

His eyes seemed to dance with new life. "I think not, my lady. And I will do my best to see that you never have cause to regret it either."

Lucas stood up and drew Season up beside him. He didn't try to kiss her, but merely held her tightly against him. She felt a tremor shake his body, and then her own body melted against his. Somehow it felt so right to be in Lucas' arms. Season closed her eyes, wondering what the future would bring. This was the first time she did not dislike the man she was supposed to marry.

Neither of them realized the front door had opened until they heard a gasp and turned around to see Rebecca staring at them in amazement.

Lucas smiled and held his hand out to his sister. "Come and congratulate me. I believe I will be a husband before you will become a wife."

Rebecca's face lit up and she flew across the veranda.

Lucas hugged both women to him.

"When did all this happen, Lucas? I never knew that the two of you were in love. I have suspected for a long time, however, that the two of you would be perfect for each other."

Lucas laughed down into his sister's face. "I didn't think anything would ever escape your notice, minx."

"Season, I am going to love having you for a sister, and it will be a comfort to me to know you will be taking care of Lucas." Turning to her brother she said, "I am overjoyed for you, Lucas. I just know you and Season are going to be happy together."

Lucas caught Season's eye. "Yes, I believe we are perfect for each other."

Rebecca's hand flew to her mouth. "We have so many plans to make, Lucas. Season you will need a trousseau, and invitations must be sent out. I think a spring wedding would be nice. Or you could have a double wedding with me and Robert? No, of course not—that would be too soon."

Lucas laughed and placed a finger over his sister's mouth. "Slow down, minx. Since there is a war going on, Season and I want a very small wedding. In fact, if Season has no objection, I had thought we would have a very private ceremony tomorrow night."

"Surely that is too soon," Season protested. "Rebecca's wedding is in two days. Can we not wait until she and Robert are married?"

"No, I believe there is no cause to delay. You will find that once I have made up my mind about something, I usually get my way."

"He's right there, Season. My brother is a very persuasive man. You may as well give in, or he will wring an agreement out of you," Rebecca stated impishly.

Season smiled at Lucas, silently thanking him for his thoughtfulness. She knew the need for haste, and was glad that he had realized she would want a private ceremony.

As Season's father rode up the drive and dismounted, Lucas took her hand and led her toward the front of the veranda.

"I believe we should tell your father the happy news," he said, smiling. Then he leaned close to Season and whispered in her ear. "You have made me a very happy man, my lady."

Chapter Twenty-Two

Hearing of his daughter's impending marriage put the duke in a jovial mood. While he and Lucas went into the study to talk privately, Rebecca took Season upstairs so they could make plans.

As the two girls sat in the middle of Season's bed, Rebecca could hardly contain her joy. "Just think, we will be sisters. When Robert and I are married, we will only be living a few miles away. We can spend Christmas and Thanksgiving together. Won't that be glorious fun?"

"What is Thanksgiving?" Season asked.

"Oh, you wouldn't know about that. It is a holiday that is set aside in America for giving thanks. We spend days preparing for the feast of venison, turkey, and more food than you can imagine. Lucas once told me it was something like England's harvest festival."

Season smiled, feeling as if she would soon be a part of this wonderful new land. Suddenly her heart felt lighter than it had in a long time. "I am looking forward to spending my first holiday at Rosemont, Rebecca. I will love having you for my sister. The one thing that grieved me about returning to England was the thought of never seeing you again."

"Are you happy, Season?" Rebecca asked, giving her a searching look.

"Yes, Rebecca, I believe I am."

"Do you love my brother?"

"I will be very honest with you, Rebecca; I like and respect your brother more than any man I know. I hope one day I will grow to love him."

Rebecca looked confused for a moment. "But why are you marrying Lucas if you don't love him?"

Season knew she couldn't bring herself to tell Lucas' sister the reason for the marriage. "I will make your brother a good wife, Rebecca; you have my word on that."

"When you get to know Lucas, you can't help but love him, Season. He is truly wonderful."

Season hugged Rebecca. "I think we both agree that he is wonderful."

The rest of the day was spent in busy preparation. Molly pressed the beautiful wedding gown that Season was supposed to have worn for her marriage to the Earl of Ransford and then to Edmund Kensworthy.

That evening when Molly came into Season's bedroom, she looked at her lady and clicked her tongue. "Such goings-on. You have near been married twice before, but this time it appears to me you will go through with it."

"This time it was *my* choice, Molly."

"Well, I have to admit this one is better than the other two, even if he is a colonist."

"Molly I never knew you to be a snob," Season said, smiling. Will you be wanting to return to England with my father, or will you remain here at Rosemont with me?"

"I will be staying with you, of course, and don't try changing the subject with me. Don't think I have forgotten the night you told me about Lucas Carrington. He's the one you met at the ball and was all dreamy-eyed over."

"Yes, he is the same man."

The maid frowned. "I remember I told you that night he was probably Lucifer himself, but I have to admit he is a handsome devil—and I like him. Probably the woman ain't yet drawn breath who wouldn't like Mr. Carrington."

Season laughed at her maid's assessment. "Molly, you are incorrigible."

Molly lifted a bundle of clothing in her arms. "This is the last of the lot. All your belongings have been moved into Mr. Carrington's bedroom, except what you will need for the wedding tomorrow." She walked to the door and turned back to Season. "I almost forgot, my lady, His Grace has asked if you will join him in the garden."

When Season reached the garden, she found her father waiting for her. He took her hand and pulled her into his arms. "I am finding this a bit difficult, Season. I believe it will be very hard to leave you and go back to England alone. I never felt that I was losing you before now."

"I will miss you, Papa," she said, resting her cheek against his. "You will never lose me, Papa. You will always be my father."

"My own dear little girl. You have suffered more than most girls your age. Let us hope all your unhappiness will be left behind now."

"I am not a little girl anymore, Papa. I am a woman with a woman's responsibilities."

He held her at arm's length. "I know you will think it is a little late in the day, but I want you to be happy more than anything in this world."

"I am not unhappy."

He sighed heavily. "I believe Lucas Carrington to be a man of honor, and he will make you a good husband. But you must never forget who you are or where you come from. You are a Chatsworth, and you will honor the commitment you are about to make to Carrington."

"I will honor him as my husband, Papa."

He kissed her cheek and said in a gruff voice. "Find happiness, little girl."

They both heard someone coming down the garden path, and Season saw Lucas come into view.

"I'm sorry if I am interrupting something," Lucas apologized when he saw Season and her father.

"No, my boy, I was just having a talk with my daughter." Mason took Season's hand and gave it to Lucas. "I now turn her over to your keeping. I am sure the two of you have many things to discuss."

Lucas felt Season's hand tremble, and he waited

until her father had departed before he pulled her into his arms. "Are you cold?" he asked.

"No, merely scared."

Season felt her senses reeling as he laid his cheek against hers. "Never be afraid of me, my lady. I would never harm a hair on your head."

"Lucas, it isn't too late; you can still back out. If you were wise, you would do just that."

He laughed deeply and looked down on her face which was clearly defined in the moonlight. "Be warned, Season, you cannot get rid of me by throwing yourself into the arms of my stableboy. At Rosemont he happens to be seventy-five years of age."

"You know about that?" she asked, smiling.

"Yes, your father told me."

"There will be no tricks between us, Lucas, and no lies. You are marrying me with full knowledge that I carry another man's child and knowing that I love him."

He tilted her face up to his. "I will wipe him out of your mind so thoroughly that he will be no more than a fleeting memory," he whispered.

Season closed her eyes as she felt his warm breath on her face. "Yes, Lucas, help me to forget The Raven." Her words sounded like a plea from the heart.

Lucas stared at her beautiful face and felt a jealous anger because The Raven stood, like a dark shadow, between him and Season. He bent his head and softly touched his mouth to hers.

Season knew he was going to kiss her, and she didn't pull away. She was surprised at the warmth that spread throughout her at the touch of his mouth. She felt a tingling in her body, and her lips parted as he deepened the kiss. Her head was spinning, and she was confused by the wild feelings she was experiencing. She had never expected to feel this way with anyone but The Raven. Her response to Lucas frightened more than pleased her.

Lucas broke off the kiss and smiled down at her. "I do not think it will be as hard as you suppose to wipe him out of your mind, Season."

She took a step back. "I . . . think I had better go inside now, Lucas," she said in a breathless voice.

He touched her face gently. "Yes, I believe that would be a good idea. I won't see you until tomorrow night. Sleep well, my lady love."

Season watched him disappear down the path, a look of confusion stamped on her face. Dear lord, she thought, how is it possible to have such deep feelings for two men? What if I am the kind of woman who reacts this way to every man she meets?

She shook her head and made her way quickly toward the house. Season didn't want to analyze her feelings too closely. She didn't want to think about tomorrow night at all.

Season wondered if every bride felt as nervous and unsure of herself as she did at the moment. As she descended the stairs and took her father's arm, she was anything but a happy bride. Solemnly he led her into the sitting room where Lucas awaited her. When the Duke of Chatsworth placed Season's hand in Lucas', he gave his daughter an encouraging smile.

The only guests present were Rebecca and Molly. Season glanced briefly at her bridegroom, and he nodded at her reassuringly.

The reverend cleared his throat and began to speak. "Dearly beloved we are gathered together here to unite this man and this woman in the bonds of holy wedlock."

Suddenly Season's nervousness disappeared, and a serene calm settled over her. It seemed so right that she should stand beside Lucas Carrington and be united with him in marriage. She listened to Lucas' clear tone when he answered the reverend's questions.

"Do you, Lucas Michael Carrington, take Season Marie Chatsworth to be your lawfully wedded wife?"

"I do."

"Do you, Season Marie Chatsworth, take Lucas Michael Carrington to be your lawfully wedded husband?"

"I . . . do."

In a daze, Season listened to the reverend pronounce that they were man and wife. Lucas bent down and gave her a chaste kiss on the lips, and she blinked in astonishment. Was it possible to go from being single to being wedded in such a short space of time? Could two people be united for a lifetime with just a few spoken words? She stared at the diamond and emerald ring that sparkled on her finger, and she realized she was Mrs. Lucas Carrington.

Season's father hugged her, and then Rebecca kissed her on the cheek and wished her happiness. Molly looked solemn-faced and said nothing.

Afterward, the reverend took his leave, and the small

wedding party went into the dining room where a lavish dinner had been laid out for them.

As Season sat beside Lucas, he took her hand and raised it to his lips. "Today is the first day of many happy days to come, Season."

She could do no more than give him a weak smile as she toyed with the food on her plate, unable to take a bite. She was thinking about the latter part of the evening when Lucas would take her to his bedroom and the two of them would be alone. She was afraid and nervous. How will I ever be a true wife to Lucas? she wondered.

When the wine was served, her father stood up and raised his glass. "I want to propose a toast to the happy couple. May your lives be filled with happiness, and may you remain forever young in each other's hearts."

Lucas laughingly rose to his feet and lifted his glass to Season. "To the only woman in the world who could make me give up single life with no regret—to the joy of my life, Mrs. Season Marie Carrington." His golden eyes sparkled as he took a sip of the wine, and Season felt the cold hand of dread move over her heart. How could she ever be the joy of Lucas' life when she carried another man's child within her body?

After dinner and the toasting, they all moved into the sitting room. There was no laughter or dancing as was the custom after a wedding, but for their entertainment Rebecca played the spinet and sang a lovely ballad.

Season was standing by the window, looking nervous and out of place when her father came to her. "I will be leaving you now, my dear. I have made arrangements to take ship early in the morning for New

York, then on to England."

"Must you go so soon, Papa?"

He smiled at her. "The one thing you don't need is your father hanging about just now. I will keep in touch. Lucas has made arrangements for my letters to reach you."

Season wanted to beg her father not to leave her, but she merely nodded. "I will miss you, Papa."

"Take heart, little girl. Before too long we will be together again. Come, walk me out to the carriage and tell me goodbye with a smile."

Season stood beside her new husband and watched her father's carriage until it was out of sight, swallowed up by the night shadows. She clung to the support post of the veranda and felt tears in her eyes.

"Don't look so sad, Season. You haven't been sentenced to death, you know. Being married to me isn't all that bad, is it?"

"I'm sorry, Lucas, it's just that—"

"I know. Ours wasn't the kind of wedding a young girl dreams of, was it?"

Season glanced up and saw an almost wistful look in his golden eyes. She sensed a sadness in Lucas, and it tore at her heart. She doubted she would ever know the reason he had married her, but she didn't believe it was because of any great love he felt for her.

"Come inside, it's getting cold, and I wouldn't want you to catch a chill." He led her inside, into the now-deserted sitting room. Apparently Rebecca had gone to her room to allow the newlyweds some time alone. Lucas seated Season on the sofa and then dropped down beside her.

"I think we should talk before we go upstairs, Season." He took her hand and held it in his. "I want you to know that I told Rebecca about the baby."

Season nodded. "She had to know sooner or later. Was she horrified?"

"Yes, but not for the reason you might think. She was sad that such a thing could happen to you. She loves you, Season, and will always be your friend."

"I am fortunate to have a friend like her."

"Did you take note that there were no servants in the house today other than your Molly?"

"I . . . yes, now that you mention it. I did think it strange that Molly served the dinner."

"There was a reason for that, Season. I didn't want anyone outside the few who were at the ceremony to know about our marriage. The Reverend Henderson came from Williamsburg, and he doesn't know my family."

"I don't understand the need for all this secrecy."

"I will explain then. When your—our—child is born, he will grow up here on Rosemont. I do not want the slightest hint of scandal attached to his name. As far as the world is concerned he, or she, shall be my child. Will you agree to this?"

"Yes, but—"

"Allow me to finish. The neighbors will be told that you and I were married in New York last spring. We will use the excuse that you were betrothed to my cousin Edmund and we fell in love and married secretly. Everyone likes to hear about heartrending, undeniable love. People will speculate for a time, but

382

after a whiile they will accept what we tell them as the truth."

"Lucas, I understand why you are doing this and I applaud your kindness, but I hate deception. I am not sure I could ever tell a convincing untruth."

He cupped her face in his hands. "You will, Season. This is for the sake of the child. This child will carry the Carrington name. If the child turns out to be a boy, Rosemont will one day belong to him. If you think about what I have said, I'm sure you will be able to tell a convincing lie when the occasion calls for it."

A tear ran out of the corner of Season's eye and rolled down her cheek. "I believe you are the kindest, dearest man I have ever known. I still cannot believe you are doing this for me."

He laid his face against hers and felt the smoothness of her skin. "Don't give me too much credit, Season. One day you may find out that I am as selfish and deceitful as the next man. Perhaps even more so."

She raised her face and looked at him. "I will never think that of you, Lucas. I may not love you, but I like you more than anyone I know. If you will be satisfied with my high regard and the deep friendship I feel for you, I will be a good wife to you."

"That's a good start. Many marriages have started off with much less."

"I suppose there have been countless numbers of such marriages."

"You have had a long day," he said in a deep voice. "Would you like to retire now?"

Season plucked at the satin trim on her wedding

gown. "Do I . . . is it really necessary for us to sleep together?"

His mouth twitched with amusement. "Yes, I'm afraid we must. We could not very well have the servants spreading the word that the master and mistress of the house sleep apart, could we?"

"The servants all know we slept apart until now."

"That's true, but they will be told, like everyone else, that we were keeping our marriage a secret. They will expect to find you in my bed."

"I have my doubts that we will fool anyone with that story, Lucas."

"Yes, we will. I found out from your father that your capture by The Raven is the best-kept secret in England. The few who know about it in New York won't talk because it makes them look bad. General Clinton doesn't particularly want to look the fool. Colonel and Mrs. Tibbs fear that your father will retaliate against them for not keeping a closer watch on you."

"What about Edmund?"

Lucas smiled at her. "How cleverly you turned the subject away from our sleeping arrangement." Then he surprised her by scooping her up into his arms and carrying her up the stairs.

When he entered his bedroom, he placed Season on her feet. "I believe Molly has moved all your belongings into my bedroom. I am not sure where she put everything, but I have no doubt that if you search you will find what you require."

He turned and left abruptly, leaving Season standing in the middle of the bedroom. Her eyes scanned the large room. It was twice the size of the one she had been occupying. A soft cream and yellow Persian rug lay on the floor, and the bed coverings and curtains were yellow and cream.

She noticed her gown and robe draped across a yellow satin chair and knew Molly must have placed them there for her. She thought it a bit strange that Molly didn't come to her, since it had been her maid's custom to help her undress for bed.

Butterfly wings seemed to be beating in Season's stomach as she removed her wedding gown and pulled the nightdress over her head. To calm herself she picked up the ivory-handled brush on the dressing table and ran it through her hair.

Walking over to the bed, she hesitated. What was she doing here? She was married to a man she didn't know very well. She thought of what her wedding night would have been like had she married Lord Ransford, or even Edmund Kensworthy, and that gave her the courage she needed to climb into bed.

Pulling the covers up to her chin, she waited for Lucas to return. She didn't fear him, but she wasn't ready to perform her wifely duties either.

The air was cool and crisp as Lucas stood on the veranda staring out into the night. For the first time in his life he had come up against a situation that he didn't know how to handle. How could he tell the woman he loved to forget the past and The Raven? He wanted to tell her to look to the future with him. He wasn't at all sure how to approach her. He had never before been at a loss as to how to handle a woman, but his love for Season ran deep. At times it was a wild and uncontrollable passion. But she didn't love him. How would he succeed in erasing The Raven from her heart when she carried his child within her body? He wondered how it was possible for a woman like Season to love a man who had treated her so badly. Was it possible for a woman to love a man whose face she had never seen?

Lucas sat down in a cane-bottomed chair and propped his long legs up on the porch railing. It was his wedding night and he was as nervous and unsure as an unshaved youth with his first love. Season was the first woman he had ever loved, and she loved a dark image of a man who had gotten her with child and then abandoned her. Standing up, he entered the house and climbed the stairs slowly, like a man who was going to his own execution.

Chapter Twenty-Three

Season had blown out the lamp, so the bedroom was bathed in the soft light of the moon which filtered through the window. She was trying hard to prepare herself mentally for Lucas' return. She kept reminding herself over and over that Lucas was her husband, but it didn't seem to help with her anxiety.

When Season heard the door open, she slid down under the covers and waited tensely. The sounds she heard indicated that Lucas was undressing, but he didn't say a word to her. Finally, when she felt the bed dip under his weight, her stomach muscles tightened into knots.

"Season, relax. For the moment, I want no more than to talk to you."

"I'm . . . listening." Her body was rigid, and she was anything but relaxed.

He reached over, took her hand, and began gently massaging her fingers. "I have a dilemma, Season; perhaps you can help me with it."

She felt herself begin to relax just a bit. "I will try, Lucas."

"In about a week I have to make a trip to New York. As much as I hate to leave you, it is unavoidable." His hand moved slowly up her arm, and Season shivered at his soft touch.

"I didn't know you would be going away so soon," she said, trying to digest what he was telling her.

"I would take you with me, but that's quite impossible. In your condition, you should be here at Rosemont where you can be taken care of. Besides, I doubt you will be too anxious to face Edmund, just now."

"I don't mind not going. You are right about me not wanting to face Edmund. I would rather remain here, but what is your dilemma?"

"The problem I am faced with is not knowing if you would be angry with me for abandoning you so soon after our wedding. Believe me when I tell you I would much rather be with you than go to New York." He slowly pulled her head over and rested it against his shoulder.

"Of course I will not be angry, Lucas. What kind of a wife would I be if I complained when my husband had to go away on business?"

Lucas ran his hand over her soft hair and wrapped a curl around his finger. "Perhaps I hoped you would be more upset at the thought of being parted from me. That isn't the case though, is it, Season?"

She sighed as his hand drifted down to her chin and traced its outline. "I will be happy to see you when you return, Lucas." Her heart was beginning to beat faster as he pulled her tighter against his hard body.

"Will you, my lady?"

"Yes, of course."

Lucas rested his face against hers and she could feel his warm breath stir her hair. "I will be thinking of you every day we are parted, Season," he whispered against her ear. "I doubt that I shall think of anything but you."

Season felt the warmth of his nearness spread throughout her body. Suddenly she felt that she wasn't good enough for him. Lucas deserved a wife who had never been with another man. She felt as if she were somehow cheating him.

"Lucas, I am so ashamed," she said, burying her face against the mat of curly hair on his chest.

He turned over on his side and drew Season around so their bodies fit snugly together. "Never be ashamed with me, Season. If I find no shame in making love to you, then neither should you."

It felt so good to be in his arms. For the first time in many weeks Season felt cherished. "Does it not matter to you that you were not the first man to . . ."

He tilted her face up and touched her lips ever so lightly with his mouth. "Nothing matters, my lady, but that you are in my bed and that I am about to make you mine as no other man ever could."

Season couldn't stop the tremor that shook her body as he nuzzled her ear. "After tonight there will be no doubt in your mind as to whom you belong, Season," he whispered against her lips.

"Lucas, how could you want me?" she asked, as his lips moved to the arch of her neck.

"I want you more than I have ever wanted anything.

I think you knew it the night of the ball in New York," he murmured against her silken skin. "Did you not sense something between us that night?"

Season smiled as her arms went about his neck. "That night I thought you were so handsome, and I hoped you would turn out to be Edmund Kensworthy. I was devastated when I found out you weren't my intended husband."

He laced his hands through her silken hair and raised her face so the soft moonlight would fall on her. "Were you now? That's very interesting."

She smiled. "I must confess, I thought you were the answer to a young girl's dream of the perfect hero. You are quite the most handsome man I have ever met."

His golden eyes blazed when he realized what they had lost. They had both been drawn to each other that night, but The Raven had stepped in and destroyed what might have been. Lucas knew Edmund would have presented no serious problem. He wondered if Season would have become his bride more willingly had he courted her after that night. Still, there was no reason for regret. After all, Season was now his wife, and he had all the time in the world to woo and win her. But first he wanted to wipe away her memory of The Raven.

"You found another hero after that night didn't you, Season?" he whispered. Lucas watched as her delicate brows came together in a frown.

"Lucas, I am your wife, and I will do for you all the things a wife is supposed to do for her husband, but I do not ever want to discuss The Raven with you. Please do not ask me about him again."

He raised a golden curl to his lips, and the sweet scent caused his senses to reel. "It's just as well, Season. I do not want three people in my marriage bed."

Season felt the sting of his words in the very depth of her heart, and she reached out and touched his face. "There is no one here but you and me, Lucas." The moment the words left her mouth, she remembered the baby she was carrying and knew he was also remembering that fact.

His hand moved down to the ribbon on her nightdress and he untied it slowly. Pushing the gown off her shoulders, his hand then moved over her breasts. "I will make you so thoroughly mine that you won't even remember the time you spent with The Raven," he whispered.

Season felt his lips nibble at the hollow in her neck, and her body came to life. Somewhere deep inside a voice told her Lucas would take what until now had belonged only to The Raven. She fought against that voice. Lucas was her husband; she didn't want her memory of The Raven to haunt her tonight of all nights. Lucas had been kind to her, and she wanted to repay him in the only way she could—if not with her heart, then at least with her body.

As her hands drifted around his shoulders, she remembered the feel of another man's back beneath her fingertips, and when his mouth drifted down to play with the tips of her swollen breasts, she remembered the feel of another man's lips. As he pulled her forward and raised her nightdress over her head, she remembered The Raven performing the same deed.

"Please, Lucas, I cannot!" she cried out. "This is

wrong. Please don't force me to do this."

"I will use no force, Season. What I take from you tonight will be freely given," he said, as he rubbed his chin against her face. "Is it wrong because you want me? You do, you know; but you are fighting against it." His hand drifted down to her stomach, and his warm caress sent a tremor through Season's body. "You may deny with words that you want me, Season, but your body will lend the lie to your true feelings. I can so easily make you want me, you know." To demonstrate his point, his hand moved lower to the tangle of hair between her thighs, and he massaged her gently.

Season threw her head back and bit her lips to keep from crying out. The Raven had awakened her body, and she hadn't realized until now that she hungered for the touch of a man's hands. "Lucas, you are making me . . . I want to . . ."

With one hand he continued to massage her between the thighs, and with the other he pulled her face up to his. "Say it, Season," he demanded in a hard voice. "Say that you want me."

Her senses were not functioning properly, and her body felt as if it were under the domination of a master at pleasing women. "I want you, Lucas," she whispered, before his mouth settled on hers in a passionate kiss. Season clung to Lucas' shoulders as if they were her life line.

She felt, rather than heard, Lucas groan, when she opened her mouth to his plundering tongue. When The Raven had made love to her, it had been dark, and she had never seen his face. Now the room was bathed in soft moonlight, and she could clearly see Lucas' face; still, she couldn't separate the two men in her mind. Both men awakened her body to a passion that surprised her.

Suddenly Lucas seemed to be driven by a strong impulse. He knew Season was fighting against the feelings he had aroused in her body, and he was wildly jealous because she was thinking about The Raven on their wedding night. He wouldn't be satisfied until his name was on her lips.

"Damn you, Season," he ground out between clenched teeth, "I warned you I would never share my wedding bed with another man's ghost." His hands were rough as he pulled her beneath him and spread her legs apart. With a forward thrust, he entered her body and felt her tremble beneath him. He thrust forward and back, making hard frenzied movements, as if by sheer willpower he could drive away the man who stood between them.

Season felt a stabbing pain and wondered why Lucas was being so rough with her. She bit her lip, not wanting to cry out. Burying her face against his shoulder, a sob escaped her lips.

When Lucas realized he was hurting her, he tensed. What devil was driving him? He remembered the child Season carried and gentled his movements. "My sweet, sweet love," he said, sprinkling kisses over her tear-streaked face, "forgive me."

Season was moved to tears by his tender words, for she realized that she must have hurt Lucas by reminding him of her love for The Raven. Reaching up, she touched his face and guided his mouth down to her lips. "Love me, Lucas," she whimpered. "Make me love you."

His smooth gentle movements caused a slow-burning fire deep inside Season. She closed her eyes and allowed the sweet feelings he aroused to wash over her.

"Season, open your eyes," Lucas told her. "I want you to see who is mastering your body. I insist that you look at me!" he commanded.

She gazed directly into passion-laced golden eyes, and there was no doubt in her heart or mind about who was giving her body the pleasure she craved.

"Say my name, Season, so I will be certain you know who is in possession of your body," he whispered.

"Lucas," she answered in a breathless voice. "It is you, Lucas, my husband."

Swiftly, he thrust forward, his body trembled, and Season felt an answering climax within herself.

Lucas rolled onto his back and pulled Season on top of him. He ran his hands over her back and hips. "You are mine, Season. After tonight there will be no ghost between the two of us."

She laid her head against his shoulder. She felt cherished and safe, but she didn't know whether she felt love for this man who seemed to demand it of her. He had given her his name and made her the mistress of Rosemont, he had given her body what she had craved, and all he seemed to ask for in return was her heart—such a simple thing, and yet her heart couldn't be given at will. Deep inside she knew she still loved the father of her child; yet more than anything she wished she could give her heart to the man who had given her his name.

"Go to sleep," Lucas whispered against her ear. "You have had a very emotional day, my little wife."

Season sighed contentedly and closed her eyes. The warmth of his body lulled her. She felt herself drifting off to sleep while Lucas' hands moved soothingly over her back. He seemed to be consoling her as one would a troubled child.

Lucas heard Season's soft breathing and knew she had fallen asleep. Her body was soft against his as he ran his hands over the silken hair that spilled over his chest. Inside him the demon still lurked. He had satisfied Season's hunger tonight, but he knew that a shadow still stood between them. How long will it take me to wipe The Raven from her mind? he wondered. He wasn't certain that he would ever be able to win her heart.

He felt his body awaken again with a burning hunger, but he pushed his need aside. He was very aware of the child Season carried, and he didn't want to do anything that would cause her to lose it. Closing his eyes, he laid his cheek against her sweet-smelling hair. His heart seemed to swell with love, and it was such a new feeling that he didn't know how to deal with it. Season sighed in her sleep, and he kissed her cheek.

"Sleep, little love," he whispered. "Find your forget-fulness in sleep."

Season awoke when Molly entered the room and pulled the heavy curtains aside to let bright sunlight stream into the bedroom.

"You had best be up and about, my lady. Mistress Carrington's fluttering about and declaring there's going to be another wedding in this house today."

Season sat up and blinked her eyes. "Has Robert Wolf returned from Philadelphia?"

"Yes, and Mistress Carrington will be needing your assistance to make all the preparations. I don't know what this world's coming to with two weddings taking place in such a short time." Molly gave Season a guarded glance. "How does Mr. Carrington feel about the baby you are carrying, my lady?"

Season blinked her eyes. "How can you know about the baby? Did someone tell you?"

Molly gave Season an all-knowing smile. "Ain't I been looking after you most all your life? Don't I know everything that concerns you? I ain't said nothing because I was waiting for you to tell me. I know what all this secret wedding was about."

"I could never hide anything from you, could I, Molly? If you know that much, you must also know that the child I am carrying belongs to The Raven."

"Yes, I know that. If I was you I'd forget who the real father was. Mr. Carrington saw fit to marry you, and you owe him an awful lot."

Season smiled. "I believe you like Lucas, Molly."

"I suppose he's as good as some and better than others," the maid admitted.

Season's eyes moved to the pillow next to hers and she saw the imprint where Lucas had slept beside her. "Where is Mr. Carrington, Molly?"

"He ate breakfast bright and early and said to tell you he was going over to the Wolf Plantation to help

Mr. Wolf with the wedding plans."

Season threw the covers aside and started to get up before she realized she wasn't wearing her nightgown. Blushing a bright red, she pulled the bedcovers over her nakedness. "Molly, I want a bath, and make it quickly," she said hurriedly, trying to cover her embarrassment. "If there is to be a wedding today, we have many things to do."

Molly smiled knowingly. "I must say you look the blushing bride this morning."

"The bath, Molly," Season reminded her maid firmly.

"I'll just bring your breakfast up first, and when you've eaten, then I'll prepare your bath," Molly stated, moving to the door. She wanted to remind Season that she still exercised some authority over her life.

When Season was alone, she reached for her robe, pulled it on, and belted it about her waist. She felt strangely light-hearted today. Remembering the night before, she smiled to herself. Lucas had penetrated the wall she had built around her heart. True, he had only cracked it, but she had hopes that he would soon pull it down all together.

The day passed quickly with everyone busily preparing for Rebecca's wedding. Hand-delivered invitations were sent out to friends and neighbors, and food had to be prepared. Season directed the packing of Rebecca's clothing and belongings, and had them transported to the Wolf Plantation.

By the time Season helped Rebecca into her wedding gown, she was exhausted. Standing back, she observed her sister-in-law, and smiled. "You look lovely, Rebecca. I just know you are going to be happy."

"I am a bit nervous, Season. Did you have butterflies in your stomach when you married Lucas?"

"That's a very good way to describe the way I felt, but put your fears aside. You are marrying a man who loves you, and you love him. Your marriage will be wonderful. I know you are going to be happy."

Rebecca hugged Season tightly. "No one will know that Robert and I were married just one day after you and my brother. Lucas said over breakfast this morning that he was going to announce tonight that you and he had been married several months ago."

Season motioned for Rebecca to turn around, and she studied her closely. "I have just the thing you need for a finishing touch."

Rebecca watched as Season opened a small black velvet case and removed a string of lustrous pearls. "I want you to have these as a gift from me to you."

Rebecca touched the pearls wistfully. "They are very beautiful, but I could never accept so valuable a gift from you, Season."

"Nonsense. I want you to have them." Season smiled. "Of course, you may not want them when you learn that they were given to me by Queen Charlotte for my twelfth birthday. She and my mother were good friends and every year she sends me a birthday gift."

"The queen gave you these?" Rebecca said in an awed voice. "Sometimes I forget that your father is such an important person."

Season fastened the pearls about Rebecca's neck. "I am much more important now than I ever was before, Rebecca. I am Mrs. Lucas Carrington of Virginia."

Rebecca hugged her sister-in-law. "I shall always treasure the pearls because you gave them to me, Season."

Neither of them knew Lucas had entered the room until he spoke. "I have missed you today, Mrs. Lucas Carrington of Virginia," he said softly.

Rebecca noted the twinkle in her brother's eyes and the blush on Season's cheek and giggled. "La, one would think the two of you are but newly wedded. This is supposed to be my day, remember?"

Season smiled as she crossed the room. "I will leave the two of you alone. I need to go to the kitchen and see if the food is ready."

Lucas reached out and took her hand. "Have you taken over the running of my house then, madame."

She smiled up at him. "I have been well trained for just that function. You will find me to be a very able housekeeper, Mr. Carrington."

He raised her fingers to his lips. "Until later," he said, his golden eyes dancing.

When Season had gone, Lucas turned to his sister. "You look beautiful, Rebecca. I believe for all your faults, I am loath to part with you."

She went into his outstretched arms. "I will miss you too, Lucas, but thank goodness we will be no more than a few miles apart."

"All I want is your happiness. I can let you go, knowing Robert will take good care of you. I just left him, and he is most anxious to make you his bride. If ever any man loved a woman, he loves you."

Rebecca looked at her brother and her soft brown eyes shone. "We are both fortunate, Lucas, for we love two very exceptional people."

He hugged her tightly. "Come, the guests have begun to arrive, and your bridegroom waits impatiently."

Season stood beside Lucas, whose hand rested on her arm, as Rebecca became Mrs. Robert Wolf. She felt a prickle of envy at the touching way Rebecca and Robert gazed into each other's eyes. How fortunate Lucas' sister is to be marrying the man she loves, Season thought. She could feel Lucas' eyes on her, and she looked up to see the soft light reflected there. She definitely felt something for this man, but she couldn't yet put a name to her feelings.

When the ceremony was over, the happy couple was soon surrounded by well-wishers.

When Season noticed Marlana Bartlett approaching her and Lucas, she tried to fade into the background, but Lucas placed his hand about her waist possessively and kept her beside him.

"Lucas, you have allowed your sister to beat you to the altar," Marlana said, standing on her tiptoes and kissing him boldly on the lips.

Lucas pushed Marlana away and gave Season an apologetic glance. Seeing the look that passed between Lucas and Season, Marlana turned poisonous eyes on the woman she thought to be her rival.

"I see you are still lingering in Virginia, Mistress Chatsworth. You must find our climate agreeable."

Season glanced at Lucas, wondering if he had caught the biting undertones in the woman's voice; but he seemed not to notice as he studied the tip of his boot.

"I sometimes find the climate more agreeable than the people, don't you, Mistress Bartlett?" Season retaliated.

Marlana took Lucas' arm and pulled him away from Season. "I would like to talk to you, Lucas," she said, staring at Season with icy blue eyes.

"Whatever you want to say to me can be said in front of Season, Marlana," he answered.

"Very well, but she may not like what I have to say. There is considerable gossip going around the country about her remaining at Rosemont for such a long time. I think you should be aware of what people are saying."

"Can I assume you defended Season when people spoke ill of her, Marlana?" Rebecca said, coming up beside Season and taking her hand.

"Well . . . I hardly know her, and I don't feel qualified to defend her," Marlana said indignantly. By now other people had gathered about them to hear the exchange between Rebecca and Marlana.

Lucas gave Season an encouraging smile and pulled her closer to him. "Ladies and gentlemen, may I have your attention," he said, raising his voice. "I realize today is my sister's day, and I don't intend to steal her thunder, but I know she will forgive me if I make an announcement."

By now he had everyone's attention; all present waited for him to continue.

"Many of you have met Season Chatsworth. It was just pointed out to me by Marlana that there is much speculation going about as to why she is staying with my sister and myself. I would like to take this opportunity to clear up any misunderstanding. Season is in truth the daughter of the Duke of Chatsworth. I met her some time ago in New York, and I am happy to tell you she gave up her father's illustrious name to become Mrs. Lucas Carrington."

Season watched the color drain from Marlana's face as the wedding guests began to murmur among themselves. Lucas held up his hand and a hush fell over the crowd. "I hope you will all welcome her to Virginia, because she will be living here from now on."

Season was unprepared for the warmth of the people who now came to her side. She received so many best wishes and dinner and luncheon invitations that her head began to swim. It didn't escape her notice, however, that Marlana Bartlett and her mother were not among the well-wishers.

The house seemed strangely empty after the newly married couple and their wedding guests had departed.

When Lucas had excused himself and disappeared behind the doors to his study, Season had easily assumed the role of mistress of Rosemont and had supervised the straightening of the house and the disposal of the clutter created by the wedding party.

When at last everything was cleaned to her satisfaction, she walked out onto the veranda which had become a favorite spot of hers. The western skies were painted a glorious wash of color as the dying rays of the sun reflected off the gathering clouds.

She smiled when Lucas came up beside her and slipped his arm about her shoulders. "You did me proud today, Mrs. Carrington. I was the envy of almost every man present. The valley will talk of little else for weeks to come. They will rave about how fortunate I am for having married the loveliest woman who ever drew breath."

"You flatter me," Season said. She was unaccustomed to receiving such compliments, and she thought her husband might tend to exaggerate a bit. "I saw a wistful look in many young ladies' eyes, and anger in Mistress Bartlett's. I believe I walked away with the catch of the county."

Lucas turned Season to face him, and she saw a strange glow in his eyes—as if the dying sunlight were reflected in their golden depths. "We are alone now," he said, lowering his head and nuzzling her neck.

Season wanted to move away, but she felt a slow warmth move over her as his mouth caressed the smooth column of her throat.

"Suppose we go to our room, Season," he whispered in his deep voice. "I have thought about you all day. I am impatient to be alone with you."

"I don't think—"

His lips covered hers, cutting off her protest. Season's heart fluttered as he deepened the kiss. Raising his head, he took her arm and guided her into the house. When they reached the staircase, he lifted her into his arms and carried her to their bedroom.

The room was aglow with the rosy hue of the last dying embers of the sun, and Season trembled as his head dipped to nuzzle her ear while he leisurely unhooked the back of her gown.

Lucas spoke no words as he removed her gown and tossed it aside. As his eyes caressed her body, Season boldly gazed back at him. She could tell that he was pleased by what he saw, and that thought caused her heart to beat faster.

She was unable to speak when he started unbuttoning his shirt. She wanted to turn away, but her eyes swept the wide expanse of his muscled shoulders and were then drawn to the black curly hair on his chest. He removed his boots, and when his hands went to his trousers, she watched, fascinated, as he stepped out of them and dropped them to the floor. Season had never seen a naked man before, but she knew that Lucas was as perfect as a man could be. With his long powerful legs, his flat stomach, and his handsome face, he was magnificent! Her eyes followed the dark hair of his chest, down past his thighs to his swollen manhood.

"My, God, you are tempting me, my lady," he said in a gruff voice. "Did no one ever tell you not to look at a man like that?" He pulled her into his arms.

Season threw back her head and parted her lips. "You looked at me first," she purred. Then, startled by her own daring, she wondered if he would think her too bold. When her naked body came up against his, a tremor shook her and her flesh seemed to tingle.

"Season, will you fault me if I say no woman has ever stirred my blood as you do?"

"I know there have been many women before me," she admitted.

"There have been many before you, but there will be none after you," he said in a deep voice. "Can you say the same, Season?" he asked. Picking her up in his arms, he carried her not to the bed, but to the thick, shaggy, white rug in front of the window. As he hovered above her, she reached up to him.

She knew when she looked into his soft golden eyes that he was silently waiting for her to answer his question. He wanted to know if she would break her wedding vows should The Raven come back.

"I will never dishonor you, Lucas. I would die before I would ever shame you."

He lowered himself beside her and pulled her into his arms. "I wonder if you could withstand the test?"

His exploring hands moved slowly and sensuously down her throat and across her breasts, gently caressing the rosy tips. She groaned with pleasure. When one hand moved down her stomach to lightly rest against her inner thigh, she couldn't seem to breathe properly. His touch was so gentle it was as if he thought Season a fragile thing, as if he feared she might break.

"You are so lovely," he said in a gruff voice. "I ache for you. Do you ache inside, Season?"

She was inacapable of answering when his head moved down to sprinkle kisses over her stomach. Yes, I ache inside, she thought wildly. He had set her body on fire, and he knew it. Her hands moved up to untie the queue in his ebony hair, and his dark locks flowed about his shoulders, blending with her golden hair. Drawing his face up to her lips, she spoke. "I ache, Lucas," she admitted at last.

Lucas' breath caught in his throat as he tasted her sweet lips. He had wanted to master her tonight, but in truth, she had become the master. He wanted to bury himself in her silken body, to make her part of his flesh. He thought of all the puny feelings other women had aroused in him in the past, and he knew he would never want anyone but this golden-haired seductress.

When he guided his swollen member into her warm, moist body, he thought the sensation he experienced was a little like dying. He was losing his grip on sanity. This woman he had married was stealing his mind as well as his heart. He couldn't bear to think that he must leave her in a few days.

Season felt wave after wave of pleasure flow through her body. When Lucas' hot mouth devoured her lips, she emitted a strangled moan of pleasure.

As Season's soft arms twined around his neck, Lucas buried himself deeply inside her. "You are mine, Season. No one can have you after tonight."

"No, no one," she breathed.

"I have waited an eternity to find the woman who could feed the hunger that raged within my body. I have found her, and she is you, my wife."

"Lucas . . ." She groaned. He seemed to be caressing her inner body, to be making her drift on an endless sea of pleasure from which they both soared to the heavens on an endless, pleasurable journey.

As his burning lips bruised her mouth, he tried to erase all memory of The Raven from her mind for all eternity.

Season felt that her whole being was feather-light, floating. Then her body shuddered, and she knew she had reached the highest point of ecstasy. She heard Lucas groan as one tremor after another shook his body. She knew she had given all of herself to him, because he had demanded it of her. He had mastered her and would take nothing less.

"My love, my lady," he whispered against her ear, and suddenly Season remembered another voice and other hands that had caressed her body. A sad and unwelcome loneliness swept into her heart, and she knew that even now Lucas hadn't succeeded in wiping out the memory of her dark lord of the sea.

A sob escaped her lips as Lucas rolled over and pulled her against him.

"What's wrong, love? Was I too rough with you? I didn't hurt the baby, did I?"

"I . . . feel as if I have wronged you, Lucas, and betrayed him at the same time." The words were out before she could stop them, and she felt Lucas stiffen.

Season clapped a hand over her mouth. What had she said? Looking up into his golden eyes, she saw the anger smoldering there. She tried to move away from him, realizing what she had said; but he jerked her against him. She waited to hear his angry words, but they were never spoken.

When he released his grip on her, she watched him stand up. "Damn you, Season, you are determined to throw happiness away with both hands. What can I do to make you see what you are doing?"

"I . . . am sorry, Lucas."

'Are you?"

"Yes. Oh yes!"

"You cannot have us both, Season. You are going to have to decide which of us you want."

"Lucas, I'm your wife. I told you how I felt about The Raven before we were married. Knowing this, you still wanted me. I am trying to be a good wife, but I cannot forget him overnight."

"Are you my wife? By law you are, but I wonder what that means to you." He began to dress, and she watched helplessly as he tucked his shirt into his trousers.

"I was going to leave next week, but I think it would be a good idea if I were to leave now, Season."

"Lucas!"

"Be silent!" he commanded. "I don't wish to hear anything you have to say at the moment. I don't know how long I will be away, but you will be taken care of. If something comes up that you can't handle, I know Robert will be glad to help you."

Season scrambled to her knees, wanting to call him back as he picked up his jacket and walked to the door.

Without a backward glance, he left the room, shutting the door quietly behind him. She had the strongest urge to run after him and beg him not to go. She hated herself for causing the hurt she had seen in his eyes. He didn't deserve to be compared to another man. Lucas had offered her his love, and she had thrown it back in his face.

Crawling onto the bed, she pulled the covers over her. Even now The Raven had reached out to destroy her, and in the process he had destroyed any tender feelings Lucas had for her.

She listened to the sound of a lone horseman riding away and knew that Lucas was gone. Season cried tears of despair when she realized what she had done to her husband that night. She couldn't really blame The

Raven; it had been she who had dealt Lucas a cruel blow.

Lucas urged his horse into a faster gallop as he raced into the night. He wanted to put as much distance between himself and Season as he could. She had become his one weakness, and she had torn his heart to shreds tonight. Perhaps it was best to give her some time to consider things. With him away, she would be able to think more clearly.

He desperately wanted to turn his horse and ride back to Season, but he wouldn't allow himself to give in to that weakness.

"Damn you, Season," he said aloud. "Damn you for making me love you!"

Chapter Twenty-Four

Lucas had been gone for over two weeks, and Season was having a hard time dealing with her guilt. She knew she had been the cause of his early departure, and she wished he would return so she could apologize to him.

The days seemed endless. Although she tried to keep busy, the manor house seemed to run smoothly with very little help from her. Drucilla had been running the household for over forty years and was more than competent.

Each night Season sat down to a solitary dinner and wished that Lucas would come home. She was finding that she missed him more than she had thought she would. The house seemed so empty without him.

She was only happy when she rode out on horseback to enjoy the crisp fall air. Then she was reminded of Chatsworth, where she had been isolated from the rest of the world, where she'd had no one to talk to except the servants who looked after her comfort.

Season always received smiling greetings from the

slaves who worked the plantation, and she was learning to call many of them by name. The overseer, Mr. Walls, was an elderly man who had been at Rosemont for twenty years. He was always polite to Season, but they very rarely exchanged more than a friendly hello.

She missed Rebecca, who had gone to Williamsburg with Robert for their honeymoon and wouldn't be back for another week.

Season could do nothing but mark the passing of time and wait for Lucas to return. She tried never to think of the man who had stolen her innocence aboard the *Andromeda,* but she carried with her a grim reminder of him—the baby growing in her body.

One warm day Season allowed Molly to lace her into a gray velvet riding habit. She placed a matching gray hat on her unbound hair, set it at a rakish angle, and picked up her riding crop. Feeling almost lighthearted, she headed for the stables and mounted a gray gelding called Wildfire. Then she rode away from the house, across the meadow.

After Season had ridden a good way, she pulled up her horse and dismounted. The countryside was awash with brilliant autumn colors, and she drank in the beauty that surrounded her. Trailing its reins, the gray grazed near the stream. It was so peaceful that Season removed her hat and allowed the warm breeze to tangle her golden hair.

Leaning back against a tree trunk, she closed her eyes and listened to the soothing sounds of the stream. Brightly colored leaves drifted down about her, and she sighed contentedly.

Season hadn't been resting very well at night, but

now she felt drowsy and vaguely realized she was about to drift off to sleep. The riding crop she had been holding dropped from her fingers, and her head slipped over to one side. Soon she drifted into a sound sleep.

Wildfire continued to graze on the dried grasses, unaware that his rider slept.

As the afternoon wore on, no one came to disturb the mistress of the manor. Finally, dark clouds covered the sun, and the warm breeze turned chill. Season awoke, feeling cold. She blinked her eyes and slowly stood up. She had a strange, uneasy feeling when she looked up at the sky and saw the storm clouds gathering.

Walking down to the stream, she dipped her hands into the cool water and splashed it on her face. A quick glance told her that Wildfire had not deserted her while she slept. She supposed she would have to return to the house, but she hated the thought of spending another lonely evening.

"Why so melancholy, my lady?" The deep raspy voice she knew so well had come from behind her. Season didn't need to turn around to know The Raven had come! Her heart was beating wildly, and she could hardly breathe as she turned her head to see him step from behind a tree.

"What are you doing here?" she asked, edging her way toward Wildfire. She knew she had to get away as quickly as possible, but she feared The Raven might try to stop her.

A strong breeze lifted his black cape and spread it out behind him. He stood with his legs spread arrogantly apart, his hands resting on his waist as if he were still aboard the *Andromeda*. "I have been watching you sleep for a long time. Do you know how beautiful you are?"

Season took another step toward Wildfire and was exasperated when the horse shied away. "You didn't answer my question. Why are you here?" she asked again.

Even though the black helm hid The Raven's face, she could feel him staring at her. Suddenly he moved, so quickly that he seemed to swoop down on her. She would have run from him, but he blocked her escape route, trapping her between himself and the stream.

"I will scream if you come near me!" she threatened. "I hoped never to see you again."

"There is no one to hear you scream, my lady. I made sure we were alone before I showed myself," he said in an amused voice.

"My husband will kill you if he finds you on Rosemont land. You had better leave quickly."

"I also made sure he was away before I came. I must say I was amazed to find you had married an English sympathizer. You didn't waste much time, did you? The last I knew you were to marry Edmund Kensworthy."

"How do you know Lucas isn't at the house and might come looking for me at any moment?" she asked, as tiny prickles of fear and excitement tickled her neck. What if he has come to take me away again? she thought, frightened.

"I make it my business to know everything that concerns you, my lady." His hand reached out and captured hers. "I even know you are carrying my child. Could you not have waited until I came back before you married Lucas Carrington?" His voice seemed to hold a note of accusation.

"How dare you say this to me! You left me alone and dependent on strangers. The child I carry may be yours by deed, but it belongs in fact to my husband."

He held her chin in a tight grip and forced her to look at him. "Do you love this man?"

Season pushed his hand away. "That is no concern of yours. I would suggest you leave at once." A part of her was frightened of him, while another part wished he would take her in his arms and soothe her battered heart.

"Suppose I told you I have come to take you away with me? Would you come freely, my lady?"

She whirled away from him. "You must be mad to ask such a thing of me! I am married, and I would never dishonor my husband in any way!"

The Raven seemed to tower above her. "He has no right to you—you belong to me. Do you ever think of golden beaches, of the night you willingly gave yourself to me? Come with me now and we will sail the seas and tempt fate."

Season threw her head back and tried to conceal her indecision. The Raven was offering her what she had once wanted more than anything. Now it was too late. How dare he come back into her life as if he had not abandoned her. If Lucas had not offered her the protection of his name, she would have been shamed before the whole world. No matter what her feelings were for The Raven, she would never let him persuade her to leave Lucas.

"I will never go with you, Raven. I want you to leave

now and never . . . come back."

The gloved hand that brushed across Season's face was gentle, and she closed her eyes. "I know your husband is away from home. Come away with me now, my lady. You know you want to."

Her eyes flew open. "What makes you think I would want to go away with you. What kind of life would I have locked in your cabin aboard the *Andromeda?* What would I do? Wait for the times you would remember I was alive so you could come to me and—"

"Make love to you," he finished for her.

"Go away! I don't want you here," she cried in a strangled voice, backing farther away from him.

"I could dispose of your husband, and you would be free to marry me," he suggested in an amused voice.

"You wouldn't dare! If you ever harmed Lucas, I would hate you until I die." Season moved closer to him and clutched at his black cape. "Promise me you will never hurt Lucas. Promise me now!"

"If he means so much to you, my lady, perhaps I should get rid of him. It would solve one of my problems."

"Lucas is no problem to you."

"Ah, but there you are wrong, my lady. He has what I treasure most in life."

"If you mean me, you didn't treasure me enough to keep me with you."

"I thought you wanted to be free of me. Did I not do you a favor by turning you over to Lucas Carrington? Besides, when I allowed you to go, I had no way of knowing you were carrying my child."

Season made a leap for the horse's trailing reins and would have mounted had a hand not gone around her waist. To her surprise, however, The Raven lifted her up and placed her in the saddle, but he kept a hand on the reins.

"I will be back a week from tonight. I will be waiting for you right here at eight o'clock."

Season jerked the reins away from him and whirled the horse around. "I will not be here," she said.

"You will come. I know you wouldn't want to keep me waiting. Remember, one week from tonight, right here."

Season applied the whip to her horse, and the animal leaped forward. She rode away without once looking back. Her heart seemed to be keeping time with the horse's hooves, and something inside her wanted to return to The Raven so she could throw herself into his arms. Even now she loved him.

Once she came within sight of the plantation house, she slowed her pace. Why had The Raven come? she wondered. What did he expect of her? He had said he knew about the baby, but he hadn't sounded over-joyed. Perhaps he wanted her to betray Lucas. He might want her to extract some information from him. No matter how much she loved The Raven, she would never betray Lucas.

The Raven watched Season depart, a dull ache deep inside him. He had wanted to tell her how happy he was about the baby, but he hadn't found the right words. He had tried to stay away from her, but something had pulled him back. He had asked her to come to him next

417

week, and he knew she would come. At that time, he would find out how deep her feelings for him were.

Three days had passed since Season had seen The Raven. She was supervising the cleaning of the books in the library, when Molly came in with a strange expression on her face.

"You aren't going to believe who's here, insisting he see you right away, my lady?" the maid said, placing her hands on her hips.

"I have told you repeatedly not to call me 'my lady,' Molly," I am no longer using that title."

"Just because you aren't using it, don't make you other than what you was born."

Season sighed exasperatedly and she wondered if Molly would ever see reason. "Who wants to see me?" she asked, removing the apron she had tied about her waist earlier.

"None other than Sir Edmund Kensworthy, my lady, or ma'am, or whatever you want me to call you."

"Edmund is here?"

"Yes. I told him to wait in the sitting room, but if I'd had any sense I'd have sent him on his way."

"I wonder what he wants?"

"Like as not he'll tell you when you see him," Molly said, sailing out of the room.

Season dreaded the thought of seeing Edmund again. She paused at the sitting-room door and straightened her hair before entering.

Edmund rose from the settee when he saw Season.

"Edmund, what are you doing here?" she asked,

noticing that he wasn't wearing his uniform.

"I might ask you the same thing. If my memory serves me right, you were supposed to marry me, but I find that instead you married my cousin, Lucas."

She walked over to the settee and seated herself, then she motioned him to a chair. "I had thought you would be glad to be free of your obligation to me. Did my father tell you that I am married to Lucas?"

"Oh, yes. He made quite an ado about how happy you were and he said you would be residing in Virginia."

"I still don't understand why you are here, Edmund. You are out of uniform, and if you are caught, you will be arrested as a spy."

"Oh, is the lady concerned about me?" he asked sarcastically. "I am truly touched."

"Why did you come here, Edmund? You know you shouldn't be here with Lucas away." She couldn't help thinking that Edmund's behavior was very peculiar. He was giving her a strangely uneasy feeling.

"I came here to kill my cousin, Lucas, and to get some things straight between the two of us, Season. Let's just say I wasn't overjoyed to be left waiting at the altar. I had my mind set on having you as my wife. Lucas is as good as dead."

Season stood up and faced him. "I will never allow you to harm Lucas, and he wouldn't like the way you are talking to me. If you are wise, you will be gone before he finds you on Rosemont."

"When I left New York, your husband was still there. I might say he seemed to be enjoying himself without his wife. You might want to ask him about a certain

Lady Southerland. They seem to be very good . . . friends."

Season felt her face burn. How dare Edmund imply that Lucas was seeing another woman. "State your business and then leave, Edmund. I have neither the time nor the desire to trade insults with you."

He stood up and walked slowly over to her. Season watched as he withdrew something from his pocket, and she gasped when she saw it was her diamond and emerald necklace. The last time she had seen the necklace had been in Maude's bedroom in Tripoli! Quickly she looked at Edmund, searching his face for an answer.

She picked up the necklace and held it out to him. "How did you get this? If you have this necklace you must be . . . No one could have this but The Raven!"

Edmund's eyes narrowed as he studied Season's face. "Will you betray me?"

Season felt a sob rise from deep inside her. Edmund couldn't be The Raven! He just couldn't be! She could never have felt love for Edmund Kensworthy. Yet he must be. There was no other explanation for how he had gotten her necklace.

She arose on shaky legs. "I . . . feel ill. I cannot talk to you now. We can meet as planned, and I'll talk to you then, Edmund."

"Where and when will you meet me, Season?" he asked looking at her strangely.

"I told you I will meet you as we planned," she said, knowing she would never allow Edmund to harm her husband. Not even if he were The Raven.

"Tell me where we meet, so I may know that you

remember," he said, watching her closely.

"At the stream, at eight o'clock Friday night—just as you said the other night. Why do you come to me and tell me that you are going to harm Lucas? I didn't take you seriously the other night down by the river, Edmund."

"Let us just say I have been brooding on what my cousin robbed me of. Lucas hasn't long to live, Season. I always knew I would have to kill him one day."

Season saw Edmund's eyes glaze over, and she shivered. "Surely you must be mad. How can you think I would stand by while you harmed Lucas?"

"I don't see you as much of a threat, Season. Just do as you are told, and you won't get hurt. Tell no one you have seen me," Edmund warned.

"Just leave now," Season said, feeling sick inside. How could Edmund be The Raven? And yet it all fit together. He was in a position to know every move the British made.

She moved to the door, thinking that if she didn't get away she was going to really be sick. She raced up the stairs, and when she reached her bedroom, she picked up a cloth and wet it in the pitcher on her washstand. Then she placed the cloth on her face. She was trembling so badly she thought she would never make it to the bed.

Please, no! The Raven cannot be Edmund, she prayed silently. She had loved The Raven, and she was going to have his child. She could never love Edmund! Nonetheless, Edmund and The Raven were one and the same. How else could he have the necklace? Had he not as much as admitted to her that he was The Raven?

Season turned her head into the pillow and cried out in anguish. "I love him! But how could I love a man like Edmund, a man who would betray his country?"

Season felt so ill for the next four days that she could hardly get out of bed. Molly wanted to send for the doctor, but Season stubbornly refused. She knew what was wrong with her, and no medicine a doctor could prescribe would heal a broken heart. Each day she had hoped and prayed that Lucas would come home so she could confide in him. If Edmund was The Raven, she would have no qualms about telling Lucas of his treachery . . . yet could she? He was the father of her baby.

As Season watched the sun go down, she paced the floor, waiting for the time to pass. She knew what she had to do now. She couldn't allow The Raven to kill Lucas. She must deal with him in her own way. Several times she checked the pistol to make sure it was loaded. She knew very little about shooting a gun, but tonight she would have to learn.

Would she be able to kill a man? She had to. Edmund had not only betrayed his country, he had also threatened to kill Lucas. There was little doubt in her mind that if she didn't stop him he would do just that.

As Season rode away from the stables, the night sky was alive with thunder and lightning, but so far the threatened rain had not fallen. She was overcome with a feeling of dread because of what she had to do. She had forced herself to think of The Raven not as a man she had loved, but as the enemy. How could she have been so wrong about a man? How had he been able to fool her so completely? It was still hard for her to realize that Edmund was the man who had stolen her heart.

The gun she carried in the lining of her cape felt like a heavy weight. Tonight she would take a man's life, even though tomorrow she would live to regret it!

As a streak of lightning flashed across the eastern sky, Season saw the river in the distance. Her hands tightened on the reins, and she slowed her horse to a walk. She was in no hurry to keep her meeting with Edmund, The Raven, or whatever he called himself. Tonight she would commit murder to save her husband!

Chapter Twenty-Five

When Season neared the stream beside which The Raven would be awaiting her, she slowed her horse to a walk.

When she reached the water's edge, she dismounted and allowed her eyes to scan the darkness. Lightning streaked across the sky and thunder rumbled in the distance. Wildfire was acting fidgety, so Season ran a soothing hand over his silky coat, trying to ease his fright.

Season didn't bother to look about for The Raven because she knew that when he was ready he would show himself to her and not before. She was in no hurry to encounter him, knowing what she had to do.

Why had she come? Surely this was madness. Just when she had almost decided to return to the house, a dark form detached itself from the shadows and appeared at her side.

"I wonder how you have the nerve to face me after the other day," she said, feeling inside her cape to make sure the gun was still there.

"Was there ever any doubt in your mind that I would be here?" The Raven asked in his raspy voice.

"You don't have to disguise your voice since I know who you are. I have to admit that you had me thoroughly fooled. I was taken completely by surprise when I found out your true identify, Raven."

"What is this, my lady? Who do you think I am, and how did you discover my identity?" She could hear the amusement in his voice. She searched the darkness, feeling confused. The Raven didn't sound anything like Edmund, but then he was disguising his voice.

"What game do you play, Edmund? I told you when you came to see me the other day to return my necklace that I knew who you were. I am just sick to find out that you are The Raven. I will admit I had actually begun to admire some of the things you stood for, but that was before I learned you had sold out your own country. When you told me you would kill Lucas I knew I had to stop you some way."

The Raven grabbed Season by the arm and held her firmly. "What are you talking about? I didn't give you a necklace, my lady."

"I don't want to play your little game anymore. I detest you. I suppose you are going to tell me you didn't threaten to harm my husband either. You really must be out of your mind, Edmund."

Suddenly The Raven became tense. "Did you tell Edmund you were coming here to meet me tonight?"

"I said I wouldn't play your—"

"Answer me, dammit! Did you tell Edmund you were coming here to meet me tonight?"

"I . . . yes, but—"

"At last, we meet, Raven," Edmund's voice penetrated the darkness.

The Raven pushed Season behind him. "I must admit you were very clever, Edmund. It seems you found my one weak spot and used her against me."

"Yes. It was a mistake to get so involved with a woman. I doubt that you would ever have been found out if you hadn't lost your heart to my cousin, Season. How very foolish of you, Raven."

Edmund stepped out of the darkness, and when a flash of lightning flickered across the sky, Season could see that he was pointing a gun at The Raven. What had she done! Edmund had tricked her; he wasn't The Raven! He had used her to get to The Raven.

"I am wondering how to handle this, Raven. I could force you to unmask now, or I could shoot you first and then remove your mask. The unmasking isn't necessary for me, you understand, since I already know who you are. It will be strictly for Season's benefit. How do you think she will react when she finds out who you really are?"

"You found the necklace, but that alone couldn't have led you to me," The Raven said.

"No, you are right. Actually, I didn't realize you were The Raven until Season told me only The Raven could have that necklace. I came here as a jealous suitor seeking revenge. How could I have imagined that my jealousy would lead me straight to you?"

"Let me guess," The Raven said. "You found the necklace among my possessions and knew it belonged to Season."

"That's very clever. I wondered how you happened to have it."

"Neither of you are making sense to me," Season said. "What has my necklace got to do with anything?"

The Raven laughed. "Edmund was nosing around in my belongings. I'm sure it was the day I allowed you to bring your . . . lady friend to my home. You saw the necklace and recognized it as Lady Season's. You knew she had worn it the night of the ball, and you wondered how it happened to be in my house. In a jealous rage, you decided to find out why I had the necklace. I think we can assume you found the necklace before you heard about Lady Season's marriage."

"That's right. Pity you don't have long to live, Raven. Can you imagine how I felt when I started putting the pieces together and realized who you were. I am now considered a deserter, because I went a little crazy when I learned that Season was married. Now I will probably get a medal for exposing you. I know I'll get a sizable reward."

The Raven reached back and thrust Season away from him. "The reward will be paid whether I am dead or alive. Which is it to be, Edmund? Do you want me dead or alive?"

"Dead I think."

"Can I have a moment to explain some things to the lady before you fire that gun?"

"No, I don't think so. I believe I will explain everything to her when you are dead."

Season saw Edmund moving closer, and she knew within moments he would fire at The Raven. She felt for the gun beneath her cape, realizing she could never

428

stand by and watch him kill The Raven. Everything was all mixed up. She had come here tonight for the express purpose of killing The Raven, and now she would be the one to save him.

"You have only seconds to live, Raven. Do you have any last request?"

"Just one, Edmund," The Raven said in his deep voice.

"Let me guess, you want to know what the fate of the lady will be?"

"My lady," The Raven said in a deep raspy voice, "I just want you to know that I never really lied to you. When I said I cared about you, it was the truth."

Season felt tears in her eyes. The Raven knew he was going to die, and he was telling her he loved her.

Edmund cocked the gun. "How very touching. Never fear, I will see that the lady is well cared for. I may not be as considerate of her as you have been, but I have plans for her. I think perhaps I'll spirit her away as you once did. Don't you think that would be justice?"

Neither man was watching Season, so she raised the gun and pointed it at Edmund, hoping she would hit the target. She realized she dared not hesitate or Edmund would shoot The Raven. The hand that held the pistol trembled so badly she had to steady it with the other one. Just as she squeezed the trigger, a jagged streak of lightning flashed across the sky, and she saw Edmund crumple to the ground, an amazed look on his face. She stood transfixed, pondering the horrible deed she had done.

When The Raven ran toward Edmund and bent down to examine him, Season felt sick. She couldn't believe she had just taken a man's life. "He's dead, isn't he? I killed him!" she cried, throwing the gun down and burying her face in her hands.

The Raven stood up and in two strides he pulled her into his arms. "Yes, he's dead."

Season raised her head to the sky, and a strangled cry escaped her throat. "I didn't want to shoot him, but he was going to kill you!"

The Raven engulfed her in the folds of his cape. "Hush, sweet lady. You must not blame yourself."

"I have committed murder! How will I ever be able to live with myself?" she cried. "I had to do it, I just had to. It was because of me that he found you!"

"You saved my life, my lady. I will be eternally in your debt." His strong arms tightened about her, and Season wanted to lean on him, wanted him to help her forget the awful deed she had just done."

"What is the penalty for murder?" she asked in a small voice.

"There is no penalty for killing a British spy, Season. Edmund was an English soldier, out of uniform. The penalty for that is death."

"That is so easy for you to say. I am torn between two loyalties. I am English by birth and American by marriage. I just killed Edmund, and he was doing no more than trying to catch a spy working against the Crown. He was never a traitor, as I suspected. He was only doing his duty!"

"Sweet lady, do not suffer so. Had the English got their hands on Edmund, he would have suffered the same fate. He deserted the army."

Another bolt of lightning streaked across the sky,

illuminating Edmund's body which lay on the ground, and Season shivered. Even if Edmund deserved to die, she was grieved that she had been the one to end his life.

"What will we do with . . . his body?"

"Because of his family, no one but you and I will ever know about the deed tonight. I will attend to everything. Do not reproach yourself."

"I must tell Lucas what I did. Edmund is—was—his cousin. He will never forgive me for what I did."

"Why must you tell your husband, my lady?"

"Because . . . he is my husband. I will not lie to him. I will also have the burden of telling him that you were here and that I killed his cousin to save you. I fear I will earn his contempt."

"Does it matter so much, my lady?"

"Yes, oh, yes. It matters a great deal. I have wronged Lucas in many ways. I should never have gotten involved with you again. Why did you have to come back?" she cried, moving out of the comfort of his arms.

"I had to see you, my lady."

"Why can you not leave me in peace? I never want to see you again."

The Raven reached out and drew her into his arms. "I wanted to tell you the other day how happy I was that you are carrying my child, but you gave me little chance." His voice was soft and caressing, and his hand moved around from her back to her stomach where his child lay.

Season was overcome with self-contempt. All The Raven had to do was touch her and she betrayed her vows to Lucas. A jagged streak lit up the sky, and she glanced up at the dark, hooded man. She was so relieved that Edmund had not been The Raven. "I am so mixed up. When Edmund came to the house the other day, he led me to believe he was you. He threatened to kill Lucas if I didn't come here tonight. I brought the gun so I could keep him from harming Lucas. I ended up killing him because he was going to shoot you." Season was trying not to cry, but tears of grief spilled down her face.

"My lady, I wish there was something I could say that would make you feel better. Edmund Kensworthy isn't worthy of one of your tears. There were many things about him that you don't know. Your General Clinton has placed a price on his head. Edmund not only deserted the army, but he killed one of his fellow officers in the process."

Season listened to The Raven's words but nothing he said could erase her feeling of guilt. "Why did you ask me to come here tonight?" she wanted to know.

"Perhaps I cannot stay away from you," he suggested. "Perhaps I had to know how you felt about me."

"I think you came here, in the hope that Lucas had told me something about the British movements. You thought I might betray his confidence. If that is your reason, let me tell you I know nothing, and if I did, I would never betray Lucas."

"Would you betray me to him?"

"No, but I will tell him all about tonight, however hard that might be."

"It is my belief you will tell him nothing. I will tend to Edmund's body, and no one need ever know what happened here tonight."

"You are wrong. I will tell Lucas everything. It is my belief that a husband and wife should not keep secrets from one another."

The Raven was quiet for a moment. "Did you tell him that you carry my child?"

"Yes, he knows."

"Did you tell him I raped you, or that you submitted to me willingly?"

"I told him the truth. Now if you have nothing further to discuss with me, I shall leave."

Season started for her horse, but The Raven caught her and spun her around. "I love you, my lady. If only I had known about the child, I would have given you my name."

"What name would that be? As far as I have been able to determine, you have no name. If you think you can come back into my life and I will willingly fall into your arms, you are mistaken."

"I love you most when your eyes flash, my lady. Did you know that when you are angry your green eyes seem to spit fire?" He removed his glove, and gently stroked her cheek. Season wanted to run, and she wanted to stay. She was mesmerized by the tone of his soft voice.

"I have thought of little else but you since the last time I saw you, my lady. Admit that you have also thought of me sometimes."

Suddenly Season realized The Raven had removed his hood! His lips burned a trail across her face. "I have thought of you,'" she admitted. Before she could move, his mouth settled on hers, and she moaned at the wild feeling that moved through her body.

The Raven raised his head. "Lucas Carrington can never have you," he said in a hoarse voice. "You will always belong to me."

When she heard her husband's name on The Raven's lips, Season realized that, without intending to, she had betrayed Lucas! Backing up, she covered her face with trembling hands. "Leave me alone and never come near me again, Raven! If you care for me as you say, you will never bother me again."

Quickly turning away, Season ran toward her horse, fearing The Raven would try to stop her. She could hear him pursuing her, and she turned just as he drew near. She raised her riding crop and struck out at him; then she grabbed the reins and pulled herself into the saddle. Spinning her mount around, she urged it forward at a run. She had to get away!

"Season, come back!" The Raven called as he ran to the top of the rise, attempting to catch her. Suddenly a jagged streak of lightning pierced the sky, striking a nearby tree. Wildfire reared on his hind legs and sent Season flying through the air. She landed heavily on the hard ground and an agonizing pain ripped through her body.

The Raven ran to Season and knelt down beside her. Finding that she was unconscious, he quickly examined her to see if she had broken any bones. He was not even aware that the first drops of rain had begun to fall. His eyes laced with grief, he carefully wrapped his cape about Season and lifted her into his arms. She was still breathing, but he couldn't tell the extent of her injuries. Looking down at her gown, he saw that it was covered with blood. He was grief-stricken, knowing it was his fault that Season had been injured; he didn't dare allow himself to think about the child. His tears mingled with the rain as he hurriedly carried her toward his horse.

Season floated in a world of darkness and pain. She dreamed she was running as fast as she could. Seeing a bright pinnacle of light ahead, she tried to reach it, but her legs were so heavy she couldn't move them. Each time she drew near the light, it faded into the distance.

Season felt that if she stayed in this world of swirling darkness she would never return to the land of the living. Something told her she had to reach the blinding light, but sometimes her pain was almost unbearable, and then she could hear herself moan. From time to time she heard voices, and she wished everyone would go away and leave her alone. The voices made her head throb painfully.

After a time the pain diminished and Season felt safe floating in the soft darkness. Her body was now cool and relaxed. Yes, she must stay in the darkness. It was too taxing on her strength to try to reach the light. It was better just to float on the soft cushion of nothingness.

Lucas sat by his wife's bedside, holding her limp hand in his and staring at her pale, lifeless face. She was so still that he would often lay his head against her chest and listen to her faint heartbeat to reassure himself that she still lived. Season's breathing was faint and shallow, but at least she still lived.

Rebecca and Robert, who had returned from their

honeymoon, waited downstairs, keeping a vigil, while the doctor stayed in the room with Season. Although he often urged his patient's husband to get some rest, Lucas refused. All through the endless days and nights, Lucas stayed by his wife's bedside, trying not to doze off lest she quit breathing while he slept. He held her hand in a firm grip, as if willing her to live through his strength, and when the doctor wanted to bleed Season, Lucas refused to allow it, knowing she was already weak from loss of blood.

Three days passed, and still Season languished between life and death. Lucas was becoming increasingly fearful that she might not recover.

Season could barely see the pinnacle of light now. It had been clear for so long, but suddenly it seemed to be shrouded in a dense fog. I am dying, she thought. I am dying, and it doesn't matter. If I let go of the light, I will be able to float in the warm soothing darkness for eternity, thinking and feeling nothing.

Suddenly a familiar voice penetrated Season's darkened world. At first the sound irritated her. No one had the right to intrude into her calm, peaceful world. The darkness was her haven.

"Season, if you die I will be cast into the bowels of hell. It was I who caused your accident. Open your eyes and release me from this torment!" the deep raspy voice commanded. "If you die, my lady, I will have no reason to live."

The voice was very familiar. Season searched her

mind, trying to remember where she had heard it before.

"You are my lady," the raspy voice continued. "I love you more than my own life."

No, no, go away, she thought. It is too much trouble to listen to you. I am so tired, I just want to be swallowed up by the calm, beckoning darkness.

The deep voice became louder and more persistent. "Damn you, Season, I will not allow you to leave me!" She felt rough hands on her arms, and she was being pulled upward to a sitting position. She tried to push the hands away, but she was just too weak to fight. Let me die, she thought; but already the pinnacle of light was becoming brighter and pushing the darkness away. She struggled to return to her safe, serene darkness.

"Season, Season," the voice persisted.

She felt a cheek against hers, and it was wet. Is he crying? she wondered. She knew who was calling her back from the darkness—it was the man she loved! Had he said that he loved her? She couldn't remember.

The Raven watched as Season's eyelashes fluttered, and she slowly opened her eyes. His heart was singing with happiness. She was going to live! He lay her back against the pillow and dropped to his knees beside her. "My love, my dearest love, you are going to be all right. You are not going to leave me," he whispered, in a voice that shook with emotion.

The room was in dark shadow, and Season couldn't see the face of the man she loved, but it didn't matter— she had never seen his face. All that mattered was that he was beside her. He had snatched her from death's final grip as no one else could have.

Her hand seemed to be heavily weighted as she slowly lifted it and placed it against his face. His face was wet, and she knew he had been crying. "You love me?" she asked in a voice so faint that he hardly caught her words.

"Yes, my lady, I love you with all my heart. I have loved you from the time I first saw you."

She smiled weakly and closed her eyes.

The Raven kissed her lips softly, and then slipped quietly out of the room. Season would live, but that did not remove his feelings of guilt. He would always carry the burden of knowing he had caused her to lose their child.

His face was masked by shadow as he made his way down the stairs and out the front door.

Chapter Twenty-Six

Season awoke slowly. Her eyelids felt as if they had heavy weights on them. Gradually, she became aware of sounds: the crackling of the fire in the grate, the sighing of the wind, and somewhere, a great distance away, the lowing of cattle. Opening her eyes a crack, she saw that it was daylight. From the angle of the light streaming into the bedroom, she knew it was early morning.

Season's mind was fuzzy. She couldn't understand why she was feeling so weak. Even turning her head was an effort. As her eyes focused, she could make out the form of a man standing by the window with his back to her.

"Lucas," she whispered through parched lips. Her voice was barely audible, but Lucas must have heard her because he turned around. Season wondered why he looked so tired and haggard. It was apparent that he hadn't shaved; dark stubble shadowed his face.

He walked slowly toward her and dropped to his

knees beside the bed. "Thank God you have come out of it," he said, raising her hand to his lips.

Season wondered why Lucas was acting so strangely. She had many questions to ask him, but she was just too weary to think.

Looking past Lucas, she saw soft snowflakes drifting past the window. How strange that it is snowing with the sun shining, she thought. It was raining!

"Go back to sleep, Season," Lucas urged. "You have been very ill. Later you can take some nourishment."

Season found it easy to do as he asked. She was so weary, and her eyes were so heavy. . . .

Several hours later Season awoke again. This time she found Molly sitting beside her bed, watching her apprehensively.

"Oh, my lady, you are awake," Molly cried, tears running down her face. "The master said you were going to be all right, but I was afraid to believe him."

"Have I been ill?" Season whispered.

Molly sniffled and wiped her eyes. Lifting a glass to Season's lips, she urged her to drink before she answered. "You have been gravely ill, my lady, but you are going to recover nicely now. The first thing we must do is get you to take some nourishment. I'll just go and fetch you some nice warm broth and something cold to drink."

Season's thoughts seemed to be in a jumble. She couldn't remenber being ill, but she was indeed hungry and thirsty. She searched her mind to untangle her thoughts. What had happened to her?

When Molly left the room, Season tried to keep her eyes open, but it was an effort. She stared into the crackling fireplace, a frown on her face. The last thing she remembered was . . . riding out to . . . meet The Raven! Then she had . . . My God, she had killed Edmund! Everything came back to her in a flash—she remembered falling from her horse!

Season's hand stole down to her stomach, which felt strangely empty. She didn't need anyone to tell her she had lost her baby. At times, in the past, she had thought of the baby as something that had ruined her life. Now she felt a deep aching sadness well up inside her. In losing her baby, she had lost her only link with The Raven.

"No, no!" she cried. "I want my baby." Tears of grief ran down her cheeks to wet the pillow her head rested upon. She had lost the child of the man she loved. Somewhere in the back of Season's mind, she could remember a voice coming to her from out of a fog. Had The Raven come to her when she lay between life and death and declared his love for her? Had he given her a reason to fight for her life? Perhaps, in her unstable condition, she had imagined the whole thing.

Molly quickly returned with a tray of food. She sat beside Season's bed and spoon-fed her the warm broth. Molly then urged her lady to sip the chilled apple juice, and was satisfied when Season drank it all and asked for more.

With some nourishment in her, Season felt much stronger. Molly helped her bathe, brushed her tangled hair, and put her into a clean nightgown. Then, moving Season to the side of the bed, she managed to change the bed linen.

As the afternoon shadows deepened Season stared into the soft glow from the crackling fireplace. Her eyes drifted shut and she fell asleep once more.

Lucas came into the bedroom and walked quietly to the bed. Staring down at his sleeping wife, he watched the steady rise and fall of her chest and knew she was sleeping peacefully. Molly had told him that Season hadn't even asked about the child. He hated to think of telling her she had lost the baby when she awakened.

He walked over to the fireplace and picked up the poker, plunging it into the fire so he could turn the log. Fiery sparks flew as the flames leaped up to lick at the log.

"Lucas."

He turned to face Season and smiled at her. "I had begun to think you would sleep the year away," he said, moving to the side of the bed and sitting down on the chair.

"I have been very ill, haven't I?"

"Yes, but you are on the mend now," he assured her. He watched as Season's eyes clouded with unshed tears.

"I have lost the baby." It wasn't a question but a statement of fact. "I lost my baby."

"Yes, and I am truly sorry, Season." His golden eyes seemed to reflect a deep sadness.

"I didn't know how much I wanted the baby until I lost it, Lucas," she said softly.

"Don't dwell on the baby, Season. Try to go back to sleep."

"No, Lucas I don't want to sleep. I have to tell you

what happened."

"It isn't necessary, Season. I would rather you recover your strength before we talk."

"No. I have to tell you, Lucas. I don't want to keep anything from you."

"Will it make you feel better?"

"No, I will never be able to face you again when you hear what I have done," she said, turning her head away. "But I have to tell you anyway."

"Season, don't trouble yourself. A man called Briggs brought you home. He told me about Edmund. He also told me how you fell from the horse."

"You talked to Briggs?"

"Yes, he brought you to the house after you were injured. He was very worried about you."

Season placed her hands over her eyes. "I cannot bear to face you after what I have done. I wouldn't blame you if you detested me."

"Season, I do not detest you. Why should I?"

"Because I betrayed you by going to The Raven."

"Why did you go to him, Season?"

"I don't expect you to understand this, but Edmund came here and led me to believe he was The Raven. I went to meet him with the thought of killing him."

"Why would you want to kill Edmund, Season?"

"He said he was going to kill you, and I couldn't allow that to happen. He led me to believe he was The Raven, and he said he was going to harm you."

"You were going to kill The Raven to save me?" he asked softly.

"Yes, but that was when I thought Edmund was The Raven. As it turned out . . . I shot Edmund to save The

Raven. Everything is so mixed up, and I feel awful knowing I took a man's life. Will I be damned forever, Lucas? Will you ever be able to forgive me for what I did?"

Lucas took her hand. "I don't think you should dwell on unpleasant thoughts. Edmund will not be missed by either the British or the Americans. There is a dispatch out for his arrest. He deserted. I do not blame you for taking his life, Season."

"But he was your cousin, Lucas."

"So he was, but we were never as close as you may have supposed. Edmund always liked to play games. This time he overplayed his hand."

"I don't know how you can be so generous with me. I will shame you before your friends when they learn that I have killed your cousin."

"No one will ever know the part you played in Edmund's death. I want to read you a letter that was brought to me by the man, Briggs. He removed a letter from his jacket, unfolded it and began to read.

Mr. Carrington,

I am compelled to tell you that your cousin, Edmund, is dead. You may later learn the details from your wife, but as far as the world knows, I killed the man.

Respectfully,
The Raven

"I cannot allow The Raven to be blamed for something I did," Season cried, turning her eyes away from

Lucas' searching gaze. I will not have him blamed for killing Edmund, when I am the guilty one."

"I believe we shall just let the matter drop, Season. You are to say nothing to anyone about what happened. The Raven will not be condemned if people think he killed my cousin. He has no reputation to protect since everyone always expects the worst from him. Just put it out of your mind."

"The Raven is not as bad as everyone seems to think he is. I have found him to be an honorable man. Since I have come to Virginia, I have learned that most people admire him a great deal."

"Even on your sickbed, you defend that man," Lucas said grimly. "Is there nothing he can do that will discourage your loyalty, Season?"

Season saw the hurt etched on Lucas' face. "I'm sorry, Lucas. I didn't mean—"

"No need to apologize, Season. We will let the matter drop."

Season couldn't let the matter drop. There were still too many unanswered questions swirling around in her mind. "What happened to Edmund's body, Lucas?" she was compelled to ask.

"The Raven took care of that." Lucas watched Season's face closely. "Who is the man called Briggs, Season? I know he is connected with The Raven?"

"I cannot tell you, Lucas. Please believe me when I tell you only that he is a friend of mine."

"I can believe that. He comes to the door every day and inquires about your health. He said to tell you if you awoke that all your friends were praying for your recovery."

Tears ran down Season's face. Dear, sweet Briggs, had been worried about her. She tried to hide her tears from Lucas. "You said Briggs comes every day? Did not my accident happen last night?"

"No, Season. You have been ill for two weeks."

Season looked bemused. "Two weeks! How can that be? I do not understand."

"As I said, you have been very ill."

Season looked at the tired lines etched on her husband's face, and she wanted to reach out to him. "Lucas, our marriage is not very old, and yet I feel I have not been the kind of wife you deserve. I wish I could make it up to you. I will understand if you no longer want me."

He looked down at her hand that rested in his. "We struck a bargain, Season. I will keep my part of it and I will expect you to keep yours."

"Lucas, I want you to know that The Raven kissed me, but nothing more happened."

He stood up and looked down at her. "What shall I do, Season? I had hoped you would forget that man and come to care for me. Was I wrong?"

She reached out to him, but he didn't take her hand. "I do care for you, Lucas. If such a thing is possible, I love two men."

"Is that meant to comfort me, Season?"

"No. If I were you, I would admit that we made a bad agreement and send me packing."

He sat down once more. "Is that what you want me to do, Season?"

"No, Lucas. I don't expect you to understand this, but I want to stay with you."

"Do you blame The Raven because you lost the baby?" he couldn't help but ask.

"No, and I think I would have died had it not been for him. I don't know if I dreamed it or not, but I heard his voice calling me back from the grave. Is it possible that The Raven came into this bedroom while I was ill?"

Season saw Lucas' shoulders sag, and she realized she had hurt him again. "I don't see how it would have been possible for The Raven to come into our bedroom since you were rarely left alone. I doubt that even he would dare do such a thing."

"I'm sorry, Lucas," she whispered.

"Where does all this leave us, Season?"

"I . . . would like to remain your wife, if you will allow it. But if you no longer want me, I will understand."

His golden eyes blazed, and a tremor shook his body. "If I want you! I pity anyone who would try to take you away from me. You are my wife, dammit, and you will stay my wife. I am jealous of every thought you have of The Raven. I am grieved that you thought it was the sound of his voice, and not mine, that gave you the will to live." Lucas dropped to his knees and nestled Season's head against his shoulder. "I love you, Season. You don't have to love me, just don't ever leave me."

"Oh, Lucas, only you can save me from myself. Don't let The Raven take me away from you."

Lucas eased himself onto the bed and pulled her gently into his arms. "No one will ever take you away from me, Season, not even The Raven."

Season leaned her head against her husband's shoulder, feeling his love reach out to her. It might be that The Raven's voice had brought her back to the living, but it was Lucas' love that would breathe life into her. She realized that as long as he held her in his arms she would be safe and secure. She knew that The Raven would return one day, but she was determined that she would never again be the cause of the pain she had seen in her husband's eyes earlier. She would rid herself of this love she felt for The Raven. Lucas was everything a woman could want in a husband, and she would try to be the kind of wife he deserved.

Over the next few weeks Season's health continued to improve. By the middle of November she was feeling her old self again. Sometimes she would think of the baby she had lost and feel sad, and in the night she was often haunted by the realization that she had killed Edmund; but these depressing thoughts seemed to occur less and less.

Since Season's accident, Lucas had acted more like a polite stranger than her husband. While she had been ill, he had slept in the connecting room, and now that she was recovered, he had not moved back into their bedroom. One night when Season was having a nightmare, Lucas had come to her and held her in his arms, keeping all the dark shadows at bay, and she often found him watching her, a strange expression in his golden eyes; but she never really knew what he was thinking.

Now, however, Season pulled on her white rabbit-fur cap and tied the silken ribbon under her chin. Lucas was taking her to see Rebecca and Robert, and she was excited since it was the first time she had been out of the house since the accident.

She slipped into her fur-lined cape and rushed downstairs, where she found Lucas awaiting her. Her heart felt lighter than it had for many days as she watched Lucas hitch a pair of white horses to a bright red sleigh trimmed with holly and strings of silver-colored bells.

He smiled at her and lifted her into the sleigh, placing a warm, fur lap robe about her. Then Lucas climbed in beside her and urged the team forward. The tinkling bells on the sleigh made a merry sound. It had been snowing intermittently for over a week, and drifts were piled high across the countryside and along the roadways.

"You are in for a real treat today, Season," Lucas said, smiling down at her. "We are invited for a Thanksgiving feast—I hope you brought along your appetite."

"I know all about your Thanksgiving feast. Since Rebecca told me about it, I have read a book on the subject. Your first Thanksgiving was held in the year 1621 in Plymouth, Massachusetts. The Indians were invited, and everyone gave thanks to God for a bountiful harvest."

He smiled, thinking how she always delighted him with her thirst for knowledge. "You seem to know more about Thanksgiving than I do."

She snuggled close to Lucas and smiled up at him. "That's because I want to know all about my adopted country."

"Careful," he said, arching an eyebrow. "You are well on your way to becoming a true American."

"Oh, I am already an American by marriage. You are a staunch Tory, Lucas, but if I'm not careful, I will become a Whig." She giggled and her green eyes danced merrily. "Wouldn't my father be horrified if he heard me make such a statement? I wonder what he would say?"

"You aren't turning into a patriot, are you?"

"I don't know—perhaps. Would you be too disappointed in me if I were?"

"That would depend on why you chose the opposite view, Season."

"It's hard to explain, Lucas, but I have come to realize that King George has not dealt very fairly with America. I always thought of him as a grandfatherly type, but he has not treated the Colonies like family."

"You aren't trying to turn me into a patriot are you, Season?" he said, chuckling.

She linked her arm through his and leaned her head against his shoulder. "Perhaps I am." Her heart seemed to lighten because she and Lucas had put their differences aside for the moment. It had been a long time since she had seen her husband happy.

He smiled down at her, now, and his golden eyes seemed to dance. "Don't try your wiles on me, Season. I have found myself to be very susceptible to your fatal charm."

She gave him an answering smile, and then her brow wrinkled thoughtfully. "Lucas, there is another thing I'm not sure I approve of. Must we have slaves on Rosemont?"

Lucas laughed delightedly. "Please, hit me with one thing at a time, Season. The world wasn't created in one day, and it cannot be changed overnight."

"Lucas, I believe if I were a man I might take up arms against the king. We should show him that he cannot push us around. After that we should start a campaign to free all slaves."

"We?"

"Yes, we."

"When did you decide this?"

"I believe it was while I was aboard the *Andromeda.*"

Lucas' mouth curved into a grim line. Season didn't even realize she had implied that The Raven had influenced her thinking. "It would be many years before you could convince the people of the South to give up their slaves, Season. You should also realize that should you become a patriot, you and I would be on opposite sides, Season?"

Her mouth flew open. "I would never disagree with you openly, Lucas—you are my husband. I know that you believe the king is right, but are you aware that my father and many of his friends in The House of Lords favor allowing America to govern herself?"

The snow had begun to drift earthward again, and a chilled wind blew down the valley. Season snuggled closer to Lucas to keep warm. He glanced down at her through half-closed eyes. "I see I am going to have my hands full with you, Season," he said in an amused voice. "You are not satisfied with trying to change me—you want to take on the whole South."

She blinked her eyes against the brilliant gold of his eyes. "I have always thought you deserved better than you have with me, Lucas."

"One day, Season, all that is wrong between the two of us will come full circle. Until that time, I am content to let matters ride."

What does he mean? she wondered. "Lucas, you have been a very kind and patient husband. Most men would have lost patience with a wife like me long ago."

He laughed. "Any man would give his right eye and his left leg to have you in his bed, my lady." He lifted her chin and kissed her on her pert little nose. "The day may come, Season, when I will ask more from you than you are willing to give. Don't praise me too highly, for when that time comes, you might rue your choice."

"I don't know what you mean, Lucas."

He turned his attention back to the horses. "One day you will know, Season."

She was confused. Lucas often spoke in riddles, and she didn't always follow his logic. Will I ever truly understand the man who is my husband? she wondered.

As Lucas guided the horses into the wide driveway in front of the Wolf mansion, a man dressed in red livery came forward and helped Season from the sleigh; then he led the horses away. Lucas took her arm and escorted her up the steps to the house.

Sounds of merriment greeted them as the doors swung open. Rebecca hugged Season tightly and then Robert pulled her into his arms. "Season you look simply wonderful—your cheeks are just glowing with health," her brother-in-law declared.

"That is due to the fresh air and the ride over," Season answered. "I love the wintertime."

"I would have thought Lucas put the blush in your

cheeks," Robert said, clapping his friend on the back.

Rebecca gave her husband a scolding glance and led Season into the parlor where the other guests were gathered. Many of the people Season had met before, and they seemed genuinely glad to see her.

The dinner was as good as Season had been led to believe, and better. There were roasted turkeys and hams, venison, duck, and fish. These were accompanied by vegetables that Season had never seen before. For dessert pies, cakes, and puddings were served.

Season sat to Robert's right, while Lucas sat by his sister at the other end of the table. There were twenty-three guests at the dinner table, and the mood was light and festive. Before long, however, the conversation turned to The Raven. One of the gentlemen present mentioned that The Raven had found a British spy not far away and had ended his miserable life. Season caught Lucas' warning glance. Apparently the man was talking about Edmund. Season was surprised to note the admiration for The Raven these people expressed. Lucas had been right, the people of Virginia didn't condemn The Raven for what they thought he had done. She wondered what they would think if they knew she was the one who had killed the spy.

"I am truly delighted to see you in such good health, Season." Robert said, pulling her thoughts away from the conversation about The Raven. "We were all very concerned about you for a time."

"I feel in the peak of health," she answered, wishing she dared ask him about The Raven. Season needed to know if The Raven had really come to her when she had been so ill, and she suspected Robert might know.

She toyed with the notion of asking him, but decided against it.

After dinner, the women moved into the parlor, leaving the men to smoke their cigars and drink their port. Season felt that she had eaten so much she would never be hungry again. She seated herself on the windowseat and was looking out the window at the falling snow when several ladies approached her.

"Is it true," one of them asked, "that your father is a real duke?"

"Yes, but I think of him only as my father."

"Do we address you by a title?"

"No, I dropped my title when I married Lucas."

"I heard you grew up in a grand palace," another said.

"Yes, Chatsworth is a castle," Season admitted.

"We heard that you had a nasty fall from a horse," an older lady said, concern in her eyes.

"Yes, but I am fully recovered now."

Noticing that Season was cornered by her well-meaning neighbors, Rebecca came to her rescue. She took Season upstairs so she could freshen up before the gentlemen joined the ladies in the sitting room.

"You will have to forgive our overzealous neighbors. They are merely curious about your past. They are really quite harmless. Many of them came by Rosemont and brought food when you were so ill."

"I was not offended by their questions, Rebecca. I suppose I never really thought much about my background until I came to America. I want very much to be accepted by Lucas' friends and neighbors."

"You don't have to worry about that. They are already charmed by you."

"Does that include the Bartletts, Rebecca?" Season asked, smiling.

"Well, not exactly. If you noticed, the Bartletts were not invited today. I thought it best to keep them away since Marlana is still upset over your marriage to my brother."

Season and Rebecca soon went back downstairs, and by then the men had joined the ladies. Season saw that Mr. Bartlett and his daughter, Marlana, had joined the party. Rebecca gave Season a guarded glance and shrugged her shoulders.

Rebecca took Season's hand. "You had better stay near me. Marlana is looking in your direction. She has been known to make trouble. As I told you, Robert and I purposely didn't invite them to dinner today, but they have dropped in anyway.

Season saw Mr. Bartlett talking to Lucas, and the man's voice was raised in anger. "Your politics are well known to everyone in this room, Lucas. If you love the English so much, why don't you take ship and live among them?"

Season moved closer to Lucas, and he smiled down at her as if he was amused by Mr. Bartlett's observation. "I am first of all a Virginian, the same as you, Gilbert. I love my home no less than you love yours."

Marlana came up beside her father and gave Season a cool glance. "One can tell you admire the English— you married one of them, Lucas," Marlana declared in a hateful voice.

Lucas still smiled. "You don't know much about men if you believe I married my wife because she was English. Ask your own father to look at Season and tell you if he thinks I married her merely because of where she came from."

Marlana's face darkened with anger, and her father cleared his throat.

"You might be surprised to learn, Marlana, that my wife agrees more with your views than mine. Only this morning she was telling me that she thought we should be independent from England."

"That doesn't excuse you, Lucas," Mr. Bartlett stated. "You are either a fool or a coward. I do not believe you are a fool!"

Season gasped at the insult, while Lucas' dark brows knit in a frown, and his golden eyes blazed. "I will not discuss my loyalties with you or your daughter, Gilbert. You are far worse than King George in trying to impose your views on others. We are both guests in my brother-in-law's home; we owe him the courtesy of agreeing not to disagree."

"Robert Wolf is willing to lay down his life for his country, while you spend most of your time buttering up the British. I resent you coming among us, and I'm sure many of our neighbors feel the same as I do," Mr. Bartlett said angrily.

Season felt humiliated for Lucas, but he didn't seem to take offense. "Very well put, Gilbert. If my company offends you, then my wife and I shall take our leave."

By now the other guests had moved closer, listening to the debate between Lucas and Gilbert Bartlett.

456

"I called you a coward, Lucas," Gilbert said, turning red in the face. "If you won't respond to the insult, then I will call you out!" Gilbert took his glove and struck Lucas across the face. Instantly everyone became silent, waiting to see what would happen next.

Lucas flinched as the glove caught his lip and blood ran down his chin. Season's heart pounded with fear as she waited for her husband's reaction. Surely Lucas would never let such an insult go unpunished.

Lucas removed his handkerchief from his breast pocket and dabbed at the blood. "I have no intention of fighting you, Gilbert. You were a friend of my father's; therefore I will allow the insult to pass. Don't ever do that again, however," he said, in a soft voice.

Season gasped, and everyone began to mumble.

"I knew it! I knew you were a coward, Lucas. Your father would not be proud of you today," Gilbert said, a great deal of satisfaction in his voice.

Robert stepped forward and took Lucas' arm. "Perhaps it would be best if you and Season left," he said grimly.

"No, no," Rebecca cried, running forward and standing beside her brother. "Lucas, don't allow it to end like this."

Lucas looked down into his sister's face. "It's best if I leave now, Rebecca. Forgive me for spoiling your party." He took Season's hand and bowed curtly to Gilbert Bartlett. "My wife and I wish you well, sir."

Season was astonished as Lucas led her to the hallway and asked the butler for their wraps.

"Lucas, how can you allow Mr. Bartlett's insult to go

unanswered?" she asked, as he placed her cape about her shoulders. "He has shamed you among your friends."

"What would you have me do, Season—kill him for expressing his views?"

"There is more to it than that, Lucas, and you know it. He insulted you."

"It isn't for you to question me, Season," Lucas replied, taking her arm and leading her outside.

As they waited for the horses to be hitched to the sleigh, Rebecca came out of the house and threw her arms about Lucas. "Please talk to Lucas, Season, and make him stay," she pleaded.

"No, Rebecca. Lucas is my husband and I will abide with what he decides."

"I will never forgive Robert for asking you to leave, Lucas," Rebecca declared.

Lucas placed a quick kiss on his sister's cheek and then lifted Season into the sleigh. "Don't be hard on Robert, Rebecca. He has his reasons for doing what he did."

As the horses started forward, Season stared at Rebecca's forlorn figure standing on the steps. "You hurt her, Lucas. You should never have taken Mr. Bartlett's insult."

"It isn't my practice to go around fighting duels with old men, and since the question of my politics never came up until he knew I was not going to marry his daughter, I question his motives now."

Season felt her stomach tie into knots. Surely Lucas wasn't a coward!

The ride home was a silent one. Whenever Season

glanced at Lucas, he seemed to be brooding, and she felt miserable.

After Lucas and Season left, Robert asked Mr. Bartlett and his daughter to accompany him into his study. When he had closed the door he turned to the older man. "I brought you here to ask you both to leave my house. I was not at all happy when you forced me to ask Rebecca's brother and his wife to depart."

Gilbert Bartlett shook his head. "You of all people should be enraged by Lucas Carrington's behavior. The two of you grew up together. You have fought bravely for our cause, and you state your politics honestly and openly while Lucas licks the boots of the English."

"Lucas married that English trollop," Marlana stated angrily. "How can you allow her into your house?"

Robert's eyes blazed. "Do not speak against Lucas or Season in this house, Marlana. I would suggest that you are speaking out of jealousy rather than patriotism."

"You dare say this to me, Robert!"

He turned back to Mr. Bartlett. "I would suggest you leave now. I will make your excuses to the rest of our guests."

Gilbert Bartlett turned red in the face. "I don't see how you can defend Lucas; he acted the coward today."

Robert laughed a humorless laugh. "Lucas isn't a coward, Gilbert. Had he accepted your challenge tonight, you wouldn't have had a chance against him.

He saved your life at the price of his own pride. I would say that took a great deal of courage, wouldn't you? Now get your things and leave."

When they reached Rosemont, Lucas lifted Season out of the sleigh, and she followed him into the house.

She removed her cloak and started up the stairs. Then she realized that Lucas was just behind her. When they entered the bedroom, she dropped her cape onto a chair and removed her bonnet.

"You think I should have fought that man just to prove my bravery, don't you, Season? I believe it sometimes takes a much braver man to walk away from a fight."

Season turned to Lucas, her eyes blazing. "You allowed Mr. Bartlett to make a fool of you. I find no honor in that, Lucas."

"You think I am a coward?"

"What I believe is not the important issue here, Lucas. What do you think?"

"I believe a wife should have more faith in her husband. She should stand beside him no matter what."

"I will stand beside you, Lucas," she said, tossing her head defiantly. "But courage is the one thing that I admire most in the world."

He grabbed her and brought her up against his body. "You are comparing me to your precious sea captain again. I have had enough of being compared to The Raven and found wanting."

"Lucas I didn't—"

"Spare me your excuses," he ground out, raising his hand in dismissal and stalking out of the room.

Season walked over to the window and watched the snow drift down. She had the strangest feeling she had failed Lucas in some way, but how could she have condoned his behavior. He had acted the coward, and she felt shame for him.

When Season went downstairs the next morning she was still tired. She hadn't slept well, and she wanted to apologize to Lucas for behaving so badly the day before. She had lain awake long into the night, mulling over the whole unpleasant incident in her mind. She now realized that Lucas had acted with great restraint in dealing with Mr. Bartlett, and she wanted to tell him how she felt.

When Season entered the dining room, she discovered that Lucas wasn't there, but a note was propped against her plate. Picking it up, she began to read:

Season, I had to leave. Urgent business in New York needed my immediate attention. Try not to think too badly of me. I am sorry about our misunderstanding yesterday. When I return we will have a long talk. I may be away for several months, so if you should need anything talk to Robert.

I remain your husband,
Lucas.

Season sank down in her chair and stared at the note. What did Lucas mean he could be gone for several months? Why hadn't he told her goodbye? She pushed her breakfast plate aside and stood up, feeling strangely empty inside. How could she go on for months not knowing when Lucas was coming home. What was she supposed to do with herself?

She walked out onto the veranda and watched the heavy snow drift down. Lucas wouldn't be home for Christmas. She would be alone, just as she had been as a child growing up at Chatsworth.

Tears gathered in her eyes. "Why, Lucas, why did you leave me without saying goodbye?" she cried, leaning her head against the veranda for support.

She watched as several men began to shovel snow from the driveway and clear a path to the stables.

Molly came out on the veranda and placed a warm wrap about her mistress. "You are going to catch your death if you don't come into the house, my lady."

Season sighed. Who would know if she just wasted away and died? She thought about The Raven. Perhaps he would, but she wasn't even sure about that.

Chapter Twenty-Seven

The days seemed endless to Season. She spent Christmas with Rebecca and Robert, but she saw the new year in alone without celebration or fanfare. Each day she waited for the post, hoping for some word from Lucas, but so far, she had received none.

January was a bitterly cold month, and Season was forced to stay indoors. She passed the time by alphabetizing the library. Each book was put in order, and she made an index catalogue, listing each book by its title. Some of the books were in bad repair, so she sent them off to Philadelphia to be rebound.

February came and went, and Season still hadn't heard from her husband. She couldn't get Lucas out of her mind. She remembered their parting and the hurtful words she had said to him. She wondered if he was still angry with her.

Season received a letter from her father. All was well at Chatsworth, but he missed her. He wrote that he would be returning to London in the spring, and

Season knew he would again be taking up his political life. She doubted he would ever be content to stay at Chatsworth for an indefinite period of time.

Sometimes, when Season lay in her bed alone, she remembered the night she had met Lucas in New York. He had been surrounded by a swarm of beautiful ladies. She often wondered if he had now found some woman to warm his bed. Then she became jealous and cried herself to sleep. Season knew she couldn't blame Lucas if he turned to another woman; she hadn't been the ideal wife. He probably thought she had betrayed him with The Raven, and after all, she had, hadn't she?

She tried not to think of the captain of the *Andromeda,* but he sometimes crept into her mind uninvited. Season knew it was wrong to let her thoughts dwell on a man other than her husband, but she had little control over her fickle heart. Indeed, she had begun to wonder if she would ever have control over her own life. Was it her lot to be always alone?

As Season watched the heavy snowflakes fall, she yearned for spring. She wanted to ride over the valley and feel the warm sun on her face, and she wished with all her heart that Lucas would return so she could apologize to him for the cruel things she had said.

The captain of the *Andromeda* stood on deck and watched the billowing sails catch the wind as he changed course. He had taken three English merchants and two frigates as prize. The crew had been celebrating the night before, for each man knew he had made his fortune. When the war was over every seaman aboard would have the wealth that other men only dreamed about.

Deep in thought, The Raven didn't hear Briggs come up behind him until he spoke.

"We have a fair wind, Captain. I sight land dead ahead. Do we go ashore at Tripoli, sir?"

"Aye, Briggs."

"You can't be too sure what our reception will be. Everyone there will know that you disposed of De Fores. He had friends among the scum there."

"We have little choice, Briggs. We need to put in for repairs and supplies. I don't anticipate trouble. That lot always shies away from a bold show of strength."

The next morning the captain of the *Andromeda* stepped ashore at Tripoli and walked slowly down the streets as if he were out for an afternoon stroll. When he entered the foul-smelling tavern, he was flanked by twelve of his crew members. Suddenly the din ceased and hostile eyes watched his progress. He looked neither left nor right, but kept his hand lightly resting on his sword hilt.

The Raven nodded his head at several of the men, but he didn't stop to talk. Finally he stood, legs spread apart in his usual arrogant stance, and scanned the room as if daring one of the pirate captains to challenge him. Angry murmurs arose, and his men came up beside him to show their support for their captain.

"If they was of a mind, sir, there could be a nasty fight," Briggs said, his eyes alert.

"Fear not, Briggs; there is no fight in this motley lot.

We could easily handle anything they might throw our way, and they know it." Even as The Raven spoke he began to move among the tables. Out of the corner of his eye, he noticed a group of men come through the door and move to his side. He smiled, knowing Maude had sent her crew to reinforce his men.

At one point a mountain of a sailor stepped angrily in front of The Raven, but when he saw the masked captain fingering the hilt of his sword he moved aside.

Maude sat with her feet propped up on a table, watching his progress. The Raven smiled and made his way toward her.

When he reached her table, he pulled up a chair and rested a booted foot on it. "I am glad to see you are well, Maude. Thank you for the support."

She leaned forward and motioned for him to be seated. "It's good to see you, Raven. I thought I might be called on to help you as you crossed the room. You always were a bold devil."

Laughter issued from behind the mask. "It would seem this lot has no stomach for a fight. They don't know how to band together—they are too busy trying to cut each other's throats."

"I would have died defending you had the need arose, Raven," Maude said with glowing eyes.

A gloved hand reached out and touched her face. "You are much too fine a woman to be wasted on this beggar's lot, Maude," he told her.

"If only you felt . . ." Maude's voice trailed off. "I heard that you rescued the Lady Chatsworth from De Fores."

"You heard right."

"Where is she now? Did you bring her with you or take her back to England?"

"As it happens, Maude, she is married and lives with her husband in Virginia."

Maude tried to see past the black leather mask. She knew The Raven had been bewitched by the lady. "I'm sorry, Raven."

"Don't be sorry for me, Maude. Let's drink and be merry," The Raven said, as he lifted a mug from a passing serving maid's tray."

Maude picked up her mug of ale and held it out to him. "What do we drink to, Raven?"

The Raven laughed deeply. "I drink to a fair wind and a fair friend. May the first always blow strong, and the second live long."

Maude took a drink of her ale. "Later, will you come to my house? On your last visit, when I kept the lady for you, I waited for you but you never came."

The serving wench passed the table and gave The Raven a saucy wink, but he nodded a negative response. He lifted his mug and took a drink before he answered. "I won't be coming this time either, Maude. We have to make some hasty repairs and then head out to sea again."

Maude sighed and, trying to act indifferent, shrugged her shoulders. "I would venture to guess that the lady hurt you badly, Raven."

"Perhaps we hurt each other, Maude."

"Will you see her again?"

"Yes."

Maude stood up and smiled at him. "Don't forget you always have Maude to help you over the rough spots, Raven. Should you change your mind, you know where to find me."

"Goodbye, Maude," he said in his raspy voice. "Take care of yourself."

Maude tipped her hat and smiled before turning away. She had a strange empty feeling, as if she would never see The Raven again. She left the tavern, knowing her crew would look after The Raven's safety while he was in port.

As Maude made her way to her house the sky didn't seem as blue as it had before. She shrugged her shoulders. Men were plentiful. She would try to put The Raven out of her heart. She knew he had never thought of her as other than a friend. The Lady Season Chatsworth came to her mind and she wondered how the lady could marry another man when she had won The Raven's heart. Maude knew she would give all she owned to have The Raven feel deeply about her.

When the *Andromeda* was under sail once more, her captain stood on deck and watched his first mate turn the wheel into the wind.

"Where do we head, Captain?" Briggs wanted to know.

"Set a course for the United States. I have just received word that the British have waged an all-out campaign in the South. They think to weaken our forces by dividing our troops; let us hope they will not succeed."

"All hell's going to break loose, sir."

"Yes. Our army in the South has been joined and

reinforced by French troops, and they now pose a serious threat to Charleston. France and Spain have formed an alliance and threaten to depose the British supremacy at sea."

"The war cannot last much longer, sir. We are getting stronger, but I do not know that we can defeat the British on land," Briggs stated.

"If the men in the Congress would only stop quarreling among themselves and give their wholehearted support to General Washington, the war would have been won long ago."

"Do we join the French and Spanish fleets, Captain?"

"No, I have received word that General Washington wishes to see me. I must find him."

As spring came to Virginia Season felt her heart become lighter. She often rode over the plantation, watching the slaves till the land and plant the seeds. Everything seemed to be reborn. Foals frolicked about in the meadows, and calves trailed after their mothers. Season couldn't help but think she would be a mother now if she hadn't lost her baby.

Each day she hoped for some word from Lucas, but nothing came. For all she knew he might be dead.

She had tried to keep busy by rearranging the furnishings, and by now she had taken over the tasks of the lady of the manor. The servants had readily accepted her authority and the house was running smoothly, but Season rarely saw her neighbors, and was never invited to their houses. She knew they resented her because she was British and because of Lucas' stand on the war.

She had heard rumors that the war had come to the South, but so far she had seen no signs of fighting.

Season refused to let herself be overcome with melancholy, although each night when she climbed into her big empty bed she ached for her husband's return. She realized more and more that they were little more than strangers. They had not been together long enough to really know one another.

Season was determined that she would care for Lucas' home and be his wife in the eyes of the world. She knew when he did return home, she and Lucas would have to come to some kind of understanding. She was beginning to resent the fact that he seemed to have cast her aside as if she didn't exist. She doubted that Lucas had even given her a thought since he had left Rosemont.

Chapter Twenty-Eight

August, 1790

The summer days were hot and humid due to the fact that it rained almost every afternoon. Season felt isolated and cut off from the rest of the world. Sometimes it seemed to her that she was no less a prisoner than she had been while on board the *Andromeda*.

Robert had taken Rebecca to Philadelphia and Season missed them terribly; they were her only friends in Virginia. She was almost sorry now that she had declined their invitation to accompany them to Pennsylvania.

She still waited in vain for some word from Lucas. She tried to tell herself that perhaps he had written and his letters had gone astray, but she had received three letters from her father so it didn't make sense that only Lucas' letters would have been lost.

On an overcast day as Season rode across the green valley, she reined in her mount at the river, noticing that it had swollen almost to the top of the banks. Heavy rains had caused the peaceful river to run rampant like a raging torrent. Glancing across the valley, Season realized in horror that should the river spill over its banks, it would damage the cotton crops and flood much of Rosemont! She wondered why Mr. Walls, the overseer, hadn't seen this danger.

Turning her horse, she urged it back toward the house. She couldn't understand why the overseer wasn't preparing some kind of defense against the flood waters. She intended to confront him for neglecting his duties.

When she reached the overseer's cottage, she jumped from her horse and banged on his door. Mrs. Walls answered the door, and her mouth gaped open when she saw the lady of the manor standing on her doorstep. Mrs. Walls was an elderly woman with gray hair that was pulled back at the nape of her neck, and her eyes were a nondescript color.

Season had often tried to talk to the woman, but had gotten no response other than a sullen yes or no. She could sense Mrs. Walls's hostility even now.

"I need to talk to your husband at once, Mrs. Walls," Season said hurriedly.

"He ain't feeling well. He's got the fever and is clean out of his head. If'n you had taken the time to inquire, you would have knowed he was sick for the past two weeks," the woman said sourly.

"Why wasn't I informed about his illness? I would have sent for the doctor."

"We ain't needing any charity from the likes of you. I been telling my man that we should just pack up and leave, but he won't listen to me. I ain't happy about living under British rule right here on Rosemont. We was just as happy before you came with your fancy ways."

Season pushed past the woman. "Take me to see your husband at once! I have no time to quarrel with you. The river is about to overflow!"

Mrs. Walls moved to the bedroom door and blocked it with her body. "You can't see him. He's too sick."

"I'll send for the doctor immediately," Season said, turning to leave.

Before she reached the exit, the bedroom door opened and Mr. Walls staggered forward. His face was pale as death and his eyes were fever bright. "Don't pay no attention to my wife, Mrs. Carrington, she don't mean no harm," he said, gripping the door to hold himself upright.

"You must not concern yourself about anything, Mr. Walls. I will have the doctor attend you as soon as possible," Season said with concern.

"I . . . don't bother about me, ma'am. I know you got your own troubles. I been hearing the rain and the river must be . . . ." As Mr. Walls gasped for breath and wavered, Season moved quickly across the room and took his arm.

"Help me get your husband back to bed, Mrs. Walls. He should never have been disturbed and I offer you my apology. He needs attention right away."

The two women managed to get the sick man back into bed and Season turned to face a less hostile Mrs. Walls. "I will send my maid, Molly, to help you until the doctor arrives. You were wrong not to tell me of

473

your husband's illness. While my husband is away from Rosemont everyone is my concern."

The older woman looked at the beautiful lady and thought she might have misjudged her. She didn't want to like the mistress of the manor, because in her eyes Season represented the enemy. "I am powerful worried about my man. I hope you won't hold what I said against me," she said slyly.

Season placed her arm about the woman's shoulders. "I'm sure you are out of your mind with worry. You look as though you are dead on your feet. I will instruct Molly to help you in any way she can. Who's the best man on the plantation to help me take charge, Mrs. Walls? I need someone who can take orders as well as give them. If we don't act fast the cotton will be ruined."

"The last time it flooded was back in 1765. At that time it wiped out the slave quarters and many people were drowned. I think Winston would be the man you are needing. My husband says he's a great help to him."

Season knew that time was against her. She had to send for the doctor and then do something about the threat of a flood.

When she reached the door, Mrs. Walls's voice stopped her. "Ma'am, Mrs. Carrington . . . thank you."

Season smiled at the woman. "Don't mention it, Mrs. Walls. All you need to think about is your husband's health, and try to get some rest yourself. In the future I hope you will keep in mind that I am more than willing to help you."

"You mean you ain't going to make us leave for the

way I talked to you?"

"No, Mrs. Walls. We all need each other. We will just forget about the incident and not mention it to your husband, or mine."

The older woman watched the young mistress leave, knowing she had badly misjudged her, but her heart was still filled with bitterness. Mrs. Walls resented Mrs. Carrington because she was British, and now her eyes gleamed spitefully; Winston had been giving her husband trouble for years. It would serve Mrs. Carrington right to have to deal with a rebellious slave, she thought bitterly.

Season mounted her horse and headed toward the slave quarters at a gallop. When she dismounted a crowd quickly surrounded her. She felt as if the weight of the world were on her shoulders as she searched the dark faces about her.

"I am looking for a man called Winston," she said, glancing back toward the river.

"I'm Winston." A mountain of a man stepped forward, a frown on his face.

"Winston, I want you to send someone to the house at once, to tell my maid, Molly, to go immediately to the overseer's cottage. Mr. Walls is very ill, the doctor must also be summoned."

"Does you want me to go get the doctor?" the big black man asked.

"No. We have a grave problem with the river, and I am going to need your help."

The big man smiled, displaying pearly white teeth. "All you gotta do is tell ol' Winston what to do and I'll do it, ma'am."

"As I told you, Mr. Walls is ill, so I am putting you in charge."

Winston looked shocked for a moment and then he raised his head proudly. He turned to the boy standing next to him and instructed him to go to the big house to do as the mistress had ordered and then to bring the doctor to Mr. Walls. That done he turned back to Season.

"I guess you'll be worrying 'bout the flood waters, ma'am? It's gotten mighty dangerous."

"Yes, the banks of the river will surely overflow and we could lose the crops as well as your homes. Tell me what you think we should do, Winston?"

"Well, I don't rightly know, ma'am," Winston replied, scratching his head. No one had ever asked his opinion before and he was taken by surprise. He looked at his mistress, pride in his dark eyes. He felt good that she had asked his advice and was determined not to let her down.

"I guess we could sandbag the banks, ma'am. That's what we always does, but we ain't got a lot of time."

"Tend to that Winston; I'm placing the full responsibility in your hands. Also, I believe if we dig several deep trenches leading toward the woods where the hill slopes, we can divert some of the water in the other direction. The flood waters will do very little damage to the wooded area. Make sure all the livestock are penned up."

"Ma'am, we ain't never done that before," Winston said, visualizing the whole thing in his mind.

"Well, Winston, I suggest we try it. Set some of your

men to making sandbags and give others shovels to dig the trenches."

He smiled brightly. "Yes, ma'am, it just might work. I'll do that right away."

"Good. I am going up to the house to change my clothing and I'll meet you at the river as soon as I can. Make haste, Winston, we don't have much time. It looks as if it might start raining again at any moment."

"Yes, ma'am," the big man replied quickly. "Winston won't let you down."

Season smiled. She mounted her horse and set off for the house at a gallop. She knew time and the weather were both against them.

She found Molly gathering up a basket of supplies to take to the sick Mr. Walls. "Has the doctor been sent for, Molly?" Season asked, stripping off her gloves and running toward the stairs.

"Yes, my lady. I was told that the river might flood. Is that the truth?"

"Yes, and we don't have much time. I am going up to the attic to see if I can find some trousers to wear. I cannot very well work in a gown."

Molly raced after her mistress and caught up with her at the attic door. "You can't go parading around in men's attire! It's just not respectable! Your father wouldn't approve of such actions."

"My father would approve a lot less if I stood by while lives were lost and crops were ruined. What would you have me do, Molly?" Season asked, exasperated.

"My lady, you aren't thinking about putting yourself in danger?" Molly queried suspiciously. "I will not allow it!"

"I will not be in danger. You take yourself off to the Walls's cottage and do what you can to help them."

Molly grumbled to herself, but did as she was told. Gathering up her medicine basket, she made her way to the Walls's. The maid couldn't help thinking she would be gald when Mr. Carrington returned so he could curb Lady Season's impulsive nature.

The afternoon seemed endless as Season labored alongside the slaves to save Rosemont Plantation. Every man and woman, and every child old enough to help had been pressed into service. No one commented on the fact that the mistress wore men's breeches and labored as hard as everyone else.

Season saw a woman who was heavy with child struggling with a heavy sandbag and she ran over to her. "You shouldn't be helping. Go up to the house and tell Drucilla to prepare food for everyone. Then you get cleaned up and lie down to rest. We don't want anything to happen to you and your baby."

The woman looked at the mistress gratefully and hurried off to do as she had been told.

As Season pushed a strand of golden hair off her forehead with a muddy hand she scanned the country-side. Looking toward the distant hills, she noticed it had already started raining there. It was only a matter of time before the rain reached them.

Several wagons were returning from the nearby beach, loaded with sand. Season thankfully watched them return. Perhaps they could just manage to beat the flood waters.

A sense of urgency drove her as she held one gunny sack after another for the men to fill with sand. The sacks were placed along the swollen banks while a dozen workers dug long trenches that led away from the fields and cabins in the hope of diverting the water down the hill and into the woods.

As Season felt the first drops of rain hit her face, she knew they must work desperately, but suddenly her feet slipped out from under her and she landed in the mud. Winston, who was standing nearby, offered her his hand and helped her up.

"This ain't no place for you, ma'am. Why don't you just go on back up to the house? Mr. Carrington wouldn't like it if he knowed you was laboring like a field hand," Winston told her.

"No, we need every available hand if we are going to lick this, Winston. Mr. Carrington would be a lot more upset if you lost your homes and he lost the cotton. What do you think our chances are of succeeding, Winston?"

He scratched his head. "I'd say our chances are between slim and none."

It was after five when their task had been completed. The part of the river which threatened the fields and cabins had been sandbagged.

Season stood beside Winston in the heavy downpour and he seemed to read her mind. "Them sandbags ain't gonna hold, ma'am."

"No, they won't, Winston," Season answered as she watched the angry river splash over the sides of the banks past the sandbags. "I believe we must now see if the trenches will do their job."

Winston nodded grimly and walked over to the place where the trenches had been dug. Heavy lumber had been stacked up against the banks to help hold the water back while the ditches were being dug. Winston motioned for several men to help him remove the makeshift dam.

Season stood tensely, her hands clasped together, hoping with all her heart that the trenches would take care of the flood waters. All those who had just stopped working held their breath as the first water ran down the ditches.

Tense moments passed while the ditches filled with the muddy water. After a while a loud cheer went up from everyone as the river began to recede!

"We did it, ma'am! We did it!" Winston shouted happily. "I didn't think we could, but it ain't gonna flood the cabins and fields."

Season laughed hysterically as her tears mixed with the rain. "You were all wonderful." She shouted so she could be heard above the rushing water. "On behalf of Mr. Carrington and myself, I want to thank each and every one of you for what you did here today. You are all to go home and get into dry clothing. I have ordered food to be prepared for everyone. We have a lot to be thankful for tonight."

As Season walked to her horse she didn't see all the adoring glances that followed her. No one looked at her more adoringly than the giant Winston. The mistress had treated him as an equal and had made him feel important. He knew he would always remember Mrs. Carrington had put her trust in him, and he felt proud that he hadn't let her down.

As Season rode back to the house she didn't know when she had ever been so tired. She was wet and muddy and her body seemed to ache all over, but never had she felt so good about an accomplishment.

She dismounted at the Walls's cottage and inquired if the doctor had come. Molly gave her a disapproving glare and Mrs. Walls stared at her in astonishment.

"Like as not, you'll catch your death, my lady," Molly declared in a clear voice.

Season smiled. "That may very well be, but we are saved from the flood."

The doctor came out of the bedroom and was thunderstruck at the sight of Mrs. Carrington in muddied men's trousers. He was too polite to voice his surprise so he told her that Mr. Walls should be up and about in two more weeks.

The doctor grinned at Season when she explained how they had diverted the flood waters. "You may not be aware of it, Mrs. Carrington, but in diverting the river, you not only saved Rosemont, but several other plantations that lay in the river's path. Many of your neighbors will be calling to thank you when they learn what you have done here today."

Season smiled and excused herself.

When she reached the house she ordered all the food to be carried out to the veranda, and she sent a young boy to tell everyone to come to the big house to eat.

When Season finally reached her bedroom she found Molly waiting there for her, preparing a hot bath and looking very put out.

"Such goings-on," the maid grumbled as she poured

bath salts into the water. "I never thought I'd live to see the day when you would dress like a man and be laboring like a common slave. I don't know what Mr. Carrington would say, or your father either for that matter," Molly stated in a disapproving voice.

Season smiled as she stripped off her muddy clothing and climbed into the sweet-scented water. "I don't know what Lucas would say, Molly, but I believe my father would be proud of me."

"What should I say?" her husband's voice suddenly filled the room.

Season sank down into the water, while Molly stared blankly at the master of the house. The maid cast Season a glance that plainly told her her husband would deal with her unladylike behavior. Then she gathered up the muddy garments and sailed out of the room.

Lucas walked casually over to Season, and she crossed her arms over her breasts trying to cover the upper half of her body from his view.

"I have heard it said that you have taken to wearing men's clothing, my lady wife," he said, smiling at her while his golden eyes ran over her creamy shoulders.

Season couldn't find her voice at first. She had gone for months without hearing a word from Lucas, and suddenly here he was acting as if he had never left her.

She watched in disbelief as he slowly began removing his wet shirt. She pressed her back against the tub when he slipped off his muddy boots. "You aren't going to do what I think you are!" she cried, thinking it was his intention to get into the bath with her. How dare he just walk in as if nothing is wrong between us! Season thought angrily.

He smiled and his brilliant golden eyes rested on Season's creamy white breasts which were plainly visible in the clear water. "I would like nothing better than to bathe with you, my dear, but alas, the tub isn't large enough to accommodate the both of us." Lucas dropped down beside her and raised her chin. "Have you no greeting for your husband after all this time, Season?"

"Season's face became flushed when she saw the gleam in his eyes. "Lucas, I'm warning you to leave me alone!" she said, pushing his hand away.

He chuckled and ran his finger down her breast. "Now isn't this pleasant? I come home to find my wife pining away for me. I understand you are restraining yourself from falling into my arms."

"How dare you, Lucas! I haven't seen you in months. You didn't bother to tell me you were leaving and I haven't received one letter from you. You suddenly appear without warning, and you expect me to throw myself into your arms as if nothing had ever happened."

His golden eyes caressed Season's face lovingly, causing her blood to pound. Feeling the pull of Lucas' magnetism, she armed herself against him. She didn't want to forgive his neglect so readily.

"Have you any notion how beautiful you are . . . even with mud on your face?" His voice was low and the sound of it seemed to vibrate in her ears.

She reached for a cloth and dabbed at her face until Lucas took it from her hand and tenderly washed the mud away. Season watched, mesmerized, as he took the cake of soap and began lathering his hands. She almost groaned with pleasure as he began to run his lathered hands across her shoulders and back. Hot waves of passion surged through her body as his hands moved slowly around to encircle her breasts and caress their satiny peaks sensuously.

Lucas' eyes held hers, and her body began to relax beneath his gentle stroking hands. Suddenly he broke the spell with his laughter.

"You have mud in your hair. What did you do—tumble in a mud puddle somewhere?" He gathered up a handful of muddy curls and began lathering them vigorously.

"I have been helping sandbag the river. You weren't home to see to it. If I hadn't taken charge Rosemont would have been flooded and you would have lost your crops."

His hands stopped. "You what? Are you telling me that Walls allowed you to take part in such a dangerous operation? I will send him packing for this!"

"Mr. Walls has been very ill and had nothing to do with it," Season said, looking at him with an angry frown on her face.

"You could have asked Robert for help, Season," he suggested ironically.

"No, I couldn't. Robert and Rebecca have gone to Philadelphia. There was no one to take control but me."

Lucas' hands were rough as he pulled her head up and forced her to look at him. "Are you telling me that you helped sandbag and dig the trenches I saw when I rode up?"

"Well, obviously not all by myself. Everyone helped. You would have been proud of Winston, Lucas. He took charge and the others followed his lead."

"Winston!" Lucas said in an astounded voice. "That slave has caused me nothing but trouble for the last three years. Mrs. Walls has urged me to sell him for fear that he might one day harm her husband."

Season looked stricken for a moment. "It was Mrs. Walls who recommended Winston to me in the first place. Why would she do such a thing if she didn't trust Winston?"

Lucas clamped his jaw tightly together. "She is a bitter old woman, but I have put up with her for years because I value Walls. I think it's time I had a talk with her."

"Let it be, Lucas. Everything worked out satisfactorily. As for selling Winston, I won't ever allow it. I do not approve of buying and selling human beings as if they were cattle. Besides, he was wonderful today. We could never have saved Rosemont without his help."

Lucas' shoulders shook with silent laughter. "Lord, you oppose me at every turn, Season. First, you turn patriot on me, and now you want to free all my slaves. You have me at your mercy, wondering what you will do next."

"Why did you come back, Lucas?" she asked pointedly. "Why didn't you just stay with your friends in New York? I have been told that you have a friend there by the name of Lady Southerland. Why didn't you stay with her?"

Lucas' hand tightened on Season's shoulder. "Where

did you hear that?"

"Edmund told me the day he came to Rosemont. Do you deny that he spoke the truth?"

"I will neither confirm nor deny the charge. If you have no faith in me, there is nothing I can say that will make you believe me."

"I have thought many things about you, Lucas, but I have never questioned your honesty. If you say Edmund wasn't telling the truth, I will believe you."

"If that is the case, I will tell you there is nothing going on between myself and Lady Southerland," he said as his golden eyes flashed.

Season lowered her lashes. "I will believe you then, but that still doesn't excuse you, Lucas."

He stood up and smiled slightly. "Am I to take it you are not overjoyed to see me?"

Season dunked her head in the water and washed the soap from her hair. She saw that the towel was hanging over the back of a chair, and knew she would have to expose herself to reach it. Anger overruled her modesty, and she climbed out of the tub and padded across the room, dripping water on the floor.

Lucas' eyes followed her and their golden depths seemed to burn into her. He noticed her long silky legs and her softly curved hips.

Wrapping the towel about her she turned to face him. "What did you expect, Lucas? Did you think I would welcome you back with open arms?"

"I had hoped so," he replied, smiling.

Season's damp hair clung to her face and her green eyes sparkled defiantly. "Perhaps the other women in your life are content to go for months without seeing or hearing from you. I have no doubt they would fall willingly into your arms, glad that you noticed them at all. If you expect that from me you will be sadly disappointed."

In two long strides Lucas crossed the room and grabbed Season, crushing her in his arms. "Dare I hope that you are jealous, Season?"

She felt Lucas tug at the towel that was wound about her, and suddenly she was naked against his body. Season had no time to react as he lifted her into his arms and placed her on the bed.

"You can put your mind at rest, Season," he said, moving his hand along her stomach and up to her breasts. "I have been with no other woman since I took you as my wife. How could I, when my thoughts are of you day and night?"

She swallowed the lump in her throat, wanting to believe him. "Why did you stay away so long? Couldn't you have written me just once?"

He could hear the pain in her voice and he dropped down beside her. "I can assure you, Season, nothing short of duty would have kept me from you," he whispered, his eyes roving over her face as if he wanted to reacquaint himself with every beautiful detail.

Season turned her face away from him, not yet ready to forgive his neglect.

He reached for her and made her face him. His eyes were soft and Season thought she saw sadness in their golden depths. "Do not turn away from me, my love. I have needed you for so long."

A sob escaped her lips and she held out her arms to him. No, she wouldn't turn away from him. Until that moment she hadn't realized how much she had missed him. It didn't matter that he had neglected her—all that mattered now was that he was here, and he really did need her.

With a strangled groan, Lucas lowered his dark head and tasted her parted lips. He had ached for Season for months, and now she was in his arms. His body cried out for the oneness that he always felt with her.

At the touch of Lucas' lips on hers, the last of Season's resistance perished. She laced her fingers in his dark, rain-soaked hair. He had been away for so long. . . . Her love-starved body melted against him.

The gentle exploration of his hands seemed to set Season's nerve ends on fire, and she was unaware that her own hands went down to the waist of Lucas' trousers.

He looked down at her hands and with one smooth motion removed his only remaining article of clothing. Season melted against him now that there was nothing to come between their hungry flesh.

She threw her head back as his mouth explored her face, brushed her ear, and then kissed both her eyelids. A weakness washed over Season as his head lowered and his mouth circled the peak of one breast and then moved on to the other.

Season was not aware of the soft purring sounds she was making as his hand brushed against the inside of her thigh. There was a need inside of her that only Lucas could fulfill. This time her mind was not clouded by thoughts of her former lover, The Raven. She thought only of her husband and his promise of perfect fulfillment.

Needles of excitement seemed to dance on her skin as Lucas rolled her over and entered her. At first his movements were gentle and slow, but as their bodies experienced a deeper need for one another he thrust forward sensuously.

Season clung to Lucas' shoulders as if she were attempting to grasp the wonderful feelings he aroused in her.

"You belong only to me," he whispered hotly in her ear. "You are mine."

"Yes, Lucas, yes," she breathed, seeking his mouth.

He groaned as she rubbed her silken body against his. "You take my breath away, my love," he gasped, his voice ragged.

He held her tightly against him as tremor after tremor shook both their bodies. When their waves of passion subsided, they both lay silent not knowing what to say to each other. They had shared a journey into ecstasy, and neither of them seemed able to put words to what they had experienced.

Season had given her all to Lucas this time, holding nothing back. Lucas had never felt more alive. He was excited, thinking that every time he took his wife in his arms she would give him the same deep pleasure.

"We are good together, Season," he said, pulling her to him so that her head rested against his shoulder.

She threw back her head and looked into his golden eyes, seeing a softness in their amber depths that she had never seen before. "I think I am beginning to love you, Lucas," she whispered into his ear.

She watched as his throat worked convulsively. "Are you sure?" The soft-spoken question revealed that he was almost afraid to hear her answer.

"Yes. I believe my love for you has always existed, but I haven't wanted to admit it."

His hand trembled as he softly touched her face. "You have no notion how long I have waited and hoped you would come to love me. I can assure you my heart has been yours since the night you walked into that ballroom and my eyes collided with the beautiful green eyes of a goddess."

"I thought you didn't like me very well that night, Lucas. You seemed so cold and distant."

"I can assure you the opposite was true. Into my life had just walked the woman I had waited for, but she had come to marry good old Edmund. How do you think I was feeling that night?"

Season traced the outline of his mouth with a delicate finger. "I told you before, as I walked toward you that night I hoped you would be the one I had come to marry. I wanted you to be Edmund."

"You were taken with me, were you?" he teased.

"I was devastated by your golden eyes."

"Season, we need to talk about him," Lucas said, watching her eyes closely.

"You mean about Edmund?" she asked, choosing to misunderstand him.

"No, I wasn't speaking of Edmund. You know very well of whom I was speaking."

"Oh," she said, wishing he hadn't brought up the subject of The Raven. She hoped that now she could put her feelings for the captain of the *Andromeda* aside once and for all. She only wanted to love her husband.

"Tell me, what are your feelings for him, Season,"

Lucas said, watching her eyes closely.

"No, I don't want to talk about The Raven. Let us not spoil what we have together, Lucas—it is still too young and fragile."

"What I feel for you is more like a devastating earthquake, rather than something fragile," he said, smiling. "Answer but one question for me, Season, and I will allow the matter to drop."

"You want to know if I still love him?" she said, turning her head to stare at the ceiling.

"Yes."

"I don't know what to say to you, Lucas. I want to be perfectly honest with you, but at the same time—"

"You don't want to hurt me?"

"Yes, something like that."

"Don't bother answering, Season, because you already have. It would seem I still have a rival for your affections."

Season saw the pain in Lucas' eyes, and she placed her hand in his and laced her fingers through his. "Lucas, I can promise you one thing—I have said this before, but I want you to believe me—I will never break my marriage vows to you."

"What you are saying is that you may love The Raven, but you won't allow him to bed you."

"Lucas, please don't torture me like this," she pleaded. "I cannot help how I feel."

"If The Raven were to come to you tomorrow, you wouldn't allow him to touch you?" he insisted.

"You have my word that I would not allow him to touch me, ever."

Lucas rested his cheek against Season's. "But you

still love him, Season. That is what tears me apart inside. How can you love two different men? My heart is so full of loving you I have no room for anyone else."

"Please, let us not talk of it any longer. You said you would only ask me one question. Tell me what you were doing in New York?"

"I was mainly running errands for General Cornwallis. You would be bored with the details," he replied, wishing he could block The Raven from her mind. He didn't want to share his wife with anyone, especially not The Raven.

"I have heard my father speak of Lord Cornwallis. I wonder if it can be the same man?" Season asked, glad to change the subject.

"I doubt that there are two men running around with the same title, but there is something I have been wondering about ever since I got home. Tell me, Season, whose idea was it to divert the river by digging trenches?"

"Mine. It seemed the sensible thing to do."

He laughed and pulled her tightly against him. "I am married to a genius. It's so simple I wonder no one has thought about it before now."

Basking in Lucas' praise, Season yawned and snuggled closer to him, as he stroked her hair. She was so tired. . . . Her eyes drifted shut.

Lucas looked down at his sleeping wife, and smiled, thinking there was no one to equal her. He kissed her cheek softly.

"Sleep, my dearest love . . . you earned it."

Chapter Twenty-Nine

As August gave way to September the cotton was ready for picking. To Lucas' relief the rains had stopped and the white fluffy cotton balls were heavy on the stalks.

At Season's urging, Lucas had placed Winston over the other field hands and had been rewarded by a more productive working arrangement. The picking was going so smoothly that Lucas wondered why he hadn't thought of putting a slave in charge of the cotton fields long before now.

Several of the neighbors had dropped by to pay their respects. They had heard that Season had kept the river from flooding, and they openly offered her their friendship. Lucas was glad that they were showing their appreciation to his wife. He realized that they were more inclined to offer their hands in friendship to Season than they were to him, for many of them still resented him for his support of the English.

For weeks now Season and Lucas had walked hand

in hand, at peace with life. For the time they had both forgotten this was a war-torn land.

"Where do you ship the cotton after it's picked, Lucas?" Season inquired one day.

"Like everyone else in Virginia, Rosemont cotton will be stored. For the last five years we have kept the cotton in the building in back of the slave quarters. I had almost decided not to plant cotton this year, knowing there was no market for it. But like my father before me, I am a planter, and I like to see things growing. No matter how long this war lasts, I suppose Rosemont will continue to grow her crops."

"Lucas, surely our cotton mills have not shut down just because there's a war. America needs her industries, now more than ever."

Lucas smiled at his wife, because she had said *our* cotton mills. "For your information, Miss Question-all, we have no cotton mills."

Season looked at Lucas, aghast. "Surely you jest? Why is that possible when we have the land and the resources to maintain a cotton mill? Where do you send the cotton to be processed, Lucas?"

"To England, my dear. Because the cotton manufacturers in England have kept the machinery out of America. They want us to sell them our raw cotton and then buy back the finished product."

"That is shameful. I am appalled by the unfairness of it. Surely someone has the ingenuity to build a mill. Perhaps we could do that, Lucas."

He laughed and pulled her to him. "I have very little doubt that, given time, you would do just that, Mrs. Carrington. I think there is nothing you cannot do, if you put your bright little mind to it."

"I'm serious, Lucas. Why do we in Virginia stand for such treatment?"

"In case you haven't noticed, Season, there is at this moment, a war going on for just that reason . . . and for several other reasons."

"Yes, and you are on the side of the ones who wish to capitalize on your own industry. I cannot understand why you can allow this to happen without raising your voice. Don't you see what's going on here? Open your eyes and look at what they are doing to us, Lucas."

"Season, until a few short months ago you, yourself, were them, and not us."

"Yes, but it took me very little time to see the truth. You have lived here all your life, and still you are blind to what is happening."

His golden eyes lost their humor and glinted dangerously. "I will not discuss this with you, Season. My family has been living on this land for three generations, and we don't need someone from England telling us how to run—"

She turned on him. "You dare say this to me when you allow England to dictate to you on everything else. Open your eyes and wake up, Lucas!"

Lucas looked as if he might say something, but instead he clamped his lips together and walked away. Season stared after him, realizing that they had just had another quarrel.

That night over dinner, Lucas was silent and brooding, and Season was hurt and disappointed because he had treated her like an outsider. Just when she thought they were beginning to get to know one another, Lucas had to shut her out again. She decided to apologize to him after dinner. After all, he knew more about the situation than she did. Perhaps she had expressed her views too freely.

When dinner was over Season followed Lucas out to the veranda. He seemed miles away from her as he stared up at the darkened sky, hardly aware that she stood beside him.

"Lucas, can I speak to you about something?" she said, moving closer to him.

"I believe we voiced all that needed to be said this afternoon, Season," he stated dryly, without looking at her. "I have no wish to quarrel with you again."

"I just wanted to apologize to you for what I said this afternoon. You were perfectly right, Lucas. What you do is none of my concern. It's just that I have come to love this land. One day our children will grow up here, and I want them to know a life of freedom."

He was silent as he turned to stare at her. "No, Season. It is I who should apologize to you. I was very harsh with you today, but you must try to understand that if your views were to reach my friends in New York, there could be some very grave consequences."

"Are you more concerned with what your friends in New York think of you, Lucas, than what your friends here in Virginia think? Good Lord, I don't understand you in the least. This is your home. The people here are your friends and neighbors."

He gripped the porch railing tightly. "You came here to beg my pardon, and still you remind me of my shortcomings. How can you profess to love me, Season, when you not only don't trust me, but you have so little faith in me? Sometimes I think you cannot see past your nose."

"I do believe in you, Lucas. I just think you have been influenced by the wrong people. I may not be able to judge the situation or the war fairly, but I do know right from wrong. England is wrong, Lucas. America has the right to self-rule. There is no freedom in this country."

He sighed heavily. "Lord, will this never end. I grow weary with this war."

"You cannot be near as weary of this war as those who have lost fathers, husbands, and sons." Season's accusation hung in the air and she covered her mouth, realizing what she had just said.

"So you think me a coward? This isn't the first time you have implied that."

"Lucas, please, I didn't mean to say that—it just slipped out."

"You think I am a coward or you would never have voiced such a thought. My life has been one upheaval after another since you came into it. Had I been wise, I would have run for my life the first time I ever set eyes on you."

Season felt the prickle of impending tears. "Perhaps you should have run that night, Lucas. You would have been doing us both a favor. We are worlds apart in our thinking, and I wonder if we will ever be able to bridge the gap that separates us?"

Lucas lookled up at the sky again. "Season, Season, why do we tear each other apart? I was wondering how

I could tell you I have to go away again. Perhaps you will now be glad to be rid of me."

Season turned and walked away. She paused at the door and glanced back to Lucas. "Don't bother writing me this time either, Lucas. If you do so, your letters will go unread and unanswered."

Lucas wanted to call her back, but he knew nothing he could say would lessen her hurt. He realized how he must look in her eyes, and in some ways, he was the coward she accused him of being. He was too much a coward to reach out for the happiness he knew he and Season could find together. Something always seemed to tear them apart. He wondered if it would always be this way for the two of them.

That night Lucas rode away from Rosemont and Season cried herself to sleep.

By the end of September the cotton crop had been picked and stored in the storage barn with the previous years yield. The dried sticks had all been plowed under, and the fields lay dormant.

The war was raging in Virginia, and the opposing armies drew nearer to Rosemont Plantation. Season could often hear the distant gunfire, and she was torn between her two loyalties. She prayed for the day when the war would come to an end. Perhaps when the hostilities stopped, she and Lucas could end their differences.

Season spent Christmas with Robert and Rebecca, otherwise she would have spent another solitary holiday. As it was, she felt alone and deserted again.

This time she didn't blame herself for driving her husband away. Lucas was wrong in what he believed. She would never be able to understand how he could desert his home and side with the opposing army.

Season didn't receive a letter from Lucas but several packages arrived. He sent her some new dresses and a diamond necklace and earrings. Uninterested, she put these items away. It seemed that Lucas thought he could make up for his absence with expensive gifts, just as her father had.

January was bitter cold, and Season rarely went outside. She had contracted a heavy chest cold which she couldn't seem to shake.

Molly, in her usual blunt manner, swore that the main thing wrong with her mistress was that she had been deserted by her husband.

On one cold bleak January afternoon, Season sat before a roaring fire trying to keep warm. She had taken several doses of honey and brandy, but still she couldn't seem to shake her cough. She heard several riders coming down the drive, and soon Molly came bustling into the sitting room, her face flushed with excitement.

"You'll never guess, my lady. There is a whole troop of our soldiers out front! Lordy, it's going to be good to see English faces again."

"How many are there?" Season wanted to know.

"I can't tell for sure, but there must be near fifty."

Just then there was a loud pounding on the door, and Molly hastened to answer. In the sitting room, Season could hear the exchange that followed.

"I am aide to Brigadier General Benedict Arnold,

499

ma'am. Is the man of the house home?"

"No, the mister is out, but Mrs. Carrington is home."

There was a long silence and then she heard the sound of boots in the entryway. Molly opened the sitting-room door and was about to announce the intruder when he brushed past her. Season rose just as a tall man swaggered into the room.

"I am Brigadier General Benedict Arnold, ma'am. I am told your husband isn't at home." He waited for the beautiful woman to speak, thinking she would be impressed by his title.

"I have heard of you, General Arnold. What I heard was that you sold out your countrymen."

Arnold's face grew red. "You would do well to keep a civil tongue in your head, madam. I have it within my power to lay your house to ashes."

She laughed insultingly. "I do not doubt it, Mr. Arnold, but I do not think you will."

"Don't test me, madam, for I am of half a mind to set a torch to your house this very day. Where is your husband? I suppose he is off fighting with the American rabble."

"My husband is in New York with General Clinton. You may have heard of him; his name is Lucas Carrington." Suddenly, Season was seized by a fit of coughing and had to sit down to catch her breath.

Arnold's eyebrows shot up. "I have heard of your husband, madam. It is said he dallies with one side while his countrymen fight his battles for him. It is said he will not lose no matter who wins the war."

"State your business, sir. The hour grows late and I do not wish to stay here long conversing with a poltroon. You are not welcome in this house." Season knew Lucas would be angry with her for being rude to Benedict Arnold, but she couldn't abide the man.

Arnold laughed. "Your information is a bit mixed up, Mrs. Carrington, I believe your husband will come nearer to being a traitor than I."

Season's eyes flashed. "What do you want? State your business and leave."

"I have come to ask permission to headquarter in your house and to put my troops in your barns. After speaking with you, I will not ask your permission. You will have your bedrooms made ready for me and my officers."

"You are badly mistaken, sir, if you think you will sleep one night beneath my roof. I cannot prevent you and your men from sleeping in our barns, but I will not permit you to sleep in my home."

"No, it is you that is mistaken, madam." Arnold crossed the room and threw the door open, calling for his aide.

"Just a moment, General," Season's voice rang out. "I think you do not know whom you are addressing. Have you ever heard of the Duke of Chatsworth?"

He turned to her and sneered. "Of course, and I have also heard of King George. What has that to do with anything? I hope you aren't going to try to convince me that you know either one of them."

"You would do well to listen to me, General. I am in fact the Duke of Chatsworth's daughter. I don't think either my father or the king would take kindly to your visit to my home today."

She saw doubt in Arnold's eyes. "I don't believe you,

madam. What would the daughter of Lord Chatsworth be doing in the middle of Virginia?"

"Shall I tell my father that you called me a liar, sir? I wonder what that would do to your new career?"

"I believe we will just settle this right now. Where is the English maid who answered the door?"

Molly must have been listening at the door because she immediately came into the room looking as if she were ready to do battle. Season knew her maid was mortified by General Arnold's treatment of her.

"You there," Arnold said, pointing at Molly. "Give me the title or last name of this lady before she became the wife of Lucas Carrington."

Molly fixed the man with an angry glare. "My lady was, and is, the Duke of Chatsworth's daughter. You, sir, would be well advised to leave as she has asked you to."

Benedict Arnold's cheeks puffed out and he cleared his throat. He wasn't sure if the maid was telling the truth, but he couldn't afford to make a mistake. "I am truly sorry, my lady. I hope you will forgive and forget my rudeness to you earlier. Had I known who you are, I would merely have paid my respects and left. I blame my behavior on the hostility that has been directed at me by the families in this valley. Not one family will receive me and my men."

"I will neither forgive, nor forget your behavior here today. I will now ask you to leave my house. Since the hour is late and it is cold outside, I will allow you and your men to sleep in our barns. I trust you will be gone in the morning, and I would not be pleased if you or your men were to destroy any part of this plantation."

Benedict Arnold sputtered and started to say something, but apparently thought better of it. Clicking his heels together, he bowed stiffly. "Your servant, my lady."

Season looked at the man haughtily. "I trust you will instruct your men to respect my husband's property. Molly will show you out."

He nodded, knowing he and his troops would pitch their tents down by the river. He couldn't afford to offend the daughter of a man so powerful in England.

Season's eyes were blazing as she watched him depart. She couldn't respecst a man who had turned on his own country, and she doubted that Arnold would receive a warm welcome if he ever reached England. She was sorry that her own countrymen would be sleeping in the cold tonight, but she would not permit that man to stay under her roof!

She thought of Lucas and of what Arnold had said about him. No, she told herself, surely Lucas couldn't be classed with Benedict Arnold.

Molly returned after showing Arnold to the door. "I never thought to see the likes of him, my lady. What's the world coming to when a lady is insulted in her own home?"

"It wasn't he who started the insults, Molly. I had heard about his betrayal of his country, and I merely pointed it out to him."

"I heard you well enough through the door. You can hold your own when you are of a mind to."

"I am not feeling very well, Molly. I think I will go to bed early," Season said, standing up.

"You go right ahead, my lady. I'll bring you a nice

dinner and put a hot poultice on your chest. My mother always said there was nothing to draw the poison out of one's lungs like a hot poultice."

"I'll take the dinner, Molly, but I will not allow you to put that smelly concoction about my neck," Season stated, walking toward the door.

The house was dark and everyone had gone to bed, but Season was feeling restless so she threw the covers aside and walked over to the window. She stared at the distant campfires that dotted the riverbank. Those were her countrymen down there, and she felt torn inside. She now considered herself an American, and yet her heart ached for the land of her birth.

She hoped the time would never come when she would be forced to choose sides. It was easy to defend a point of view, but when it came right down to it, could she turn her back on England? Yes. When it came right down to it, she would stand with the land of her husband's birth. How ironic it is, she thought. I want to defend the American cause, and Lucas stands with my former countrymen. Perhaps she had burned her bridges behind her when she had ordered Benedict Arnold out of her house. She doubted that Lucas would be pleased by her action.

Season felt the chill of the room seep into her body, and she shivered. A light snow began to fall and the wind whistled down the valley. She crossed the room and climbed back into bed. When she finally fell asleep, her thoughts were very troubled.

Chapter Thirty

Season slept very fretfully. She dreamed she was aboard the *Andromeda* and the wind was blowing in her hair. She could almost smell the warm sea breeze and feel the golden sun on her face. In her dream a man was standing just behind her, but she couldn't see his face. She held out her hand and the man took it, then moved into the light. The man was wearing a leather helm! His hands went upward to remove the mask and she saw that he was Edmund! Backing away, Season tried to run, but her feet wouldn't move. When she turned around again she saw Edmund's dead body and realized she had killed him. Suddenly there was another man behind her and she turned. He also wore a leather mask. He reached out and touched her face and she tried to escape him. But his soft touch seemed to draw her to him and he raised his face and kissed her lips.

No, no, this is wrong, she told herself. I promised Lucas I would not betray him. But The Raven merely laughed at her pleas and his warm lips settled on hers.

Season suddenly sat up in bed, fully awake. She was trembling, and it took her a few moments to realize that she had only been dreaming. She was trying to fight off her drowsiness when she heard a faint sound at the foot of her bed. The room was dark, but she tried to see what was in her room. Perhaps I am still asleep, she thought.

Then Season's heart began to drum and she knew she was awake as a dark shadow moved toward her. She couldn't see him clearly, but she knew The Raven was in the room with her!

"You have come back," she said in a shaky voice.

"I couldn't stay away. I had to see you," came the deep raspy reply.

"How did you get into the house? Are you aware that there are English troops camped by the river?"

"No one can keep me from you. Not the whole British army."

Season felt him touch her face and she moved out of his reach. "Go away or I will scream."

He sat down on the bed and pulled her unwilling body into his arms. "You will not scream, my lady," he said confidently. "Are you not glad to see me?"

"You shouldn't have come here. Please, I want you to leave now."

"No, I will not leave until you tell me how you are feeling. I had heard that you were ill."

"How did you—"

"I have my sources. Tell me how you are feeling?"

"I had a fever, but I am fine now. I have only a lingering cough."

He touched her forehead. "You feel cool—you are no longer feverish."

"Now that we have established that my health is good, will you go? Although I don't see why you should be concerned about my well-being."

"I am always concerned about your welfare. You should know that by now."

"If you don't leave I will send someone to blow your ship out of the water. I know you must be anchored off the Virginia shore."

"Tsk tsk, but you are bloodthirsty. I am also thirsty," he said, leaning forward to touch her lips, but Season turned her head aside, realizing he wasn't wearing his mask. He knew it was dark in her bedroom and she wouldn't be able to see his face.

"I despise all men," she said scrambling off the bed and running toward the window. "You think all you have to do is say a few pretty words and all will be forgiven. I am weary of hearing pretty words. I wish you would leave me alone! How much more do you think I can take?"

The Raven leaped across the bed and lifted Season in his arms. "It is far too cold for you to be up, my lady. The place for you is in the bed." He placed her on the bed and pulled the covers up to her neck. "Now, isn't that better?"

"No, and I am still angry with you."

"Tell me why are you mad at all men. We are not such a bad lot when you get to know us. Perhaps you are speaking of your husband. Do you tire of married life so soon?"

"I will not discuss Lucas with you."

He sat down beside her, and she played with the ring on her finger. "Perhaps I will leave if you will give me but one small kiss."

"No! I will not."

"Surely you wouldn't send me out on such a night without a kiss from your lips to warm my heart."

"If you have something to say, Raven, say it and leave. I will not allow you to kiss me . . . besides I promised Lucas I wouldn't—"

"Wouldn't what, my lady?"

"Please leave me alone, Raven. Leave me with some shred of decency. I beg you to allow me to retain my honor."

"My sweet lady, I never intended to make you suffer. I will leave if it is your wish, but please do not send me away without a taste of your lips." His hand clamped on her chin raising her face to his.

"I dare not," she whispered, as her heart swelled with love for this man whom she didn't really know. She had once thought she would know The Raven if she ever saw him unmasked, but now she wasn't so sure. Not after what had happened with Edmund.

"Would you deny me one little kiss just because of a promise you made to your husband?"

"Would you respect me if my word was so easily broken, Raven?"

"Say that you don't really want me to leave. Give me at least that much."

"You must go. I would not want you to be captured by your enemies."

He pulled her tightly against him and laid his cheek to hers. "You have bewitched me, my lady. I would risk any danger for just a smile from your lips."

His deeply spoken words sent a thrill through Season's body. "You shouldn't be saying these things to me," she said, trying to hold on to her sanity.

"I have to make a confession, my lady. I have been through hell, for I know it was my fault that you lost our baby. If only I could hear you say you forgive me, then I could leave with a lighter heart."

Season wished she could see his features, if only to know whether he was sincere, but his face seemed to blend with the night shadows. "If I say I forgive you, will you go and never return again?"

"Would you be speaking the truth?"

"Not exactly. Because of you I have killed a man. I do not blame you for the accident that took my baby, but I do blame you for the fact that I committed murder to save your life. I will never forgive you, or myself."

"You were not at fault, my lady. Had you not killed Edmund, you would have lived to regret it."

"I regret it now! Just go away, Raven."

"If I do leave, I cannot promise to stay away from you, my lady. Something keeps pulling me back to you."

Season tried not to listen to his words. From past experience she knew The Raven could use words to his best advantage. "You must go," she said, pushing him away. "If the soldiers return they will arrest you."

"Would you care so much? Perhaps you would view my arrest as justice. I have heard you say many times that you would like to see me hanged."

"I would like to see . . . the last of you."

"I wonder if you speak the truth, my lady. If you hate me so much, why have you told no one what you know about the crew of the *Andromeda?* There are many things you could have told Lucas Carrington about me and my men, yet you did not. I wonder why."

"How do you know what I have told my husband?"

"I have ways of finding out about you, but you haven't answered my question. Another thing you might think about, if you wanted to see the last of me, you could have allowed Edmund to kill me that night."

"I do not intend to answer any of your questions. Do you see no shame in entering a married woman's bedroom? What if someone were to find you here?"

"No one will ever know I have come to your room unless you tell them. I seem to have no shame and no pride where you are concerned. Allow me to stay with you for a while and talk. You have my word I will not try to touch you . . . unless you want me to."

"What good would it do for me to ask you to leave? I have done so repeatedly, and still you are here. Why don't you seek out a woman who would be more willing than I to entertain you in her bedroom?"

"Alas, I cannot, for since the first time I tasted your lips, I have wanted no other." His voice was deep and disturbing as always, and she hated the way her heartbeat increased at his pretty words.

Season got out of bed and walked over to the fireplace, but she found no warmth there since the fire had gone out. "You will never make me believe you have been standing on the deck of the *Andromeda* pining away for me. I know you better than that, Raven."

He moved closer to her. "'Tis true, my lady. But most of all I have been in the depths of hell, thinking you blamed me for the death of our child." He pulled her into his arms. "I admit I have wronged you in many ways, my lady. Say you forgive me and release me from this torment."

Season closed her eyes because she could feel tears

gathering. She knew that The Raven was speaking from his heart. No matter how he may have teased and goaded her in the past, she felt The Raven was sincere this time. She could feel his suffering like a pain within her own breast.

"Oh, yes, I forgive you all. In your pain, I also feel hurt," she cried out.

He clasped her hands tightly together. "I love you, my lady. Should I never gaze upon your face again, I would take a vision of you to my grave."

A sob tore from her lips. "You are far more fortunate than I, for I have never seen your face, yet I shall remember you for the rest of my life."

"I am tempted to light a candle so you might gaze upon my face, my lady. You have but to say the word and I will reveal myself to you."

"No, I have no right to know your true identity. Do not give me knowledge which might later be used to betray you."

She heard him take a ragged breath. "Would that I were your husband, my lady. I would count myself the most fortunate of men."

Season tried to shut out what he was saying. He had no right to say such things to her—and she had no right to listen to him. "Raven, I will ask one thing of you. Something happened and it has been bothering me for some time."

"You have only to state what you wish from me, for I can deny you nothing."

"After the accident, when I lost the baby, did you come to me?"

"Yes."

"Then it was not a dream?"

"I came to you hoping to give you back your life. I knew it was because of me you lost my . . ." His voice sounded very strained and he couldn't continue.

She wanted to cradle his head against her breast and tell him that she felt the loss of their child as deeply as he. She wanted to tell him that she loved him, but she couldn't break her vow to Lucas.

"I will say this to you, Raven, and then I want you to leave and never come to me again. I would have died had it not been for you. When I heard your voice you literally pulled me out of death's grip. You saved my life and I will be eternally grateful for that."

The Raven seemed tense and undecided. "Do you love Lucas Carrington?"

"Yes."

"Surely you cannot love him. Was it not my voice you heard when you were so ill? That is the proof that you love me!"

"I will always keep a special place in my heart for you, but I will never allow you to take anything away from my husband, Raven."

"You may think you love your husband, but every time he takes you in his arms you will think of me." He moved to the door and paused. "I will come to you but one more time. When this war is ended I will seek you out. At that time I will ask you to decide whether you love me . . . or Lucas Carrington."

Season didn't know he had left until she heard the door close softly. She started shaking and fell to her knees, burying her face in her hands. Dear God in heaven, she loved two men, and in her mind she couldn't decide which one of them she was betraying.

Chapter Thirty-One

June, 1781

The war between the United States and England raged on. General Charles Cornwallis advanced through the South and on into Virginia. He sent dispatches to General Clinton urging him to bring all-out war to the South, but Lord Clinton feared if he sent troops to Cornwallis' aid, he would weaken his forces in New York. Not knowing where to commit his forces, Clinton ordered Cornwallis to take up a position in Virginia and hold it at all cost.

Cornwallis marched his troops toward the Chesapeake, pursued by Lafayette who had been hounding his rear. Making for the sea, Cornwallis hoped to be rescued by the British fleet. What he didn't count on was the aggressiveness of the French so he became hopelessly trapped between Lafayette and the sea.

An urgent dispatch went out to General Clinton in New York, asking him to hasten his troops to the South or the war would be lost.

A cloud moved over the moon, shrouding its light and casting the land in dark shadow. The only sound that could be heard was an occasional night bird calling from deep within the dense forest.

General George Washington's troops were camped at the edge of the woods, and many tents and campfires dotted the land. It was a warm night so the soldiers lay upon their bedrolls, under the open sky. None of them noticed the dark shadow that detached itself from behind the trunk of an oak tree, moving as silently as a cat stalking its prey. When a sentry advanced, the intruder dodged quickly behind the thick foliage of a wild honeysuckle bush and waited for the guard to pass.

Shortly thereafter, the dark shadow circled, just outside the light of the campfires, until he came to the big tent that was set apart from the others. Looking over his shoulder, the man cautiously entered the tent.

General Washington sat on a campstool, a grim expression etched on his face. His head was bent over a map which he was studying intently. He was so deep in thought he hadn't heard the dark, cloaked figure enter his tent, and he spun around when he heard the deep, raspy voice.

"I am sorry to be late, General, but I had a little trouble crossing the Hudson."

Washington stood up and shook hands with The Raven. "I'm glad you could make it at all. Did you run into any problem entering my camp?"

Laughter emerged from behind the black mask. "I met with no resistance. Had I been the enemy, you would now be dead or my prisoner."

Washington smiled as he motioned for The Raven to be seated. "I will have to speak to my officers and see if they cannot set up a more impregnable camp."

The Raven seated himself and glanced down at the map, noting that it was a sketch of the Virginia coastline. "I received word only last week that you wanted to see me. I came as quickly as I could get away."

The Raven studied the face of the man who had been his friend for many years. Washington was a tall man and carried himself proudly, but tonight The Raven could see traces of weariness on his rugged face. His eyes looked as if he hadn't slept in many nights.

"I will close the tent flaps if you wish to take your mask off. No one will enter unannounced, and I can offer you some brandy. Lafayette sent me a case of the best French vintage."

"I dare not chance it, General. Too much depends on keeping my identity a secret. I left my men on the other side of the river and there is every need for haste."

Washington sat down wearily and rubbed his temples. "I often think of the roll you play for your country. If you are ever caught, it will be the hangman's rope for you, but after all this is over and the smoke has cleared, you will never receive the recognition you deserve. Few are aware of the important part you have played in this war; yet I shall always be grateful for the secret information you have funneled to me. Many times, your information has helped turn the tide of battle. Had you not been so useful to me as a spy, I would have insisted you take a commission in the army."

"I'm not doing this for glory or recognition, General. Like yourself, I am an American, and I do what I can for love of country." He smiled. "As for being in the army, I never was much good at following orders."

Washington studied The Raven's gloved hands. "I have never had a son of my own, but as a result of this war, I have come to know two very fine young men who could have been the sons I craved. Lafayette is one . . . you are the other."

"I am and always shall be your friend, sir," The Raven answered. "You have my deepest respect."

Washington nodded his head and laced his fingers together. "As badly as I hate to do it, I find I must call on your services again. I desperately need your help."

The Raven pushed his black cape aside and leaned forward. "I am yours to command, as always."

"Do not be so quick to commit yourself. What I am going to ask you to do will be very risky. It could turn the tide of the war, one way or the other. I don't have to caution you that this will be very dangerous."

"You have piqued my curiosity."

Washington stood up, unrolled the maps, and motioned for The Raven to come closer. "Lafayette has General Cornwallis trapped at Yorktown," he said, pointing at the coastal town of Virginia.

"Yes, I had heard that. Cornwallis is expecting to be saved by the British fleet. I have considered joining the French fleet when they do battle with Admiral Groves."

Washington's shoulders seemed to sag. "What I will

ask of you has nothing to do with a sea battle. I want you to convince General Clinton that I am going to try to retake New York!"

The Raven swung his head up and Washington knew he was stunned. "Why, General?"

"I'm going to Virginia, and if Clinton finds out he will send the fleet ahead of me. I want him to hold his forces in New York."

"I see. This could be the final push."

"I am going to help you all I can. I will make a great show of crossing the Hudson so it will be easier for you to convince Clinton that I am heading for New York."

"When will this all take place, General?" The Raven wanted to know.

"I haven't even told my own officers. They think I am making plans to swing up to New York. I hope to make the crossing on August twelfth. I don't have to tell you what's at stake here. It is most imperative that Admiral Groves does not pull his fleet out of New York!"

"I can see that the timing will be very important, sir. Should I convince Clinton too soon, he would have time to advance on you at the Hudson, and the British fleet could still rescue Cornwallis."

"That is only too true, but I will leave the timing strictly up to you. There will be no glory in this for you, Raven. As a matter of fact, only you and I will ever know of the part you will play to turn the tide of war in our favor. Your only reward will be in knowing you have served your country to the utmost."

"That is all the reward I have ever wanted. Let us hope I can convince General Clinton."

The Raven extended his hand and General Washington gripped it tightly. "Have a care, my friend. You are walking a dangerous road. I fear after this your usefulness as a spy will be ended; General Clinton will have figured out that you tricked him."

"Good luck to you, General. May God go with you."

The Raven slipped out of the tent and faded into the shadows. He left the camp as easily as he had entered it earlier, no man aware of his coming and going, with the exception of General George Washington.

August 1, 1781

General Henry Clinton looked over the sea of faces and listened to the drone of voices. These social affairs always bored him. He was a military man and didn't care for all this elaborate entertaining when there was a war going on. He didn't want to make the same mistakes his predecessor, General Howe, had. Lord Howe had seemed more interested in amusing himself than in winning the war, which was why the British government had made Clinton Howe's replacement.

"This is quite a turnout, Sir Henry," Lucas Carrington said, coming up beside him.

"Where have you been?" General Clinton asked sourly. "I left word at your lodging three days ago that I wanted to see you, Lucas."

"I am sorry, sir, but I have been out of town. Was it not you who sent me to Philadelphia?"

"Yes, yes," the general said impatiently, "but that was over a fortnight ago. You certainly took your time getting back to me. What did you find out?"

Lucas smiled at Lady Southerland as she danced by and indicated to him that he should meet her later. "Actually, sir, I found out very little. From what I was told, Washington is hoping to swing south and retake his home state of Virginia from Cornwallis."

General Clinton's brow furrowed. "Is it your opinion that I should commit the British fleet at Yorktown to reinforce Cornwallis, Lucas?"

"That was the advice I got, but I'm not sure I agree with it. My informant tells me there is something big in the wind."

General Clinton stared at Lucas. "Just what are you implying, my boy? You know I always value your advice. You have never yet let me down."

"This is my advice for all it's worth. If I were you, I would hold the fleet here in New York for a few weeks longer. It isn't at all unlikely that Washington wants you to think he is going to swing south to join Lafayette, when in truth he will try to retake New York. Washington is no fool, and he knows New York is the more important of the two. I believe he will head here."

General Clinton pondered Lucas' advice. "Yes, I can see the sense in what you are saying. I will wait for a week, two at the most. If by that time, Washington has not swung his troops south, I will know he is planning to advance on New York. By God, I would love to get my hands on him!"

Lucas Carrington smiled. "Who knows, Sir Henry, the war may be drawing to a close. Perhaps your meeting with Washington is closer than you think."

"You may be right, my boy. Let us hope so. I long to return to England. Perhaps the king will recall me as soon as this rebellion is put down."

"I would like to return to Virginia, myself. I have a young bride waiting for me."

General Clinton smiled knowingly. "I don't blame you, my boy. You have every reason to go home. Tell me, why don't you bring that beautiful wife of yours to New York?"

"Season prefers to stay in the country, sir. She has no liking for New York."

"If she were my wife, I'd be damned if she would be there and I here."

Lucas laughed. "I can't argue with that, sir."

General Clinton looked uncomfortable for a moment. "That was a nasty business about your cousin, Edmund. The word is around that Edmund was The Raven, that he was done in by one of his own crew members. Do you believe that?"

"No. I have heard that he was killed by The Raven."

"I never thought Edmund would desert the army. He always seemed to be a good soldier, but then one can never tell about such things. I believe he went a little crazy when he heard that you married Lady Season."

"I feel partly responsible for his death," Lucas said in a soft voice.

"Nonsense. He was very unstable. It is well that Lady Season married you instead of Edmund. I believe the two of you are well suited to one another."

"I can't argue with that either, sir," Lucas said, smiling to himself. "If you will excuse me, sir, I believe Lady Southerland is motioning for my attention."

"Lucas, it has never been my habit to interfere in

other peoples' lives, but I think I should warn you about the gossip that is circulating about you and Lorona Southerland. I am sure you wouldn't want any word of this to reach your wife in Virginia."

"I have often been the target for wagging tongues, sir. I can only say in my defense that there is nothing between Lady Southerland and myself besides friendship."

General Clinton looked as if he didn't entirely believe Lucas, but he only nodded his head. "Don't keep the lady waiting, but have a care about your lovely wife in Virginia."

Lucas bowed politely and took his leave. He saw Lorona Southerland step out into the garden and started after her. However, just as he reached the door, Mrs. Tibbs stepped in front of him to block his path.

"I was wondering how your wife is faring, Mr. Carrington." Mrs. Tibbs said, looking at him with disapproval.

"Season is well, Mrs. Tibbs," he answered, smiling.

"I wonder why you never bring Lady Season to New York, but then I suppose that would curb your outside activity, would it not?" she said, nodding toward the garden where Lorona Southerland waited."

"I'm sure I don't know what you mean, Mrs. Tibbs. Lorona and I are just friends."

"Hmm, a likely story," she said, brushing past him and heading into the dining room.

Lucas frowned as his eyes followed Mrs. Tibbs. He hoped the lady wouldn't take it upon herself to inform Season about his meetings with Lorona Southerland.

As Lucas stepped out into the garden Lorona came

up beside him. "I saw that Mrs. Tibbs had you cornered. I don't think the lady likes me overmuch, Lucas."

"I don't think I am very high on her list either. I will be glad when this farce is ended," Lucas said, taking her arm and leading her around to the front of the house.

He helped Lorona into the carriage and climbed in beside her. As they pulled away from General Clinton's home Lucas stared out into the night.

Lorona leaned forward and placed a hand on Lucas' arm to get his attention. "You love your wife very much, don't you, Lucas?" she asked.

"Yes, very much."

"I saw your wife when she first came to New York. She is very beautiful. This separation must be hard on both of you."

"The war will not last forever, Lorona."

"I get the feeling you don't want to discuss your wife with me."

"The one thing I always admired most about you, Lorona, was your quick perception. Do we go to your house or mine?" he said, changing the subject.

"Let's go to mine, it's closer."

"What does it matter? I suppose we have given the gossips enough to talk about," he said, sighing heavily.

"Lucas, I know you love your wife, but you must be very lonely. I myself have been very lonely since Tom died. We could help each other over this rough time. Everyone already believes the worst about us."

Lucas smiled. "If I were not so much in love with my wife, Lorona, I might just take you up on your tempting offer. I am sure you will not take it personally if I decline. Good lord, I must be out of my mind to turn down such a tempting offer. Before I met Season I would never have hesitated to please a beautiful woman."

Lorona laughed. "I hope the new Mrs. Carrington knows how fortunate she is?"

Lucas smiled. "Perhaps you will tell her, if you ever meet."

"I don't think that would be a good idea, Lucas."

He laughed. "Nor do I. The last thing a wife wants is to have her husband's virtues pointed out to her by another woman."

"I still think she is most fortunate, Lucas."

"I am the one who is fortunate, Lorona. Season is like no other woman I have ever known."

"Pray that this war is soon ended, Lucas, and you can return to your wife."

"I believe the wheels of war have begun to grind down even now, Lorona."

August 20, 1781

The allied forces, commanded by General George Washington, had crossed the Hudson River. When General Clinton heard of the crossing he felt that he had made the right decision by ordering the British fleet to remain in New York waters to defend the city from the American general's expected attack. It wasn't until the American army crossed the Delaware heading south that it became obvious to Lord Henry Clinton that he had been tricked! Consequently, George Washington marched unopposed to join Lafayette at York-town. Meanwhile, the French fleet reached the mouth of the York River, trapping Cornwallis' forces between them and Lafayette's land forces.

When the British fleet, commanded by Admiral Groves, finally arrived to help their surrounded troops it was too late. The French fleet gave battle, and managed to outsail, outshoot, and outsmart the British. Admiral Groves was forced to take his crippled fleet back to New York for repairs, leaving Cornwallis to fend for himself.

September 28, 1781

The French and American forces, commanded by General George Washington, surrounded the British and German Hessian troops. It wasn't until October sixth that Washington began the attack. The battle raged for twelve days, until Cornwallis knew he had been defeated. The war was, at last, nearing an end. America had won an important battle and was well on her way to being free!

October 19, 1781

The British and German forces marched out in front of their posts. Their uniforms were neat and tidy, while the American troops were a rag-tag lot. Many of the Washington's soldiers didn't have uniforms. There was a sharp contrast between the opposing armies. As the

American troops drew up parallel to the British and Hessians, the line stretched for more than a mile.

George Washington was sitting on horseback, patiently waiting for Cornwallis' surrender. The British general couldn't bring himself to hand over his sword to Washington, whom he considered no more than a traitor. He ordered his second-in-command, General Charles O'Hara, to offer the sword to Washington. But Washington, aware of the insult aimed at him by Cornwallis, refused the sword. Washington's deputy, General Lincoln, accepted the token of surrender in place of his commander in chief.

It was with great reluctance that the British officers ordered their men to disarm. Many hated glances were directed at the American soldiers as the defeated army stacked their weapons in a huge pile.

Lafayette's young face was eager as he looked at General Washington. "It is over, sir. The war is ended," he said, smiling proudly.

Washington looked toward the sea where he could see the *Andromeda*'s sails catch the breeze as she headed out to sea. He smiled to himself, thinking of how The Raven had managed to come ashore to watch Cornwallis' surrender. No one else would ever know that The Raven had kept the British fleet in New York long enough to allow him and his troops to reach the South and defeat Cornwallis.

Washington turned back to Lafayette, a grim expression on his face. "There will yet be battles to fight, but for all intents and purposes, the war is ended. I am weary of this war and will be glad to become a planter again."

Chapter Thirty-Two

Season was sitting on the veranda, going through the mail. She knew she wouldn't receive a letter from Lucas, and she couldn't really blame him for not writing her. After all, she had told him she would not read any letter he wrote. Still, each day she waited and hoped for some word from him.

Picking up a letter with unfamiliar handwriting she broke the seal. She smiled to herself when she saw it was from Mrs. Tibbs.

My Dear Lady Season,

I take pen in hand to say how surprised I was to find out you married Lucas Carrington and not his dear cousin, Edmund Kensworthy. I do hope you know what you are doing, my dear. I heard of dear Edmund's death and many of us think he just didn't want to live after he lost you.

I hope you won't think I am prying, but I think someone should tell you that your husband is seeing a lot of a certain widow, Lady Lorona Southerland. I don't approve of gossip, but I myself have seen the two of them together. It's easy to see they are more than friends. I do not wish to upset you, but I think you should know what is going on.

I send you my highest regards and wish you all that happiness can bring.

> Your loyal friend
> Edna Tibbs

Season placed the letter on the table and stood up. Tears of anger at his betrayal blinded her. How could Lucas do such a thing? Her heart shattered into a million pieces and an agonizing sob broke from her lips. Lucas didn't love her—he couldn't—not if he found pleasure in another woman's arms. Edmund had warned her that Lucas was seeing Lorona Southerland, but when Lucas had told her it wasn't true she had believed him. Mrs. Tibbs would never have written and accused Lucas of being with the woman if she hadn't believed it to be the truth.

She walked into the house and slowly climbed the stairs. In the last letter she had received from her father he had asked her to come home to Chatsworth for a visit; perhaps she would do just that. She would wait a few more days for Lucas to come home, and if he didn't, she would consider her father's suggestion and return to England.

*   *   *

Season was arranging a bouquet of fall flowers in a vase when Rebecca came running into the house, her cheeks glowing and her eyes shining.

"Season, it's over, it's over. We have won!"

Season was trying to make sense of Rebecca's excited clamor. "What are you talking about? What's over?"

"The war is over. America is free!" her sister-in-law cried excitedly.

Season almost dropped the vase she had been holding. Her hands were shaking so badly she spilled some of the water onto the floor, so she placed the vase on the hall table. As she watched Rebecca dance gleefully around in a circle, Season's heart sank. She was happy that America had won her independence, but she couldn't help feeling a painful ache because the land of her birth had suffered defeat and humiliation.

"Where did this happen, Rebecca? When did you receive the word?"

"At Yorktown! Robert came home this morning and told me all about it. As soon as I could get away, I rushed over to tell you. General Cornwallis surrendered to General Washington yesterday!"

Season closed her eyes. Her life seemed to be filled with conflicting emotions. She didn't know whether to laugh because of the victory or cry because of the defeat.

Rebecca seemed to sense Season's torment and she hugged her tightly. "I know how you must be feeling, but perhaps the time will come when our two countries will become friends again. After a period of healing on both sides, I believe that's just what will happen."

"I pray what you say will come to pass, Rebecca. I am so torn within my heart."

Rebecca took Season's hand and led her into the sitting room. Once the two girls were seated, Rebecca smiled. "We must look on the bright side. You have been alone so much, because of Lucas' absence. Now that the hostilities have ceased my brother will be coming home to stay."

"Yes, I suppose you are right. I wonder how Lucas will handle the end of the war?"

Rebecca sighed. "I wonder about that myself. I hope our friends and neighbors will put aside their hostile feelings toward Lucas. In time, my brother will come to know that he was misguided in his choice of a government for the United States."

"I pray that is so, Rebecca. Lucas did what he thought was right, just as Robert did what he considered his duty. They stayed friends despite the difference in their political views."

"I know Lucas felt strongly about his loyalty to the British. Right or wrong, he has always stood up for what he believes in." Rebecca defended her brother.

"Have either you or Robert heard from Lucas?" Season asked softly.

Rebecca looked at Season and saw the tiny shadows under her eyes. She couldn't understand why Lucas neglected his bride so shamefully. "No, we have heard nothing. Have you still not received a letter from him?"

"No, nothing since he left," Season saw no reason to tell Rebecca of what Mrs. Tibbs had written about Lucas and Lady Southerland.

Rebecca patted Season's hand. "Try not to fret. One

day soon Lucas will come home. I just know he will! If he has not written, there must have been a good reason."

Season stood up and walked over to the window to stare out at the trees with their bright autumn colors. She had many reasons to distrust Lucas, and she didn't know if she ever wanted to see him again.

She didn't tell Rebecca that she had received a letter from her father asking her to come home. He had written that the war was going badly, and he feared for her safety if she remained in America, thinking she might become the target for revenge. He thought she might be in danger since the colonists seemed to despise everyone and everything British, and he felt it would be wise for her to come home to Chatsworth until things cooled down.

Season had almost made up her mind to return to England. Now that the war was over she would give Lucas one more week to come home. If by the end of that time he hadn't put in an appearance, she would pack her belongings and sail for England and Chatsworth.

In the early evening Season walked in the garden, watching the multicolored leaves drift to the ground. It had been over two weeks since Rebecca had told her about the end of the war, and still she had heard no word from her husband. Her trunks were packed and tomorrow she and Molly would sail for England.

To Season's surprise, Molly had been the one who put forth the loudest objection to their departure. She had adamantly aired her view that she didn't consider it proper for a wife to desert her husband without first letting him know she was leaving.

Season allowed her eyes to move over the land. It was painful to be leaving Rosemont, and Virginia. She had come to love it here and considered this her home.

She shook her head. What right did she have to expect fidelity from Lucas? He had once said he loved her, but she had doubted the sincerity of his words. She had been his wife such a short time; still she didn't feel obligated to sit at home alone while he paid court to another woman. If she had owed him a debt, she considered it now canceled.

Turning her footsteps back to the house, she felt the sting of tears in her eyes. She would go back to her father and hope she would never hear from Lucas again. She was so absorbed in her misery that she didn't see the shadow that moved from behind an oak to stand in her path, but when Season heard the deep raspy voice her head snapped up, and she stared at the dark cloaked figure.

"Were you not expecting me, my lady? I told you when the war was over I would come to you one more time."

Season could hardly catch her breath. "What are you doing here? Go away and leave me alone!"

"Are you not glad to see me?"

"No, I am quit with you and Lucas Carrington. I want nothing that will remind me of the grief I have suffered because of you both."

The Raven chuckled. "Could your ill temper be caused by the fact that your husband and I have neglected you so shamefully?"

Season's temper soared. "You may find cause to laugh at me, but I can assure you I find no humor in anything you have to say. For your information my trunks are all packed. By tomorrow I will be on my way back to England. I never want to see you or Lucas again!"

"Lucas was a fool to leave you for so long. You are feeling neglected and who can blame you."

Season's eyes blazed. "Move aside and allow me to pass, Raven. I am in no mood to listen to you. I cannot take much more from you or Lucas."

Suddenly The Raven seemed to tense. "Have we both hurt you so badly, my lady?"

Season could feel tears gathering in her eyes. "I just want to go home."

The Raven was quiet for a moment; then he reached out and pulled Season into his arms. "If it is your wish I will take you to England," he whispered against her ear. "If you do not wish to go to England, I will take you back to the island where we once swam in the sea. Would you like that?"

Season closed her eyes, feeling The Raven pull at her heart. There was a time when she would have given her life to hear him say those words to her. Now it was too late. She was a different person from the innocent girl he had once known. She had felt love for two different men, but neither loved her. Season knew that deep inside she still yearned for a true and lasting love. She wanted a man to love her totally and wildly. Neither Lucas nor The Raven had been able to satisfy that need. Both of them had asked more of her than she was willing to give.

Season raised her head and stared into the black leather mask. "No. I cannot allow you to take me to England, and I will not go with you to your island. After tomorrow I will never have to think about you again."

The Raven touched her face with a gloved hand. "Actually, my lady, you have little choice as to whether you want to go with me or not. You see, I have come to take you away, with or without your consent."

Season stepped back a pace. "Surely you aren't saying . . . you wouldn't try to—"

"I believe the word you are having difficulty with is 'kidnap,' Season. I abducted you once before, this time it will be even easier."

"I will scream, Raven. You can't just come to my home and spirit me away as you did before. There are many here at Rosemont who would stop you."

"There are those who would try," he said, reaching out and lifting her into his arms.

Season struggled when he placed a hand over her mouth. She couldn't believe this was happening to her again! Surely The Raven couldn't be so bold as to abduct her a second time! She ceased struggling when he lifted her over his shoulder and carried her toward the back of the garden and out the gate. He had removed his hand from her mouth and Season knew if she were of a mind to, she could scream loudly enough to bring someong to her rescue. She considered the consequences if she were to call for help. Whoever challenged The Raven, would surely lose his life.

Once outside the garden, The Raven placed Season

on her feet and she saw that a carriage was waiting for them. Looking back at the gate, she wondered if she could outrun The Raven.

"Don't try it, my lady. I would only come after you and cause us both a great deal of trouble."

"I despise you!" she spat out. "You are a black-hearted pirate."

He merely chuckled. Scooping her into his arms, he placed her in the carriage and then climbed in beside her.

Season moved into the corner and faced him defiantly. "How can you justify what you are doing to me, Raven? The last time you abducted me, you had a cause—this time there is no excuse. I don't know why you are doing this!"

"It's really very simple, my lady. I want you."

"Lucas will never stand for this. I am his wife and he will hunt you down."

"Your husband will have a very difficult time tracking us, my lady. The *Andromeda* leaves no tracks to follow," The Raven declared in an amused voice.

As the carriage raced on through the night, Season realized the hopelessness of her plight. She stared into the darkness, barely able to see The Raven since he blended in with the shadows. Suddenly she realized that he had braved danger to see her. Was he not risking his life by kidnapping her? Surely that must mean he loved her. She thought of Lucas, he hadn't even bothered to come home to her when the war had ended.

Season felt an ache deep within her and she wished with all her heart that it was Lucas who sat across from her. She realized in a flash that it was her husband she wanted to be with and not The Raven. She knew suddenly that even if Lucas didn't want her, she still couldn't betray him.

"I will never allow you to touch me, Raven. If you think you can win me over as you did the other time you abducted me, you are sadly mistaken," Season declared in a voice that shook with emotion.

Before The Raven could answer, the carriage came to an abrupt halt. He opened the door, jumped to the ground, and pulled Season into his arms.

"No, I will not go with you," she declared, kicking her feet and trying to escape his grasp.

The Raven merely laughed as he strolled down the sandy beach. When Season continued to struggle, he plopped her across his shoulder and she pounded him on the back with her fists.

When they reached the longboat that rested on the shore, The Raven placed her in it, and Season lapsed into silence, knowing she was wasting her energy.

In the dim moonlight she recognized the men who were rowing the boat out to sea, but she was too angry and upset to acknowledge any of them.

In her mind she pictured Molly's distress at finding her mistress missing and she imagined Lucas coming home and finding her gone. If he discovered she was with The Raven, would he think she had gone with him of her own free will? That thought made her feel empty inside and tears gathered in her eyes. She wished with all her heart that she was with her husband.

She wanted to beg The Raven to take her back, but

she knew he wouldn't listen to her. She had been planning to leave Lucas anyway, but not this way—never this way. The man who had married her and then abandoned her had stolen her heart. It was he who fit the realization of her youthful fantasies.

Suddenly Season wanted to feel her husband's arms around her. She ached to be held tightly by him. A sob escaped her lips when she thought of never seeing Lucas again.

The longboat bumped against the hull of the *Andromeda,* and Season had no time to think as The Raven lifted her into his arms and climbed the rope ladder. Season didn't voice her protest as he carried her below, knowing it wouldn't gain her anything. Once in his cabin, he placed her on her feet.

"Put out to sea," The Raven said to someone who stood just out of Season's view.

"Aye, aye, Captain," Briggs replied.

The Raven closed the door softly behind him and turned to Season. As he took a step in her direction she moved back a pace.

"Don't do this to me," she pleaded. "Please allow me to go back to my husband."

"Were you not going to leave him tomorrow? Why would you want me to take you back to him?"

"I don't expect you to understand this and I am not sure I understand myself. . . . I love Lucas and even if he does not love me, I want to be with him."

The Raven stood so still it was almost as if he had been turned to stone. "You are right, my lady, I don't understand. You were prepared to leave him tomorrow.

I happen to know your trunks were already packed. Why should you suddenly decide that you love your husband?"

"I . . . it was a mistake to think I could run away from my heart. I had learned that Lucas has been seen with another woman. I suppose I was hurt and wanted to hurt him in return."

"What did you hear?"

"I . . . do not want to discuss it with you. It concerns Lucas and myself."

"I know what you are referring to. You think your husband betrayed you with Lady Southerland."

Season looked at The Raven. "How could you know that? If you tell me one more time that you have ways of finding out everything I'll scream. Everyone but me seemed to know my husband is in love with another woman."

"Believing this, you still want to return to Lucas Carrington, my lady? Would you not be better off with a man who loves you?"

"You?"

"Yes, me."

"No. I once thought that I loved you. I suppose it was because you made me feel things that I had never experienced before. Perhaps I do love you in a way. There were many times when I couldn't separate you and Lucas in my mind. I will say this about you, Raven, I admire many things about you. I found you to be a man of very strong loyalties and convictions. You fought valiantly for what you believed in . . . but I don't love you. How can I love a man whose face I have never seen? I love my husband."

"If you were blind and had never seen Lucas Carrington's face, would you still have loved him?" The Raven asked.

"Yes, I suppose so. One experiences love through the heart, not through the eyes."

"What does your heart tell you about me, my lady?" he asked softly. Season sat down on the edge of the bed and was surprised when The Raven knelt down beside her. She could feel the ship rock as the waves lapped against its hull. "I told you I admire you."

He removed his glove and touched her face softly. "It's more than your admiration I crave, my lady."

When Season felt his touch, a shiver of delight passed through her body and she was momentarily startled. How was it possible that he could so easily make her react to his touch?

"You will get no more from me than admiration, Raven," she said quickly, trying to cover up her overreaction to his nearness.

But The Raven had seen her eyes dilate and knew what she was feeling. "I am not sure you speak the truth, my lady. I believe you will never forget what we shared. We were once bound together by the child you carried inside of you." His hand moved down to rest on her stomach, and Season quickly drew in her breath at his tenderness.

"Our baby died, Raven. I want my memory of you to die as well."

He pulled Season into his arms and she could feel herself melting against him. "No, no," she pleaded. "I don't want this. Please don't make me love you. I love Lucas."

"Perhaps you love both of us," he suggested softly against her ear.

Season rested her head against his shoulder as his hands ran up and down her back. "It isn't possible. How can it be?" she asked in a tortured voice. "I don't want to love either one of you; yet I do. As surely as I live and breathe I love you both," she whimpered.

The cabin became strangely silent and the only sound that could be heard was the wind catching at the canvas sails. Season sobbed in The Raven's arms. He tried to soothe her by kissing her cheek and gently rubbing her back.

"It would seem that neither Lucas Carrington nor myself are worthy of your love, my lady. We have both taken too much from you and have given back very little in return. Why should you waste your time with either of us?"

"I . . . want to go home, Raven. Please take me back," Season pleaded.

"By home, do you mean back to your husband?" he asked, almost tenderly.

"Yes. Take me back to Lucas."

"Will you forgive him for what you think he has done?"

"I don't know if he will want my forgiveness. I don't think he wants me."

"What if you were to find out that your husband has been faithful to you as far as other women are concerned, but you learn that he has deceived you in other ways, Season?"

"I don't know what you are talking about," she said staring at the leather mask The Raven wore, wishing she could see his eyes.

"What would you think of a man who had deceived those who trusted him, my lady? What if you were to discover that I had lied to you time and time again? Would you ever forgive me, ever believe in me again?"

Season stood up and turned her face away. She didn't know what point The Raven was trying to make, but for some reason he was frightening her. "I don't want to hear anything you have to say against my husband. You and Lucas were on opposite sides in the war, but that doesn't give you the right to condemn him."

When Season turned back to The Raven he seemed to loom over her. "You are very quick to his defense, my lady. Could it be you truly love your husband and would forgive him many things?"

"Yes. Is love not forgiving? I once hurt Lucas by implying that he was a coward. He told me then that a wife should believe in her husband. I now know he was trying to tell me to trust him. I do trust him, and I want him to know he can trust me. He will think that I went away with you of my own free will. I wish there was some way I could let him know I would never betray him."

Season watched as The Raven's hands went up to his leather mask. "If you are willing to forgive Lucas Carrington, my lady, then perhaps you will also forgive me. There is no longer any reason for me to hide my face from you, for I know you would never betray my secret."

Season caught her breath as she watched him slowly lift the leather mask. Her heart was drumming within her breast as she waited to see the face of the man who had divided her heart in half. She watched him step out of the shadows into the dim halflight of the cabin.

A loud sob escaped her lips and she shook her head in disbelief. "No! It cannot be! You are trying to trick me," she sobbed, placing her hands over her face. "Dear God, say it isn't true!"

Chapter Thirty-Three

"Did you mean what you said about forgiving me, my lady wife? Since I am both men who have wronged you, there will be twice as much for you to forgive."

Season covered her mouth with her hands and backed up against the wall of the cabin. "I don't understand, Lucas—how can you be The Raven? You are the last person I would have suspected. Surely there is some mistake."

His golden eyes sought hers and she saw a softness there. "Did you think after I had tasted your sweet lips that I would ever let you go? Have I not told you as The Raven and as myself that I loved you."

"You don't love me or you could never have deceived me so, Lucas," she said, feeling she had been betrayed.

"Come and sit beside me and I will try to make you understand why I had to deceive you, Season." The searching gaze he gave her revealed his deep need for her understanding.

She walked stiff-legged toward him and sat on the

edge of the bed. "I don't think you will ever be able to make me believe anything you tell me, Lucas. You should be ashamed even to face me."

He sat down beside her and stared at the ceiling. "There is no reason you should forgive me Season, but I will tell you my reasons for deceiving you, and then leave the final decision in your hands. If you so desire, I will take you back to your father. But should you find it in your heart to forgive me, I will consider myself the most fortunate man. Ask me any question and I will answer it honestly."

"I want to know about the beautiful widow, Lorona Southerland," she stated quickly, her jealousy coming to the fore.

Lucas smiled slightly. "I did pay marked attention to Lady Southerland, but not in the way you think. Lorona was born in America. She married Lord Southerland and was a devoted wife to him until he died. She was also a spy and my only contact with George Washington. Since she was a woman as well as an American, she was able to carry my messages to Washington without arousing anyone's suspicion. No one but myself and General Washington knew that her true loyalty was to the land of her birth."

"Did you ever kiss her?" Season asked, looking deeply into his golden eyes and trying to discern the truth from all the lies that divided her and Lucas.

"No, never. Lorona knows how much I love my wife. If you believe nothing else, Season, believe that I never kissed another woman after I came to know you on board the *Andromeda*. I was too much in love with a green-eyed seductress who had stolen my heart."

"What about Maude? I know she was expecting you to make love to her the night I was locked in her bedroom. You must also have seen her again if you got my necklace from her. Dear lord, now I know what Edmund was talking about that night down by the river. He knew who you were!"

"That is true. He had every intention of unmasking me after he killed me."

Season shook her head in disbelief. "I don't understand any of this, Lucas. Did Maude know who you were?"

He touched her cheek. "No. Maude had no notion of my true identity. I will admit that Maude and I were once lovers, but I have made love to no one since the first time I came to know the joy of your body. Briggs brought me the necklace after he learned you had been spirited away by De Fores. Because of the necklace Edmund realized I was really The Raven. He had been watching me for some time. I suppose he found the necklace before you and I were married. Tying the loose ends together, he came to the right conclusion about me."

"Poor Edmund didn't deserve to die. I will never forget that it was I who ended his life." Her eyes shone brightly with tears. "I couldn't let him kill you that night."

"Put all that is bad behind you, Season. Remember only that I love you."

"How can I trust you?" she said, blinking her eyes. Everything you have ever said to me has been a lie."

"Not everything, Season. I never lied to you when I declared my love for you, and I will never again tell you anything that is untrue as long as we live, you have my word on it. I will not blame you should you never forgive me—but I hope with all my heart that you will."

"Why didn't you tell me you were The Raven, Lucas? You allowed me to make a fool of myself. How you must have laughed at me when I confessed that I loved you a moment ago."

He softly touched her golden head. "No, I didn't laugh," he said softly. "I felt overpowering joy, because I had waited a long time for you to say you loved me, Lucas Carrington, and not me as The Raven."

"You still haven't told me why you kept your identify a secret from me after I was your wife," she said, wanting to believe him, but afraid to trust her heart.

"I wanted to confess everything to you many times, Season, but I suppose I was a coward. At first, I couldn't tell you who I was because you were one of the enemy. Later, I couldn't tell you because I feared you would turn away from me in anger when you found out the man you had married was also the man responsible for getting you with child. I fell in love with you the first time I saw you. When I kidnapped you, I wasn't sure whether I did it to get my uncle back or because I wanted you. I felt sick inside that the woman I had searched for all my life had a soiled reputation, but the night I took you in the cabin and found you to be untouched, I was horrified that I had stolen your innocence."

Suddenly a thought occurred to Season. She had believed that The Raven had abandoned her when he had handed her over to Lucas Carrington, but that was not the case. Her confusion deepened.

"Lucas—"

"No, allow me to finish, Season, and then you can ask what you will. Even now, I fear I will lose my nerve." Lucas seemed not to know what to do with his hands and Season realized he was indeed nervous.

"Go on, Lucas—I am listening," she said, wishing she dared reach out and touch his hand.

Lucas took a deep breath. "After the night I had taken your innocence away from you, I made myself a promise I would never touch you again. As you know, I didn't keep that promise. That night on the beach, you were so bewitching I knew I had to have you. When I made love to you, Season, you not only filled the emptiness in my body, but you filled my heart to overflowing. When De Fores helped you escape, I was in torment, fearing what he would do to you; but in my mind he was no worse than I was, for had I not taken you against your will?"

"No, Lucas you didn't force yourself on me. I was more than willing to . . ."

He reached out his hand to touch her, but then allowed it to drop. "My foolish love. Do you not know that although I didn't force you physically that night, I wooed you into submission. You were so young and innocent that you didn't know how to fight against the feelings you were experiencing for the first time."

"Are you saying that you deliberately set out to make me want you?"

"Well . . . yes, though it pains me to admit it. I was seducing you into submission. I have never taken a reluctant woman. Of course, I must add in my defense that I thought you had been with many men before me.

I was horrified when I found you to be a virgin, but I was also delighted. Selfish brute that I am, I didn't want to think that any man had been with you before me."

"I am a bit confused, Lucas. Who was The Raven the day I was handed over to you as Lucas Carrington?"

He smiled slightly. "I persuaded Robert to play the part that day. I must say he wasn't too pleased with the notion. Robert, Briggs, and James had all three been hounding me to take you back to New York. They weren't at all happy that I was keeping you with me at Rosemont, but I just couldn't bear to part with you. I suppose, deep down, I hoped I could make you love me as much as I loved you."

"I take it then that both Robert and Rebecca know you are The Raven?"

"Robert knows, but Rebecca does not."

"Why did you ask me to marry you, Lucas?"

He looked into her eyes and she saw a soft glow in his golden gaze. "I would have thought that was obvious. I loved you and couldn't think of any way to convince you to marry me. I would never have turned you over to Edmund, Season. When I found out you were carrying my child, I knew I had the means to convince you to marry me. I wanted to shout to the world that I had planted my seed in you, but instead I had to act as if I were being magnanimous by offering my name to another man's child."

Lucas tilted Season's chin up. "When you lost my child I was devastated because I knew it was my fault."

"No, Lucas, I will not allow you to blame yourself for the loss of the baby. If either of us is to blame it is I."

"Perhaps, you are, after all, forgiving me, Season. But I, alone, was responsible for your accident. I will have to live with that guilt for as long as I live."

"If I can forgive you, Lucas, why then can you not forgive yourself?"

Season saw a misty look come into his golden eyes. "My God, Season, are you saying you forgive me?"

"Yes, I forgive you, Lucas," she whispered, feeling the sting of tears in her eyes. "I know now what you went through when I lost the baby, Lucas."

She saw his throat muscles working and knew he had indeed felt strongly about the loss of their child. He looked away from her and spoke in a hoarse voice. "For days I thought you would die, Season. You cannot imagine the hell I lived through as your life hung by a thin thread. Finally, in desperation, I spoke to you in the voice of The Raven, hoping you would respond—and thank God you did."

Season was beginning to recover from the shock of knowing her husband and The Raven were one and the same. She now realized why she had loved both men. "Lucas, you were a very convincing actor, because I thought you were jealous of The Raven."

"I wasn't acting, Season. The strange part in all of this is that I became insanely jealous of my other self. I was competing with myself for your love. I hated the fact that you seemed to love the part of me that wasn't real. As The Raven, I seemed to have a part of you that I could never possess as myself. I waited and hoped for the day you would say you loved me—Lucas Carrington—which you did tonight. Although at one time you told me you were beginning to love me, that wasn't good enough. I wanted all of you, Season."

He turned to her and pulled her into his arms as if he feared she would draw away from him. "Have I killed the fragile love you have come to feel for me, my lady? Will you ever be able to look into my eyes and say that you love me?"

Season raised her head and touched his face. "I am looking into your eyes, Lucas, and I love you. I am a bit confused and I don't understand everything that has happened, but I know I love you."

Lucas' hand trembled as he reached out and touched her lips. "My dearest lady wife, I have done nothing to deserve your love, but selfish beast that I am, I want you—heart, body, and soul."

Season saw tears gather in Lucas' eyes and a sob escaped her lips. "Lucas, my dearest love, how could I not love you? We are from enemy countries, and both of us will probably be condemned for our love, but nothing can keep me from loving you."

"Not even the fact that I deceived you over and over?" he asked, still not able to realize she had forgiven him.

She pressed her cheek against his. "Not even that. You can call yourself Lucas Carrington, The Raven, or whatever name you choose, and I will still love you. Even when I thought you were a coward I still loved you."

"You did sorely wound me that day, Season. I wanted to be the man you would be proud of, but I had to bear your contempt in silence. I feared you would hate me even more should you find out the truth about me. Even now it's hard to believe you do not fault me for playing the friend to your country when, in truth, I was their worst enemy. Let no country stand between you and I, Season."

Season raised her head and he saw sadness in her green eyes. "I love you even though our countries stand apart, Lucas. Sometimes it is hard to know where my loyalty lies."

"You are my wife, Season. We should allow no loyalty to the king on your part, no loyalty to my country on my part, to rip us apart. Allow me to bind you to me so firmly that nothing can ever separate us. The war between our two countries has ended; let us lay down our weapons and love one another."

Season was still reluctant to give her love to Lucas wholeheartedly. "Why didn't you ever write to me, Lucas? You were gone so long and never sent me any word."

"Most of the time I was at sea, Season, and unable to communicate with you. At other times, I suppose I was punishing myself. I would have liked nothing better than to have received correspondence from you. I also felt that you didn't want to hear from me. At one point, I did write you a letter and confessed to you who I was. I suppose I thought it would be easier than facing you with the truth. But too many lives would have been jeopardized had it been intercepted, so I threw the letter away."

"I would never have betrayed you, Lucas."

His eyes rested on her lips. "Don't you think I know that. I tested you many times, but not once did you say anything that would incriminate me as The Raven. If you will remember, the day I first brought you to Rosemont I asked you if you knew the name of the crew members of the *Andromeda* and you denied any knowledge of them. I wanted to take you in my arms that day and tell you how much I loved you, but you would have been a little distressed if Lucas Carrington had done such a thing. You didn't betray The Raven to me, and later, you didn't betray me to The Raven. I can still feel the sting of the dressing down you gave me when you told me you would never betray your husband."

Lucas stood up and walked over to the porthole, gazing out into the night. "If you say the word, Season, I will put into port and have the figurehead of The Raven stripped from the *Andromeda* so no one will recognize her. Then, if it is your wish, I will sail to England and take you to your father."

He heard her come up behind him but he didn't turn around. He didn't know how she would accept everything he had told her tonight, and he wouldn't blame her if she insisted on being taken to her father. He closed his eyes and waited for her to speak.

"What will happen to The Raven now, Lucas?" she asked softly.

Without turning, he spoke. "The Raven will just disappear from the face of the earth, never to be heard from again. No one can ever know who he was."

"Will you promise me one thing, Lucas?"

He turned around and saw that she was smiling, and he felt a flicker of hope fan to life. "I will promise you the moon if you ask it of me, my lady."

"Will you speak to me sometimes in the voice of The Raven? I admit he vies for the affection I owe only to my husband. I have grown to love him also, and shall grieve if I never hear his voice again."

Lucas threw his head back and laughed. "You little devil," he said, drawing her into his arms. "I believe you are attempting to make me jealous. In your case, I will always have to live with another man's image in your heart. Must I always share you with that black-hearted pirate?"

Season threw her arms around his neck and peppered his face with soft kisses. "Yes, you will always have to share me with The Raven, for in my heart you are one and the same. I now know why I could not separate the two of you in my mind; in my heart I must have known you were one and the same."

Lucas picked Season up in his arms, placed her on the bed, and eased himself down beside her. "How will you like having a husband who will stick so close to you that you will sicken at the sight of his face? I have many things to make up to you. Do you mind being married to a simple planter, Season?"

She brushed a dark lock of hair from his forehead and smiled brightly. "I love Rosemont and I will be happy living there with you beside me. There is no longer any guilt in my heart because I love two men. I want to go home and start our life together."

He gathered her tightly against him. "All in good time, my lady. The *Andromeda* is making her final run, she is taking me and my wife to a certain island where we will spend our honeymoon. Will you like that?"

"Oh, yes, Lucas," she said, smiling. "What will happen to the *Andromeda* after we return home?"

"She is going to be stripped and repainted. Briggs

will be her captain and enlist her in trade. I fear the *Andromeda* will lead a dull existence from now on."

"I love this ship just as I love her dark master," Season admitted.

Lucas gave her a heartwarming smile. "Perhaps every year I will take you sailing on her. Would you like that?"

"Umm, yes," she said, snuggling into his arms. "Lucas, I love you so much."

Fire lit the depths of Lucas' golden eyes, and as his lips traced a pattern across Season's creamy white shoulders, she laced her hands through his ebony hair.

"We will raise strong sons and daughters, Season, and they will grow up in a free country."

"Yes, and one day I will tell them how their father spirited their mother away and stole her heart."

He brushed his lips against the gentle rise of her breast; then he looked at her in mock horror. "Surely you don't intend to tell them everything? Will you tell them their father was a pirate?" he asked, smiling.

She arched an eyebrow and moved away from him. "Well . . . perhaps I shall omit one or two details."

"Come here, wife," he said, pulling her forward and slowly unhooking her gown. "Tonight you shall have two different men making love to you, but after this you will have to be content with just your husband. I will never share you with a black-hearted pirate, The Raven."

Season parted her lips and smiled. "I will do my best to satisfy you both." Suddenly, Season had a thought that made her eyes widen. "Lucas, Rebecca and Molly won't know what has happened to me. They will be worried sick."

He chuckled. "No, I told them both that I was taking you on a honeymoon. Your trunks are stowed in the cargo hole."

"It seems you think of everything."

"I try, my lady."

"What would you have done had I asked you to take me back to England, Lucas?"

"I would most probably have kidnapped you again. I don't think I will ever be able to give you up, Season."

As Lucas drew her tightly against him, Season's heart swelled with love. She had found her love in two men who had merged into one. As his hands moved over her body she smiled to herself. Deep in her heart she knew she would always be The Raven's lady.

Season stood on the sandy beach, the wind blowing her golden hair. Shading her eyes against the glaring sun, she watched with a heavy heart, as the figurehead from the *Andromeda* splashed into the sea. She remembered the first time she had seen the raven in flight. How frightened she had been that day. Now she felt sad that it must forever lie at the bottom of the sea. Perhaps one day it will wash upon a beach to rot in the sun, she thought.

"Why so sad, my lady? I have it on good authority that you have every reason to be happy."

Season turned to face her husband. "I am sorry that the figurehead must be stripped from the *Andromeda.*"

Lucas put his arms about Season and hugged her to him. "Not only is the figurehead to be replaced, but the

Andromeda will have new paint and her name will be changed."

"Are you not the least bit sad, Lucas?"

He smiled down at her. "On the contrary—I have never been happier. I give up my wicked ways without a backward glance. The *Andromeda* served her purpose, as did her captain."

Season was warmed by the tender glow in Lucas' golden eyes. "I cannot hope to compete with your love of the sea. Will you not miss being the captain of a ship?"

He laughed and kissed her lips. "How could I miss the sea when I am your husband, my lady? To me that is a far more important role."

"I want to make you happy, Lucas. I just don't want you to have any regrets."

"You haven't asked me about the *Andromeda*'s new name, Season. Aren't you the least bit curious?"

She smiled and laid her head against his shoulder. "What is the new name?"

Lucas lifted her chin and gave her a half smile. "Her name is *Lady Season.* Wait until you see the new figurehead, I had the face carved in your image, and it looks as though her golden hair is flying in the wind."

Season laughed delightedly. "When can I see the figurehead, Lucas?"

"Not today, my lady wife. I have plans for you."

He took her hand and led her down the beach. Season felt her heart lighten as they lost sight of the *Andromeda,* and when Lucas pulled her into his arms and kissed her deeply, she melted against him.

556

Suddenly breaking off the kiss, he laughed down at her. "Tonight will be our real honeymoon, Season. We will swim in the sea and sleep beneath the stars. I have a feeling this is where I planted my seed in you before, perhaps I will do it again."

She touched his face and was overcome by her tender feeling for the man who had twice won her heart. "I want to have many children, Lucas. I want to tie you so closely to me that you will never want to leave me and go sailing the world."

He sat down on the sand and pulled her down onto his lap. "I will never leave you again, Season. If I ever do sail the world, you will go with me. I need no child to tie me to you. You have already bound me to you with your sweet smile and your lovely face. From now on, where I go, you will go."

"Will you not soon tire of me?" she asked in an uncertain voice.

He laughed and his golden eyes danced. "Not even when we are old and gray. I intended to make you my captive, but instead I became your slave. You have made me a very happy man. I never tire of the sound of your laughter or the sight of your beautiful face."

She touched his face softly and felt her eyes mist. "It is wonderful to love and be loved, Lucas. I never knew one could find such complete happiness."

Lucas rolled her onto the sandy beach and lay beside her, pulling her tightly against him. The gleam in his golden eyes made her blood flash like quicksilver through her veins. When he bent his head and captured her lips, Season felt her senses ripple like a tidal wave.

Wild primitive delight coursed through her body as he touched her breasts with a feathery, stroking motion.

"You are so enticing, my lady. I fear I cannot wait until the sun goes down," he whispered in a deep voice.

Season's whole being tingled with desire as she surrendered to her husband's kiss. I will never know loneliness again, she thought. Lucas has filled my world with love and now I belong to him.

Lucas glanced toward the rolling waves that lapped against the beach, and he realized he no longer felt such a deep kinship with the sea. He found himself wanting to return to Rosemont where he and Season could raise a family.

As his lips brushed against her satiny skin, he longed to possess her. His hunger for Season never seemed to lessen; he found renewed joy each time he took her in his arms. If only she knew how tightly she had bound him to her . . . He would spend the rest of his life proving his love to her, and perhaps, in time, she would forget all about his deception. Perhaps, one day, he would not have to compete with The Raven for her love.

"I love you more than life, Season," he whispered against her ear. "You will always be *my* lady!"

THE BESTSELLING ECSTASY SERIES
by Janelle Taylor

SAVAGE ECSTASY (824, $3.50)

It was like lightning striking, the first time the Indian brave Gray Eagle looked into the eyes of the beautiful young settler Alisha. And from the moment he saw her, he knew that he must possess her — and make her his slave!

DEFIANT ECSTASY (931, $3.50)

When Gray Eagle returned to Fort Pierre's gate with his hundred warriors behind him, Alisha's heart skipped a beat: Would Gray Eagle destroy her — or make his destiny her own?

FORBIDDEN ECSTASY (1014, $3.50)

Gray Eagle had promised Alisha his heart forever — nothing could keep him from her. But when Alisha woke to find her red-skinned lover gone, she felt abandoned and alone. Lost between two worlds, desperate and fearful of betrayal, Alisha, hungered for the return of her FORBIDDEN ECSTASY.

BRAZEN ECSTASY (1133, $3.50)

When Alisha is swept down a raging river and out of her savage brave's life, Gray Eagle must rescue his love again. But Alisha has no memory of him at all. And as she fights to recall a past love, another white slave woman in their camp is fighting for Gray Eagle.

TENDER ECSTACY (1212, $3.75)

Bright Arrow is committed to kill every white he sees — until he sets his eyes on ravishing Rebecca. And fate demands that he capture her, torment . . . and soar with her to the dizzying heights of TENDER ECSTASY.

STOLEN ECSTASY (1621, $3.95)

In this long-awaited sixth volume of the SAVAGE ECSTASY series, lovely Rebecca Kenny defies all for her true love, Bright Arrow. She fights with all her passion to be his lover — never his slave. Share in Rebecca and Bright Arrow's savage pleasure as they entwine in moments of STOLEN ECSTASY.